ASHLEY ROBERTSON

UNGUARDED

Published by Ashley Robertson Books

Copyright © 2012 Ashley Robertson

All rights reserved.

ISBN-10:   0615649882

EAN-13·   9780615649887

Thanks to my editor, Stephen Delaney, who I couldn't have finished this book without his meticulous attention to detail and expertise. And a special thank you to my husband, Baron, for his unending patience, love, and support. Lastly, I must express my gratitude to Claudia at PhatPuppyArt for creating the beautiful book cover.

More about the author can be found at
www.AshleyRobertsonBooks.com

TABLE OF CONTENTS

UNGUARDED

1

I WOKE UP IN A PANIC, gasping for my next breath. My lashes fluttered open, but everything was blurry at first, swirling, fuzzy points of light blanketed a velvety blackness. I squinted, then blinked a few times and saw that I was staring up at a clear night sky full of stars. My back was flat against the ground, my head resting uncomfortably on top of something coarse and hard. As I rolled over and pushed up with my hands, sharp pain spread through my body, letting me know I hadn't completely healed yet. But I ignored it and stood up, feeling unbalanced as I swayed. My arms flapped out as if I could fly, but I was only trying to keep from falling. After a few grueling moments, I was finally able to get it together—sort of. I cast a wary gaze around me. A forest thick with vegetation spread out on both sides, quiet and secluded, and a road weathered with age split right through the middle of it. Not too far from where I stood, the moon projected its light upon the dark surface like a mirage in a desert, and no matter how much distance I could gain, I knew I'd never reach the point where its light truly touched.

A deep sigh blew through my lips as a sense of hopelessness claimed me. Though I was certain I was somewhere on Earth, I still didn't know where exactly I was or why I was there. I glanced down and my chest tightened with panic. Red, crackled smears covered the tops of my black wedge boots, spreading in crimson trails up my jeans, which were also ripped and torn—shredded at the knees. My arms were scratched and bloody, and the white tee had definitely seen better days. I grabbed my mouth, holding back a gasp, swinging another gaze around me.

Suddenly, images shot through my mind like a projector playing old videos. There was a man holding me, running his fingers through my wavy caramel hair. His eyes were like deep, sapphire pools, coaxing me into their bottomless depths. He lowered his lips to my ear. Then, the vision cut out like interfering static. I drew in a deep breath. More images returned, and this time I could make out that the man was familiar. He was around five foot ten, brunette, and had a muscular body from head to toe. I couldn't see his eyes this time, not because I wasn't straining, but because he was blurry…no, moving really fast. He threw me to the ground. "Stay down!" he yelled. "They're coming!"

"No!" I screamed, trying to rise. "Cole!" I couldn't move fast enough. Everything was happening too fast, yet it seemed to be progressing in slow motion.

But as I rose, something grabbed me, holding me back. Long black arms wrapped around me. Slick, scaly fingers with claws the size of knives interlocked at my waist, securing their hold on me. I kicked back, then tried to squat down and twist free, but the thing's grasp was too tight, unbreakable. I looked around in a panic, scanning the area, but couldn't find a trace of Cole. I screamed—more like a shriek of pain. Panic seized me. I blinked….

The visions stopped. I remembered everything.

There were headlights off in the distance ahead of me, slowly approaching. I glimpsed the overgrown forest on both sides, then swung right and took off running, plowing into the thick vegetation and swerving around trees and bushes. Their branches were like skeletal hands gripping me, cutting into the tender flesh on my arms. But I kept pushing forward, tears building in my eyes like a stream during a flood. Cole. I'd left Cole. I needed to get back to him before it was too late. I couldn't let *them* take him. My pace slowed to a swift walk, and I closed my eyes, squeezed them shut, letting my aura guide me. My fingers pressed into my temples, concentrating, directing all of my focus on Charon, the place where Cole and I had been just before I accidentally orbed back to Earth.

A few moments later, I was standing on a land overtaken by war. Smoke rose from fresh craters blasted in the soft, sandy surface, and black ashes fell like snow. It was like a smothering fog making it difficult to see, hard to breathe. I squinted, trying to help my eyes work a little better. There were mountains all around, a small inlet of water separating them from me. The water looked black, empty, and lifeless. Small waves rushed the expansive, sandy shoreline, breaking, splashing, and then retreating back to sea. I couldn't remember why I was here. But I knew this place. I'd been here before, but this wasn't how it looked. It was much more beautiful. What happened here? The fresh smoke proved something recent had occurred. I swallowed hard, my pulse rushing up my throat. This place was Charon. Or at least *was* Charon.

Everything had come back to me, my memories connecting like matching puzzle pieces.

"Cole!" I yelled, my voice frantic, desperate, and afraid. The fact was, I was beyond afraid, because I couldn't sense him here. They must've taken him alive. If he were dead, I would've known instantly.

I walked around aimlessly, like a lost puppy, only to find more destruction. I kicked a rock the size of a tennis ball. It scuffed across the grainy, powder-like surface, leaving a trail behind it.

Then the air grew thicker—like pressure building before a storm—and after a moment, I sensed a presence, familiar, but not friendly. Gooseflesh spread across my skin and my teeth ground together. "Show yourself, Limos!" I demanded, my eyes narrowing.

There was a poof of orange, rusty colored smoke. A draft blew through, clearing some of it away. Limos glared at me, a hint of fang showing in his open mouth. He was nearly six foot, long, flowing black hair draping over his even blacker cloak, and his eyes were the color of blood. "Selene, aren't you supposed to be guarding your human?" His voice was a deep, malicious hiss.

"That's none of your business!" I snapped, eyes narrowing into a deeper glare.

Limos waved a hand in the air like he was shooing a fly. "My apologies. Though I do enjoy seeing you in human form." He stepped forward, reaching for me. His fingernails were overgrown—jagged and sharp, like miniature razors. I swallowed hard as he moved closer, leaving barely a couple feet between us. He hesitated a moment, then lowered his hands. "Ah, that's much better," he purred, sounding more like a growl. "Selene, you really are my favorite angel."

I rolled my eyes. A chill crept up my spine, spilling across the back of my head. "Where is Cole?"

"Do not worry, my child. He is unharmed. I may hold onto him for a little while. That is, unless you are willing to make a trade?"

I took a small step back. "What trade? What do you want?"

Limos half laughed, sinister, evil, like the demon he is. "Oh, Selene, my dear child. I want you. But you already know that."

I could feel my pulse quickening, shuddering up my chest, into my throat. "No. I can't!" I swung my head to the right, then slowly to the left, scanning the mayhem previously unleashed by Limos and his hoard of demon followers. "Please let him go!" Tears dripped out of my eyes, making cold, sticky trails down my cheeks. There was an emptiness in the pit of my stomach that clenched into sharp, excruciating pain.

"Tsk tsk, Selene. Was it not your fault that Cole even came here?" Limos turned, arm raised, voice loud and authoritative, saying, "Is this not my world? Look around you, my child! Your god has abandoned this place. I have claimed it for my own." He lowered his arm, took a small step closer. "Did you really think this world was not on my radar?"

I stared at him, the lumps forming in my throat making it difficult to speak. I had been wrong about this world. It had been an even bigger mistake to bring Cole here. "Limos, please. Don't do this."

Limos burst into sinister laughter. A moment that felt more like an eternity passed as I waited for him to settle down. "If only you would have followed the rules." A sly chuckle rolled off his black, dry tongue. "None of this would have happened. But I am so grateful to you, my child, that you did not follow *His* rules."

I couldn't reply. Limos was right. All of this was my fault. I looked past the demon and gazed at the water, wishing I could jump in and wash away all of my sins. But that was a human desire. Angels aren't supposed to sin. Even though we were created so differently from people, the truth is we are actually a lot alike. Angels, like humans, have the freedom of choice. We're not robots. We're real living beings. We're not immune to punishments if we make a bad choice. That was how Lucifer, one of God's most beloved angels, got thrown out of heaven in the first place.

I found my voice. "I will strike you down! You do not have any power over me. Release Cole now!" I stepped forward, keeping my focus on Limos' eyes.

He rubbed his hands together—slowly, teasingly. "My child, are you threatening me? You want me to release that vampire after you brought him straight to me? You are a fool. If you kept him on Earth where he belonged, I would have never been able to take him. Your vampire was under the protection of Typhon as long as he remained on Earth."

"Typhon will hear about this! He will challenge you!"

"That is where you are wrong, my child. I have grown stronger. Typhon will not do a thing."

I wanted to strike Limos that very moment. But I knew I couldn't. Angels can't strike demons without *His* permission. And I definitely didn't have *His* permission. If I had just kept Cole on Earth, none of this would've happened. Hindsight can be such a bitch sometimes.

Limos cocked his head sideways, watchful eyes all over me like an unwanted and prying visitor, which he was. "Are your stints of amnesia increasing when you orb?"

My eyes went wide. How did he know about that? I couldn't answer him. I couldn't let him know just how much I understood his question.

"So it *is* true?" he exclaimed. "Your eyes gave it away, my child." That evil laughter returned, rumbling out of his mouth like a tidal wave of evil. "You no longer have *him* on your side. But you're not fallen yet. No, not yet. If you were a fallen angel, then I could easily acquire you." A sly smile curved his lips. "I suppose I should test the waters and take you for my own right now!" He lunged forward, fast—so fast he was impossible to see.

I gasped, stepped back. But he was already there. Too close, his arms opened wide, ready to grab me.

Out of my body a jolt of electricity burst forth, radiating a light so bright it pierced the dark, smoke-filled world around me as if it were a miniature sun. Limos jumped back, ducking down, hands over his face to shield his eyes. He shrieked in agony, hissing words, begging me to stop, to turn off the light. I closed my eyes, stealing a moment to express my gratitude, and then sucked in a deep breath, swallowing the light inside my body as if I were a vacuum.

I walked over to Limos, crouched down beside him. He lowered his hands enough to peer at me, red eyes wide with shock. "You are still under *His* protection!" he wailed. It definitely was not a question.

I nodded, feeling a touch of a smile on my lips. "Put Cole back on Earth where he belongs, and I will forget the past few hours ever happened."

"You have won this one, Selene! But we both know your time is limited. Soon you will be fallen. And then you will be mine." Limos lowered his head, curling his body into a ball, and vanished inside the rusty orange cloud that had brought him to Charon.

I took a deep breath and rose. How was I going to get Cole back? I didn't have anyone I could go to for help. My only chance was if Typhon would help me—except going to the Underworld would not only take too much time, but came at a high price. The Underworld was off limits for angels. I definitely couldn't orb there. And even if I could, my powers most likely wouldn't work there. I'd be a sitting duck, er, angel, with demons of every kind running all around me. I cringed at the thought. No, going to Typhon wasn't my answer. Somehow I needed to get a message to him, and the only way to do that was through one of his followers. But there were two big problems with that. The first was that I'd be breaking another "angel" rule for the vampire I loved. The second was that you just cannot trust a demon.

2

I FOLLOWED MY CHARGE IN the shadows, until it was just the right time for me to appear in human form. Caitlyn Harris dashed through the double glass doors of the research center, two oversized books tucked in the crevice of her arms. She was an attractive young woman with a very promising future. Rich brown hair framed her heart-shaped face, swaying just below her shoulders as she rushed to the only available table. A pair of jeans and a red polo shirt fit snuggly around her slender, five-foot-six body.

There were several rows of bookshelves stretching to the ceiling, surrounding the study area where Caitlyn claimed her spot and pulled out her chair. After she placed her books on the table and got a little more situated, she let out a deep, satisfying sigh. She'd just leaned forward, ready to dive into her work, when she looked across the table and noticed me sitting there. Startled, she jumped back in her chair. "Selene! Where did you come from? I didn't see you when I came in here!"

I half laughed, mindful of keeping my voice low. "You were in a hurry. I don't think you noticed much of anything."

Caitlyn smiled, running a couple of fingers through her straight, silky hair. "I'm a little behind with a few of my classes. Feeling the stress of it. You know?"

I nodded. "I completely understand." I glanced down at my lap and then back up at Caitlyn. "I'm still so excited that we're both here. This past year has been amazing."

"Are you kidding? It's better than amazing. It's perfect."

And it really was—for Caitlyn anyway. She'd been accepted at Bridgeton Institute while working on getting a BA in Earth and Space Science at Florida Atlantic University. Bridgeton Institute is an elite school offering advanced programs in her field. Since I'm her guardian angel, I followed her across the country, all the way to Denver, Colorado, where BI was located.

"I'm thinking about meeting Stacey and Rob tonight," Caitlyn said. "I need a break from the books."

"Where at?" I tucked a few wisps of hair that had fallen out of my ponytail behind my ears.

"Brix. Eight o'clock."

"Okay."

"Okay you'll come?"

I smiled. "Of course."

"Stacey said that Jack might come." Caitlyn smirked. She quickly pressed her hand across her lips, covering them up.

I frowned. But kept my mouth shut. An argument about Jack wasn't on my list of things to do today.

"Don't look at me like that!" Caitlyn scolded.

I quickly diverted my attention to my lap and started tracing circles in my jeans with my index fingers. I could feel Caitlyn's glare burning a hole in my head, so after a brief, uncomfortable moment of silence, I looked up. Some of her hair had draped across her face like a curtain, and both arms were folded in front of her chest. "I'm sorry," I said, voice small and cautious. "I just think you should be careful with him. I don't know if I trust Jack." And then I added, "Yet," hoping to make it sound a little better.

"It's not about YOU trusting him! I'm the one that likes him. You should trust ME! And what about Cole? I never give you crap about him! He's the one that's shady!"

I bit my lip, holding back my angered words. Tears began welling up in my eyes. Cole. I'd been doing my best to keep him off my mind while I'd been guarding Caitlyn. She's my charge, my responsibility, my number one priority. If anything happened to her, it would be my butt on the line. But if anything bad happened to Cole, it would be my fault. MY fault. I brought him to Charon. He would've never been there if it weren't for me. The guilt was becoming unbearable. The desire to find him was pushing to the surface of my emotions.

But I needed to keep Caitlyn my first priority. And since Jack had come around, that's meant a whole lot more work for me. He was bad news. I could see the shadows surrounding his aura. He was not fully controlled by darkness, but his mind was open to it at the moment. If Caitlyn didn't take careful steps around him, her foot would get stuck in his web. One of my additional assignments had been to prevent that from happening. At all costs.

"Cole won't be there tonight," I said flatly. "I promise to be nice to Jack."

Caitlyn unfolded her arms, dropping them to her sides. "Selene, what's wrong?"

I fought to keep the tears in my eyes, but one spilled out, slicking its way down my face. "Everything is fine." I got up and took a small step back, keeping my eyes on the tops of my sneakers.

"No it's not." I heard her chair scoot back, then hurried footsteps marching my way. "Is it Cole? Did something happen with you two?" She gently rubbed my back, slow, careful strokes.

I didn't know what to say. My eyes were so full of tears, another drop couldn't fit in there. I swallowed hard. "We're just taking a little time apart." My words were choked.

"Well, you guys have been inseparable. It's okay to spend some of your time with other people. I'm sure you'll be back glued to each others' sides before long."

I sniffled, forcing a half smile.

Something caught her attention. Caitlyn wasn't looking at me anymore. Her brown eyes had slid to the side, were curving around my face. My chest tightened. I knew who it was without even looking. His black aura constricted around my spine like a boa constrictor. I stepped out of my embrace with Caitlyn and turned to face Jack, the twisted center of her attention.

"Jack." Caitlyn hopped over to him like a bunny in an open field. He was six feet tall with a toned body, square jaw, dark auburn hair cut short and spiked on top. He opened his arms and squeezed her inside them. I didn't find it affectionate. It was actually more territorial than anything else. What the heck did she see in him?

"Hey sweetie." He kissed her cheek and let go of her.

I couldn't think of a better reason to be invisible. I didn't want Jack to look at me with those possessive, controlling, snake eyes of his. "I'll see you tonight, Caitlyn," I said, and then gave a slight nod toward Jack. "Enjoy your afternoon."

"Selene! Where are you going?" he asked, voice loud and sarcastic. "Don't leave on my account." His dark eyes slanted into a glare, lips smirking just enough to show a glimpse of teeth.

I shook my head, felt a flush of heat spread all over my cheeks. "I'm not. I was already heading out when you got here."

Out of nowhere, something jerked in my stomach as if I'd been punched, but I pretended nothing had happened, since it wasn't anything to do with my human company. With anger blossoming inside, I quickly turned on my heel.

"Bye," Caitlyn called after me.

"Whatever. I guess we'll see you later," Jack said, his voice still a little too sarcastic for my taste.

"Lucky me," I mumbled under my breath.

A quick wave with my hand and I was out the doors of the research center. Massive oak trees lined the sidewalk that led to a few other classrooms and the campus café. There was an expansive, grassy park area on the right, just beyond the oaks. Shadows below fluffy white clouds danced around, careless and free. My stomach twisted into a knot so tight, it almost brought me to my knees. I caught my breath and ducked behind one of the bigger trees, then blinked away my human form, becoming invisible to everything and everyone around me—except the demon trying to get my attention.

"What do you want?" I asked with annoyance, staring into his beady, obsidian eyes. Moros looked like an oversized Komodo dragon. I'd prefer him to be in human form, but what can you really expect from a demon? His gaze slid up and down, taking in everything he saw. In my angel form, there's a luminescent glow to my skin. My white dress was a soft cottony satin and flowed all the way to my bare feet. My hair was the same as when I was in human form—caramel in color with voluminous waves, gliding down to the small of my back, and my eyes were the deepest shade of green, almost like emeralds.

"I'm with Jack today. Haven't been able to find his angel." Between each word, his forked tongue spattered hisses and sighs.

"And that's why you're bugging me? I already know his angel won't be with him today. Why do you think I'm on overtime with my charge?"

"It doesn't have to be so difficult between us. You and I both know that Jack will have Caitlyn." The hisses seemed to give his words a thick Russian accent.

I rolled my eyes. This was an endless argument that Moros started with me every time Jack came around Caitlyn, but he'd never gone out of his way to get my attention like he had today with the stomach punches. Something else was up. I didn't have to be invisible to talk to him, but it would've looked like I were talking to an imaginary friend. Besides, I was more than ready to be unseen, thanks to Jack. "Moros, this is not why you're annoying me. Get to the point. The real point!" My body started glowing like a nightlight.

Moros slithered back, squinting his reptilian eyes. "Put that light out and I will tell you."

I took a deep breath, closed my eyes, and then slowly opened them. The glow on my skin was gone. "Speak. Now."

"There are rumors spreading that Limos has Cole."

Cole. My heart split inside my chest. I needed to help Cole, but I could sense Moros was going to be more of a problem than I needed at the moment—especially since he was throwing out extra threats on my charge. Next time I meet with Raphael, my boss and archangel, I was going to give him a piece of my mind. Leaving out the part about Cole, of course.

"Selene," Moros hissed. "I like Cole better than I like Limos. Perhaps we could make a deal and I would help Cole get back to Earth?"

"I cannot make a deal with you!" That's what I said, but that silent voice inside my head was desperate to hear Moros out. So I stood there and stared at him, waiting for him to continue. Hoping I wouldn't have to ask.

"Abandon your charge for one hour, just one teensy-weensy hour, and I will tell you who can help you."

I shook my head, trying to force a "no" off my tongue, but my voice was caught on the massive lump in my throat. My chest was so tight I could barely breathe. I sucked at the air, drinking it in as fast as I could. It burned the back of my throat, penetrating my mouth with hot, fiery flames. My skin crawled with tension like there were tiny electric shockwaves zinging along my arms, crawling up my neck, spilling all over my head. I glared at Moros, feeling regret, pain, betrayal, fear, desperation.

If I betrayed Caitlyn for just an hour, Moros would help me save Cole. But what would he push Jack to do to Caitlyn while I was gone? Was it worth Cole's undead life to give my human charge over to the monsters? But all Moros was asking for was an hour. Surely I could repair whatever damage he did in that small window of time. And then I would have a lead on how to save Cole. Everything was going to work out for the greater good in the end. I just had to believe that. I was in love with Cole. Caitlyn would want me to save him if she knew what had happened. She'd be okay. She'd probably enjoy having an unsolicited hour of time with Jack anyway. And what if I can talk Raphael into putting Jack's angel back on the clock? Then at least Moros wouldn't have free reign with him.

Everyone has a choice. After a few grueling moments, I'd made mine.

After making the deal with Moros, I got the name of a vampire who could help me, and a location where I could find him. Moros and I arranged his "free" hour for tomorrow night. That meant Caitlyn was safe for now, and with that thought came a flood of relief. At least I didn't have to regret my decision yet.

Once Corrine showed up, it was time for me to get busy. Corrine was an angel, temporarily contracted to be a backup guardian angel for Caitlyn and two other charges. She was sort of like a substitute teacher. She wouldn't be the first choice for the job, but if the primary angel wasn't available then she got the call. Corrine is around five eleven, with light blonde hair cut short around her long, narrow face. The white dress looks a little misplaced on her broad, sizeable shoulders. She'd been helping me with Caitlyn for the past year. Apparently the higher-ups thought I couldn't handle round-the-clock shifts anymore. Unfortunately, ever since I met Cole, I'd have to agree with them. Even though Grote (the demon that usually trails Caitlyn) hadn't been around for a couple of days, I still couldn't help but feel a little frustrated, a little jealous, and full of a lot of guilt. No one and nothing is supposed to come before a guardian angel's assignment, and that particular someone that was dividing me from my job didn't even have a halo over his head. And now even bigger monsters had kidnapped him.

But before I could find this new vampire ally, I needed to meet with my boss. And that was definitely not going to go well. No, not at all.

3

I DIDN'T LIKE THE WAY Raphael was looking at me. His arms were folded in front of his broad chest, and his fair skin glowed, tinting it a luminescent tan. There was an inquisitive look in his gleaming blue eyes. His long auburn hair flowed like a lion's mane behind his head, while a cloak the color of fresh snow swept behind his body, reminding me of a train on a wedding dress. He took a few steps toward me, his white satin pants sliding up his bare feet. If it weren't for the cloak, he'd look just like any other male angel. But he wasn't. Archangels were the most supreme beings to exist. Every angel strived to be one, yet most weren't capable of what it took. I had been so close. But then I fell in love with a vampire.

"Selene!" Raphael exclaimed, throwing his arms in the air. "What in the world am I going to do with you?"

I stared down at the ground, took a small step back. My feet squished into the billowy surface as if I were walking on pillows. Europa, the world where angels lived, was more beautiful than any paradise I'd ever seen. There were vast meadows, rich in grasses, plants, and flowers, divided by streams of cool blue water. A snow-peaked mountain range rose up in the distance. Tens of thousands of angels floated over the fields like sheer, weightless spirits. Soft fluffy clouds hovered a couple thousand feet above the ground, casting shadows on the paradise below them. That was where Raphael and I were standing.

"Selene!" he roared. "I'm talking to you! Look at me."

My head tilted upward, eyes slowly rising to see his angry face. "I won't apologize again," I muttered.

"You left your charge! She was unprotected for seven minutes!"

"I stepped outside to go invisible. I'm sorry, I didn't mean—"

"Enough!" Raphael shook his head slowly. "Selene, you are the one who prefers human form to guard your charge. Figure out quicker ways to transform, or I will disable you from changing over!"

An argument built up on my tongue, but I knew it wasn't a good idea to go there. "It won't happen again. But perhaps if you put Jack's guardian back on, it would be easier to deal with his demon."

Raphael ran a frustrated hand through his hair. "Jack's demons are not the only things we have to keep your charge safe from." He took another step closer, reaching for me.

I took his hand. He gently rubbed the top of my fingers with his thumb. I stared at his face, waiting for him to finish lecturing me. I'd heard it a hundred times before, each time stinging with guilt a little more. He let out a deep sigh, then pressed on. "You were one of my best guardians. Everything has changed since you have fallen for this vampire. Do you not see that it is causing more harm than any good you can imagine? If you do not find your way soon, I fear you will be lost forever. Once you are fallen—"

"No!" I exclaimed. "Please. I don't want to hear it. Why am I not allowed to love? Because I'm an angel?" I pulled my hand away, turned around. I didn't want him to see the extra moisture welling in my eyes. "Then why do angels feel love at all?"

"We are created from love. It is a good thing to feel it, to know it, to touch it with our hearts, hold it in our hands." Raphael came up behind me, placing his hands on my shoulders. "That is what separates us from the darkness. And that is why you cannot be *in* love with something from the darkness."

"Cole isn't evil!" I pulled out of Raphael's grip, swinging around to face him.

"He is a vampire! They are born of darkness! They follow the darkness!"

A tear finally escaped my eye, weaving down my cheek. "But Cole is different. If he could be something other than a vampire, he would. If only I could change him, make him human."

Raphael came closer, gently placed his arms around me. "It is not possible to change species. Nor would it be possible for you to love him the way you do if he were human. You must call it off with this vampire. Before it is too late."

"Why must I pay such a price for simply falling in love? How can that possibly mean I am dark and evil when love is created from purity and light?" I sniffled, burying my face deeper in Raphael's cloak.

He let out a deep sigh. "Just because I am your superior, your mentor, does not mean I can make sense of every question you ask. It is good to love all things, both good and evil. It is our duty. Our honor. Our privilege. But we have a job to do. We are angels. We must obey those rules or we are thrown down to Earth, or perhaps some other unpleasant world, to be controlled by those in charge there. If that were ever to happen"— Raphael squeezed me tighter against him—"you would never return to Europa. You would be enslaved by demon guardians and you would be tortured for all eternity."

Those words should have been enough to make me forget all about Cole. So why wasn't it enough? Not only was I risking my charge to be with Cole, I was risking my life, my responsibilities in being an angel. I'd already lost the chance to be an archangel. How far would I go before falling indefinitely? Why was love so strong, so blinding, and yet so satisfying? Why do we risk everything we hold to be true in the name of love? When you know it's wrong, when you're certain it's not good for you, why is it still impossible to shut your feelings off?

I didn't bother asking Raphael any of these questions. He spoke in riddles, and I really didn't even think he knew all the answers anyway. But there was one more question I needed him to answer before I left. I wiped my face and started walking, gazing down at the beautiful, brilliant world just below. As if sensing there was more to say, Raphael fell in step with me. The clouds went on as far as the eye could see, so we locked arms and just walked for a while.

Once I finally built up some inner strength, I asked, "So, have you decided if you'll put Saber back on Jack? Please?" I looked up at Raphael's face. It was solemn and very hard to read.

"Why is that so important to you? Saber has a new assignment."

"Please, Raphael. Moros is up to something, I mean he's always up to something, but this time it feels different, more dangerous."

Raphael's lips quirked, but he didn't answer right away. Maybe he was seriously considering my request? I playfully tugged his arm. "Come on. I could use the help. So could Corrine. Just temporarily, until we get through whatever this is. You could put a different angel on Saber's new charge and that would free him up to help watch Jack."

Raphael stopped walking. I stopped with him. "It would be just temporary."

"Yes!" I nodded, beaming my eyes at him. "Just until we find out what Moros is up to."

"So be it. The arrangements will be made. Saber will return to Jack tonight. But once Jack's new guardian is assigned, I am pulling Saber off."

"Thank you! Thank you!" I stepped up on my tiptoes and kissed Raphael's cheek. By the time my heels hit the ground Raphael was gone. I was alone in the clouds.

I wouldn't have even needed to ask for Saber's return to Jack if we had a more efficient way of assigning new guardians to new charges. Jack had sort of been bumped to the bottom of the list since his behavior had gotten out of control. There wasn't much we could protect him from if he wouldn't listen to us. But we couldn't abandon humans indefinitely. We were angels. No matter how difficult, and evil, some people could be, there was still a guardian angel somewhere nearby—unless, of course, they were in the middle of transitioning a new guardian. That usually took about a week in human terms.

My secret mission to save Cole wouldn't stay under wraps for long. Nor would my agreement with Moros. The truth always seemed to leak out at the worst possible times. The building pressure of getting caught weighed heavily on my heart, almost as much as the guilt did. Moros was going to be livid when he discovered Jack's guardian was back on the job. But since that wasn't part of our deal, it was going to make leaving Caitlyn alone for that hour a whole lot easier, and hopefully my punishment not quite as severe.

"Hey, Selene!"

I swung around, finding Beck just a few feet behind me. His soft blonde hair spilled around his narrow face. There was a gleam in his eyes like sapphires in the sun. His skin glowed like a faint light on the horizon, shimmering a yellowish orange. A gust of wind fluttered around us, pressing his white pants against his legs. He took a small step forward, a broad smile stretching across his face. There was something in the way he looked at me. I didn't like it.

"I was hoping to catch you," he panted, voice low and soft. "I've been hearing crazy rumors." He placed his hands on his hips, arching his left eyebrow. "Are you still seeing that vampire?"

I rolled my eyes, turned around, and picked up my pace. "I'm not talking about this!"

"Come on!" He grabbed my arm, a little rougher than he should have. "Please talk to me. I'm your friend! Remember?"

He was right. He was a great friend. But ever since Cole came into my life, Beck was more of a gossiping friend. I didn't like my private business spread all over Europa like some horrible virus outbreak. With that thought I pulled free and started walking again. "I don't want to talk right now."

Beck ran up beside me. "But they're saying that you and that vampire are going to run off together. Or at least try to run off together. But if you do that Raph—"

"Cole and I are not running off together." I threw my hands in the air, already feeling exhausted. "Besides, where in all the worlds could I even go and not get caught? Nowhere! There's nowhere I can go that stays under the radar. I'd have to run forever, and quite frankly I'm not a very good runner!"

"You could do it if you weren't on assignment."

That stopped me in my tracks. I turned and looked at Beck. "Do you really think I would do that? If I wasn't on assignment, then I'd either be in limbo, or…" My stomach turned with disgust. I shook my head violently. "No, no, no! I just talked about this with Raphael!"

"Selene, please talk to me!"

There was a tightness in my throat that kept me from wanting to talk. Beck must have sensed it because his face softened. He put his arm around me. I stayed in his embrace a short while and then we walked in silence together. A couple of white doves flew by, dipping in and out of the cloud. There was a waterfall somewhere beneath us: you could vaguely hear its water surging over the cliff and crashing into the rocks. The sound brought back memories of Cole.

We were somewhere in the Denver backwoods. There was a waterfall close by calling out to us. The night wrapped around our bodies like a velvety liquid. My hands caressed Cole's stone-cold cheeks. I stood up on my tiptoes and crushed my lips against his. His kisses were no softer than mine—firm, moist, and sensual. He gripped the back of my head and brought me closer, nearly suffocating me. Gasping for air, I pulled away. "It's not fair!" I panted. "Why do you make me feel this way? Like everything is perfect and right with the world."

He gently cupped my face. His hands were cold and hard like marble, and yet there was a softness to his touch that reminded me of silk brushing across my skin. "Because I love you," he said, voice rich and intensely erotic.

The heat of those words burned inside me. My heartbeat accelerated. I could hear it slamming in my head.

He lowered his hands just below my jawline. "You're my greatest temptation," he murmured. "I can feel your desire for me." His right hand drifted down my neck, rubbing that sensitive area just before my shoulders. His left hand stayed pressed against the raging vein in my throat.

"I've never wanted anyone or anything more." I traced his lips with my fingertips, trailing down his chin, and then lower. I grabbed his tee-shirt collar and pulled him a little closer. I could feel his face drifting toward mine, but he found my ears instead of my lips. He nibbled on my earlobe, making tiny electric shocks zing through my body. I gasped, stumbling backwards. There was a tree behind me that caught my fall. Before I could catch my breath, Cole was there helping me stand up straight. "Thanks."

"Of course."

"Maybe we should sit and talk for a little while." I slipped out of his grasp and stepped toward the sound of the waterfall. "It's obvious I can't handle you touching me right now."

He half laughed. "Sure. I'll follow you anywhere."

And he did. The waterfall was just a short walk away. There was an oval-shaped pool the rushing water spilled into. A faint cloud of mist hovered over it. The trees and thick brush receded, leaving a small open field. A blanket of greenish brown grass covered the ground, a few flowers scattered about. I closed my eyes and concentrated on those flowers, pushing a tiny amount of my energy into them. They instantly brightened like sparkling stars.

I watched Cole sit down a few feet away from the water's edge. His brown hair swayed across his face like a curtain, drifting just below his chin. His beautiful dark eyes gleamed in the faint light. He wore gray jeans, black boots, and a black tee with a dragon etched on it in red. He bent his legs in front of him, hands coming to a rest on his shins. "Nice light show."

I chuckled, feeling a little embarrassed. Both of us could see in the darkness. That wasn't what my little light show was for. Actually, it seemed that whenever it was dark, we both got into a lot more trouble. "Thanks." I walked over to him, sitting down about a foot away. A little space would be good, as long as we kept that safe distance.

He stared into my eyes, a desire that penetrated deep into my heart. "I would give anything to be with you freely. The thought of your punishment hurts me beyond words."

A chill gripped my spine. I swallowed hard. "Some of my power has been stripped away. But that's done. I cannot earn it back. Please don't feel guilt or remorse. That is not the reason I chose to be with you."

He reached over and started touching my hair with slow, caressing strokes. "I know you say that. How can I love you and not feel some remorse for your losses?"

"You could call this off at anytime! You know that." I tensed and tried to pull away, but he grabbed a handful of hair and wouldn't let go.

"I don't call it off for the same reasons you don't." He pulled my face closer, finding my lips with soft, teasing kisses. In the blink of an eye, he flipped me on my back, holding my wrists above my head with one of his hands. His other hand started tickling along my rib cage. I was laughing so hard I couldn't breathe, begging for mercy between gasps. Finally he stopped and let me go.

I swung upward, punching him in the chest, but he didn't feel a thing. "I hate when you tickle me!"

"But you love me and everything about me." He cocked his head and then wrapped his arms around me, cradling me like a baby.

My head nestled against his chest. "Cole?"

He glanced down as I craned my neck to look up at him, our eyes locking onto each other in some harmonic trance.

"I love you. I love you more than I should. I love you more than life."

He tenderly rubbed my cheek. "I love you too."

"Selene! Did you hear a word I just said? Selene!" Beck's hands were on my shoulders, shaking me back and forth.

"Wh-what? Stop shaking me!" I let out a deep, frustrated sigh.

"You didn't hear what I just said, did you? What were you thinking about?"

I shook my head. "Nothing."

"I thought you would've at least laughed when I got to the part about my charge getting locked out of his room with no clothes on."

I smiled. "I'm forever tainted by the image you just put in my head."

The sound of wind chimes went off in the distance like metal bells jingling melodically in currents of air, and Beck's body started glowing brighter. "Well, I guess I gotta go. See ya later, Selene." Beck shimmered and then vanished, returning to his charge...and leaving me alone with my thoughts of Cole and what I was about to do to save him.

4

IT WAS EARLY IN THE EVENING back on Earth, somewhere near Virginia Beach. I could hear a busy highway close by—engines blazing, an occasional car horn, and a motorcycle that found a clearing and then accelerated to see how fast it could go. I stood on the corner of a residential area. Condos and apartments stretched back from the street, making me feel like I was walking through a maze. Several of the windows were lit, some revealing dark silhouettes of people moving behind them. The streetlamps lining the street looked more like glowing yellow lollipops. The type you might find in a horror movie, luring young children closer, then stealing them into the shadows never to be seen again.

The amnesia from orbing here had finally worn off, but I still felt groggy and disoriented. I looked down at my clothes, making sure everything was in order. Distressed black jeans, a grey tank top, and a pair of black boots with a two-inch heel. Long, wavy strands of my hair fell to the side, loosely pulled together with a ponytail holder. I walked slowly, cautiously. Somewhere in these shadows was the vampire ally I was looking for—along with a whole slew of vampires and demons that I wasn't. And since it was a vampire I needed, I had to be human. Demons were the only species that could see angels in their purest form.

There was movement in my peripheral vision. I swung around but didn't see anything. That eerie feeling of someone watching me made my heart slam in my throat. Then there were hurried footsteps, getting closer and closer, echoing, vibrating. I looked all around, not finding anyone. I stopped walking, took a deep breath. No matter what I encountered here, it couldn't hurt me. I was safe. I was still protected from demons. Limos had already proved that. Vampires would be a little trickier, though. I'd definitely have to use my powers. Hopefully it wouldn't come to that.

Out of nowhere something big slammed into me, taking me to the ground. I spun around and rose as fast as I could. My attacker was nowhere in site. I went from afraid to pissed off in a matter of seconds. "Watch yourself!" I called out. "You do not want to challenge me!" It's funny how anger brings along confidence.

I waited for a response but didn't get one. "Show yourself! I command you to show yourself now!" I held my right hand out in front of me, fingers stretched, then hesitated. I didn't want to use my powers, but the clock was ticking and it seemed to be the only way I'd get any cooperation. Unfortunately if I used too much energy, it would send a signal back to Raphael. When an angel uses enough of their magic, it's like activating a built-in GPS with a flashing light that says, "Here I am." Most superiors pay no attention to this, but my boss had threatened to spy on me too many times. Was he bluffing? God only knew. Obviously I'd prefer Raphael not knowing my whereabouts right now, so limiting my energy use was my only sure way. But if I lingered here too long, he'd eventually figure it out anyway, hence the ticking clock.

To my surprise, two vampires and a demon came out of the shadows, standing several feet away. The vampires were both male. One had long black hair, black leather pants, and a matching leather vest with no shirt underneath. The other was several inches taller and a lot more attractive, with brown hair and dark alluring eyes, and wore blue jeans with a white tee shirt. He sort of looked like Keanu Reeves. The demon was in human form, which I was thankful for, even though the sex was questionable. It was around five feet with short, pale yellow hair and clothes matching the vampire in leather's except for the rust-colored tee shirt.

I crossed my arms over my chest. "Who's the wise guy that knocked me down?" I already knew it wasn't the demon—demons can't touch angels—so that left one of the vampires as my culprit.

The vampire in leather stood very still, stone-faced and threatening. He took a step closer, black eyes drilling holes in me. The brunette vampire's features were softer. He seemed to watch me with fascination instead of loathing. Neither of them answered me, though.

A wry smile stretched across the demon's face. "Who's asking?"

I rolled my eyes. "I don't have time for this. I'm looking for Luke."

"Well he ain't here," the demon said.

"But you obviously know him," I observed.

The vampire in leather licked his lips, inching closer still.

The demon half laughed, shrugged its shoulders. "Maybe I do, maybe I don't."

"I really don't have time for games, guys." I exhaled slowly, a little surprised I'd been holding my breath. "I know Luke is somewhere around here."

"We don't have to help you!" the demon hissed.

"I can be Luke, if you want?" Leather Boy said.

I gave a sidelong glance at the brunette vampire. He was staring at me, eyes curious. "Can you help me out here?" I asked him.

"Leave him out of this, Blondie! I done told ya that I'd be your Luke!" In a whir of movement Leather Boy was standing in front of me, barely an inch away. He was slightly taller than me with my boots on—maybe five foot nine—and his body was rounded and thick. The black leather outfit had given him a more slender appearance from a distance. His face was hard with craggy features. His inky black eyes bore down on me, sucking at my mind like a vacuum.

"No!" I exclaimed, closing my eyes. I wanted to run but I didn't. Running away would only intensify his hunger for me. All vampires love a good chase. I used to love it when Cole chased me. He always caught me pretty quickly, but only because I let him. The moment he caught me was always the best part of the chase.

"Look at me," Leather Boy roared, reminding me it wasn't Cole I was dealing with. He seized my shoulders and started shaking me pretty hard. I squeezed my eyes, straining with every muscle in my face. "Fine! If you're gonna play hardball, well then, so can I!" He grabbed my ponytail, or at least what was left of it, and yanked my head to the side.

A small whimper slipped off my tongue. "Please don't do this. I just need to find Luke," I pleaded, voice small. I was close to using my powers, but a part of me kept hoping I wouldn't have to.

I could feel Leather Boy's breath on my neck. It was warm, evidence he'd just recently fed, but that didn't mean he'd skip the opportunity to eat again, though. My breathing was deep and short. My heart was pumping as if I'd just run a marathon. Vampires can sense fear. They can also feel the vibrations of a rapidly beating heart. But did he know I was an angel? Most vamps don't recognize our signature; however, that demon most certainly knew who I was.

"Damien, don't. Let her go." I didn't recognize the voice, but refused to open my eyes to see who it was.

"Stay out of this," warned Leather Boy, aka Damien I'm guessing, his breath still hot on my skin.

It was eerily quiet for a very short moment and then I was jerked to the side, slipping free of Damien's grasp. There was a loud *thwack* and a few other muffled noises banging and scuffing close by. I stepped back, opening my eyes. Damien was on the ground. The brunette vampire was on top of him, slamming his fists into his face. Damien held up his arms, trying to block the attack. Some big badass vampire he was now.

I saw the demon take a few steps back, shifting its eyes from the fight to me. When it saw me staring back, it flashed around and bolted away. It knew where Luke was—I was sure of it. Adrenaline shot through my body, and I was running after it before I realized my feet were moving. The sound of the vampire brawl was growing distant, though I was pretty sure I'd heard Damien begging for mercy.

"I won't hurt you. Please. I just need to find Luke!" I shouted to the demon, now about twenty feet away. The little voice in my head was tempting me to zap it with a bolt of lightning—using my energy for electricity alone shouldn't be enough to send a beacon to my boss, but if I was wrong and Raphael found out I was here, my whole plan would be blown.

"Never! I will never help you!" It growled back—literally. Its body burst into ripples that looked more like rapid waves underneath the skin. A dark cloud materialized around it, and I stopped running. The cloud hovered a little longer before completely dissolving away, leaving a deformed lion-thing in its wake. It didn't have any fur except for its raggedy, patchy mane, which was still that pale yellow color. Its skin was gray and scaly like a lizard's. A loud growl rumbled from deep inside its throat, after that it lowered its head close to the sidewalk, red eyes glaring at me. Then, surprisingly, it took off running the other away instead of lunging at me in full attack mode. I was left standing alone, debating over and over in my mind if I should use my powers to track and hold it until it talked. My only other option—go in and ask nicely—had just failed miserably.

Pain and hopelessness in their rawest forms expanded in my heart, tightening my chest. "Cole," I said under my breath, shaking my head slowly, my hands curled into fists, hoping that motion alone would hold me together. Though it seemed to be working thus far, I knew it wouldn't last much longer. I was on the edge, peering into an abyss of emptiness, desperate for anyone or anything that could help me save Cole.

A hand gripped my shoulder, and I startled, quickly spinning around. God, please don't tell me it's Damien back for round two. Could this day get any worse? But it wasn't Damien—it was the brunette vampire. I looked at him cautiously, warily, stealing a breath before asking, "What do you want?"

His lips curved into a small smile, revealing a glimpse of fangs. "I thought I would help you…since you've gone to so much trouble to find me and all."

I studied him for a moment. His hair looked soft and shiny, like silk lying out in the sun. It hung along the sides of his head, modestly framing his perfect, creamy face. He stood casually, arms crossed over his chest, his left eyebrow slightly raised. I'd guess his age was somewhere around twenty-five in human years, which was a littler older than the age I went for in my human form. "You're Luke?"

He nodded. "Why are you looking for me?"

Hoping the truth would be best; I dove into explaining the situation. "I was told you could help me by, um, an acquaintance. A vampire has been kidnapped by an otherworldly demon. I'm willing to help Typhon—"

Luke held his hand out. "Whoa! Wait just a minute. How do you know all of this? I can buy that you know about vampires, and even demons. But no human knows about Typhon."

I stared at him a moment, the reality of what I was doing hitting me. But I couldn't stop. I couldn't turn around and leave. Cole needed my help. More importantly, I needed to help Cole. My face felt flushed, a mixture of raw emotions and the sting from the position I was in. I swallowed hard. It was time to get real with Luke. "My name is Selene and I'm an angel."

He gaped at me, eyes wide with shock. "Aren't you out of your jurisdiction here, Angel?"

"Yes, I am. And that's why I need your help. I can't force Limos to show me where Cole is. But if Typhon knew, I believe he would do something about this."

"Did you say Cole?" He said that name with recognition, familiarity, yet there was a mischievous gleam in his eyes I couldn't quite place.

I nodded—slowly up and then back down.

"I know Cole. I just saw him the other day. He can't possibly be missing."

"But he is. Limos took him!" I said, my voice rising.

Shaking his head, he replied, "That just isn't possible. Typhon wouldn't allow *any* otherworldly demons on Earth without permission, let alone give an opportunity for one of his dark ones to be taken from him."

I looked down at the ground and then back up, meeting Luke's eyes. A lone tear rolled down my cheek. With a tight chest and muffled voice, I told him everything. How I took Cole to Charon and everything that went wrong once we were there.

He snorted in disbelief. "An angel...romancing a vampire?" He nearly spat the words. "I've never heard—"

"We've been together a little over a year. Fourteen months, one week, and three days to be exact," I stated matter-of-factly.

He considered me for a moment, as if he didn't know what to say at first. I'd never heard of any other angel-vampire relationships either, so I guess I couldn't blame him. "I'm guessing Typhon didn't know that Cole left Earth?" was what he finally asked.

"No, I don't think Cole told him."

Another minute of silence.

Luke ran his fingers through his hair. His head tilted slightly. "If Typhon decides to aid you in this, he will want something from you in return."

"I know." I explained to Luke how I'd made a deal with an Earth demon just to find him and how I was hoping Typhon would accept that as part of a deal.

"All right." Luke turned around and started walking.

I went after him. "Wait! All right what? Will you help me?"

He turned around, staring deep in my eyes. "I said all right. I'm going to see Typhon."

"Just like that?" I asked, a little surprised at his willingness to help. Especially without asking for something in return.

"Yes. And we're wasting time by discussing this anymore. We need to know if Typhon will help us."

"We? What do you mean 'we'? And why are you so willing to help me? I mean, I appreciate it and all, but there has to be something you want?"

"Let's get one thing straight, Angel! I'm not helping you for *you*. I'm helping you for Cole."

My voice was stuck in my throat. I nodded so he'd know I understood. Yet, there was something mysterious floating in the depths of his dark eyes—something that made me doubt him, or at least not fully buy into what he said.

"So I'm leaving now to go see Typhon," he went on. "I'll send word to meet with you when I get back."

I swallowed, slightly loosening up my throat so I could speak. "Okay. Thank you."

"Don't thank me yet, Angel. We will see how things go in the Underworld." Luke turned on his heel and walked away.

"I love him," I called out, desperation crushing my heart. "I love Cole more than anything. That's why I'm doing what I can to help him."

He disappeared around a corner without another word. Of course I was helping Cole because I loved him. But there was also the guilt of being the reason Cole had been taken in the first place. Love can make you do crazy things, but when you add guilt to the mix, crazy becomes stupid, dangerous, and even life-changing. Everything was moving so fast. I silently prayed that Cole's safe return would be even faster.

The next few moments felt vaguely familiar. Heat flushed across my skin, and then it felt like my insides were compressing. My vision blurred. I closed my eyes, squeezing them shut. There was a horrible, disorienting feeling as my body swayed against a blast of pressure. Right before my mind went blank and my body went completely numb, I remembered thinking that this was how I'd felt the last time I'd accidentally orbed somewhere.

My eyes shot open. I sucked at the air, then let it back out through deep gagging coughs. I looked all around, swinging my head to the right, left, and even up at the sky. Water was everywhere, as far as my eyes could see, and my legs were half submerged in it. A small wave splashed against me, some of it getting up my nose. I started hacking as I crawled up onto the shoreline. Small, jagged rocks were mixed with grainy sand, which bit into my hands and knees as I pushed up onto the compact, dryer area. My clothes were soaked, jeans torn, my tank top ripped from the collar to my armpit on one side. At least my bra still covered me up. There were cuts and scrapes all over my bare feet. Don't even ask where my boots went.

A loud grumble erupted nearby. The ground vibrated slightly, then a woman's voice shrieked out. Moments later, her voice echoed against the rocks, singing and chanting. Its high-pitched notes reminded me of being at the opera, but its demonic vibe reminded me of Anthemusa, a demon water world filled with sirens and aquatic serpents. A siren was a water demon. And I was sitting smack dab in the center of their world.

I pulled myself up, using some of the rocks to do so, then steadied my balance on the uneven surface. A siren was approaching, I could feel her presence prickling on my skin a few minutes before I saw her gliding through the water toward me. Her lower body was hidden beneath the surface, most likely riding on one of those wretched aquatic snakes. The upper half of her was very curvy and feminine. It was in a solid form, even though it was made completely of water. She even appeared to have long hair flowing behind her. She came to a stop about twenty feet away, still half covered by the waves rushing by. "What do we have here?" she asked. Her voice was expressive and sharp, each word sounding like part of her enchanting song.

I shook my head, finally gaining my memory back and feeling annoyed with yet another orbing accident. "I apologize for coming here. I mean you no harm and will be going soon."

"Oh no, don't go," she purred as she floated a little closer. There was definitely something under her but I couldn't see enough of it yet. "Please stay for a while. Sing with me, angel. Our voices can rain down on the land in a beautiful harmony."

"I don't think so. Like I said, I'll be going soon. Please respect that."

She frowned. Tiny drops of water fell from her arms as she raised them above her head. "You cannot leave. You just got here." Her eyes darkened. They looked like bottomless water pits. "I will not let you go. Not until you sing with me."

Sirens knew that angels wouldn't sing with them. But they still couldn't handle a refusal of any kind. Why in all the worlds did I accidentally orb here? I took a small step back but couldn't go much further. A wall of rocks, about waist high, prevented me from moving. Unless I turned around and climbed over it, I wasn't going another step, but there was no way I was taking my eyes off the angry siren.

She slithered a little closer. I swallowed hard. Please, God; tell me I still have my powers. I searched inside myself, pulling at the corners of my heart and mind, willing the energy to come to me. Instantly, I could feel it swelling in my veins. My arms tingled with the electricity from inside my body. I opened my hands wide, letting the power move to the tips of my fingers. I moved my hands out in front of me, very slowly and cautiously. The siren stopped approaching, her eyes glaring at me.

The sound of wind chimes erupted in the distance. I let out a deep sigh of relief, and my body started glowing a radiant creamy white.

"No!" she wailed. "No, you cannot go! I will get you. If you ever return, I will get you!"

I flashed her a smile as I closed my eyes. And then I was sucked away—far, far away from Anthemusa.

5

THE TRANSITION TO MY HUMAN CHARGE went a lot smoother when I was called to her side, versus the other times when I did the orbing myself. This time I didn't have any amnesia to recover from, so I sat on my twin-sized bed, in invisible form, staring at Corrine across the room, fully aware that if looks could kill, I'd be six feet under. Thankfully they didn't. Another reason I was thankful was because I couldn't sense Grote—or any other demon for that matter. Before I could ask if the usually bothersome demon had showed up while I'd been gone, Corrine gave a final roll of her eyes and vanished.

I could hear Caitlyn using the hair dryer in the bathroom. Protective instincts pulled me from the bed like a magnet drawn to iron. I floated across our square-shaped dorm room, giving one backwards glance at Caitlyn's side. It was a mess. Gray sheets strewn all over the bed and a lavender comforter rolled up on the floor. Her small wooden desk was just beyond her bed, in the corner of the room. Papers and books were scattered everywhere, and a laptop was sitting somewhere in that mess. It literally looked like a cyclone had hit her half of the room. Mine, however, was in perfect condition. Sheets folded neatly on the bed. Books and papers stacked and organized on my desk. Of course, having magical powers is a plus to keeping things neat and tidy.

I used a little magic to shape-shift into a pair of dark skinny jeans and a red velvet, scoop-necked top as I approached the bathroom. "Cait, I'm home," I called out to her.

When she didn't respond, I gave a loud knock on the door. "Cait, it's me," I yelled.

The hairdryer stopped and then the door swung open. "Where have you been? We're going to be late for Brix!" She looked me up and down and her face softened a little. "Oh," she said, sounding a bit startled. "I didn't realize you were already dressed and ready to go."

I shrugged. "Of course I'm dressed. What time is it anyway?"

She raised her left wrist, bringing her white, leather-strapped watch close enough to read. "Almost seven-forty. We needed to leave five minutes ago!" She rushed to the closet in the back of the room, frantically looking for shoes to go with her faded torn jeans and a Hawaiian black tube-top, one jumbo-sized white flower stitched to its front. Her makeup looked perfect—not overdone, but very natural with a little powder, bronzer on the cheeks, and a smudged brown line under both eyes. She wore her hair down with a few stray pieces swooping across her face, just above one eye.

I used a little more magic to throw my hair into a low ponytail and shift into a pair of tan wedge sandals while she was fishing out her other black, peep-toe pump. We left our dorm, heading straight for the parking lot, walking as quickly as our shoes would let us. I concentrated on keeping Caitlyn steady and balanced. Tripping over uneven pavement, or one of her own feet, wouldn't be a good way to start the night.

Caitlyn drove a newer-looking cherry red Honda Accord. She rushed into the driver's seat and fired up the engine as I got into the passenger side. We rode in silence, her attention mostly on driving and getting us there as fast as humanly possible. There was a pedestrian that didn't look before attempting to cross the street. Miraculously, and with a little angel help, she swerved around the panicked person and kept going. There was no such thing as a "near miss." There's always a guardian angel behind it, keeping the car on the road while you're texting, or helping the car turn sharper to avoid hitting someone or something.

Brix was a lounge connected to an average-rated hotel, The Desiree. There was a dining area to the left, where they offered bar bites and tapas-style food choices, which was just another word for small portions. To the right was the bar, the counter stretching across the entire left side of the room. A couple pool tables were off to the side with a handful of bistro-style tables and mini chairs scattered around them.

There were also about a dozen angels hovering closely to each of their charges, and about half that number of demons. Guardian angels were required to be with their human charges at all times—even when those pesky demons weren't present. That was why substitute angels, like Corrine, were created. Believe it or not, people seem to find just as much trouble without the help of anything dark provoking them. It's amazing how many "close encounters" humans have had with death, only to repeat the same mistakes over and over again expecting different outcomes. If I were human, I'd be thanking God every second for placing a guardian angel to watch over me and keep me safe.

Stacey and Rob were sitting at the far end of the bar, their guardians, invisible to everyone but me, close by them. Stacey was barely twenty-one and had the cutest blond pixie cut framing her face. She wore flared jeans and platform sandals, which made her five-foot-seven body look a few inches taller. Rob was at least six foot, maybe a little more, with short brown hair that looked blonder in the sunlight. In the subdued, smoky atmosphere in here, though, it appeared a darker brown.

"Caitlyn! Selene!" Stacey wailed in excitement. She jumped up and rushed toward us, arms stretching around in a tight group hug.

"Hey girls," Rob said in his usual low, unexcited voice.

Caitlyn and I smiled at him as we broke free of Stacey's grasp and found our seats at the neighboring bar. Caitlyn glanced around the lounge, most likely checking to see if Jack had arrived yet. She frowned and grabbed the specialty drink menu lying on the counter. I guess that meant no Jack yet. Goody for me. But I could sense Saber close by, so it wouldn't be good for me much longer. I breathed a sigh of relief that Raphael had put Jack's guardian angel back on him. Maybe it'd make Jack more tolerable this evening.

"How's biology going?" Stacey asked Caitlyn. "Still struggling to keep an A?"

Caitlyn shrugged. "I guess it's going a little better than the last time we talked."

"A little better?" I chuckled. "I'd say a lot better. Mr. Henrickson has fallen head over heels in love with her. He'd pass her whether she earned the grade or not."

Caitlyn gently elbowed me in the arm. "Hey! Watch it! You don't know what you're talking about."

Stacey took a sip of her drink. "You guys wanna play a round of pool? Rob and I against you two?"

Caitlyn glanced at me with a brow raised and I nodded. "You're on," Caitlyn said as she motioned the bartender over. She ordered a club soda for me and a draft beer for herself. The bartender immediately asked for her ID. She dug in her messenger bag and pulled out a driver's license that read "Dianna Lynn McCord." Dianna is twenty-two and has a vague resemblance to Caitlyn. The bartender studied it a moment longer and then handed it back. As he turned to get our drinks, Caitlyn let out a sigh of relief.

I leaned over, my lips close to her ear. "You need to get rid of that fake ID before you get in trouble."

"Yes, Mother," she hissed, giving me a very obvious roll of her eyes.

With our drinks in tow, the four of us made our way over to one of the pool tables and got on with the game. About a quarter of the way through it, Caitlyn and I were in the lead with three solid balls sunk. Rob was studying the striped balls on the table. Stacey glanced at Rob and then turned her attention back to me and Caitlyn.

There was a slight magnetic pull in my aura: Saber was getting closer. I looked up and saw him and Jack coming into the lounge. Jack was tucking a cell phone into his jeans pocket. Perhaps he was finishing a call outside before coming in. He quickly saw us and made a beeline for Caitlyn. Saber trailed behind him, invisible to everyone but me. He was tall, slender, fair-skinned, and had bushy golden hair framing his rectangular face. His deep green eyes threatened to burn a hole in me. I half smiled and shrugged. I guess he *was* upset over getting reassigned to Jack.

Caitlyn and Jack hugged, long and lingering, and then Jack looked over at Rob. "Who's winning?"

Rob pointed at Caitlyn with the tip of his pool stick, then at me. "These two."

"Good girl," Jack said in Caitlyn's ear, just loud enough for me to hear. I was standing no more than a couple feet away, wishing more than anything I was invisible. Then I remembered the look on Saber's face and was thankful I was in my human form.

Rob took his turn and knocked in two striped balls at once. Jack headed over to the bar, Caitlyn following right behind him. Stacey was cheering Rob on as he leaned down and made another scoring shot, and that's when my stomach jerked into a knot, hard enough to nearly bring me to my knees. I swallowed hard, my fist rubbing small circles against my waist.

"You okay?" Stacey asked. Her eyebrows creased as she stepped toward me.

"Yeah, I'm okay," I replied, nodding. "I'll be right back. Gonna run to the ladies room."

"You sure?" Stacey placed a hand on her hip.

I smiled. "Yeah. Be back in a minute." I dashed away, heading for the bathroom. When I got out into the lounge area and saw no one was there, I went invisible. Then I rushed back into the bar area, not wanting to leave Caitlyn unattended with Jack.

The bartender was handing Jack a Miller Light. Saber was standing near the bar and immediately noticed my form. "Selene," Saber hissed.

"Not now."

"I was happy with my new charge!"

"It's not like you won't see your new charge again. Watching Jack is temporary. I needed your help."

Saber's face softened a little. "What do you mean, you need my help?"

I started to answer but once again my stomach twisted. I looked back and saw Moros heading straight for us.

"Not this clown," Saber said, rolling his eyes and stepping back.

"Yes, this clown," Moros hissed. "I'm expected to be here. However, *you* are not." Moros' glowing red eyes glared at Saber.

"Well, I'm glad to be here then," Saber replied.

A deep growl reverberated off Moros' tongue. "This isn't acceptable," he hissed.

I swallowed hard. Was everything I'd done about to be exposed?

"What are you up to, Moros?" Saber asked, glaring down at the demon.

"Me? Up to something?" Moros erupted into laughter trailed by hisses.

"It's no wonder the archangel put me back here," Saber snapped. "You're out of control!"

Moros instantly stopped laughing. "We'll see, Angel Boy. Perhaps I should give you a reason to be here." In a flash, Moros jumped into Jack— literally. His Komodo dragon body completely blended into Jack's human shape, leaving no trace of the demon. Then Jack, possessed by Moros, grabbed Caitlyn by the shoulders and started shaking her violently.

"Jack, stop it!" she screamed.

Saber flashed to Jack and stepped into him, a little more gracefully than Moros had. I was already next to Caitlyn, pulling her out of Jack's grasp. Tears streamed down her face as I tugged her a couple more steps away. Rob and Stacey came up beside us. Their guardians stood cautiously, waiting to jump in if one of their charges got involved. Stacey's arms stretched out and Caitlyn fell inside them, crying hysterically.

Rob stepped closer to Jack. "What the hell's wrong with you, man?"

Jack's body twitched side to side, then Moros went flying out of it across the bar, landing on the other side of the pool table. Jack shook his head, gasping for air, then placed his palms on his temples. "I don't know."

Saber stepped out of Jack, wiping his hands together. "Where's that wretched demon?" he asked me.

I gestured with my eyes across the bar. I could tell he wanted to go after Moros, but the situation between Rob and Jack wouldn't allow it.

Rob got closer to Jack, almost getting in his face. "You can't treat a woman like that!"

Saber approached his charge, and Rob's angel floated a little closer as well.

Jack shook his head, still looking a little dazed but with anger flaring in his eyes. "That ain't no woman. She ain't been with a man yet!"

Rob pushed Jack in the shoulders, causing him to take a couple steps backward. "Get the hell out of here, you loser!"

Jack started to move toward Rob.

The guardian angels were sending calm, soothing vibes into their charges, trying to deflate the anger and encourage a more peaceful solution, but it didn't seem to be working.

Suddenly the bartender shouted, "Not in my bar! Ya'll going to fight, take it somewhere else."

"How could you do that to Caitlyn?" Stacey yelled, holding my distraught charge against her body, arms wrapped tightly around her.

Jack started backing up, inching his way to the door. Since everyone's attention was on him, I glimmered back into human form. Conveniently I'd been behind Stacey, and Caitlyn's face was buried in her shoulder. I rubbed Caitlyn's back and whispered, "It's okay, sweetie."

Stacey jumped and looked back. "Where the heck did you just come from?"

"Uh," I shrugged. "The bathroom."

Stacey released Caitlyn, and she scooted straight into my arms and resumed crying. "Did you see what just happened?" she asked through sobs.

I nodded slowly, then realized she couldn't see me. "I saw enough of it," I said, my voice low and seething, then glanced at Stacey. "I'm taking Cait home."

"Do you want me to come with you guys?" Stacey asked, raising a brow.

I shook my head by way of an answer.

"I'll see you later, Caitlyn," Jack called out. He still lingered in the doorway, a smug look all over his face.

"The hell you will," Rob shouted, his right fist waving in the air.

Jack flashed a broad smile, then turned and left. Saber rushed after him, Moros trailing right behind them. Their fight was far from over. My fight with Moros would be coming—he'd see to that sooner rather than later, I had no doubt.

I patted Caitlyn's back, soothing her the best I could as Rob made his way over. "What a jerk. Caitlyn, I'm so sorry."

"I don't want to talk about it, please. Selene, I want to get out of here." Her voice was muffled against my shoulder, a few gasps between each word.

Rob nodded. Then he reached for Stacey's hand. She eagerly took it.

"Thanks for the offer," I said to Stacey. "But I'm going to get her out of here and we'll call if she needs anything."

Stacey mouthed a silent "okay" and then I led Caitlyn out of Brix. After everything that had just happened, I should've been more focused on Caitlyn. But the foremost thing on my mind was Cole, and when—or if—Luke would get back to me with an answer from Typhon.

6

CAITLYN PASSED OUT shortly after getting back to our dorm. After tucking her under the covers, I kissed her on the forehead. Then I sat down on my bed across the room and watched her sleep, thankful not to hear her crying. My knees were pressed against my upper body, my arms cradling them. A pressure built up in my chest and spread into my throat. I sniffled a few times, then swallowed hard. My eyes prickled, eventually spilling out wet, sticky tears.

I wasn't quite sure how long I cried for, but the minute I sensed *its* presence, I stiffened. I wiped my face, slowly looking over at the door, which was closed and locked—not that it could keep out the unseen. I shimmered invisible to the world of humans and waited. *It* didn't keep me waiting long.

A thick, black, smoky-looking shadow floated up from underneath the door. As it rose, two long arms stretched out, their stick-shaped fingers pointing at me. The rest of its body looked like one big blob of goo—except for its big, neon green eyes. "Hello, Angel," it said. There was an indentation of a mouth on its face, blending in with the goo, and when it spoke, its body rippled like waves.

I cocked my head to the side, feeling vaguely amused. "Who are you? Where's Grote?"

"Oh, Grote will be joining us shortly." It erupted in laughter, sinister and somewhat intimidating. Its whole body jiggled, and its green eyes darkened as if filling up with smoke.

I grimaced. "Lucky me, I get two of you tonight. If either of you wake her up, you'll surely regret it."

Its snickering stopped. "Maybe that would scare Grote, but I do not feel pain. It will be such a pleasure to disappoint you."

That statement just set me off. I threw my legs over the side of the bed and got up. My body started glowing, shimmering a whitish-yellow light all over. The demon floated backward, instantly colliding with the door. It threw its arms over its eyes and squealed like a baby pig. "I thought so, you fool!" my tone vehement. I took a few more steps toward the demon, my body brightening. "Do you still wish to challenge me?"

"No," it shrieked. "Please stop. Shut that off!"

"I asked you what your name was, beast! Now tell me what it is!"

"Morton! It's Morton," it wailed. "Please, Angel! Turn it off!"

I half laughed, folding my arms in front of my chest. I dimmed my body a little, but kept a faint glow all over so he wouldn't forget my power. "Your name is Morton?" I asked, sounding surprised. "Morton doesn't sound like a very beastly name."

Morton lowered its arms, gaping at me with those big, smoke-filled green eyes. "My master named me. It is a wonderful name. Don't speak about things you don't know!" It floated a little closer, hovering a few feet above the ground. "My master wishes that I help Grote for tonight."

"Fine! But don't forget who I am and what I can do!" I exhaled a deep breath of air, blowing Morton back against the door. "Do not awaken my charge!"

Morton looked up at me, appearing shaken—as much as a gooey blob can look shaken—and replied, "I won't. I won't bother her while she sleeps."

I turned around, walked back to the bed, and sat down. Morton stayed by the door, eyes sliding from Caitlyn to me. It never said another word the rest of the night. Grote never showed up, which was no surprise. Either Morton was lying or Grote had blown it off—or maybe it was both. But you just couldn't trust a demon. I'd learned not to take anything they say to heart.

Caitlyn woke up around eight o'clock in the morning. I (along with Morton) followed her around the first half of the day. She moped around, looking sad and depressed, dragging herself from class to the campus research center, to another class, and then straight back to the dorm where she collapsed on the bed, burying her face in a pillow.

I flashed a warning look at Morton, then went in the bathroom and turned visible. I shifted into a pair of jeans and a gray camisole. I walked out of the bathroom and saw Morton still floating by the door, his eyes locked on my charge. I headed straight for Caitlyn, placing my hand on her back. "How are you doing, sweetie?" I asked.

"Horrible." Her voice was muffled in the pillow, the words choked on her tears.

"I'm so sorry." I rubbed small circles on her back, patting in between them to try to comfort her.

She raised her head out of the pillow and looked up. Her hair was matted to her face, partly covering her eyes. "Can you believe he hasn't called to apologize?" she sniffled.

I shook my head and watched her, not really sure what to say.

Morton floated over and whispered, "Don't worry, he'll call you," and I knew she'd feel those words as an impression inside her mind.

If he calls, don't answer. He's not good for you. I pushed my thoughts into her head.

"When he calls, you should take it," Morton said right away. He was already annoying me.

No you shouldn't. He doesn't deserve to hear your voice.Why reward him for his horrible behavior last night?

Morton started to say something, but I was done with this angel versus demon battle. I closed my eyes and exhaled slightly, sending him flying into the wall once again. I glanced at him, challenging him to speak one more word with my eyes, and then looked back at Caitlyn, hoping she hadn't noticed. All of a sudden, "E.T." by Katy Perry blurted out from somewhere behind my charge's bed, seizing her full attention. Her eyes lit up as she crawled forward and reached for her purse on the desk. She pulled out an iPhone and tossed the purse back. She stared down at the illuminated screen as the song stopped playing, then quickly raised the phone to her ear. "Hello." She waited a short moment and then repeated, "Hello."

Morton floated closer. I flashed him a glare, then returned my attention to Caitlyn.

She slowly lowered the phone. "It was Jack. But I didn't answer fast enough." She stared down, gripping the phone tightly in her hand. "Should I call him back?"

"No way! Absolutely not," I replied.

"Yes you should. He'd love to hear from you," Morton said. "He's calling to apologize."

I could feel Caitlyn's comfort in the demon's logic and I rolled my eyes with disgust. "Cait, just give it a little more time. Please."

"No more time is needed," purred Morton.

Caitlyn let out a deep sigh. "Maybe you're right." She looked up and met my eyes. "He doesn't deserve to talk to me yet, does he?"

"No, baby, he doesn't," I replied as I leaned forward and hugged her. She returned the embrace.

Morton floated closer, voice low and steady. "Just go ahead and call him. He's sorry. What he did wasn't that bad. Call him, call him, call him."

I squeezed Caitlyn tighter and inhaled a deep breath. Energy zinged through me, causing gooseflesh on my skin. I locked eyes with Morton and opened my mouth, carefully shooting forth my energy with barely a puff of air so Caitlyn wouldn't notice, and again he flew to the back of the room, crashing into the wall. Then I took another breath, easing some of the power inside me.

"You can do that all you want, Angel, but I'm never going to stop!" Morton yelled. He started floating back toward me and then the room rippled and warped. Morton froze. "Who's coming? Who did you send for?"

I half laughed. Caitlyn pulled back and looked at me. "What's so funny?" she asked.

"Nothing. I, um, I just remembered I needed to be somewhere five minutes ago." I leaned close and kissed her cheek. "I'll be back in a few hours. Will you be okay? Do you need me to bring you anything?"

She shook her head. "No, I'm fine. Thanks."

I jumped up from the bed and started walking toward the door. Morton glared at me as I passed him and then Corrine appeared. Her body shone brightly enough to blind the annoying demon. He swayed back against the wall, cowering behind his arms. "Turn it off," he squealed.

I smiled at Corrine, then left the room. Once I confirmed I was alone in the hallway, I shifted back to invisible. The moment I did, a demon appeared. It was a goblin-looking creature about three feet tall, with a black body and dull red eyes. "The charge is not unguarded!" I exclaimed, folding my arms in front of my chest. My body instantly gleamed.

The demon jumped back, throwing its clawed hands over its eyes. "Please don't. I'm not here for the human."

I let my light fade, raising a brow. "Then why are you here?"

The demon peeked out through open, bony fingers. "I'm here for you. Luke sent me."

I couldn't help but think what perfect timing that demon had.

I stood on a street corner, just off Atlantic Avenue, in Virginia Beach. I could hear the ocean's waves crashing against the shore, but I couldn't see the water from where I was standing, though I could feel the moon's pull on the tide as it rose and the sun set. There were restaurants and shops lining the streets, which seemed to go on for miles. Joggers, rollerbladers, and tourists passed back and forth with an occasional car—with a supped-up muffler, overdone speaker system, or both—zooming down the street. I had been waiting for nearly fifteen minutes, but there was no way I was going to start complaining about it. I still couldn't believe Luke sent for me the moment Corrine showed up to watch Caitlyn. It was as if it was meant to be. Maybe if I kept telling myself that, it'd come true.

I shook off the thought, wrapping my arms around my chest. The first chills of the fall season were here, sifting through my light gray cardigan and making me thankful I'd worn it over my tank top. I'd also shifted into a pair of jeans and boots. A small chrome butterfly clip clumped a few wisps of hair together on the right, preventing it from falling in my face, and the rest of it fell in loose waves to the small of my back.

Suddenly, my skin zinged like static electricity, indicating something dark was approaching. I unwrapped my arms and waited, but it didn't keep me waiting long.

Luke walked out of the shadows about thirty feet away. In the blink of an eye, he was standing right in front of me. He wore faded jeans and a white tee with a picture of a Tootsie Roll Pop and the words "How many licks does it take?" across the top. His brown hair was soft and glossy, parted evenly down the middle and falling just below his ears on both sides. "Hello again, Angel," he said with a gleam in his eyes.

I wasn't in the mood for polite small talk. "What did Typhon say?"

A sly smile creased his face. "Come have coffee with me and I will tell you." He walked past me in human steps and turned left down Atlantic Avenue. A *vampire* wants coffee? Slightly amused, I followed—not that I really had a choice.

Cliff's Kona's was only a few blocks away. Since I didn't want to be recognized as an angel by those from the spirit world, I masked my aura as I walked through the doors. It was big for a coffee shop, with dozens of small tables spread around an expansive room. There were dark blue vinyl love seats in three of the corners, with plenty of wooden end tables for people to set their coffees on. The walls were sky blue with pictures of other coffee shops painted on them—a few from France and Italy, and a few with more of an island theme. There was a heavyset man sitting on one of the love seats with a newspaper in his hands. A couple of college-aged guys occupied two of the tables. One of them was an angel—in human form. The rest of the guardians (and demons) were diaphanous, hovering around each of their charges. Even though they could physically see me, masking my aura prevented them from sensing my angelic waves. Very few angels had this ability, and I was so very thankful it hadn't been stripped from me—yet.

Luke ordered an iced green tea for me and a chilled vanilla latte for himself. After retrieving our drinks, we went over to the table furthest away from the other customers and sat down across from each other.

"Vanilla latte, huh?" I teased.

Luke smiled, big and beautiful, a trace of fang glistening through his lips. "Don't knock it 'til you try it."

I set my tea on the table and crossed my left leg over my right. "Why the formalities? Why not just tell me what I need to know in the alley where you had me meet you?"

The smile faded and, as he leaned closer, his eyes darkened. "Don't worry about what I do or why I do it. Do you still want my help or not?"

I stared at his eyes—deep, dark pools of mystery. I could feel them poking at the corners of my mind, making tingles scatter around my head, then spill down my neck. My body tensed. I couldn't look away. I inhaled a deep, slow breath. My fingers sizzled with energy, but I pushed it away. I couldn't tap into *any more* of my powers; as it was, masking my aura was probably pushing it. And I knew it was just a matter of time before Luke figured that out (though I was certain that action alone wouldn't have been enough to alert Raphael).

He pressed a little further, digging deeper inside me, and I had to let him do it. Seconds dragged by, or maybe no time passed at all. Panic seized me as I felt him slithering through my head, slimy tentacles slicking inside the most private sectors of my mind, prying and prodding into my deepest, darkest secrets. The moment he had complete control over me, he

44

pulled out, leaving me feeling dirty…and violated. I quickly looked away, blankly staring outside the window, and hugged myself. I let out a breath without realizing I'd even been holding it. "You bastard," I murmured.

"Why'd you let me in?" he asked, an inquisitive tone in his voice. "From what I've heard about angels, you could've stopped me."

I looked over at him, careful not to meet his eyes this time. "Don't worry about why I do things and I won't worry about you."

A sly smile curved his lips. "How about *you* tell me what I want to know because *you're* the one who needs help from me."

I swallowed hard, keeping my eyes on his lips. My hands dropped to my lap. "Please just tell me what Typhon said. Will he help me…um…us?"

Luke took a sip of his latte and set it down. "I can see we're not going to be able to work together on this. Perhaps I should be going now." He stood up slowly, cautiously.

I reached forward and grabbed his hand. "Please, don't go!"

His fingers intertwined with mine and, in a sudden blur of movement, he pulled me up against him. I felt dizzy and afraid, but I didn't try to pull away. I was all in with Luke, with no other options. I'd never felt more weak.

His lips were close to my ear. I could feel his breath—a chilling warmth brushing my skin. He'd recently fed and stolen the heat from his victim. "Answer my question so I can answer yours, Angel. Why didn't you stop me from getting inside your head? I really didn't need to know all of *those* details about you and Cole."

Cole. Just hearing his name created instant tears in my eyes. "I love him so much," I breathed against Luke's chest. "I didn't stop you because I can't stop you. I can't use too much power or my archangel will find me. If he finds me, he'll stop me. And if he stops me, I may never see Cole again."

Luke released me. I looked up, meeting his eyes this time. They were just eyes, no threat to penetrate my mind. A few moments passed in silence, then we both returned to our seats. Not wanting to seem afraid, I broke the silence. "I've answered your question, now tell me what Typhon said."

Luke sipped his latte and leaned closer. "My master didn't believe me at first. He sent a messenger spirit to confirm the information, which is why I didn't get back to you sooner. The boss was beyond pissed when the spirit returned and confirmed everything you'd said was true. Limos is hiding, and my master is forming a small army to bring him in. You must have a horseshoe up your ass, Angel, because my boss didn't want anything from you. The information you gave was enough. You're free to get back to *whatever it is* you do."

"But what about Cole? What will happen to him?"

"He'll be just fine, unless"—Luke's brows furrowed—"he's killed while the dark army is retrieving him."

I swallowed hard. "But Limos has an army of his own. He'll fight back! What if he—"

"If Cole dies then it's *your* fault, now isn't it?"

The way he said that made my chest tighten. I slumped in the chair, staring at the table. There had to be another way! Even though I knew Typhon was stronger than Limos, that didn't guarantee Cole would make it out alive. There was only one thing that did, but since I didn't trust Limos—or any demon for that matter—I wasn't one hundred percent sure that would even work.

"What is it? What are you thinking about?" Luke asked. "You should be happy with the results of this, with no penalty to you."

"No penalty?" I exclaimed. "You have no idea the price I've paid to be with Cole. You cannot begin to grasp what I will do to get him back!" I stood up, looking down at Luke. "Thanks for what you've done to help. I'll take it from here."

As I turned to leave, Luke grabbed my arm. "Wait."

I made eye contact with one of the college guys (not the angel). He quickly returned his attention to the book in his hand. His guardian sat across from him and was also reading something. I'd been so blinded by desperation and anger, I'd forgotten all about others being present in this coffee shop. I took a deep breath and turned around to face Luke. "What do you want? We've put on enough of a show for these *people*."

Without a word, he wrapped his arm through mine and started walking. Not wanting to make more of a scene, I went along with him. As we exited Cliff's Kona's he said, "What are you going to do? I want in on it."

7

CAITLYN WAS GETTING DRESSED when I returned to her. While she'd been under Corrine's guard, she'd managed to not only talk to Jack, but to also arrange to meet with him. Since tonight was the night I'd agreed to leave Caitlyn unguarded, Moros must have been ecstatic. Morton was gone and Grote still hadn't shown up, but that didn't mean they wouldn't be around later. Saber was my only hope tonight. I'd been working on a way to explain why I needed to leave for an hour. But so far, I hadn't come up with anything.

I decided to stay invisible since Caitlyn probably wouldn't want me coming with her anyway—plus I needed to talk to Saber. I followed behind her as she pulled up to Eat, a popular restaurant with a Latin-American theme. Caitlyn glanced in the mirror on the back of the visor, then got out of the car. I could sense her nerves racing as she headed toward the entrance. A water fountain trickled beyond a few of the outdoor benches. A few light fixtures hung from an overhead lattice covered with bougain-villea sprouting bright pink flowers, their faint light created shadows that blended with the darkness.

I felt Saber before I noticed Jack walking out of the shadows, eyes gleaming in the soft light. Caitlyn went to him and they embraced—so much for my advice he wasn't good enough for her. Where was Moros? I didn't sense him anywhere. How strange, but it might turn out to be convenient for my upcoming absence. Saber appeared beside me and we followed the lovebirds inside.

Music vibrated through the restaurant, just loud enough to hear that the words were in Spanish. Caitlyn and Jack followed the hostess to a table for two in the back corner. They were handed menus and then promised someone would be with them shortly. I couldn't help but keep wondering why there still weren't any demons on either of our charges. Then I finally thought of a plan.

"Selene," Saber pouted, "I'm obviously still stuck with this wretched human. I'd hoped a replacement would've been found before now."

"I'm really sorry about that." I said it, but I didn't mean it.

"Sure, whatever."

"Where's Moros?"

"Why would I know where that despicable monster would be?"

"I, um, I figured he'd be here since Raphael put you on Jack." But the fact that Moros wasn't here was actually working to my benefit. "Anyway, that must explain why *they* need a meeting with me."

"What meeting? What are you talking about?" Saber put a hand on his hip and cocked his brow.

"Um, you know, that *meeting*. They need me to come…*now*."

His face went blank for a moment and then he exclaimed, "Uh-huh! I heard about that! You're finally gonna get it, aren't you?" His cheeks turned red and his features softened. "Oh, sorry, Selene. I didn't mean it to sound like that. I hope you don't get in more trouble, since you've always been nice to me, but honestly, you're gonna get something for your recent behavior. Everyone is talking about it."

Relief flushed through me. *This plan is working*, I thought. "So, you've got everything handled here, right?"

He nodded. "Of course, of course I do! Go on now before you get in more trouble for keeping *them* waiting." He shooed me away. The last thing I remember thinking before I orbed was how easy that whole thing went.

My body was shaking. I felt pressure on my shoulders and face, and heard a voice so distant I couldn't understand what it said. I tried to look, but couldn't see beyond a blurry wall. Iridescent light flitted around a dark roundish shape, as if it—or I—was underwater. The voice grew louder, but was still muffled beyond recognition. My heart pounded so hard, I could feel its vibrations in my ears.

The voice got closer, louder, and the ringing in my ears faded. There was a molten, coppery taste in my mouth, warm and wet. I blinked, and finally could see more clearly. A man was above me, shaking me with one hand while his other arm pressed firmly over my mouth. "Angel! Angel! Wake up!" he was yelling. I recognized his voice, but it wasn't enough to confirm who he was.

I pushed his arm off my mouth and scooted back, my elbow grinding against concrete. "What are you doing?" my voice demanded with a hint of outrage.

His lips compressed, but he didn't answer. Yet the look he was giving me spoke volumes: confusion, worry, and relief.

I cast a wary gaze at my surroundings, then glanced back at the man. We were in some sort of alley, but I wasn't sure where. There were sounds of a dance club off in the distance, the pulsing music no more than a soft buzz drifting along a light breeze, which also brought musky scents of old trash, urine, and booze. My senses started swirling out of control, anxiously seeking my memory; all the while I was trying to keep my cool and not freak out, because I knew this guy, and I knew I was supposed to be here with him. I closed my eyes, relaxing my mind and suppressing my panicked emotions. It took a few moments to find that calm, soothing place in my head, but once I was there, it was as if nothing else was around me. Then, I opened my aura, willing it to find that piece of me that was lost—the part that had been stripped away when I'd been caught orbing places I wasn't supposed to go. And that's when I remembered where I was and who I was with. Luke—a vampire. And he had just given me blood. *His* blood. I was gagging the next instant, trying to spit it out. "You can't give me that," I hissed. "It's poison to me!"

"I thought you were dying." He sounded concerned, with a soft, uneven voice.

"Angels don't die," I replied dryly. I spit a few more times, trying to get as much of his blood from my mouth as I could. But a metallic flavor lingered deep in my throat, and I knew I'd ingested some of it. No angel really knew for sure what the blood of a dark one would do to them, since none had ever drunk it. Fear crawled up my spine, but I pushed it to the back of my mind, knowing time was of the essence. And I'd already wasted enough of it with my little blackout-amnesia stint.

"Then what the hell happened?" he demanded, folding his arms together in front of him.

"Don't worry about it!" I stood up but lost my balance and started to fall. In a flash, Luke was there holding me up.

"What's happening to you, Angel? You better tell me right now! You better not jeopardize *our* plan!"

I shook my head, then leaned against his chest. It was hard like marble—just like Cole's was. "I won't screw this up! I want Cole back too!"

"Well, you're in no condition to go anywhere right now. You can't even stand without me helping you."

I didn't say anything back because he was right. I couldn't stand on my own—not good. The blackouts and amnesia were even worse. The thought of orbing again scared the hell out of me, but I'd be doing it soon to return to Caitlyn.

I couldn't tell Luke what was happening to me...or should I? I let out a deep sigh and asked, "How long was I out?" Nope, better to not tell him.

He gave me a suspicious look, then released me. I didn't fall this time. Goody for me. "Just shy of thirty minutes."

"Thirty minutes?" I repeated to him, sounding shocked. That only left me thirty minutes. Would that be enough time? If I needed a similar recovery period, then I was already screwed. *Just great. Too late to turn back now.* I turned on my heel and headed down the deserted alley.

"Where are you going?" All of a sudden Luke was next to me, holding my hand.

"I just need to be moving, that's all." I pulled my hand free and kept going, feeling suffocated by the stress of my situation, a situation that could, once again, quickly become a debacle.

"Well you're going the wrong way if you want to meet Huron." Luke retrieved my arm and pulled me back the other direction.

He didn't let go until we arrived at some hole-in-the-wall bar. I immediately closed my eyes, bringing the shield over my aura. Since there wasn't a sign anywhere, I had no idea what this place was called. The minute we walked in, cigarette smoke and stale vomit crowded my nose. There was a pool table—with barely enough room to actually play—and a bar area in the back. About a dozen barstools surrounded the old wooden countertop. There were six others in here, including the bartender. We sat down and waited for service. No one paid us any attention until the bartender made his way over to us. His appearance told me that there was some American Indian in his family tree—at least when he'd been human—and I knew this must be the friend Luke had told me about.

"Luke," the bartender said in a friendly tone, confirming by observation, "good to see you, my old friend." They shook hands.

"Huron, this is Angel," Luke replied, then looked at me. "Angel, this is Huron."

Huron's chubby cheeks pulled into a smile as he reached a hand toward me. "It's Selene. My name is Selene." I took his hand in mine, returning the smile.

"Nice to meet you, Selene." He let me go and looked back at Luke. "So what is it you need me for again? You said someone was in trouble?"

"I won't bore you with all the details. They're not important anyway." Luke shifted in his seat and leaned closer to Huron. "An otherworldly demon took a friend of mine, and me and Angel here have a plan to get him back, but we need your help with that."

"What do you need me to do?" Huron asked, watching Luke with solemn eyes.

"I need you to rally a few vamps, and demons too, that are willing to go to Charon. That's how we're getting our boy back."

Huron rubbed his chin. "Well, the vamps won't be a problem, but the demons might. Charon, huh? Won't the boss have a problem with that?"

Luke laughed. "The boss is already on it."

"But your plan isn't part of the boss's?" Huron inquired. What a smart undead man he was.

"The less you know, the better, ole buddy."

Huron flashed a knowing smile. "How long before you need 'em?"

Yesterday, I thought.

"Yesterday," Luke replied. Was he reading my mind? Impossible! I quickly shook off the thought.

Huron nodded and let us know he'd be in touch as soon as he could. Luke and I had left the bar, heading back to the alley so I could discreetly orb back to Caitlyn, when a terrible, stabbing pain struck my chest. An agonizing cry rushed out as I pressed my hand over my heart, collapsing to my knees.

"Angel, what's wrong?"

I couldn't answer. It hurt too bad. I'd never felt anything like this before.

Luke picked me up in his arms. "Hold on. This might make you feel dizzy, but I gotta get us somewhere more private."

There was a whir of movement all around, flashing lights, and then more of that horrendous chest pain. My fingers massaged through the cloth of my shirt, desperately trying to find relief. But the pain was deep inside, throbbing spasms cutting through the center of my heart. I remembered Caitlyn, my deal with Moros, and immediately I sensed something was wrong. It was as if the wind was knocked out of my lungs, and I struggled to find my next breath. Something had happened to her. I just knew it. The sharp, shuddering pain intensified, and it felt like I was about to pass out. I was disoriented beyond words, leaving me speechless. Where was Luke taking me?

When the dizzying movement stopped, I saw concrete walls everywhere. Even the floor and ceiling matched the gray décor. It reminded me of a basement. Luke laid me on an old, scratched-up sofa, gently placing a pillow under my head. "Just lie here a minute, I'll fetch you some water," he said.

I sat up, still in pain but finally able to speak. "No. It's not necessary. I'm fine."

"The hell you are."

"It's not your concern," I hissed, feeling a pressing urgency to return to my charge. "I've got to go. Send for me when we're ready." I closed my eyes, placing all my focus on Caitlyn. Everything warped around me, then went completely dark.

It was twilight. Oversized red rocks surrounded me as I ran. The ground was hard, with an inch of dusty orange sand on top—which slowed me a little. I could sense the clearing coming up ahead, then the amphitheater just beyond that. The Red Rocks Amphitheater, I thought. I could hear a man laughing in the distance. The voice was ever so familiar. Cole.

I kept up the pace, not daring to look back for fear it'd slow me down. Cole might seem far away now, but he'd be on me in seconds if I weren't careful. Then I'd never hear the end of it. Although I'd let him, he'd already caught me the last six times. It was time for me to break his winning streak.

I rushed past the clearing, shape-shifting my boots into a pair of sneakers, then leapt on the top row of stadium seating. The amphitheater was built on the side of a mountain, and the seating sloped downward from the direction I'd come. I lunged for the next row of seats and something crashed into me from the side. Just before I hit the ground, there was a swish of movement. My face felt cold against the rushing air, but it didn't last more than a second. Then I was standing at the base of the stadium and not particularly happy about it.

"I won," Cole said from behind me, wrapping his arms around my waist.

"Dang it! I almost had you!" I exclaimed in defeat. "A little magic never seems to be enough!"

Cole half laughed. "So tonight it's your magic's fault. Or at least your inability to use more of it."

I elbowed behind me, hitting his rock-solid abdomen, feeling a slight aching tremble spread through my arm from the impact, and I wished even more that I could use my powers. "I'm just saying, you'd never have won if you weren't using your vampire magic."

"Ha," he scoffed, gripping me a little tighter. "Selene, you're a sore loser. Admit it!"

I wiggled around and looked up into his eyes. "I wouldn't say I was sore about this." I stepped up on my tiptoes and kissed him. My hands went straight to the back of his head, pulling his face closer. I smashed my lips against his, my tongue sliding back and forth on them. He accepted my invitation and opened his mouth. My tongue moved in a practiced motion, staying clear of his sharp fangs. It didn't take long for him to take over and do a little mouth exploring of his own. My body felt dangerously hot all over, my breath coming in short bursts between kisses.

He pulled my hair to the side as he left my mouth and trailed down to my neck, leaving a cold wet trail on my skin as he moved. I could sense his mouth on top of my vein; could feel the smallest prick of his teeth, but not enough to break the skin. "I know that's what you want," I purred.

His reply was a muted growl as he gently sucked on my neck.

I grabbed a handful of his beautiful brown hair and pressed his face harder against me. "Go ahead. It's okay. Just don't take enough for them to notice."

"I can't. We can't," he mumbled. His sucking traced the edge of my chin, then back up to my mouth.

He kissed me hard and violently. His fingers instantly found the button on my jeans. I grabbed his hand as he unfastened them, and moved it around to my butt. He pulled back and looked at me, disappointment flashing in his eyes. "That's not fair."

I stepped away, pulling free of his hands. "None of this is fair. I want you so bad. I want all of you. And I want you to have all of me. But this"—I pressed two of my fingers against the vein in my neck—"is all I can offer you."

"You know I want to taste you more than anything, but I love you even more than that."

"But I can give you the best blood you've ever had. I can make it taste exactly how you like it." I sighed and turned around.

Suddenly Cole was in front of me, forcing me to look at him. "Selene, I want to, but even you said it was a horrible idea. If they found out—and you were pretty sure they would—they'd finish you off for good. What if they didn't send you to Earth? What if they sent you to another world, and then I'd never see you again? We can't risk it. I can't risk it."

He was right. Every single word. Tears welled up in my eyes. "But I want to feel even closer to you. I love you, Cole."

He put his hands on my arms. "I want to feel closer too. But you shouldn't tempt me. Next time I might not be able to stop." His lips crushed mine, making that little reality check become a blur.

Then everything around me was hazy. There was nothing around me. Cole was gone. "Cole!" I screamed. "Cole!" Panic seized me. I couldn't breathe. Then I remembered Cole was missing. We'd been at the Red Rocks last month. I'd been looped in a memory from my past.

I closed my eyes, then opened them. I was on a cloud—in Europa. Raphael stood several feet away, his back facing me. "You're finally awake," he said without looking.

I swallowed hard and nodded. Then I realized he couldn't see that and said, "Yes."

He slowly turned. His hair didn't flow like it usually did. It lay flat to the sides as if it was wet. He stared at me with flaming blue eyes. "You have no idea what you've done."

I cowered at his voice and instantly knew something was wrong with Caitlyn. "What's happened?" I asked, my voice small and weak.

"Did you even sense she was in danger? Did you?" he roared, and his body flared in golden hues.

I shook my head. My throat was so tight I couldn't answer aloud.

"I didn't believe it at first! But then I discovered you were nowhere to be found! Moments later, I could feel you orbing and I snatched you!" He moved closer, glaring down at me. "Stand up and face me, Selene! Right now!"

I didn't move at first. I just gaped at him, completely scared out of my mind. But then I grew more afraid of what he'd do to me if I didn't obey him. Slowly, I stood up, but I'd never felt more small. My eyes stung with the threat of tears as I looked up at Raphael's face. I'd never seen him so upset. "What happened? Please tell me," I begged.

Suddenly, blue flames shot out of his eyes and burned straight into mine. I gasped, but couldn't move, standing paralyzed as the heat filled my body. Unbelievable pain shot out with the blaze, torching my insides like dried wood. In my head I pleaded with him to stop, but was so distracted by the pain I couldn't push my thoughts into his mind. The heat intensified and I felt nauseated and wobbly. Pressure swirled around me, warping and twisting like a tornado crunching metal. This must be what it was like right before *falling*.

And just when I thought I'd be orbed to another world, Raphael stopped. The blue flames left me and receded back into his eyes. My whole body shook as the heat within it simmered. Then Raphael spoke, loud and authoritative: "Return, Selene! Return to Earth and see for yourself what you have done!"

8

I WAS IN A ROOM THAT REMINDED me of a hospital. There was a sink to my left and a blue-patterned curtain straight ahead, the eerie sounds of buzzing and beeping coming from behind it. Styrofoam-like squares covered the ceiling. With a turning stomach and constricted throat, I walked toward the curtain and drew it to the side. I wasn't prepared for what I saw. "No!" I cried out, collapsing to the floor.

It took me a few minutes to pull myself together enough to crawl the remaining distance that separated me from my charge. I pulled myself up, using the edge of the twin-sized hospital bed, and stared at the beaten body lying on it. A cast covered Caitlyn's left arm, while purple and bluish-colored bruises mottled her right. A blanket, tucked under both arms, concealed her legs. Her once beautiful face was discolored beyond recognition, and her right eye was swollen completely shut. A tube about an inch in diameter hung from her mouth, connecting her to one of the beeping machines to the left of the bed. Other tubes and wires protruded from her body in various places.

I swallowed back bile as I turned around, unable to look at her another moment. *I did this. It's my fault! I did this to my charge!* Now if I could just find a hole to crawl into so I could hide and never come out!

Raphael materialized beside me. His cloak was wrapped around him, blanketing his body. A golden seal of a dove, about the size of my hand, pinned it together below his neck. He stood stoically for a moment, then

UnGuarded

put his hand on my shoulder, causing the cloak to flow open. At his touch, my skin instantly radiated orange. Since I was too ashamed to look at him, I stared down at the floor. The bottom of my white dress was dirty and torn. It looked like I'd been running through a mud puddle—a giant mud puddle.

"Selene." My body shivered as he said my name.

"Wha-what ha-ha-happened to her?" came my small, broken voice.

He didn't answer. The silence was killing me. I gave a long sigh and asked again.

"Saber was fighting three demons while two more slid under the radar and possessed Jack. Those demons used Jack's body to beat your charge unconscious, just before some innocent bystanders intervened and stopped him. He fled the scene, but the police have him in custody now."

"Five demons?" I repeated, dumbfounded. *Five demons?* I hadn't expected Moros to conjure up so many at once. Without a doubt, I knew Grote and Morton showed. But I'd been expecting that, and knew Saber could handle all three of them with his eyes shut. So who were the other two demons, and why were they ordered to attack my charge? Most of the time, demons were unorganized, and they definitely didn't follow orders well—unless the orders were coming directly from Typhon.

Interrupting me, Raphael asked, "Did you make a deal with one of those dark ones?"

I felt the truth flush my face. I glanced over and could tell Raphael noticed it. Too late to lie now, so I nodded.

Raphael removed his hand from my shoulder and closed his eyes. "I knew it was true, but I didn't want to believe it. You were so close, Selene. So close, and yet so far away. How can you love something dark this much? You've given up everything for him!"

I knew he was referring to me almost becoming an archangel, like him. I had given that up for Cole—amongst a few of my angelic powers. One of those lost powers was healing. Every guardian angel has limited healing abilities that they may only use on their charge. Since I'm Caitlyn's primary guardian, only my powers of healing could've worked on her. I wouldn't have been able to heal her all the way, but at least it would've been enough to awaken her from the coma she lay in.

"Will she wake up? Will she be okay?" I asked, my voice sounding small.

"I don't know."

"But you are shown the future!"

He turned and faced me, his deep blue eyes penetrating mine. "No! I am shown the *possible* future. There are factors that can change the outcomes I see."

"What were you shown? What *might* happen to Caitlyn?"

"I haven't seen her path yet." Raphael gripped my shoulders again, fingers pressing as his face drew close. "Now tell me, are there any more deals you've made with demons—or any dark ones for that matter?"

My throat felt tight. I started to look down at the floor, but Raphael shook me aggressively, forcing my gaze back up to his. "Do you love that vampire *that*"—his eyes gestured toward Caitlyn—"much?"

My stomach clenched with distress. "I *do* love him, but I love her *too!*"

A nurse came in to check on Caitlyn, but since I was in angel form she couldn't see me—or the very angry archangel standing in front of me.

"Your love is twisted, Selene! Your charge is supposed to be your priority! Now tell me, have you made any other deals with *any* of the dark ones?"

As I started to answer him, wind chimes went off in the distance, but these weren't for me. Raphael's eyes flared a deep blue. "When I return, you will answer my question," he threatened, and then he disappeared.

Since archangels didn't have charges, I knew those wind chimes meant something else. But since I'd never be an archangel, I'd never get to see for myself where it was the highest supreme beings went.

Four days passed by. Not once did I shift into human form, nor did I leave Caitlyn's side. There hadn't been a single demon on her either—not that her condition merited much attention from them. She was in a coma, being fed through a tube, with no vital response to anyone who came to visit her. The doctor informed Caitlyn's mother (Andrea), who got in last night from Washington, that if nothing changed in the next few weeks, there wouldn't be anything more the hospital could do for her. Now Andrea stood over Caitlyn, grief filling her face beyond what any parent should feel. A female angel I didn't know accompanied Andrea, along with a demon I'd never seen before either. I ignored them both, keeping my attention on my charge's mother.

"Baby girl," Andrea whispered as she scooped Caitlyn's hand inside her own. "Please wake up. Please show me this is all a bad dream."

When no response from Caitlyn came, Andrea fell into the chair beside the bed and sobbed for the hundredth time. Each time she did that, pain cut my insides like sharp claws were tearing into me. I'd been sitting on the foot of the bed, unable to stop looking at my charge. Finally, exhausted from my own guilt and despair, I hugged my knees against my chest and cried with the grieving mother.

"Please," Andrea wailed, "please wake up."

Nothing.

"I'll be more available if you do. I'll get a different job that will allow me to come see you more. Please, baby, please wake up." Andrea leaned over and gently stroked her daughter's cheek. "Lord," she prayed, "I know I've made so many mistakes, but please don't take my baby girl away from me, please. Let her wake up. Let her wake up now, please."

The only response was *beep, beep, beep* of the nearby machine keeping Caitlyn alive. Then something that sounded like an air pump went off. It hummed a few minutes, then went silent again. Andrea was still praying over Caitlyn, getting no answers, no responses.

The guilt pressed down, harder and harder, suffocating me inside a bubble of despair and loss, and I needed to release it, get it off my chest, and catch a much-needed breath. So I finally spoke with a voice only audible to the unwanted spiritual audience. "I'm sorry. I'm so sorry for what I've done. Cait wouldn't be in this mess if it weren't for me. I wish I could change the hands of time and give your daughter back to you—happy and healthy just like she was before this happened. I love Cait! I really do. But I love him too and I'm just so very sorry." Ashamed, I buried my face back into my knees.

"I've heard of you, Selene," spoke a soft voice I didn't recognize. "I'm sorry this has happened. I'm Natalia."

I peered over my knees and saw that Natalia was the unknown angel in the room—Andrea's guardian. Both she and the demon stood on either side of the grieving parent. Natalia was about my height with long hair the color of chocolate. Her white flowing gown was similar to mine—except for the torn and muddy part I had at the bottom. The demon was just a black floating glob of smoke with greenish eyes. It had chosen not to materialize all the way. With it being outnumbered, I didn't blame it one bit.

"This is all my fault," I explained to her. "I feel horrible for what's happened."

"But Selene, you know everything happens for a reason. This was supposed to happen."

I always hated that response when humans used it. I hated it even more now coming from a fellow angel. "Spare me the dramatics," I said, sounding more sarcastic than I'd meant.

"Sorry, but you know it's true. Everything will work out in the end. It always does."

I didn't say anything. This was *so* not the speech I wanted to have.

"So what's it like," Natalia asked, "to be in love?"

I felt my eyes widen. Did an angel just ask me that? But I still answered her with, "You know what love feels like."

"Not that kind of love. You know what I mean. What does it feel like to be *in* love with someone else?"

Should I answer her or pretend I didn't hear? There was nothing more I could lose, so why not go for it? "There's nothing else like it," I said under my breath. "Loving him is perfect and wonderful, amazing and satisfying. And it's not just because I love him, but because I'm loved by him in return. I felt weightless every time we were together. I long for him when we're apart. Even now, after all of this, I still think of him. I still love him and want him here with me. Humans have it so good to be able to experience this kind of love so freely."

Natalia just watched me with an unknowing gaze. It almost looked like pity. It hurt, but was nothing compared to the stabbing pain in my chest. Cole. Each day that passed without getting him back left me feeling more desperate, empty, and lost. Even after all of this, I still wanted him.

Luke hadn't sent for me yet, which was probably a good thing. There was no way I could leave Caitlyn alone again—even though her current state made demonic attacks unlikely. Plus there's the orbing problem. Having amnesia was bad enough, but the unconsciousness was worse. What if I couldn't wake up in time to see the plan through? After all, I was the bait. The whole thing wouldn't work without me—awake.

It had been my idea to give myself up for Cole, but Luke's suggestion had been better, and would provide me a way out. First, I'd be masking Luke's aura. Then he and I would be taking a trip to Charon. As soon as we arrived, Limos would sense me and come straight for me. I was to offer myself to him in exchange for Cole. If Limos took the bait, then I'd arrange the time and meeting place. Hopefully by that time, Huron's mini army would be in place and I'd be taking all of them with me upon returning to Limos. He wouldn't suspect a thing since I'd be masking everyone's aura but mine. Once Cole was in sight, Luke and the mini army would jump Limos and whatever minions he had with him, and I was to use that distraction to grab Cole. Then orb us all back to Earth. This could really work, right? Well, it had to since there wasn't a Plan B.

I'd been so heavy in thought I hadn't noticed that Natalia and the demon were gone. *Uh oh.* I felt like a sitting duck. I wasn't really sure how long he'd been standing there since he obviously had his aura hidden from me—on purpose, no doubt. But feeling his presence now, I looked behind me and met his eyes. "Hello, Raphael," I said.

His auburn hair gleamed brighter, like shimmering gold laced with ice. "Oh, to know your thoughts, Selene. I sure hope they're about your duties to this innocent charge."

I couldn't get my voice past the lump in my throat. *Thank goodness he can't read minds.*

Raphael moved around the bed and stood close to Andrea. Her sobs had simmered and she wasn't praying anymore. Anger glared in her red, swollen eyes. Her shoulder-length brown hair looked sticky around her face. She stood up and headed out of the room, to where her spiritual followers were probably waiting, with one long glance back at Caitlyn as she pushed through the door.

"It's been decided that you're to remain this charge's guard," Raphael said.

Believe it or not, I'd somewhat expected that. If I was going to get cast down from Europa, it would've happened back at that last meeting with Raphael. But he'd held back then, which meant my time wasn't all the way up—and that meant there was still a chance I could get Cole back.

Raphael's voice deepened. "But do not forget the thin ice on which you stand."

I felt my eyes widen as I nodded. An eerie moment passed in silence, then I asked, "Were you shown anything yet?"

He shook his head, steady and slow. "No, but since you're so eager to hear about her possible future, I'll be happy to share the path with you once it is shown to me."

I gestured toward the machines flanking Caitlyn's bed. "Her stats haven't changed. Isn't there any way you can help? You're more powerful than I ever was."

"You know I can't—"

"But if she doesn't get better… No, she has to get better. What if her mother decides to unplug the machine? No parent would want their child to live like this. The doctor has already gone over the options."

"Selene, you cannot worry about things that have not happened. You only control the now, and you must give whatever positive energy you have left to your charge. Hold her, pray over her, lift her up with all the love you can harness."

"But I've already done all those things," I pouted.

"Do them again, and again. Never give up. *He* is always listening and watching."

I gave a long sigh, trying to hold the tears in my eyes. Raphael shook his head and vanished—without another word.

Five minutes had barely passed when I sensed a dark presence. I refused to acknowledge it at first; I knew this demon wasn't here for Caitlyn—it was here for me. I glanced over and saw the same demon Luke had sent to retrieve me before. It didn't speak—neither did I. I couldn't leave without knowing Corrine would be here, or at least some other angel that could keep watch of my charge.

"Go on," I hissed at the demon. "Let him know I'll be there as soon as I can."

The demon nodded, then vanished inside a cloud of grayish smoke. Then, to my relief, Andrea returned. She had a bag of food from Subway in one hand, a book in the other. Good, she planned to camp out for a bit. Natalia and that same demon from before now flanked either side of her, which was all I needed to come up with a plan.

I explained to Natalia that I needed to get some air, which was partly true. I couldn't stand to be in the hospital room another moment. Maybe it was her pity for me, but she bought it, and I was thankful. Natalia was a little nervous about me leaving, but she promised she could handle Fizer, the demon currently tracking her charge. I glared at Fizer and promised hell if it tried anything while I was away. It cowered back, bringing a small smile to Natalia's lips.

I didn't linger another moment, didn't want Natalia changing her mind. I orbed off, heading straight for the vampire who'd summoned me.

9

I'D BEEN PASSED OUT EXACTLY thirty minutes, with just a little disorienting memory loss. Luke was across the basement while I lay on his sofa, waiting for my dizziness to wear off so we could leave. He kept a watchful eye on me as he paced back and forth. He'd already expressed doubt (and a little concern) at least five times. He was working on the sixth, saying, "I know you're holding out. What is it? What's wrong with you?"

"For the last time, there's nothing wrong. We just need to plan on me passing out for thirty minutes when we get to Charon. I'll mask both of our auras now, and when I come to, I'll lift the mask off of mine."

Luke stared at me a moment and then submitted. "Fine. If you say so."

I sat up, thankful the dizziness was gone. "Come here."

Without seeing any movement at all, Luke was sitting next to me. Startled, I half laughed as I brushed my hands against my jeans.

"What is it?" he asked.

"Cole used to sneak up on me like that."

Luke smiled, a glimpse of fang showing. "Our speed is one of the perks to this, for sure."

"Hopefully it will be a *perk* to our little plan. Vampires have always been faster and better skilled at fighting, compared to demons."

"Touché."

I leaned closer, holding my hands open, palms facing his face. Then I started moving them very slowly around his body.

"Will this hurt?" Luke asked.

A vampire asking me if something hurt? I'd heard it all now. "No, you won't feel a thing."

It only took a minute to finish masking him and another minute to do myself. I scooped up his hand and asked, "You ready?"

He hesitated a moment, then replied, "Ready as I'll ever be. Since I've never *orbed* before, can you just tell me a little bit what it's like before we go?"

Interesting. Luke really was nervous about this. Cole had seemed more excited, but maybe it was because we had something more positive to look forward to, like being in each other's arms without the threat of getting caught—or so we had thought—only Raphael hadn't been the one to catch us. Oh, how different things would be if he had. Cole would've been returned to Earth and I would've been reprimanded and sent back to my charge. Then I'd never have had a reason to leave Caitlyn unguarded and she'd be awake and happy, carrying on with school, her friends...and Jack.

"Angel," Luke said. "Is there a reason you're not answering me? Is there something I should know before we *orb*?"

"Sorry, um, no. There's nothing you need to know. Your skin may tingle a little while we travel, but we'll be there in a few seconds so you may not even get a chance to feel anything. You're already accustomed to moving fast anyway."

That answer seemed to comfort him. Luke's grip tightened. "All right. Let's get this over with then. Shall we?"

I smiled, closed my eyes, and concentrated on Charon.

When I opened my eyes, I was standing in a deserted, war-infested-looking terrain. Some strange, and yet slightly familiar man, was next to me, holding my hand. Startled, I shook him off, stepping back one slow step at a time. "Wh-wh-who are you? What's going on?" I frantically looked around as fear prickled up my back. There were mountains off in the distance, rippling black water separating them from me. My feet were partly covered by ashy-looking sand—or maybe it was just ashes. I peered over at the man—no wait, not a man. I closed my eyes momentarily, breathing in his essence. My eyes flared open. "You're a vampire!" It wasn't a question.

He gaped at me, eyebrows raised. "You've got to be kidding me. It's Luke. I'm Luke."

He approached but I backed up. "Don't come any closer!"

"Angel, what are you doing? This isn't funny!" His hands hung at his sides, balling into fists.

"Don't even think about fighting me!" I warned.

Luke the vampire glared. "I wouldn't dream of it, Angel, but you're really starting to piss me off!"

I took a few more backward steps and closed my eyes. A tingling heat spread over me.

"What are you doing?" the vampire shouted.

"I'm getting out of here."

In a blur of movement he was gripping my arm, shaking me. "Angel! You cannot leave! We have a deal to make with a demon before that! Quit acting like you don't know why we're here! More importantly, quit acting like you're gonna leave *me* here!"

"Let go of me!" I yanked my arm, but the vampire's grip didn't loosen the slightest. "Release me now!"

Luke let go and looked me up and down. "Wow, you really had me fooled. I honestly believed you loved that vampire enough to pull this off. Turns out you just used him to bring me the same fate."

"What are you talking about?" I hissed.

Luke ran his hands through his hair. "How did you project those memories of Cole to me when I glimpsed your mind?"

Cole. I knew that name. An avalanche of memories gushed through my mind. I grabbed my head, pressing into the skin, trying to ease the pressure. It throbbed badly, warping my vision. I closed my eyes, squeezed them shut, my whole body trembling as images blurred inside my mind. It was Cole. The man I love…no, vampire I love. Cole was why I was here in the first place, with…with…

"Luke," I breathed. "I remember. I'm so sorry." I walked to him and grabbed his hand. It was stiff and cold.

"What-the-hell-just-happened?" Luke roared.

Crap. I guess I should have explained what had been happening to me every single time I orbed somewhere I wasn't supposed to go. But I just didn't want him knowing I had a weakness—not yet anyway. And though I still wasn't sure if I could trust him, as I stared into his anger-filled eyes, I felt guilty for not mentioning it. "My orbing has been a bit…dysfunctional lately," I offered by way of explanation.

His brows furrowed together, his gaze hardening. "What do you mean by 'dysfunctional'?"

I shrugged. "Blacking out, a little memory loss, and sometimes I end up in strange places."

His fingers tightened around mine. "Don't you think you should've told me those little details *before* we orbed anywhere? What the hell else aren't you telling me, Angel?"

My guilt intensified, making me defensive. "You didn't have to come with me this time!"

"Yes I did!" he shot back. Then he let me go and started pacing in a small circle nearby. He kept running his hands through his hair while refusing to look at me. Obviously, he was very upset, but it had been his idea to tag along even though he wasn't needed until I struck a deal with Limos. I remembered how Luke had said he wanted to "scout out" the place and also keep an eye on me in case anything went wrong, and it made me feel even worse.

"I'm sorry," I called out. And I meant it.

He stopped pacing and locked eyes with me. His voice came deep and loud: "I'm sure glad I *did* come so I could learn about your little secret *before* I start a war with my own damn kind!"

I cowered from his voice, but felt the need to get back to why we were here. I couldn't stand the horrible memories I had of this desolate place, and being here pushed each one of them to the front of my mind. "Luke, we're here now. Let's just get on with this. Please." I gave a small smile and started walking toward him.

Luke's features darkened with anger, but I ignored him the best I could, releasing the mask that covered my aura. "It's showtime," I mouthed.

There seemed to be a reply on the tip of his tongue, but thankfully he refrained and took off in the other direction. I guess he was exploring the surroundings and finding the best place for him and the army to take cover when we returned.

After waiting impatiently a few minutes, an orange cloud of smoke appeared. Moments later, Limos materialized, statuesque and tall, with dark, blazing-red eyes looking down at me. "Selene." His voice slithered in my ears. "I wondered how long it would take for you to return, my child."

I took a small step forward, finding courage in my desperation to get Cole back. "I'm here to make a deal."

Limos laughed, deep and guttural. "And what makes you think you're in any position to make a deal with me?"

I glared at him. "Because you want me! You'd be willing to make a deal if *I* were the offering."

As he tilted his head to one side, Limos' clawed hand gently rubbed his chin. "You have my attention."

"I thought so. I'm willing to make a trade, me for Cole. Release him back to Earth and I will be yours."

The demon moved closer, leaning down so our eyes were level. "Why in all the Earths would you do that for a lowlife vampire?"

I couldn't stand being this close to Limos. I wanted to back up, or at least look away. But I knew that if I did, he wouldn't believe my offer. So I swallowed down my fear and spoke in a very calm voice: "I'm willing to give myself for Cole, because I love him. That is all you need to know. You cannot comprehend love or anything of its nature, so do not try to understand why love would make me do this. Just concern yourself with the fact that if you agree to my terms and take the deal, then I will be yours."

Limos reached for my face. My body instantly lit up—a bright, radiant light. He flinched and threw his arm over his eyes, retreating several feet. "You are still protected!"

"Yes I am." I stole a deep breath and continued. "But that doesn't mean I can't give myself to you. Like I said, you'll have to agree to my terms."

"If I can't control you, then what is the point of having you?"

I let my light fade as I approached the cowering demon. "What point is it to have me if I'm not obedient? I'm offering my obedience to you."

Limos straightened, his eyes locking onto mine. "Allow me to touch you and we shall have an agreement."

I turned away, staring off into the blackness. Luke was nearby; I could feel his presence on my skin. My chest tightened as I considered what Limos was requesting. All angels were protected. When we're in the presence of danger and the emotion of fear is released, an automatic shield from *him* surrounds us, causing our lights to shine big and bright. No angel had ever tried to shut that off. But perhaps no angel had ever had a reason to even try. In my haste to get Cole back, I never considered Limos would require this of me. Now I didn't have time to think about it, nor did I have other options. There wasn't enough time for another plan. Either I find a way to remove my sense of danger, or this deal would not be made.

I gave a long sigh as I turned to face the demon. "When can I have Cole back?"

"By the death of three days from now."

"Where?"

Limos chuckled but it wasn't pleasant. "We must meet here, my child. Typhon's Earth is not within my perimeters at the moment."

I put my hand on my hip. "I thought you'd grown more powerful?" I said it like a question but it sounded more like an insult.

Limos growled, his eyes glowing a deeper shade of red. "That is not your concern, nor is it part of this deal!"

I'd hit a nerve—goody for me. But I'd also confirmed that Limos was afraid to enter Typhon's territory, which meant Limos was even weaker than I'd thought. So whatever minions he'd have at our little meeting at midnight three days from now would be more inept than him. Luke's army shouldn't have any problem defeating all of them... including Limos.

I cleared my throat. "You understand," my tone crisp, "that if I meet you here to get Cole back, then you must allow me some time to return him to Earth before I give myself to you."

"That is correct." He rubbed his hands together, claws scraping against each other. "I will even allow you extra time for your little amnesia problem."

I pondered what he said, then replied, "Okay. After I take Cole to Earth, I will need at least twenty-four hours before I can attempt to return here."

His eyes slanted into a glare. "That is far too long!"

Feeling confident, I inched closer. "Take it, or leave it! That is my offer." I closed my eyes and forced away any fear that might have been lingering inside me. "If you agree to the terms, you may touch me."

I squeezed my eyes, concentrating as hard as I could on Cole. All of this was for him. Even though the words I said to Limos were truthful, the unsaid reality gave me strength. Limos would never really have me. I wouldn't leave Charon without seeing for myself that Limos was destroyed. Then, and only then, would I orb Cole and everyone helping me back to Earth.

Suddenly, I felt claws tracing my cheek—not hard enough to break the skin, but still digging in. I opened my eyes and watched Limos as he touched me. I could sense his uneasiness, but it wasn't strong enough to make him remove his hand.

I'd done it. Somehow, I'd really done it. I'd suppressed my fears and allowed a demon to touch me. My insides felt so tangled I thought I would suffocate. I could feel my aura growing darker, leaving behind a filthy residue…one I might never be able to wash away. I'd been so confident mere moments ago, while now I felt nervous, insecure, and violated. I tried to swallow, but I couldn't feel anything past the throbbing of my heart penetrating my body like an earthquake.

A smile stretched across Limos' black, demonic face, revealing a glimpse of yellow, pointy teeth. No more words were needed. The agreement was made. Laughter erupted from his mouth as he vanished inside the same orange cloud that had brought him here.

"Selene…"

I jumped back about a foot, then swung around to see Luke. "Don't do that!" I breathed.

"Sorry. I just saw that demon was gone, and I wanted to see if you were okay." He gently rubbed my arm. "Are you?"

I brushed him off. "I'm fine. Did you have enough time to check the place out?"

He nodded, his mouth curled in a grin.

"What?" I asked.

Luke pointed to an area about thirty or forty yards out. There were about a half dozen massive boulders lying at random angles. "You couldn't have picked a better spot to meet this demon. Those rocks are a perfect place for me and the others to take cover—not too far away, and plenty big enough to hide all of us."

I rubbed my arms, still feeling grimy from Limos' touch. I forced a small smile and took Luke's hand. "Let's go. I can't stand being here another second. We can talk more back at your place."

"Fine, but you'd better just pass out this time because I don't think I can handle another memory lapse."

Like I have any control over that, I thought. Then, I gave his hand a gentle squeeze and closed my eyes. Moments later, we were sucked inside a blur of motion, and then everything went black.

I regained my memory after nearly twenty minutes of arguing with Luke—I'd been unconscious for a half hour before that. I sat on his sofa, rubbing my temples with the tips of my index and middle fingers. My clothes were filthy—ashes and dirt plastered all over my jeans and tank top, but even they felt cleaner than my soul. I glanced toward the back of the basement and saw Luke sitting at the table, arms tightly folded in front of his chest. Ashy-colored smears coated his black tee shirt, while his gray jeans seemed to conceal most of the remnant leftovers from Charon. Even through the dirt and grime, there was an attractiveness to him, a sincere form of affection expanding from the depths of my heart, settling on my bones like rich, viscous honey. He was genuinely helping me, or helping Cole, but either way he was seeing this through. Some vampires really weren't bad—I'd met two of them.

Luke caught me looking at him and I hurriedly turned away, feeling heat flush my cheeks. I bit my bottom lip, staring down at the floor. "I need to return to my charge," I mumbled under my breath.

"Fine. But if you leave before telling me what the hell is going on, then you can count me out."

My hands curled into fists, my breathing grew shallow. "But you can't quit. You're supposed to help get Cole back!"

Luke stood up and stepped toward me. "I heard the agreement you made with that demon. You don't need me to get Cole back." There was a blur and then Luke was kneeling in front of me. He grabbed my chin, held it steady as his eyes searched mine. "What you need me for is to cover your *ass*! If I don't go with you, then you'll have to keep your deal with that demon."

I felt my eyes widen. "That's not—" I stopped before saying "true." Luke was right. I'd been ready to do this on my own but he'd stopped me and offered to help. But what I hadn't realized—until now—was that Luke was actually helping *me*. If it weren't for him, I'd be giving myself to Limos with no way out. Was Cole worth it? Yes—absolutely. But it was also awesome having a way out.

Luke's grip tightened on my chin. "Are you talking, or leaving?"

If I told him my situation, it would weaken my position even more than it already was. But I couldn't afford to lose his alliance against Limos. Feeling backed in a corner, I gave him the only answer I could. "I'll tell you, but, I have a question of my own for you."

"Nice try, Angel, but it's me first on this one. Now spill it!"

"I'm falling," I cried out. "I'm falling because I'm in love with a dark one." My fists squeezed tighter, and I could feel my nails digging into my palms. Luke's position never wavered. He held my face, his eyes soft and curious. It reminded me of Cole, the way he looked at me just before everything changed. Flashbacks of what had happened, and why, appeared with such clarity, it was as if I were in that moment all over again.

Cole and I were somewhere near Estes Park, surrounded by mountains, trees, shrubs, and wildlife. A river ran to my left, the water humming and splashing over the rocks. Stars lit up the hazy, black sky like tiny flashing beacons. Cole stood behind me, his arms wrapping tighter around my waist. His face nudged up against the back of my head, lips brushing my ear. "Are you sure about this?"

I twisted around and gazed up into his eyes. "Yes."

He caressed my chin with his strong, firm hand, fingers gently stroking. I gasped, unable to completely catch my breath. I licked my lips, then his mouth was on mine, kissing me hard. I gripped his hair and pushed down, forcing his lips below my mouth. His tongue slicked along my skin until it stopped on my neck. He growled—low, rumbling, and hungry. I felt his sharp fangs prickling my skin just before he bit into me.

Luke's hands were on my shoulders, his face close, his eyes burning with understanding. "You let Cole bite you? You've been bitten by a vampire?"

I nodded slowly, bravely meeting Luke's eyes. "I knew there was a price to pay if Cole and I went further. I'd already lost some of my powers just because I was with him. But it wasn't until after he bit me the first time—"

Suddenly I was pinned against the wall, without having even felt myself move. Luke's hands pressed my shoulders harder into the cold, bare stone. His face was close; the chill of his breath was on my cheek. "I cannot believe you let him bite you!" he went on, raking me with his gaze. "More than once, for that matter!" A low growl vibrated in his throat, spilling out of his mouth. "I've never tasted an angel before."

"Stop it!" I screamed, fear slithering up my limbs. "What are you doing?"

"You have no idea how tempting you are, Angel." His soft, moist lips brushed my cheek as the hardness of his body pressed closer.

Panic seized me but my light never came—though it should have. But I pushed that concern out of my mind and closed my eyes, trying to focus on Caitlyn. *Back with Caitlyn, back with Caitlyn*, I repeated over and over in my head. I could feel my body flickering with energy—like a faint light flashing on and off, the way a light bulb does right before it completely burns out. And then, all at once, it stopped.

"I'm sorry." It was Luke's voice. I was still in his basement, but I didn't feel him on me anymore. I opened my eyes and saw him standing across the room.

"You're sorry?" my tone laced with ice. I rubbed my arms, trying to ease the violent chill. "How dare you!"

He frowned, keeping his gaze somewhere off to my right.

"Don't you have anything to say?" I demanded, anger surging within. "Why did you do that to me?"

Still he wouldn't look at me. Several uncomfortable moments passed in deafening silence and I watched him suspiciously from across the room, impatiently waiting for him to answer me, but it wasn't long before I realized he obviously wasn't going to explain himself—which didn't sit right with me at all—not that there was anything he could say that would have justified what he did.

Another minute of silence passed before he stepped twice in my direction. "Stay where you are! Don't come any closer!" I warned.

He held out his hands, waving them slowly, gesturing his surrender. "Angel, I won't hurt you."

I wasn't buying that for a second. "Do you take me for a fool? How can I believe you after what you just did? You took advantage of me while I was weakened from orbing. What were your intentions once you had me against the wall?"

A sly smile curved his lips. "I wouldn't have hurt you, if that's what you're thinking."

"Answer the question, Luke!"

"You're the first *angel* I've ever been exposed to. Controlling myself around you has been somewhat"—a slight shrug of his shoulders—"difficult. And now that I know you've been tasted...well, let's just say it'll be a bit more challenging."

Wasn't that just great? Not only were vampire's insanely crazy when it came to their food, but they were also extremely territorial. Combining the two—like I had with Cole by dating him and letting him drink from me—was extremely intimate for them, and there was no way on this world, or any of the others, that I was getting that close to Luke.

"I'm in love with Cole," I furiously reminded him. "I will not permit anyone else to drink from me—ever."

"I know that," he snapped, bitter acceptance flashing across his face.

As I met his gaze levelly, my body finally lit up, fierce and radiant. Excitement and relief filled me as a joyful sigh burst off my tongue. Luke took a couple steps back, shielding his eyes with his arm.

"How can I believe you'll help me get Cole, now after all this?" I asked, a huge part of me ready to end this alliance right now.

"I'm not helping you get Cole, I'm saving you from that demon!" he shot back, then added more harshly, "Remember that!"

"But *if* you save me from Limos, I'll return to Cole. Not you."

"You're not telling me anything I don't already know, Angel."

There was something in his voice that I couldn't quite place—sadness, disappointment, or maybe it was both, but there was definitely no mistaking the raw hunger in his eyes, a need so absolute I feared it, wished I didn't know it existed, and yet at that moment, I'd barely begun to learn the extent of his insatiable appetite.

I let my light fade since Luke no longer felt like an immediate threat, and for that I was grateful. Still, no matter how I looked at it—or how much I didn't like it—I needed his help. My plan wouldn't work without him. But why was he willing to help me if not for Cole? I just didn't know. Friendships between vampires always seemed to be heavily based on two things. Either someone helps you and now you owe them a favor, or you do something for someone and now you're calling in that favor—hence Huron's willingness to help Luke with barely any questions asked. And since Luke was making it crystal clear that he was helping me—not his friend Cole—I couldn't help but wonder what in all the worlds was I going to end up owing him? "I need time to think about this," I said at last.

Luke lowered his arm and smiled. "Well, you have three days."

10

TWO DAYS HAD PASSED, and Caitlyn's condition still hadn't changed. Neither had the situation with Luke. I was sitting on the foot of my charge's hospital bed, hunched over, my face buried in my hands. Caitlyn and Luke weren't my only problems. While orbing back to the hospital, I'd accidentally ended up in Anthemusa again, and had a déjà vu experience with that horrible siren. Only this time when I didn't sing with her, she threatened to torture me for all eternity. I was worried she'd get her wish if I ever ended up in her world without the ringing of chimes to save me.

I'd been away from Caitlyn so long that Natalia had been forced to send for Raphael. She told him that I'd needed space and that she'd agreed to watch Caitlyn while I was gone, but that when I never returned—and Andrea was ready to leave—Natalia had had no option but to call him. Raphael put Corrine on my charge, then focused his energy on finding me. But when he couldn't sense me, he knew something was up. The wind chimes had gone off just as that siren was dismounting her sea snake to come at me.

When I arrived in Europa, I told my boss how I'd orbed back to Caitlyn but ended up in Anthemusa. I, of course, left out all the parts before that. Raphael was more distraught than I would have ever imagined, and shortly after that, he released me back to my charge. I'd been sitting at the foot of her bed, in angel form, ever since.

There'd been many visitors to see Caitlyn—coming with smiles, leaving with tears. Rob and Stacey were here about an hour ago. Stacey was a complete wreck by the time they left. Rob wrapped her up in his arms, trying to comfort her, while keeping himself steady and calm at the same time. No easy feat—I knew that personally.

Still, for the whole past hour, my mind was racing in loops about what had happened with Luke. Cole had expressed his territorialism for me on countless occasions, so I was very familiar with just how jealous vamps could get. But I wasn't Luke's—I was Cole's. Despite that, Luke was behaving as if I should be his, and I feared that little preview of his temper would only be the beginning if I chose to continue my alliance with him. Add the fact that I had less than twenty-four hours before that dreadful meeting with Limos, and my problems just kept getting worse. I wasn't prepared to go without Luke. I needed his help, but could I risk bringing him with me now, after what had happened? I was in the biggest mess of my existence, and I seemed to be digging myself deeper in the hole.

So, I welcomed the distraction when Corrine appeared. She hovered in the back corner of the room by the window. "Raphael has requested a meeting with you."

"About our charge?"

"I don't know, Selene," she smarted. "I'm just here to relay the message, and"—she glanced over at Caitlyn—"watch her."

"Fine." I returned her tone. "I'll be back when I can." I closed my eyes and vanished without bothering to say good-bye. When I opened them, I was in Europa. No fainting. No amnesia. No disorientation. I never got those unpleasant side effects when I was following the rules—though it still didn't bring a smile to my face. Instead of a cloud, I stood near a waterfall, humming and splashing upon the rocks. Mist sprayed off the overflowing water, hovering like a hazy sponge above the pool below. Lush green grasses coated the ground, feeling cottony-soft on my bare feet. There were colorful wildflowers everywhere. It reminded me of springtime in the mountains back on Earth.

Since Raphael wasn't here yet, I went to the water's edge and sat down. I took the torn and muddy edge of my gown and submerged it under the cool, crisp water. I rubbed back and forth, scrubbing the fabric as hard as I could, but when I brought it up out of the water, nothing had changed. The filth still clung to it—as if it were now a part of the dress. The rips weren't something you could just sew up anyways. What I wore was merely a reflection of my aura, a mirror into my soul, which was no longer perfect and clean. I was beyond repair.

I sensed Raphael behind me and turned, gazing up at his face. He smiled slightly as he moved closer, sitting down beside me on the grass. "Selene." The smile faded as he continued, "I have been shown the futures of your charge."

"Will she be okay?"

He took a deep breath. "No, she won't. There are two possible outcomes, and both of them end in her death on Earth."

"No!" I wailed, pounding my fists into the grass. My heart rammed against my chest, I could hear its violent rhythm in my ears. "What happens to her?" I asked, my voice small.

Raphael rubbed my back but it provided no comfort. "One of her paths reveals she won't awaken from the coma. After months of holding out hope, it is decided by her mother to pull the plug. The other path shown to me was that your charge will wake up, but her brain is severely damaged."

"How damaged?"

"She'll be in a wheelchair and won't be able to care for herself." He paused a moment, then added, "And she will not remember anyone from her life before the accident."

A surge of tears built up, nearly choking me as a massive gash ripped through my heart; then everything inside me seemed to freeze, leaving me empty, numb, and more broken than I'd ever known an angel could feel. My head slumped to the side and clumps of wavy hair fell over my face. Raphael brushed some of it away, but it swooped back down like a falling curtain. Without looking up, I asked, "Isn't there anything I can do? Anything *you* can do? To help her."

"Yes. We let her go. Her suffering will soon be at an end."

I peeked up through my fingers. "Please, Raphael. It's too soon. She has so much life ahead of her."

His face softened as he reached for me, removing my hands from my face. Instead of letting go, his fingers intertwined with mine. "You may have disappointed me beyond words, but you are still a wonderful asset and I will not lose you. Do you understand?"

I shook my head. "But if my charge dies—"

"You will be reassigned another charge, and some of your powers will be returned. You have been given another chance."

Was I hearing him right? Another chance? But what about Caitlyn? "What do you mean by another chance? I don't want a new charge! I want Caitlyn healed! If my powers will be returned, then give them to me now so I can help her!"

His grip tightened. "It is not completely up to me how this will work. Caitlyn is going to die on Earth. Her spirit will go on to live with *him*."

I knew that his answer should comfort me, knowing that Caitlyn would move on to the light, but it was just too soon. It wasn't her time. She still had a life to live on Earth, and because of me that time was being cut short.

"You were always so stubborn," he said, his voice softer. "Please just let this go, Selene."

My breathing grew shallow, my chest compressed with sorrow. "But I—"

"You have been chosen. *You!* You've been given a second chance when most other angels would surely be fallen and forgotten."

I jerked away from him, throwing up my hands. "But why me? What have I done to deserve this? It's my fault Caitlyn will die. My fault! How can I possibly be reassigned after that? What if I make the same mistakes all over again? What if another charge will die at my hands?"

A wave of anger flushed his face. Raphael glared at me, taking several deep breaths. "You will obey me! A new assignment will be given and you will take it! Do you understand?"

I swallowed hard, desperately seeking the right words. "If you were me, you'd try to find a way to help your charge."

He leaned over, delicately brushing his thumb across my cheek. "No. If I were you, I'd accept this second chance, and be happy my charge was moving on to a place where she could no longer suffer."

I gave a long sigh. Time. I needed time. "Can you please give me some time to think about everything?"

Raphael looked at me, hard, his gaze unfathomable. "You can think about this all you want, but the decision is made. I'll give you a week to say good-bye to your charge."

Grief welled but I forced it down; still there was nothing I could do about the numbness inside, filling me almost to the point I'd suffocate on it, thinking about how I wasn't ready to say good-bye to Caitlyn. How could this be happening? I leaned over and picked up a shiny, black pebble, and tossed it into the pool. Ripples danced across the water like subtle vibrations. "Why have I been given a second chance?" I asked, my voice soft.

"I can't answer that question. It is as it is. But it's been a great help for you not having that *vampire* around."

Vampire. Cole. His name stuck in my throat, and it took me a moment to respond. "That *vampire* will return"—my voice was full of certainty. "He'll be back on Earth—"

"You are forbidden to fall back into whatever relationship you had with that dark one! You're better off without him, so I suggest you pray that he doesn't return! I cannot promise a third chance for you, Selene!"

My chest tightened, and the clenching in my stomach intensified. My heart burned as if acid were being poured over it. I wanted to defend Cole and our relationship, but it was pointless to even try. Raphael would never understand. No one would. Shrugging my shoulders, I shook away those thoughts.

My archangel placed his hand on my arm and said, "I'm sorry if I'm hard on you, but it's only out of love. You're an angel, a magnificent guardian. Now go to your charge and prepare your good-byes."

"I'm not ready to see her yet," I said somewhat absently. "I need to be alone for a little while."

He nodded slowly. "Of course. Corrine will stay with her then, as long as you need."

I stared at him, unable to say another word. His face softened, then he disappeared. I felt defeated. Caitlyn was dying. And all of this was my fault. Slowly, I got up, though my shoulders stayed hunched as my feet tracked along the edge of the pool. I had just chucked another pebble, gazing out at the sparkling water, when another angelic presence appeared behind me.

I swung around to face my new visitor. "What do you want, Beck?"

He waved his hands in front of his tan, shimmering chest, in full surrender. "Sorry, I just thought—"

I marched forward, pressing my fingers into his shoulder. "Don't patronize me! You were spying! I know you heard everything that just went down!" I lowered my hand and stepped back. Through squinting eyes, I asked, "So, why are you here?"

His head dipped and a wave of his soft, blond hair sloped across his face. He brushed it back with his hand. "I thought I could offer some help. There might be a way to save your charge, but it's risky and dangerous."

My hands settled on my hips. "What are you talking about? How?"

"First"—he swung his head to the other side—"you must give me your word that you'll tell no one that it was *I* who spoke of this to you."

"Fine. Yes," I replied, impatience in my tone. "Now tell me."

Beck walked past me and kept moving slowly along the edge. "You could sacrifice yourself for your charge."

I rushed over, falling in step with him. "What do you mean? How would I do that?"

He flashed me a look like that of someone telling something they shouldn't: mischievous, arrogant, and transfixed. "I meant it exactly as I said. You could give your life for hers."

"I never knew that was possible," I stated in disbelief. "How do you know about this?"

"It was written in the ancient sea scrolls of Rhea. Their contents claim that a guardian angel, stricken with grief over the looming death of their charge, surrendered their breath so that the charge would get a second chance at life on Earth."

"Surrendered their breath? How? You mean the angel became fallen?"

Beck stopped walking and stared at something far across the water. "Selene, no one knows for sure what that means. But what if it doesn't result in an angel falling? What if the angel merely ceases to exist?" He glanced at me, studying me with his eyes. "All I know is that the angel who made the sacrifice was never seen again, nor were the scrolls of Rhea."

"But we can't 'cease to exist,'" I replied, dumbfounded, my mind seeking memories, sifting through hundreds of thousands of years, trying to find anything that would support my friend's story. Maybe there were one or two cases where an angel seemed to just vanish, but was that enough to justify Beck's claim? It's not like I had a lot of options—none, actually—so did that make me desperate enough to grab onto anything that might be able to save my charge? Maybe it did. After all, Beck was an old friend and he was only trying to help me. "How do *you* even know about these scrolls?" I eventually asked.

"Sicily overheard her archangel telling Vitas about it," he informed. "I guess it's some kind of old, silly story that gave both of them a great laugh. But after they finished talking about it, her archangel made the comment that 'there was always truth behind fiction.'"

"And that comment gave you the impression those scrolls really exist?"

He nodded. "I believe so. You could always ask your archangel for confirmation."

I snorted. "Yeah right! He'd never confirm that, even if it were tr—"

"And," Beck interrupted, "I did overhear a conversation between a couple of demons not too long ago, one of them mentioning the very same scrolls."

I harrumphed. "That confirms nothing!"

"Doesn't it though?" he asked, brushing a hand through his hair. "It's not like I was asking those demons for information. I accidentally over-heard one of them say that the scrolls were well guarded—or something like that. I can't remember verbatim what that thing said, to be honest."

Could this really be an option? Though I believed Sicily's gossip much more than I'd ever trust a demon, and yet my old friend did have a good point. If the demon didn't know Beck could hear it, then there'd be no reason for it to lie, would there? Still, even if I considered this, Raphael would never approve, and I told Beck so.

"You've never been a saint at following the rules" was his quick re-sponse. "At least it's another option."

Fresh hope sparked inside me, fueling excitement…and an idea. "We should go to Rhea and look for those sea scrolls. What have we got to lose?"

"Wait just a minute!"—Beck's temper flaring. "I never said anything about me going anywhere!"

"But you said you could help!"

He settled a little, voice returning to his normal tone. "I *am* helping by telling you this in the first place. I will not accompany you, should you choose to go."

Feeling disappointed, and losing some of that renewed hope, I asked, "Why would you tell me this option but not offer your hand in aiding me?" I raised my eyes and glared deep into his. "You know I cannot go to Rhea alone."

Beck met my gaze squarely. "I said it was risky and dangerous. That place is swarming with demons and God only knows what else. Besides, I can't cloak myself the way you can. They'd spot me coming a mile away. But promise me if you go, you'll take your boyfriend with you."

Cole. I bit back the pain of not having him here to help me, though ob-viously the rumors of Cole's kidnapping hadn't spread through Europa… yet. "But you hate that I'm close to a dark one. Why would you encourage me to bring him?" My gaze narrowed. "And better yet, why are you even helping me?" Skepticism pushing forward in my mind.

He brushed his fingers across my cheek. "Because you're my friend."

I stared into his eyes, trying to discern the truth. Beck and I used to be friends—really good friends. But we'd grown apart this past year, mostly because I'd given my heart to a vampire. And though he hated my choices, he still assured me that he would always be there—friends forever, and all that sort of stuff. I mentally weighed my options. What other choice did I have? This was the only way I knew of saving Caitlyn. And that meant it was worth the risk. As I looked in my old friend's eyes, I finally found the sincerity I needed to see. He really wanted to help me. Instantly, my throat constricted, but I was able to squeak out a "Thank you."

Beck gave a slight nod, amusement crinkling the corners of his eyes. "Praying it goes in your favor," he noted, then vanished.

I was too choked up to say good-bye anyway.

My thoughts pressed heavy in my mind. Caitlyn was dying, but at least I'd been given new hope on how to save her. Somehow I needed to give my breath for hers. But how could I do that? And could it really end up killing me? Or the more pressing question: Am I willing to die for my charge? Shivers raced down my arms and my stomach turned. I hugged myself, finding no comfort to the menacing chills. There had to be another way, but I wouldn't know anything without getting my hands on those sea scrolls. What if giving my breath didn't mean I'd die? Beck had said the angel that attempted this was never seen again. But that didn't mean the angel died.

One thing at a time, I scolded myself. The first thing I needed to do was get Cole back—then I could worry about the possibility of going to Rhea. Cole. Just the thought of his name sent my heart pounding. Even after everything that just happened, saving him from Limos was still my number one priority. But now if I didn't take Luke, I wouldn't be free to go to Rhea and find those scrolls. The clock was ticking. The air around me seemed thin. Pressure swelled in my head, throbbing at my temples. I rubbed them with my palms and released a deep sigh. My decision was made and it was time to inform my ally.

11

I ORBED TO CENTRAL PARK, in Manhattan, which was where I sensed Luke's essence. My annoying orbing side effects had finally worn off, and I had just finished masking my aura. I stood against a tree, in angel form, watching a few joggers climbing a hill in the distance. Their angels floated above them in iridescently lit shapes. Demons slicked the ground beside them in shadowy formations of black, globby smoke. The sun hung below a hazy gray sky, slowly dropping beyond the line of trees. A gust of wind rushed the sidewalk, stirring burnt cigarette butts, tattered napkins, and stained plastic cups along its route. The hustle and bustle of the city could be heard miles away—the rush of traffic, honking horns, and the occasional emergency vehicle blaring its siren.

What in the world is Luke doing here? I wondered, then closed my eyes and concentrated on his essence. He was close. I followed his scent until I saw him standing under a cluster of overgrown trees, physically hidden in their shadows. Luke wore faded jeans with a gunmetal, bomber-style leather jacket. His brown hair was parted down the middle and slicked back on the sides, very similar to Keanu Reeves' hair in *The Matrix*, once he'd become the badass Neo. The joggers were almost passing him and I could taste Luke's hunger, could feel the saliva thickening in his mouth. That's what he was doing in the park! I dipped behind a tree and turned visible, shifting into a navy cotton tank and skinny jeans tucked into a pair of black combat-style boots. I wore my hair down, and the wind forced it sideways as I dashed toward Luke. He was prowling out of the shadows, his eyes fixed on one of the joggers.

"No! Luke! Don't!" I exclaimed as I approached him.

He flashed around and locked eyes on me, then licked his lips. "I knew I'd be seeing you soon," he purred, as the unknowing joggers safely moved past him. Luke took a few steps my way, smiling. "You look"—his eyes slid up and down my body—"delicious."

Instantly, heat flushed my cheeks. But how could he have that effect on me? It wasn't possible. I hated him for what he'd done, and I was only here because I needed his help. Nothing more! I shook it off, feeling a little mortified, mostly because I knew Luke had noticed. "We need to talk," I demanded, shrugging off my embarrassment.

He nodded slowly, then leaned down and brushed his nose against my hair. "You owe me a meal."

I gripped his forehead and pushed him back. "You can feed when we're done talking."

There was a blur of motion, then he was standing behind me, his arms trapping my body inside a firm grasp. His lips were buried in my hair, trailing along my earlobe. Tingles spread like tiny electric currents along my skin. I tried to speak, but couldn't get my voice around the tightness in my throat. His body pressed closer into mine, and I knew I had to either use my power to teach him a lesson, or I could…

I closed my eyes and went invisible. After all, there wasn't anyone else around to witness me doing it. His arms crashed together as he fell forward, but in a flash he caught himself and jumped up—more gracefully than a cat. His eyes were searching around frantically. "Angel! Where are you? I didn't mean to do that. Come back!"

There was a park bench several feet away. I sat down, crossing my right leg over my left, then shifted back to human form. "Enough of the games, Luke. Please."

He flickered to me and sat down—a little too close for my comfort so I kept my guard on high. "But you're just so damn tempting." He leaned over and sniffed my hair, seemingly lost in the scent for a brief moment before sitting back and casting a dreamy gaze my way. "It's not my fault," he added innocently.

Yes it *was* his fault; he needed to get better control over his appetite and I told him so. "You can't have me now, or ever," I carried on impatiently. "You're going to help me get Cole back and then you will never see me again." I reached over and grabbed his arm, shaking it with a little force. "Are you okay with that?" I let go and leaned back into the bench, feeling the hard, smooth wood on my back.

Luke ran a hand through his hair. "Fine," he grumbled.

I smiled softly, feeling the sweetness of victory, though I'd be keeping my senses alert around him for sure. "How is Huron coming with our... um...*backup?*"

He assessed me, his expression unreadable. "Everything should be set with that. There are six vampires, three demons, maybe more when we show up tonight."

"Can the demons be trusted to show? They have no alliance with anyone."

"They do what Huron tells them," he assured with no trace of doubt in his voice.

"Why? How does Huron have that kind of control?" I leaned forward and some of my hair fell across my face. In an instant, Luke's fingers were there, brushing it out of my eyes; then he quickly retreated back to his space on the bench. I took a deep breath, ignoring my racing heart as best I could. All the while, I stared into his dark, mysterious eyes and saw more than hunger, more than a thirst for my blood. Lust—pure, raw, and unde-niably present lust, and that definitely was not good. But the plan to save Cole (and me) wouldn't work without him, which left me no choice but in sticking with him.

Luke was the first to look away. He stared at the ground and said, "Everyone helping us tonight owes Huron a favor, and—"

"Wait a second!" I exclaimed, pondering how he even knew I'd still want his help. "How did you know I'd still need your help? Us spending any more time together whatsoever is absolutely the worst idea ever!"

"I knew you'd want my help because there's no way on this Earth, or the others, that you'd really give yourself to that demon if you didn't have to," he stated in a monotone of resignation.

He had me there. I shrugged, then asked, "So what were you saying about favors being owed to Huron?"

"In a nutshell, Huron owes me a favor, and all the dark ones helping us owe Huron."

"Do I even want to know why he owes you, or why any of the others owe him?"

Luke shook his head. "None of that is important."

I was curious, but I wasn't going to press him for fear that if I showed too much interest, he'd mistake it for me caring enough to know—which I didn't. Shaking my head, I looked away. There were a few more people approaching from down the hill. A younger-looking man wearing gray cargo pants and a matching hat while the woman with him appeared slightly older. She pulled her cream-colored cardigan tightly around her body, then reached down to take the hand of a five- or six-year-old little girl. The girl's blond hair was in cute little pigtails, and she wore a Hello Kitty top with sneakers that lit up in flashing lights around her toes. There was an entourage of spiritual followers directly behind them, a few extra angels in place for the little girl.

Luke's body stiffened. I could feel it in his aura, and in the way he shifted on the bench. Instinctively, I grabbed his hand. It was cold and hard, like polished marble under silk. "No!" I warned under my breath. "Not them! Not that little girl!"

It was eerily quiet for several racing heartbeats. Then Luke said through gritted teeth, "Angel, you cannot sit here and forbid me to eat anyone that passes, all the while not offering me anything else from you."

I turned and caught his eyes glaring at me. There was a hunger inside them that provoked a familiar fear in me. It reminded me of all the times I'd been with Cole when he hadn't fed. It was intense, intimidating, and very scary, but Cole was able to control himself—at least until he was no longer with me. Cole also promised that he never killed a victim. He'd just drink from them, heal their wounds, and then erase any memories they had of it. For reasons I couldn't explain, I needed to know Luke ate the same way. I needed to know he wasn't a murderer.

Without taking my eyes off his, I asked, "Do you spare them? Or do you finish them off?"

He licked his lips as he tightened his grip on my hand. "What do you—"

"Don't play dumb with me!" I hissed. "You know what I'm talking about!"

"I spare them. How much more do you like me now?"

Swallowing hard, I pried my hand from his hold. "Sorry, it was none of my business, and I don't like you, therefore it's impossible to like you more." I stood up, running my hands over my arms, a cool breeze prickling my skin. "Are we meeting at Huron's bar?"

"Wait a second." He jumped up beside me, but kept his hands to himself. "Where are you going?"

That was a great question. I had no idea, but I still wasn't ready to go to Caitlyn, and Europa was out of the question. I would've loved to do a little research on Rhea, but I doubted I'd learn anything until I got there. Should I ask Cole to help me? What if I lost him all over again? I couldn't bear it if that happened. I needed to keep Cole safe. Once I got Cole home, he could never leave Earth again. As I stared at Luke, I realized that he was the only one who could help me get those scrolls. But I knew that even asking him for that would be a huge mistake. Unfortunately, going to Rhea alone was out of the question. And since Beck wouldn't go with me, it really left only one option.

"Will you walk with me?" I asked as I turned around and headed up the hill, away from the humans.

Luke didn't answer, but I felt him fall in step beside me. We walked for several minutes, listening only to the howl of the wind and the busyness of the city off in the distance. Since there was really no way to candy-coat my request, it was time to just ask and get it over with. Not that I felt any more confident about needing his help once again. "After we return from Charon, there's another task I need your assistance with."

"And what would that be?" His voice was piqued with curiosity.

I took a deep breath and told him everything Beck had told me about Rhea, the scrolls, and how I could give my breath to save my charge. For reasons I couldn't explain, I also told him about being offered a second chance, a new charge, and the possibility of regaining most of my lost powers. When I finished, I glanced over at Luke and saw he was looking at me. Not wanting to take my eyes off him, I stopped walking. He instantly stopped too. He grabbed my hand and gently guided me over to stand by a towering oak. His eyes were wide as he asked, "Why wouldn't you just take the second chance? You get your powers, a new charge, and a new little life. Why is it so important to try to save a dying human? What if you're the one who dies instead?"

I shrugged, still not really sure I believed an angel could actually die, but I'd never seen the scrolls, and I didn't know what kind of power they held. What if giving my breath for my charge in turn wiped away my very existence? Was it possible? "It's my fault Caitlyn is in this mess," I finally said. "I at least need to try to make it right by her. I'm not saying that I'm willing to give my life for hers, but there's no way to even know what 'giving my breath' means unless I get those scrolls."

"But what about the other angel that did this? He's dea—"

"No! We don't know that for sure. No one has seen or heard from him, but that doesn't confirm his death. He could be alive, in hiding, or he could be fallen."

Luke put his hands on my shoulders. "That doesn't make any sense! Why would sacrificing himself for his charge cause that angel to go into hiding, or even better, why would he become fallen?"

I swallowed hard as my eyes slid toward the ground. "I don't know. I don't have all of the answers, but neither do you." I glanced back up. "There's no way to know without going to Rhea. Will you help me, or not?"

Luke's head tilted to the side and the wind shifted slightly, blowing his brown hair behind him. "Will Cole be joining us?" I didn't like the cockiness in his voice.

"No!" I exclaimed. "Once Cole's back on Earth, that's where he'll stay. I'm not risking him again!"

He released me, stepping back, his eyes never leaving mine. "Oh, I see, I'm the one who's dispensable!"

"It's not like that!" I argued. "I love Cole! I can't risk his life…again! Just because I've asked for your help doesn't mean I want something bad to happen to you."

He squinted slightly, inquisitive. "If I say no, are you still going?"

I fisted my hands at my sides. "Yes." Though I wasn't sure how I'd pull that off yet.

The family of three had almost reached us, causing a brief interruption. Luke's body stiffened, his ears and nose twitching. He closed his eyes and took in the air around us. I grabbed his hand, gently squeezing. His grip tightened as I pulled him closer, then whispered, "It's okay. They're almost past us. Please, fight it and spare this family altogether."

He gritted his teeth as he answered, "I'll let them go, but I must feed before we leave Earth tonight."

I nodded. "But why'd you come all this way just for a meal?"

"I don't like to eat where I live."

I remembered Cole saying the exact same thing when I asked him why he'd travel so far to find blood. He'd told me that he never wanted to risk someone remembering him, even though he'd always load them up with vampire charm. Since vamps could move so quickly, it was a breeze for them to go several states away for food, then return home within the same

90

night. Sometimes Cole would stay away for a couple of days loading up on tons of blood—a binger, he'd called it—and then when he'd return home he wouldn't need to eat again for several weeks.

At last, the family had passed us; I could see them in the distance, striding up another hill. The little girl was in the middle, holding each parent's hand and swinging back and forth. I could sense the joy from her guardians and hear the little girl's giggles, but then the wind shifted and carried them away for good.

I pulled my hands free and started walking. Luke followed. The wind blew my hair sideways, in the opposite direction of Luke, giving him, I was sure, a perfect view of my neck. "If you'd just let me feed from you, we could go together to Huron's," he pressed.

Heat flushed my face but I quickly shrugged it off, half laughing. "Nice try, wise guy."

"It would entice me to go with you to Rhea," his voice mocking.

"There's no way you're drinking my blood. Period. End of story."

"Fine!" he smarted. "The next person who comes along will be dinner, then."

"Fine!" I returned his tone. "Now quit avoiding answering me! Will you come to Rhea with me, or not?"

His pace slowed as he stole a glance at my face. "Stay with me, we'll go to Huron's together, and I'll think about it."

I looked away and sped up. He did too. "And if I don't?"

"Then my answer is no."

"But if I stay here with you, then you'll only think about it?"

"That's right."

"This is so not fair," I pouted. "What will we do for *four* hours?"

"Don't worry about it, Angel. By staying here, you'll be accompanying me everywhere I go. We might actually have some fun."

I wanted to laugh at the ironic situation. I'd come here to let Luke know I still needed his help tonight, and then I'd never be seeing him again. Now, if I didn't spend the next four hours with him, he might not help me get those sea scrolls. But even if I did stay here, he still reserved the right to tell me no. It was a win-win for Luke. Quite possibly a lose-lose for me. But could I risk leaving and definitely not having his help? I knew the answer, and I hated it. I gave a deep, long sigh, shaking my head in defeat. "Fine!"

His eyes lit up like fireworks. He clapped his hands together as he said, "You've chosen wisely, Angel."

"For the record, these next four hours are going to be pure torture."

Luke started laughing, and once he calmed down a little, he replied, "You don't know that for sure."

He gestured toward a bench and I followed his direction. "Have a seat and I'll be back in a jiffy."

"Where are you going?" I asked, sitting down.

"Since you won't feed me, I need to go…"

"All right. Never mind. I'll be right here, waiting ever so patiently."

He leaned down, whispering "I know you will" in my ear.

12

THE SKY WAS A THICK, HAZY blackness distorted by the millions of flashing lights throughout the city. Lampposts—like white glowing balls on iron sticks—lined the sidewalks. The streets were filled with vehicles, mostly old orange-colored taxis, moving slower than the many thousand pedestrians. Car fumes intermingled with the street meat vendors located on just about every other block. Luke held my hand, dragging me along behind him, pushing through the sea of people, heading towards someplace that promised a good time. With such a heavy demonic presence here, I could only imagine the fun Luke had spoken of.

Since the final descent of the sun, it had gotten chillier—much chillier. Thankfully, numerous skyscrapers and countless towering luxury hotel chains surrounded us, blocking some of the wind. We turned on 83rd, finding it much quieter than the other roads we'd traveled. Luke's brisk pace slowed, which meant he didn't need to drag me anymore, so I tugged my hand free and immediately rubbed my exposed arms. He glanced back and said, "Angel, you're freezing! Here." He slipped out of his leather jacket and draped it over my arms.

"Thanks." I pulled it tighter around me. "Is there somewhere private I can go to, um, change into something more appropriate?"

He smiled slightly, not a hint of fang showing. "Shopping isn't on our agenda."

"I don't want to go shopping. I just want to shift into something a little warmer." My jeans were fine, but the tank top wasn't even close to keeping me warm.

He took my hand again, focusing ahead of us as he asked, "How do you plan on getting out of those clothes without having anything to change into?"

I sped up so it wouldn't look like he was still dragging me. "I can shape-shift into anything I want."

"What a cool trick." He glanced over, both eyebrows arched. "But will you forget who I am if you do that, and ruin our short time together?"

"No, I mean, I haven't ever had problems shifting before. Just orbing." So far, anyways.

We took a sharp right turn and walked straight into a small bar. The oval-shaped sign hanging above the door read "Nicco's" in cursive letters lit up in red. Black-and-white checkered tiles expanded throughout the tiny space. About a half dozen wooden tables with white cloths lined each side, leaving an open path down the middle. There were a few people sitting on either side, an angel and demon with each of them. Luke gestured toward the back, where a small rectangular sign promised the restrooms.

After ducking into a tiny stall, I shifted into a boyfriend-style gray sweater, then headed back out to meet Luke, who was waiting for me in the front by the door. "Nice trick," he commented, then took his jacket, put it on, and tugged me back out into the cold, busy street.

We walked for several minutes before arriving at our destination. The building was so tall that when I craned my neck, the top of it was hidden in darkness. Wide marble steps led up to a row of massive windows with tall glass doors between them. The glass was thick and smoky-looking, obstructing any views of inside. Luke opened the door and I followed him in. Warm air rushed me, instantly removing the chill. An older man—no, he was a vampire—approached offering to take our coats. His short gray hair was slicked back, exposing his shiny forehead and bushy white eyebrows. He wore a long-sleeved black button-up shirt tucked into loose-fitted black pants. There was a chrome skull-and-bones belt buckle centered across his waist. What in the heck kind of place had Luke brought me to?

I watched the old vampire hang Luke's jacket and my sweater in a closet by the front doors. Then he returned and had us follow him down a short, tight hallway. The floor was covered in 12x12 squares of black marble, and the lacquered walls were the color of red wine—or blood. There were a few large pictures hanging on both sides of the hall with thick, black frames and images of recumbent figures during the Renaissance Era. Three gothic-style light fixtures hung about six feet apart from each other, radiating faint, cream-colored light. Ahead of us was a set of black double doors, intricate iron detail surrounding their peepholes.

On the left wall, the old vampire pressed a small round button that resembled a doorbell. Moments later, the door on the left opened and techno music instantly pulsed in my ears. *A soundproof party room for vampires*, I thought, as I followed Luke inside. Directly in front of us, purple, red, blue, and white spinning lights zigzagged across a dance floor. People and beings were everywhere—humans and vampires, angels and demons. There were round couches in the back with red and black curtains pulled to the sides. High-top tables were scattered about, but none with any chairs. Most of the dancers were using them for drink holders as they lost themselves to the music. In the back right corner was a DJ booth with three young, human men wearing oversized headphones.

Luke turned left, pulling me along. The bar was this way. It had a retro-looking glass countertop that stretched along most of this side of the club. Red leather barstools crowded around it, only a few of them empty. A few plasma TV's displaying some kind of eerie laser light show hung from the ceiling behind the bar. There were a few bartenders rushing around—my senses confirmed they were all vampires. Luke sat down, and I squeezed into the stool beside him. He raised his arm as one of the bartenders looked our way. "What do you want?" he called out.

"Water," I said.

He lowered his arm as he swung an astonished look at me. "C'mon, Angel! Live a little. Have one drink with me." Luke arched his brows. "Just one drink?"

I leaned closer, placing my lips near his face as I attempted to shout over the music while still keeping our conversation private. "There's a war tonight. Some will die. I don't want drinking alcohol before we go to be on my conscience. Plus, it doesn't affect me the same as humans anyway."

"Me neither. I need double the amount to even feel the slightest head tingle. So there's really no reason we can't just have one. It'll loosen us up before we dance."

"What?" I gasped, leaning back in the stool. "I'm not dancing!"

A sly smile curved his lips as he silently mouthed, "Yes you are."

Luke turned away just as the bartender arrived. She looked young and was very pretty. Her blonde hair was short and cropped around her face. The stretchy black mini with matching black corset showed off just how curvy her figure was. She stretched across the bar and planted a small kiss on Luke's cheek.

I flushed and quickly turned away, hoping Luke hadn't noticed. The music was thumping so hard it felt like my head was vibrating. I took three deep, long breaths, then rotated back around. The bartender was gone and Luke was staring at me with a huge smile on his face. "Jealous?" he asked, just loud enough to hear.

So much for keeping it hidden. "I'm ready to go," I said through gritted teeth.

"No way! We just got here. But we can go somewhere a little more private while we drink these." He raised his hands from the bar, a green-colored martini drink in each.

"Forget it! I said I wanted water!" I whirled up, bound for the exit.

"Well, if you leave," he shouted, "you can forget Rhea, and what the hell, you can forget me helping tonight too!"

That stopped me cold and I swung around, staring daggers at him. "You wouldn't! You gave your word!"

He snickered. "Let's go over here." Luke headed off through the sea of dancers. I didn't follow. I glared at the back of his body until he disappeared.

I had a choice of either going after him, or leaving. If I left, I'd be on my own tonight, and then I'd never beat Limos, or even have the chance to go to Rhea. I wonder how that whole second chance thing would work if I was a slave to a demon. Would Raphael be able to get me back? Would the second chance still be offered? If I didn't stay, I'd be guaranteeing Caitlyn's death, and maybe mine too. I needed Luke's help.

"Shoot!" I mumbled under my breath as I closed my eyes, focusing, then started walking in the direction of Luke's essence.

The moment I got to the dance floor, a smoke machine went off and a thick, fumy cloud swallowed me. My eyes shot open, momentarily losing Luke's aura. Suddenly a heavyset black lady collided into me, then danced off, shaking her butt and bopping her arms. I rolled my eyes and started pushing through the cluster of dancers. A tall guy with dark hair and tan skin grabbed my arm, pushing me backwards. His hips swayed side to side, then he grinded against my thigh. I pulled free, taking several steps back before hitting something hard that stopped me. Two muscular arms stretched around me from behind, aggressively pushing me side to side. I tried to turn around, but the arms tightened, holding me in place. Instantly, I ducked down into a low squat and slipped away. As I started to make a run for it, I was intercepted by yet another set of arms. The smoke kept filling in thicker and thicker, constricting my ability to catch my breath. I wanted to go invisible, but there were just too many humans in here. I couldn't risk it.

The music roared louder, pulsing inside my ears. The multicolored strobe lights glistened on the heads of those closest. I still couldn't see who held me, and the sea of people and beings seemed to have doubled in size. The fog was even thicker, mixing with the musky smell of sweat and alcohol. I'd had enough of feeling like a caged animal. After jerking my body right, slipping out of the grasp of who- or whatever held me, another set of hands lashed out, and I could've sworn there were demon claws protruding from them. I dropped down low and started inching my way to freedom. After a few heartbeats, someone rammed into me, taking me down to the floor. My head hit hard, then I rolled over to the side, the taste of molten copper filling my mouth. Just great! Now I was bleeding in a club loaded with vampires. All I could see were feet everywhere, jumping, tapping, and skipping around. I spun back over and pushed up with my hands, and instantly I was engulfed by another set of strong arms. I twisted around, trying to push out of the unwanted embrace, when I noticed a familiar vibe.

Relief rushed through me as I glanced up at Luke's face. His features were soft, a slight smile curving his lips. His hair appeared wet and numerous strands were out of place, but it actually looked good. Without thinking, I threw my arms around his neck and hugged him. "Thank goodness it's you," I breathed against his shoulder.

He pulled me close. "You've been having fun without me." I could feel his nose in my hair, sniffing me. "You're bleeding!" he exclaimed.

I inched my lips to his ear. "I bit my tongue. It's nothing. It'll heal. Let's get off this dance floor. Please."

Luke nodded, then guided me toward the back of the club. We passed the oversized round couches and came to a few square-shaped private rooms. He gestured left, and as soon as we entered a room, the music's volume must've decreased at least ten levels. It reminded me of how you could hear the busy city from the middle of Central Park, faint and distant. There were two plush red love seats along the left and back walls. In between them was a black ottoman with a large red and gold crown stitched in the center with a chrome tray sitting on top, holding the green martini drinks.

Luke gestured for me to sit, and I went for the love seat on the left wall. As I sat down, I noticed a massive fish aquarium in front of me, taking up the entire right-side wall. It was illuminated just enough to show the teal and green coral and the shadows of hundreds of small fish. Luke handed me the martini as he nestled in next to me.

I took the glass and stared at it. "I told you I can't drink this."

His eyes slanted into a glare. "Well, you don't really have a choice now. You smell like blood! If you don't want to accidentally get bitten, then you need to wash away the smell with that drink."

I returned his glare and replied, "I can just shift it away."

"No! Forget using any more of your powers until later tonight. Just take a few sips. It's an appletini with caramel on the rim of the glass. Vivian said you should like it."

"Who's Vivian?" I snapped, and immediately regretted my tone.

"Your jealousy can only mean one thing, Angel."

I looked away and mumbled, "I'm not jealous."

I felt a whir of motion, then Luke's mouth was next to my cheek. "Yes. You. Are"—his breath a warm chill on my skin. "Now drink some of that before I drink you."

I shrugged my shoulders and took a small sip. My lips puckered at its tartness, but then my tongue was left with a tangy, sweet aftertaste. The drink reminded me of a green apple Jolly Rancher, and there was no proof in its flavor that it contained any alcohol. I took one more tiny sip, then set the mostly full martini back on the tray.

"That's better, but I can still smell your blood," Luke said, setting down his glass. He studied me a moment, then added, "You got it on your shirt." He pointed to an area near my tank top's scooped collar.

"I'm probably covered in dirt too. I can't believe how rude those people were."

"You've never seen a demon-possessed human?"

Yes, I had. "That explains their behavior!" I exclaimed, sitting a little straighter. "No one would let me off the dance floor. I bet they thought they could use my body as a host."

"How? They can do that to an angel?"

"Of course not!" I scoffed. "But none of them know I'm an angel since my aura is masked. To them"—I gestured back toward the dance floor—"I look like any other human."

Luke draped his arm around my shoulders. "You don't look like any ole human to me."

Heat flushed my cheeks, and my chest tightened. Why was he affecting me like this? Why were my nerves racing through my body like mini currents of electricity? I didn't know, but the longer I sat tucked under his arm, the more intense I felt—an inferno building and growing until I'd either explode or melt away. I swallowed hard and nudged him. "You can't say things like that"—my voice breathless as I shimmied out of his embrace.

He shot me a frustrated look. "Quit acting like I have the plague. We're just two friends trying to enjoy ourselves before we go into a gnarly battle later. We only have another hour, so ease up! Will you do that for me?"

"Why only another hour? I can orb us—"

"No!" He scooted closer and put his arm back around me. "No orbing until we leave Earth. *I'm* taking you back to Virginia Beach."

"What? You don't have a—" I realized what he meant. "You're offering to carry me to Huron's?"

He nodded, smiling like a little boy on Christmas morning.

I'd never traveled that way with Cole; would it be appropriate to do it with Luke? I'd hate to spark unnecessary jealousy in Cole once I got him back. But Luke was his friend, and we were working together to help him. Surely Cole would be okay with whatever things Luke and I did together to accomplish his safe return. In my mind I went back and forth with it another minute, then nodded at Luke.

"Great! It's settled!" He grabbed his martini and held up the glass. "Cheers!"

I sat there gaping at him. Then his eyes got darker and deeper, and I felt my whole body start to tremble. I tried to turn away but couldn't move. My breathing quickened and my heart began pounding against my chest. I could feel him at the edge of my mind, moving closer and deeper—all the places he shouldn't be. There was so much pressure everywhere, threatening to suffocate me. Fear seized me.

Then, suddenly, he was gone. I was me and he was him. "Jerk!" I hissed, starting to rise, but his hand was on my arm pulling me down. "Let. Me. Go!"

"Wait! Let me explain! I didn't mean to do that. It's because of your blood! I swear! Please don't go."

I stole a minute to collect myself, then asked, "What do you mean it's because of my blood?"

"I never feed without *alluring* my prey. I couldn't help it. The way you were looking at me, mixed with the fresh scent of your blood. Angel, you're almost irresistible."

"It seems like I am completely irresistible!" I scoffed. "If that happens again—"

"It won't. But maybe you *should* shift into another shirt."

I peered around. There were lots of people and beings scattered outside our private little oasis, but they all seemed so distracted, and there was no real good view of Luke and me from out there anyway, so I shifted into a fresh dressy tank. Luke's eyes widened, then he said, "That was efficient."

"It beats going through that cluster"—I gestured toward the dance floor—"to find the bathrooms."

"How do you plan on dancing with me if you don't want to go back out there?"

"I'm not dancing with you!"

Luke took my hand and stood up, pulling me along with him. "We can just do it right here," he whispered in my ear, then tugged me away from the sofa and around the ottoman. He twirled me under his arm, pulling me close against his chest.

"Luke, please! I don't want to do this!" I begged, but then he tossed me backward and whirled me around as he pulled me back to him. "Luke, st—" He spun me again, then dipped me low. I could feel my hair graze across the ground as he brought me back up. His hands landed on my hips and he slid me side to side, mimicking his own movements. Another argument built up on my tongue, but it was silenced as he twirled me again. His hand gripped my back, firm and hard, guiding me along with each step. He pulled me closer, holding me tighter, then released me with a powerful thrust. I triple-stepped back, losing my balance, but Luke was already there with both hands on my hips, steadying me. We swayed back and forth, then he swooped me up in his arms, holding me like a baby as he twirled around and around. Then he dipped me again while still holding me steady, secure in his arms. As he pulled me back up I started laughing uncontrollably, and obviously it was contagious. Luke burst into laughter and I lost track of time as he stood there, holding me, both of us giggling so hard my cheeks started hurting. I gazed up into Luke's eyes and our laughter trailed off. His face was closer, but I never saw him move. He squeezed his arms more firmly around my body. My breathing sped up, and my chest tightened. Then his lips brushed across mine, sensual and soft, igniting a fire within me like flames on gasoline. I couldn't think straight, my thoughts were a blur; every part of me wanted Luke—needed to feel him kissing me. There was a perfect balance of fire and ice, the warmth of my breath and the soothing chill from his. Without thinking, my arms snaked around his neck, and my lips pressed harder against his. Something between a groan and a growl escaped his mouth, then his right hand slid up into my hair, tugging and pulling, while his other hand kept holding me under my knees. His tongue slid across my lips, slowly open-ing them with each stroke. An inferno of lust clung to my spine, burned up my neck, and spilled out onto my head. For a brief moment, we were whirling and spinning, then I was lying on something firm and squishy, with Luke on top of me and my legs wrapped tightly around his body. My hands slipped under his shirt, rubbing all over his back, and as his body pressed closer my fingernails dug into his skin. Luke growled, deep and guttural, then breathed, "Angel."

Suddenly, reality shook my body like an earthquake, my hunger and need completely silenced by panic and guilt. "No, we can't!" I shouted, pulling my hands free of his shirt, then placing them on his shoulders and pushing as hard as I could. He barely moved an inch.

His eyes bore down into mine. "Don't do this," he begged, his voice breathless and panting.

I pushed harder, holding his body at arm's length. "Luke, we can't. Please."

His shoulders slumped back, his face softened, and then in a flash of motion he was sitting beside me, my legs draped over his thighs. "Angel, I..."

I sat up in a rush, swinging my legs away from Luke and shifting my position, careful not to sit too close. Cole. *What about Cole?* I scolded my-self, leaning forward, burying my face in my hands. How did all of that just happen? How could I have let it happen? But it felt so good being close to Luke, filled with so much desire and warmth. It was similar to my times with Cole, and yet so very different. It was wrong, so very wrong, but it'd felt so right just moments ago. But it wasn't, and I knew it. I raised my head and glanced at Luke. He was watching me, eyes cautious and sad. "I'm not mad at you," I said at last, slumping my shoulders and taking slow, deep breaths. "This was my fault too. I'm sorry. This can never happen again."

"But what if I want it to? Angel, it felt too perfect being close to you. Feeling your body pressed against mine. There's something between us and you can't deny it!"

My mind was reeling; my heart was beating out of control. He was right. I couldn't deny it, but none of that mattered. I loved Cole. So how was it possible to feel something for Luke? My body started trembling, and Luke's hand was instantly on mine. "Are you okay?" he asked.

My chest tightened with anguish. I tried to speak, but couldn't get my words over the lump in my throat. I swallowed a few times, and it helped a little. Dang it, why couldn't Luke have gotten me the water I'd asked for? I reached for my drink and took a small sip, then said, "Listen to me. Cole will be back tonight and then everything will be back to normal. I've been lonely and missing him so much. I'm sorry for letting this happen tonight. We need to stay focused. Please, I can't do this without you, Luke."

His expression hardened as he shook his head. "No problem," he mumbled as he stood up.

"Where are you going?"

"To grab one more drink before we go." He stormed off, in human steps, and I watched him disappear into the sea of dancers.

13

WE ARRIVED AT HURON'S bar after a couple long hours of traveling in Luke's arms—since he had to carry me. A silent frustration had prodded my heart the whole way, unspoken desires floating in the air between us. I hoped my mixed feelings for Luke were only filling the empty void of not having Cole here with me. Once I got Cole back, everything would return to normal, and the unexplainable attraction to Luke would disappear. It had to.

We were about a block away from the bar when Luke set me down. I assumed we'd just walk the rest of the way in human steps, so I turned and headed up the sidewalk. Suddenly, Luke's hand was on my shoulder, holding me in place. "Wait."

I took a deep breath and turned. "We don't have much time."

"I know, but this can't wait. I need to say it now." He ran his hand through his hair. "If anything happens, I mean anything bad, I just want you to know...I want you to know that I care about you."

That clenching in my stomach returned. What was happening to me? I was a complete wreck without Cole. It wasn't possible to feel something for Luke. Was it? I looked down at the ground, stealing a moment to collect my thoughts. We were less than an hour away from the fight of our lives. There was no guarantee we'd come out of this victorious. What if we couldn't defeat Limos? What if his army proved greater than ours? And what if—just thinking this broke my heart into a million pieces—Cole was already dead? I shook off the thought immediately, refusing to believe Limos would have killed him before he'd gotten what he wanted—me. Surely the stress of my situation, and the fear of the unknown, were the reasons I was feeling anything for Luke, and he had to be feeling out of sorts because of that too. He just *thinks* he cares about me, when in fact, I'm filling a need for him also. I glanced up at his face and simply couldn't acknowledge what he'd told me. So I tried to sound positive when I replied, "I wish I could tell you that everything was going to be okay. But I have no idea what to expect with Limos. We can only pray that things work out in our favor—we get Cole, and we all get out…in one piece."

He half smiled. "Even when you get *your* vampire back, I'm still going to care about you."

I shook my head, feeling a stab deep in my heart as I tried my best to ignore that. "You're getting him back too. Remember, Cole's your friend?"

Something strange flitted in his eyes, then they changed back to their normal deep and mysterious pools, threatening to swallow me inside them. I gasped, certain he was about to enter my thoughts, but nothing happened. Without saying another word, Luke swooped me up in a big bear hug. I resisted at first, but then the reality of his words hit me like a ton of bricks. Maybe he really *does* care? What if Luke dies trying to help me save Cole? Caught up in the moment, I wrapped my arms around his neck, squeezing tighter and tighter. Time seemed to stand still as we held each other, then his lips slowly brushed across my cheek as he pulled away.

I sighed, then turned and headed off toward Huron's. I couldn't hear Luke behind me, but I felt his closeness tingling on my skin as he followed me. We walked inside the musky, smoky bar and went straight to the back. Huron set a mug full of foamy beer in front of some old, raggedy-looking vamp, then he looked up at us and nodded. His eyes slid to the side, directing us. Luke got in front and led me to the furthest right corner of the bar. A cracked, wooden door spilled us into a short, narrow hallway. We followed it to the end and arrived at another door. My angelic senses were going haywire, cautioning me not to proceed, but when Luke opened the door and walked in, I stayed right behind him.

The medium-sized room was dimly lit and overcrowded with dark ones. In the center was a poker table with six vampires sitting around it—all of them with cards in their hands. A few more vamps were seated in wooden stools along the side wall. They'd been watching the poker game, but now their eyes were on me and Luke.

There were three demons at the very back of the room. I instantly recognized Grote, Caitlyn's former nuisance of a demon, and one of the four that had helped with her attack, leaving her to die. Grote was in human form—well, sort of. He was around five foot tall with curly brown hair perched on the tops of his shoulders. He wore black leather pants and matching combat boots. His bare chest and arms were pale and scaly—like a cross between a gator and a vampire—and his eyes were bright orange with black, diamond-shaped pupils. One of the other demons looked very similar to a panther, but instead of black fur, thousands of razor-sharp whiskers covered its body, and its eyes glowed red. The other demon looked like an oversized centipede with a deep green body and red spikes all over it.

I grabbed Luke's arm, pulling him close, then whispered, "I know one of those demons. I don't trust him."

"I don't trust any of the demons," he breathed in my ear, "but I trust Huron."

"Hello, Suh-leeen," Grote hissed. "I had no idea it was *you* I'd be helping."

Anger clawed my spine and I felt my eyes narrow. "Because of you, Caitlyn is dying!" I took a few steps toward the demon, but Luke grabbed my arms from behind, holding me back.

"You know that isn't true," Grote said, scowling. "The charge is dying because you weren't there to keep her safe."

"No!" I exclaimed, pushing forward while Luke's grip tightened, keeping me where I was. "Who orchestrated the attack? You demons"—I gestured toward the two beside Grote—"are never *that* organized. Tonight, you're here for Huron. Who were you following when you attacked my charge?"

Grote's lips curved into a sly smile. "Wouldn't you like to know?"

"Was it Typhon?" My voice was getting louder. "What would he have to gain from killing my charge?"

Grote burst into sinister laughter. As he shook, flickers of light danced across his skin. The other two demons swayed back and forth, as if trying to laugh in their creature forms. My chest felt constricted, my heart heavy with anger and grief. Luke tugged me back a little more and I slumped down, Luke's hard chest against my back. I let out a deep breath without even realizing I'd been holding it.

The vampires along the side wall, one middle-aged woman and two twenty-something men, were watching me: stone-cold, expressionless.

The vampires at the table had returned to their poker game—except for a younger-looking redhead. She must've been barely sixteen when turned into a vampire. Her skin was flawless and smooth like porcelain, and her eyes were like black, bottomless pits. "Enough!" she roared, keeping her eyes on me. The room fell silent, and I could've sworn I saw Grote cower and take a step back from the corner of my eye. She set her cards on the table and stood. A black rocker-styled tee hung loosely over her skinny, dark blue jeans. She fluttered to me, swift and graceful, standing no more than a foot away. We were about the same height, giving me too good a view of her eyes. I hurriedly looked to the side, finding the only unoccupied space in the room. The wall was off-white with numerous cracks running up and down, just like the rest of the walls in the room. I felt the vampire's fingers brush across my face, below my lips and along my chin. I gasped, sucking in a deep breath, attempting to step back but being already squished up against Luke. "Why won't you look at me?" the young vampire purred.

"Back off, Annabel!" Luke said, his voice deep and authoritative. As I focused on the wall, I felt the vibrations of his words against my back.

"Oh, Luke, I just want to know why the lovely angel here won't look at me." She cupped my face, and I could feel her staring at me.

There was a blur of motion, then suddenly Annabel was flying across the room, just missing the poker table and hitting the wall beyond it before crashing to the floor. The vampires at the table were looking at me, obviously unhappy about the distraction. Luke was beside me now, eyes slanted in a glare and fangs exposed. "I said back off!" he roared.

Without seeing her move, Annabel was now standing just behind the table. Her mouth was bloody and she was snarling, crimson drops falling from her fangs. "That really wasn't necessary!" She sprang up, coming straight for us.

Luke jumped in front of me, but she was intercepted by one of the poker-playing vamps. He was tall and slender, thick brown hair cropped above his ears. He was standing—one arm stretched in front of him, holding Annabel by the neck, over the table, in the air. In what seemed like slow motion, he swung her to the side and set her down beside him. "Know your place, Annabel," he said, then looked at me. "After we help you tonight, our debt will be repaid." He looked back at Annabel and added, "And that is when you can get to know the angel a little better. Do you understand?"

Annabel nodded, slowly. "I'm sorry, Argon, I must've lost myself in her scent."

"If Annabel even thinks of trying anything," Luke said through gritted teeth and fangs, "she'll be going through me first!"

"So quick to bounce into the arms of another woman," Annabel smarted, glaring at Luke.

Argon elbowed Annabel in the side. "You can play the scorned jealous lover later. Right now, there are some things to go over."

Luke and Annabel had been in a relationship? I felt my own wave of jealousy wrap around my spine, pulling at the corners of my chest. I glanced over at Luke and he was clearly seething, fangs still exposed. I took his hand inside mine, giving it a gentle squeeze, then looked at Argon and said, "There isn't much time before we need to leave. I think we'll get along best if Grote and Annabel keep their distance from me."

Argon nodded. "I couldn't agree more. Now tell me…Selene is it? Tell me, why are you even helping a vampire?"

My throat was instantly dry. But there really was no point in keeping secrets from my allies, right? I didn't have a backup story to tell anyway. "I'm in love with him."

Several gasps sounded throughout the room. I sensed something unsettling coming from Luke, a minute tremble within my grasp. It reminded me of my last run-in with the siren, how my hands shook with anxiety, the sharp anger from being in her world in the first place, the swirling uncertainty of when I'd hear the chimes, or that maybe this time I wouldn't hear them at all. Because of that stupid kiss, now Luke was feeling confused and unsure of me, where I stood with him, with Cole, and how things might change once Cole was back. All because of a kiss that I couldn't take back, couldn't make disappear from our memories, and sadly, a part of me didn't want to forget. And it scared me more than anything we were about to do in Charon.

When I glanced at him, his face was hard and unreadable. I knew he didn't like hearing what I'd just said, but it was the truth and every being in this room deserved to know what they were risking their lives for…even Grote, though it wouldn't have bothered me the slightest if he never made it back to Earth.

Another male vampire at the poker table stood up. He was shorter than Argon but just as slender, with long dark hair swooped back in a low ponytail. "You're in love with a vampire? How is that possible?"

Suddenly, Grote started laughing, pulling everyone's attention his way. All the vampires swung challenging glares at him. His laughter turned into a gagging sound, like he was pretending to clear his throat instead of laugh. After that, he fell completely silent.

All eyes were on me again, and the shorter vampire repeated, "How is it possible that you love a vampire?"

"I don't know why I love him, if that's what you're asking." I shrugged my shoulders. "We don't choose love, it chooses us."

"But you're an angel. How can you, an angel, love one of us?" The short vampire stretched his arms, waving at everyone else in the room.

I stepped forward, taking a deep breath. "It is forbidden, and I have paid the price for loving him."

Luke stepped up beside me and tugged his hand away. There was something harder about him now. "Dustan, I don't see how your question pertains to anything. If you have any real questions, then ask them now."

Dustan's head cocked to the side. "How can you say that? I think it's very important to know why an angel of the light is helping a vampire of the dark. We are all risking our lives for this!"

"No!" Luke exclaimed, pointing his finger at Dustan. "None of you would be alive if it weren't for Huron!" Luke's finger swung side to side, pointing at every single being in the room. "Let us remember that when we go to war tonight. You owe it to Huron to give this battle everything you've got."

Annabel stepped forward, her eyes flaring the deepest blue I'd ever seen. "But what does Huron owe this angel? Why would he cash in our debt to help *her*?"

"That's none of your business!" Huron came in and stood beside me. His black hair was pulled back into a long twisting braid. "If you have a problem fighting tonight, then leave now!"

An eerie silence spread throughout the room, then Argon said, "We are all here to stand and fight. There is no trouble. Forgive us."

Huron smiled. "Good." He looked over at Luke. "Are there any other details we need to go over before leaving?"

"Yes." My voice was calm but stern. "I can give us the upper hand by weakening the enemy with my light."

"Your light will blind all of us! And we'll all be destroyed!" That came from a very angry-looking Grote. A little melodramatic, are we? But with his comment, a hushed commotion spread throughout the room. All the vampires looked unsettled, anxious bickering rolling from their tongues.

"That's not true." I was trying my best to stay calm, but Grote was really pissing me off. "To keep your presence hidden, I am masking your auras. But this will also allow you to be in the light for a brief time."

"How can that be?" Annabel's face softened, her head tilting slightly to the side.

Grote let out a deep growl. "Her light will destroy us all!"

"Silence!" Argon swung around, glaring at Grote, then flashed his fangs at everyone else in the room.

I locked eyes with Argon, nodding my thanks. "I give my word that all of you will be safe from my light as long as you are standing by me. If you become a threat, I cannot promise your safety any longer."

"What she means," Luke explained, "is that if you turn on her and start fighting with the enemies, your light pass will be expired. Got it?" He looked around, making sure everyone understood. Their widened eyes and bobbing heads were a great clue that they did.

"And one more thing," I added. "My orbing—"

Luke grabbed my hand, squeezing uncomfortably, and I stared. Something flashed across his eyes, warning me to keep silent. I inclined my head, letting him know I understood. Luke glared around the room, then said, "Angel will be orbing us to Charon about thirty minutes early so we can all safely get to our posts. There is an enormous boulder to the north of our landing point. You can't miss it. All of you are to head straight there and take cover. I'll be helping Angel get into position and then I'll come join you."

Smart move, Luke! He knew I'd need time to recover from orbing, and he obviously didn't want anyone here to know about my little issue. Especially with Annabel hot on my tail, so to speak. In my haste to get on with things, I'd almost shared a fatal weakness with every single dark one in this room. Sure, they were helping tonight, but after that, all bets were off. Thank God Luke had cut me off. I felt my emotions get tangled in my chest, and all I could do was squeeze Luke's hand, hopefully letting him know how much I appreciated what he'd done.

"When do we attack?" asked Dustan.

"When I give the signal," Luke replied.

"Listen up, everyone." Huron bellowed like a commander in the military. "Luke is in charge. Do exactly what he says. If anyone screws up, then your debt ain't paid and you still owe me. Those who listen and *succeed* are free of my claim to them. Now let me know you all understand what I'm saying."

A dozen heads were nodding, even the two demons in creature form. My mind was reeling, wondering what in the worlds Luke had done for Huron to earn the debts that all those dark ones owed, not to Luke, but to Huron. Luke had told me that I didn't want to know why Huron owed him, and at that time I'd thought the less I knew the better. But now my curiosity was burning a hole in my mind, making me feel I couldn't live without knowing the details. It wasn't a good time to bring this up, though, so I shrugged it off the best I could, storing it in the back of my mind for later. Hopefully, once I got Cole back, I wouldn't want to know anymore. Hopefully. But I was starting to doubt my ability to say good-bye to Luke once that time really came.

14

I WAS SECURELY TUCKED INSIDE a firm, chilly grasp while gazing intently at familiar grayish-blue eyes. Darkness surrounded me, thick and suffocating, with foggy light gleaming from a few distant stars. The eerie silence was steadily interrupted by the sound of waves crashing on a nearby shore. It didn't occur to me to freak out, mostly because I felt comfortable with this beautiful, familiar stranger. His fingertips stroked my cheek, gentle and slow, fending off remnant traces of anxiety.

"Angel, are you with me?" He ran his fingers through my hair, finding a few tangled spots but kept tugging through them. "We only have a few minutes, and if that demon shows up early—"

My breath caught as I pulled myself up, using his neck as support. "Luke. Where's everyone else? Did they make it okay?"

He helped me stand, keeping his arm around my back. "Yes. They're in position. Are you ready?"

I gave a slow nod. "I recognized you…knew you wouldn't harm me." I shrugged, stepping out of Luke's embrace to face him. "I couldn't remember your name, but yet I knew who you were. That's never happened before."

"Maybe you're already getting some of your powers back?" he suggested, then switched back to the task at hand. "What will you use as a signal for us to attack?"

"My light." Then I added, "You won't be able to miss it."

In a whir a motion, Luke's lips brushed my cheek, and then he was gone, presumably behind the oversized rock where I sensed the masked essence of my makeshift army. My thoughts were heavy, my anxiety back in full force. There was the overwhelming realization that I was moments away from getting Cole back. Cole. Oh God, please let him be okay…and in one piece.

Once I removed the mask from my aura, it was a "hurry up and wait" situation. Silence filled the air, nipping through my skin, prickling against bone. Unease slithered up my spine, clenching at the base of my neck, squeezing, taunting. But thankfully, Limos didn't take long. All of a sudden, orange smoke churned the air about ten feet away from me. My body tensed as I waited for the demon to materialize. At last, he stood in front of me. His eyes flared red as the trails of smoke faded. "Selene." His voice made me shudder. He pulled his cloak's hood back, folding it behind him. There was a gray flakiness to his skin, and his eyes seemed to gleam a brighter crimson.

"Where's Cole?" Need I say more?

He clapped his hands together, rubbing them, his claws scraping with the friction. "Straight to the point, I see." It didn't sound like a question. "So be it." He stretched his arms, hands rising toward the sky, then started chanting: "Om-ma, de-le vicci, losa duro mia…"

I glanced around, anticipating the soon arrival of his summoned minions. They didn't keep me waiting long. After numerous puffs of more orange smoke billowing in the area behind Limos, several demons appeared. Some were in human form; others ranged from mutated tigers or jaguars— to bull looking-thingies with too many horns—to some kind of oversized dinosaur-bird creature. I counted about twenty of them, including Limos. One of the human-looking demons with dark flowing hair and obsidian eyes approached, dragging something heavy with silver chains behind him.

Cole. His name shivered through me the minute I picked up his essence. He was barely alive, if that's what you could even call it. Anger seized me, instantly filling me with more rage and vengeance than I'd ever felt before. Light burst from me as if my whole body were a flamethrower. In unison, all the demons cowered back—except for one. Limos stood his ground, not even shielding his eyes. His laugh came out loud and sinister, then he roared, "Backing out on our deal so soon, my child?" He lunged forward, crashing into me, and rode me to the ground. I broke his fall, knocking the air from my lungs, but a new surge of rage flowed through me.

"Now!" I screamed, refocusing everything inside me on the light. It blasted brighter, radiating neon yellows, sparkling whites....

Limos struck me across the face, and I saw starbursts in my mind. "You're outnumbered. Concede to me now, or die."

"You may be able to touch me," I said, my teeth grinding together, "but you cannot kill me." I swung sideways, throwing Limos off.

I glanced around and saw Luke and the mini-army fighting all those demons with everything they had. The jaguar thingy was knocking Annabel around, but then Dustan came to her aid and twisted its head off, a killing blow since vamps were the only creatures I knew of that could actually kill other dark ones without permission. Argon was wrestling with one of the human-looking demons, and I started to search for Luke when my senses told me to turn around—which I did just as Limos was charging straight at me. His hand slashed out, claws ripping into my face. I cried out, jumping back, then sprang up in the air, my fist crashing into Limos' head as I landed. He sidestepped, then swung at me again, but this time I felt a rush of wind as he just missed. His eyes glared, his face seething with fury. "You're mine! Or no one's!" In a rush, he was on me; I never had time to get out of his way. His massive body towered over me, long arms stretched around me in what felt like a bear hug, but when he squeezed tighter, I knew he wasn't hugging me—he was trying to crush my insides.

I tried to get away, but my consciousness was starting to waver. And since that had never happened to me before while fighting a demon, I had no idea what to do. My light had always been enough to handle any of the dark ones, but now, because I'd let Limos touch me, he seemed to be immune. But what could a demon really do to me? I needed to shift back to my angel form, but I couldn't concentrate on any one thing long enough to do it. My breathing grew shorter and shorter, and I felt my light getting duller, dimmer. Soon, it wouldn't be enough to hold back Limos' minions, and that would put my allies at risk. My spine iced with violent chills as my head throbbed with panic...and the possibility of failing.

Soon after that, blackness took me.

"Angel," came a cool, soothing voice.

My eyes shot open as I turned over, then started coughing up blood. Stabbing pain shot through me each time I hacked, and my insides felt like mush.

"Are you okay? What's happening to you?" Luke asked. He hovered over me, looking confused and afraid.

I rolled on my side, then pushed up. Sharp pain shot through my left side and I instantly fell back down. "I don't...I don't know. I couldn't shift into angel form. That's never happened before."

Luke gave me a hard, penetrating gaze. "Will you be able to get us back home?"

"Where's Limos?" my voice laced with anxiety. "Where's his army?"

"They're dead—all of them. We lost a couple of our vampires and one of the demons."

"Demon?" Please let it be Grote.

"Yeah, the wicked-looking caterpillar."

Brief disappointment, then, "Cole! Where's Cole?"

Luke looked behind him, then back at me. "He's over there, in pretty bad shape. Worse than you."

"Take me to him"—my words short and breathless. "Round up everyone who's left and gather around me."

He nodded once and scooped me up in his arms. My head rested against his shoulder, my whole body throbbing each time he stepped. "Will taking my blood help you heal?" his low voice rumbled.

"No, I don't..." But I'd never tried it before, so how would I *really* know? I'd always believed vampire blood to be poisonous to angels, but I never got sick when Luke had tried giving me his blood before. Would it help me? I didn't know. All I knew was that I sure needed something, and I needed it now. Otherwise, our trip back to Earth might be postponed. "Can we try?" My question seemed to take him by surprise, because his grip tightened. "Ouch!"

"Oh sorry, I just...wasn't expecting you to say that."

"Is there any way to keep this private?" The thought of drinking another vampire's blood with Cole lying right there seemed dirty and wrong, plus I didn't need the other vamps and demons getting any ideas.

A whoosh of air, then Luke set me down in front of a small outcropping of oddly shaped rocks. I could see the rest of our allies standing around a hump of silver chains, keeping a short, safe distance. Cole. He was chained in silver, and God only knew what his condition really was. "Is he conscious?" A huge part of me hoped he wasn't.

Luke shook his head, then raised his wrist to his mouth, ripping the skin open with his fangs. He placed the bleeding wound in front of my mouth, and when I hesitated, he encouraged, "Go on, before it heals."

Luke's blood flowed in tangy, molten globs down my throat. Hundreds of years of my life, countless memories with my charges long before Caitlyn was ever born, flashed inside my mind. Some had died due to disease and famine, some lost their lives to war, and then there were a few that lived their lives to the very end—until old age claimed them. Of all of them, there was never a death where the blame lay fully on my shoulders. Accepting this was difficult, but it was the truth, and I couldn't let her die because of me. Any doubt I had about giving my life for hers had just been brought front and center in my mind, and guilt seemed to drive the undisputable answer on home—though I'd wait to make the final decision once I was in a little better shape.

My thoughts were shaken as Luke pulled me off his wrist. "You can't take any more without seriously wounding me."

I sat back, wiping the blood from my lips with my fingers. Surprisingly, I felt better…much, much better. A wave of elation washed over me, and all the edginess was gone. My body felt stronger, and it wasn't hurting that bad anymore either. Ripples of electricity seemed to flow through my veins, sending shockwaves across my skin. I could feel Luke's desire for me—more intensely than I'd ever felt—and my ability to sense things seemed heightened too. Feeling overconfident, I tried standing, but my legs gave out and I fell—though Luke was right there, arm stretched around me, holding me up. "Thanks," I said.

His mouth quirked. "I see you're feeling better."

I beamed at him, amazed at how good I really felt. "I never knew this was possible."

"Glad to know I made you feel better." A pressure thickened in my chest. Luke swooped me up in his arms and headed toward the others. His steps weren't torturous anymore, and it felt like my insides were mending. My cracked bones seemed solid and unbroken, and it was easier to breathe, even with the tight chest. Soon, I'd be walking on my own again.

Once we arrived where the others stood, Luke set me down—very hesitantly. I could feel jealousy swell up inside him, and as I looked over, I understood. Cole. I crawled the short distance separating us, my body sinking in the soft, grainy sand, a few sharp rocks digging into my shins through my jeans. There were concerns and questions coming from what was left of our army, but their words faded in and out.

Luke's aura hardened the moment I reached my vampire lover. Cole's face was dirty and smeared with blood, leaving him almost unrecognizable. I touched his cheek, gently stroking his dry, cracked lips. "Cole"—my voice was a whisper as I looked down at the rest of him. His body seemed crushed beneath the silver chains—bruised, bloody, and with numerous broken bones. Tears sprang into my eyes and my throat constricted. I stared at his face, voice soft and begging, "Baby, wake up. You're safe now."

With no response, I flashed angry eyes at everyone around me. "Help me get him out of these!" I grabbed at the chains, pulling and yanking, needing a little more strength to get them off.

All eyes widened. Argon took a small step forward. "We can't touch those. They're made of silver."

I'd forgotten all about that tiny little detail. Silver was toxic to vampires, even though alone, it wouldn't be enough to kill them. Then I had another idea and waved my hand at Grote. "Get over here and help me take these off him."

"But we're ready to go home," came a high-pitched whining voice. I glanced over to find it belonged to Annabel.

"We're not going anywhere until these chains are off!" was my icy reply, and it seemed to get some action. Both Annabel and Argon flashed warning looks at Grote, making his twisted smile fade. He approached, knelt down beside me, and helped me get the chains off without one single word. Smart demon.

Once we were done, Grote carried the chains a few yards away. Upon his return, I motioned for everyone else to approach. Cole would need days to recover, and God only knew how much blood, but I could sense that his death was no longer a worry. I still couldn't get up on my own, so I stayed on the ground next to Cole. Annabel bounced forward, taking my hand, while my other one remained on Cole's chest. The rest of the vampires grabbed onto each other, and Argon connected our chain by taking hold of Annabel. Luke was toward the back, searing with jealousy and keeping some distance between us. *Solving one problem, only to create another*, I thought, then closed my eyes and focused on home…sweet…home.

15

IT WAS TWO AND A HALF DAYS LATER, and Cole's recovery was moving slower than predicted. Still unconscious, he lay on an old brown leather sofa that had been brought in the back room at Huron's bar and squeezed between the poker table and wall. A blood bag was hung from a hook on an electronic, metal-looking contraption, and a long, narrow tube ran down from it to lodge deep in Cole's throat. An IV would've been pointless, since vampires usually heal too quickly—even though Cole wasn't healing fast enough for my taste.

Once we got back, I'd made almost a full recovery—unbeknownst to anyone but Luke that there was ever anything wrong, thank God. Oddly, though, I still didn't feel like my normal self, and I couldn't help but assume it had something to do with me drinking Luke's blood. Being a strong and mighty vampire, I'd expected Cole's progress to be the same as mine. Apparently Limos had tortured him terribly, and delayed any healing with those silver chains. It was a shame Limos was already dead. There were several ways I would have loved to pay him back.

Although Huron's hospitality was appreciated, I couldn't help but wonder if it was still only because of his debt to Luke—who sadly I hadn't seen, or sensed, since shortly after our return. While enduring those annoying orbing side effects, Luke had stayed with me and was familiar just like before, until the symptoms wore off and complete recognition kicked in. But since he took off immediately after that, I didn't get a chance to talk to him about it. His absence brought an indescribable sadness to my heart. And I didn't like feeling that way.

With their slates wiped clean of Huron's debt, the remaining vamps and demons had fled—except for Annabel. No, she'd stuck around as if only to annoy me, poking her head in periodically to check on me, then retreating from my repeated threats. I assumed she was helping Huron work the bar, not that I'd left this room to go see for myself. On one of his several trips back here, Huron had told me that as long as I was under his roof, I'd be safe from Annabel. He couldn't promise the same once I left, though. I didn't think she could hurt me—without my permission of course—but these new feelings I had brought caution, and I didn't want to push my luck with her yet.

A little good news in all of this was that I hadn't heard a peep from Raphael. Good. He really was giving me my space, presumably thinking I was preparing my final good-byes for my charge. So I guess that meant Corrine was still watching Caitlyn, and no changes had happened with her condition, good or bad.

Still, I'd had plenty of time to ponder my revelation about dying or falling—either way I'd no longer exist as an angel—for Caitlyn back on Charon. Once Cole woke up, I'd be seeking Luke out to see if he planned to help or if he was done with me for good. There was a sharp pang in my heart considering the latter, bringing to light that I *did* have feelings for Luke. Even as I stared at Cole's face, seeing life slowly come back to him, memories of Luke and I kissing traipsed through my mind—followed by a hefty amount of guilt.

I sat on the floor with my legs tucked under me, my back leaning against the side of the sofa. Faint movement and the feeling of being watched had me swinging around to find Cole's deep blue eyes locked onto mine, wide with unspoken things. "Selene?"

With instant tears streaming down my cheeks, I wailed, "You're okay," then wrapped my arms softly around his neck. "I was so worried. I prayed every second that I'd find you alive."

He hugged me back, light and gentle, his body still on the mend. "I've missed you." His mouth brushed through my hair, settling on my ear. "I love you."

More tears fell and my body tensed. I leaned back, staring down at my lap. "I missed you too"—my voice a hushed whisper. Then I raised my face and met his eyes, my guilt morphing into curiosity about what happened on Charon. "What did Limos do to you?"

Cole sat up—it was a bit of a struggle—and I helped him get into a comfortable position. "Where is that wretched monster? Stay away from him, Selene. He was only using me to get you. He wants your power so he can use it to defeat Typhon and rule the earth along with his other lowly worlds."

"Limos is dead," I said at once. "And all those who helped him."

He gave a hard, penetrating gaze. "How?"

I filled him in on my alliance with his friend and how he'd put together a small army of dark ones to go with us to Charon, which was how Limos and his helpers were destroyed. I briefly touched on Huron and that we were in a back room of his bar. And once I got to the part where Huron was helping us because of the favor he owed Luke, Cole gaped at me, confused, and asked, "Who's Luke?"

"He's your friend...," I tried to explain, but my words trailed off as doubt crept in. I remembered Luke saying, "*Even when you get your vampire back, I'm still going to care about you.*" And the look in his eyes when I'd said, "*You're getting him back too. Remember, Cole's your friend?*"

Realization slapped my face, hard and uninvited. Luke *didn't* know Cole, and they were *never* friends. I sat back, nervously running my hands across my jeans, feeling breathless and uneasy. My body started shaking and I fought to regain composure. Cole put his hands on top of mine, holding tightly enough to get me to look at him. His eyes were burning blue flames and I hurriedly looked down at his chin. "What haven't you told me, Selene? I can taste your fear. Why would you be afraid of me?"

"Nothing," I stammered, my heart almost pounding out of my chest. I closed my eyes, stealing a moment to calm myself. Then at last, I said, "I just don't understand why Luke would lie to me about being your friend."

He shot me a frustrated look. "Why would that cause you to fear me? Don't we owe this guy for saving my life, and yours?"

I nodded slowly, feeling a lump barrel its way up my throat.

A brief moment passed with thick silence, then Cole lowered his lips to my neck. "What are you doing?" I asked, even though I already knew the answer.

"I've missed you so much." The chill of his breath tickled my neck. "And those blood bags aren't enough to get my strength back. I need you,

Selene. I need to taste you right now." His fangs plunged underneath my skin before I had a chance to respond. Shivers spread through my body like tiny electric currents and I sighed with pleasure, tilting my head to give him a better vantage point.

That's when everything seemed to happen at once. Cole growled, deep and guttural, then shot back to the far side of the sofa. With his body hunched over, his eyes flaring with rage, he roared, "Is that *his* blood I taste in you?"

I'd never said a cuss word in all of my existence, but at this moment, several of them built up on my tongue. "I can explain, please let me explain."

He chuckled, but it wasn't pleasant. "How? No! Better yet…why?!"

"Limos beat me up pretty bad," I said in a rush. "And I needed to get everyone back to Earth…including you."

"You? Get beaten up?" was his hysterical reply. "Are you freakin' kidding me? How can an angel get beaten up? It's just not possible!"

I dug my nails into my palms, fighting back the tears that tried to choke me. "More of my powers were stripped. My human form has grown weaker." I stole a deep breath, then added, "And I was too weak to change back to my angel form after I fought Limos."

"So you drank blood from some other vampire?" Each word drug out, ending in another snarl. "It's no longer a mystery why he stuck around to help you now! Is it?"

Cole was right. Luke had stuck around only to help me, but still I'd thought he was Cole's friend, and that that had been the reason he originally got involved. "But I didn't know, I swear it! I was injured and not thinking straight. Please, Cole," I pleaded. "I never meant to hurt you by doing this. I just wanted to get you home."

His face only hardened, brows creasing as his eyes slanted more. "You-gave-him-your-blood!"

I scooted closer but he shook his head. "Don't," he warned.

Tears flooded out of my eyes, my vision a complete blur. "Cole," I begged. "Please don't do this. I've waited so long to get you back. Everything I did was for you." Remembering that kiss with Luke back at the club, a wave of guilt pressed down on my heart. *Not everything*, my mind smarted. My body started trembling with feelings I couldn't begin to describe. Fearing Cole would see right through me, I turned away, facing the door, and used all my strength to suppress that horrible memory.

"Look at me!" he roared, his voice echoing in my ears.

I obeyed, my eyes dreadfully seeking his. And then he did something he'd never done to me before. Without warning his hard, penetrating gaze dug deep inside my eyes, and within seconds he was completely inside my mind. His swift intrusion left me breathless. Cold sweat instantly covered my body from head to toe. I was shaking so badly, it felt like I was having a seizure. Panic seized me. Then, everything went eerily numb. I couldn't feel anything at all, as if I were paralyzed. But after a beat, something that felt like hot, sharp tentacles gripped my spine and slithered up to my neck. It was on top of my skin, inside my body, leaving me suffocated and violated all at once.

Invisible hands wrapped around my neck, squeezing until I could no longer breathe. I tried to cry out, but couldn't speak. Then, as quick as it had happened, it was over. Cole was in front of me, both hands holding my face. There was a glimmer of knowledge in his eyes, and I braced myself for what came next. He sprung back, clearing the poker table and landing across the room. His head shook violently. "No, no, no!"—the sound of denial in its rawest form. "How could you?" I could barely recognize his voice.

The words "I'm sorry" could hardly begin to express my remorse. But I said them anyway, hoping it would help him forgive me.

Cole waved a hand in the air. "Selene, do you realize what you've done?"

I shook my head, unable to think clearly enough to form a response.

He lowered his hand and shot me a lasered glare. "You're mine!" He wasn't yelling anymore, but there was a firmness in his voice that scared me more than his previous high volume. "You're mine," he repeated. "But now that monster has marked you!"

Marked me? What did he mean by that? He'd never told me anything about vampires "marking" people before. "What are you talking about?" I asked once I found my voice.

His look turned icy. "You took his bloo—"

"But I never gave him any of *my* blood!"

"That doesn't matter, even though your blood is very special." Pain filled his words and dug into my heart. "Whoever takes the blood of a vampire is marked forever. Selene, you belong to *him* now."

"Then why didn't you ever give me *your* blood?" I wailed, rising to move closer to Cole. He didn't back away or stop me this time. His arms folded around me and I held him back. "I can't belong to him," I mumbled against his chest. "I love *you*."

He released me and grasped my chin, tilting me to face him. "I love you so much"—pain and loss filled his voice. "Every minute with that wretched demon, I dreamed of being in your arms." Pink tears streamed down his cheeks. "I never thought you'd ever allow vampire blood to swim in your veins. Or trust me, I would've offered. But now not only have you been marked by another vampire—which I do believe you had no intention of doing—but you've also betrayed me to him." He paused a moment, sadness building in his eyes. "Though I'm willing to bet that betrayal was driven by the new blood bond you share with him," he added at last.

I felt my eyes widen, and my breath caught in my throat. I hadn't been attracted to Luke until after the first time I'd caught him giving me his blood. Even though I'd tried to spit it out, I remembered the metallic taste in my throat and knew with certainty that I'd ingested some. That had to be the reason I kissed him. And now, with more of his blood swimming inside me, who knew what mess of emotions that would create. Panic surged up—I desperately wanted to flush Luke's blood out of me. Maybe if I drank Cole's it would help? "I'll take your blood now. Please!"

Cole's eyes narrowed. "It doesn't work that way. I can't erase his blood from your system, and with you being an angel, I have no idea how long it will linger inside you." He let go of my chin and ran his hand through his messy, beautiful, dark and silky hair. "Just the thought of your lips on his makes me crazy."

I cringed. "I know there are no excuses, but I was an emotional wreck without you"—words flowing in a rush of desperation. "I made a mistake. Please, Cole. Forget that his blood is in me and be with me. There must be a way to flush him out. I'll do whatever it takes."

His mouth quirked. "When a vampire marks you, it's forever. If you were human, traces of his blood would be in you forever—and even add many years to your life."

"But I'm not human. I can get rid of him! I know I can." But the truth was, I just didn't know, but I'd do anything, say anything to keep Cole with me.

"I don't know," came his flat reply. "I need time. And I'm certain that other vampire will try to claim what is his."

"I'm not his!" I hissed.

His head sunk low. "In my world you are."

My fingernails punctured my palms, and I just kept squeezing. I stared at Cole, empty of words, the realization of what he'd just said threatening to suffocate me. Oh, how I wished it would. Whether or not Luke had the right intention for giving me his blood, he'd never said a word about what it meant. And there was no way he didn't know that he'd be marking me as his if I took it. Sure, it might have helped heal my human body quicker, but now I could feel the change his blood brought inside me and I knew what Cole said was true. "I'm sorry," I mumbled under my breath, but I knew Cole could hear it as if I'd screamed it at him.

His mouth compressed, but he said nothing while he cupped my face and stared intently at me. A lone tear fled from his eye—the lightest shade of pink. *Blood mixed with water*, I thought, then placed my hands on top of his. They were shaking.

Suddenly, Cole's lips were on mine—a blast of fire and ice. Then, as quickly as he'd kissed me, he was standing across the room, wiping his lips as if trying to get something off of them. "I can't even kiss you without feeling him in you," he spat. "I'm sorry, Selene. I need to get out of here. I'll find you when I'm ready."

"But what if..." I bit my bottom lip, staring down at my palms where my nails had dug away the skin. Cole was already gone, and I wondered if I'd ever see him again. I'd never even had a chance to tell him about Rhea, or the fact that I'd decided to give my life for Caitlyn if it came to that. Why hadn't Luke told me what it meant to take his blood? If he had just been trying to help me, he could've at least explained that part of it. Or maybe because we'd kissed, he felt empowered to make such a move, hoping for exactly the outcome that just happened? *That stupid kiss*, I scolded myself. Even if Cole did get over the whole me-drinking-Luke's-blood thing, I knew he'd never get over the fact that I'd kissed another vampire. I started crying harder, uncontrollably, and I screamed in agony, trying to release some of the horrible pain. When nothing happened, I screamed again, and again, slamming my clenched fist into the poker table. After that, I shifted invisible and orbed away, before Huron or Annabel would come looking for me.

I was high up on the side of a mountain, sitting on a chunk of exposed granite. My bare feet dangled over the ledge as I stared blankly out ahead of me, not really seeing anything but the crowded thoughts inside my mind. It'd been nearly a day since Cole left me, and I'd come to this place—somewhere near the Garden of the Gods in Colorado—to think. I was numb and bitter, angry and sad. But mostly, I was just lost because I knew there'd be no real way to get Cole back. Unfortunately, I couldn't put all the blame on Luke, either. I'd participated, and it was pointless to come up with lame excuses.

It felt like I was stuck in limbo, with no real assurance of where to go or what to do next. There was no way I could go to Caitlyn until I got what I needed from Rhea. And hopefully, at that point, I'd have some good news—preferably for both of us. Raphael was still giving me my space, thank God. Staying far away from him and Europa was actually a great thing for me right now. So I pondered my only two options: finding Luke and probably getting into some kind of major confrontation, or just going on to Rhea by myself. Selfishly, I still wanted Luke to come with me. He'd proven himself a huge asset by having my back on Charon. But I felt hostile toward him because of the deceitful way he'd given me his blood, even though when I played devil's advocate on the matter, he could've only been trying to help me heal. So after tossing around the idea of going on my own, I felt it had more merit. I could stay in angel form, which had apparently become my stronger suit, so to speak. And I wouldn't have to worry about bickering or arguing or any other relational-type problems. Cole was gone. Venting on Luke wouldn't get him back.

Once my overactive mind simmered, I was able to get a good view of everything around me. Pine trees were spread out along the slope. Smooth, speckled granite rocks of all shapes and sizes protruded near clusters of trees and along a few steeper drop-offs. Through a clearing, a herd of elk appeared like ants, meandering near a small creek toward the base of the mountain. I took a deep, crisp, and refreshing breath, looking up toward the sky. Thick gray fluffy clouds hovered directly above, while off at a short distance their color changed to a deep blue, then morphed into blackness, the sun completely hidden behind them.

The sound of breaking twigs and snapping branches pulled my attention away from the darkening sky. I closed my eyes, sensing the auras of everything around me. My breath caught as I jumped up in panic. *That's not possible*, I thought, staring down at my body, desperately making sure I was in my angel form—which I was. I took a few steps away from the edge, my torn and muddied white dress dragging along the ground; then Luke appeared out of the shadows of some brush. I jumped, startled, then reminded myself there was no way he could see me. That reassurance didn't last long.

"Angel! I hope you weren't planning on going to Rhea without me!" He moved closer, coming to a stop a couple feet away.

"You can see me?" I said aloud, while also wondering it to myself.

"See you? I could smell you all the way from Virginia! I had no idea you were really *this* far away, though." He brushed his hands along his jeans. "Sorry I'm a bit dirtier than when I set out."

His clothes weren't *that* messy. Maybe his jeans had a few darker spots, but his solid-gray tee looked fine. Maybe the dirt just blended into it. I glanced around, feeling anger and confusion taking charge of my emotions. "It isn't possible for your kind to see me like this."

He eyes slid from my feet to my brow. "You look beautiful in that, uh…is that a wedding dress?"

"Wedding dress? Hardly!" I scoffed. "This is my angel form, and you're not supposed to be able to see me like this!"

His head dipped to the side. "Well, I swear, I *can* see you." In a flash, he was directly in front of me, a few inches away at most. "And you smell better than you have ever smelled before." Then his lips were on mine, cold, hard, and sloppy. I gasped in disbelief, grabbing his chest, then pushing with all my angelic strength. He should've flown somewhere far off the side of the mountain, but he only budged a few feet.

"None of this is possible!" I exclaimed, turning away, the first rumblings of thunder echoing around us.

He gripped my shoulder and swung me around. "Then explain to me how it's happening! This is real! I see you, I can smell you." His grasp tightened, fingers digging into my skin. "I'm touching you."

His eyes darkened—flaming black orbs. My body shuddered and I hurriedly stared at the ground. "Don't you dare!"—my voice full of warning. "Please go. I don't want you here."

"Angel, look at me, please." His voice was softer but still firm. "I promise you can trust me."

I waved a hand, feeling my anger thicken. "Trust you? You gave me your blood and never bothered to warn me of the consequences."

"I thought you were dying! I was only trying to help you!"

I raised my head, briefly glimpsing the clouds flicker as lightning danced behind them before settling my hardened gaze on Luke. "So you *did* know what your blood would do to me?"

Acknowledgment flashed across his face, hardening his features. "Your condition wasn't good. I offered my blood on impulse, not thinking you'd really take it." His voice was rising, almost yelling, as he pressed on. "There wasn't time to explain the side effects of drinking my blood, nor did I have a clue that any of that would happen with you! You're a freaking angel!"

And that's when my body lit up like a beacon at the same instant the thunder roared another reverberating threat. Streaking white and yellow light, bursting from every pore of my luminescent skin, radiating my anger, frustration, and most of all, my broken-heartedness. But when I realized that Luke wasn't affected—he was standing tall and staring straight at me as if nothing were happening—I gasped in astonishment, then dropped to the ground as my light faded.

In a flash, Luke was on his knees beside me, one arm wrapped around me in a comforting way. "Are you okay?"

A flush of anger surged though me and I scowled. "Okay? Okay?" This was the edge most psychotics stood on, right before jumping off. "Do I look okay to you?" I gripped his shoulders and pushed back as hard as I could. He gasped in shock as he tipped over, his back crunching against the ground. In a rush, I was on top of him, swinging my fists at his face, the sides of his head, and anywhere else I could hit him and cause pain. Both of his arms shot over his face, blocking most of my blows. Then he reached out with one hand, trying to grab me and hold me back—while keeping one arm securely over his face for his own protection. Twice, my captured wrist slid free, but the third time he was able to keep his hold. His fingers dug in with victory, but I still had one free hand to swing with.

My fist landed on his upper cheekbone with a *whaack*. His fangs burst out in an enraged growl. In a whir of motion, he flipped me over, my back smashing against rocks and twigs with the weight of his body straddled on top of me. He held both my wrists over my head in just one of his hands. He ground them into the uneven rocks, his deep obsidian eyes boring into mine, spittle dripping from his fangs landed on my nose. His free hand was on my chin, compressing and pinching. "What the hell is wrong with you?"

"I hate you…" My breath caught in my throat. I'd never said anything like that before. It wasn't possible for me to hate. Only dark ones could feel such an emotion. "Let me go," I begged, my words broken by a thunderous crackle, a bolt of lightning flashing across the sky. "I won't attack you again."

Hesitantly, Luke got off me, but didn't retract his fangs. "Angel, I swear I didn't mean for anything bad to happen to you—or with your *boyfriend*."

Anguish melted inside me and I buried my face in my hands. "I just released all my light, and nothing happened to you." I sniffed. "And now I'm using words that should never be in my head."

He pulled me up and brushed some of the debris off my back.

"Were you trying to hurt me?" he asked, peeling my hands away from my face and lifting my chin.

Our eyes met, but this time I didn't even try to look away—since now they were a softer shade of grayish blue—and I stared blankly into them, overcome with more pain than I could bear. "I just want you to leave me alone."

He stroked my chin. "Can't you see that's not possible?" He paused a brief moment. "Even if I hadn't given you my blood, I'd still be here with you. Granted, now that you've drunk from me, some feelings have grown stronger. But I swear, I didn't know! I had no idea what my blood would do to you. Your body seems to be reacting to it the same way a human's would." His gaze grew harder, penetrating; then he grinned wolfishly. "I'd be lying if I said this was upsetting to me. I kinda like knowing where you are, feeling your presence the way you can sense mine. Please don't pull away, let me help you."

I shook my head, my whole body trembling. "You took Cole away from me! I didn't even have a choice. If I'd known, I would've never taken your blood."

"Bull crap!" he exclaimed, eyes narrowing. "I didn't force my blood in you! I asked, and you took it! And I didn't force you to kiss me either!"

My hands curled into fists and my breathing grew shallow. As much as I hated to admit it, Luke was right. Though that first time he gave me his blood was a bit questionable. Still, I'd done all of this to myself. The earthly temptations had proven too great. I should've listened to Raphael and never transitioned into human form. He'd always warned me about the consequences, but I'd ignored him. At some point I'd become somewhat addicted to my human form, reveling in emotions I'd never felt as an angel, experiencing things I'd never done, yet so many of those things were forbidden. Still, if I'd stayed in my angel form, none of this would've happened. Of course, I'd never have loved Cole either, and the thought of that crushed me. Was it worth it to experience love in such a way that words couldn't even begin to describe it? To be loved more than an angel had ever known and also love someone with that same degree of emotion? And I didn't even know how to think or feel about Luke. The way he'd hurt me and angered me and yet I still had a softness in my heart for him. How could that be? Was it possible that I loved him too?

Heat flushed my cheeks, and I quickly shoved those thoughts away. This just wasn't the time for my messed-up love life, which I wasn't even supposed to have in the first place. I took a step back, finding Luke's eyes, and reluctantly admitted he was right. "Even though you were blackmailing me," I added with a hard press of my lips.

"Wait just a minute…," he started to argue, then just shrugged his shoulders.

"What?" I demanded.

"Nothing, it's not worth it. When are we leaving?"

"You're not coming!" was my icy reply.

"Please, Angel! Don't be stupid about this. Who better to kill demons for you than me?" He came close, placing his hands on my shoulders, the thunder reverberating once again. "Don't do this alone. I want you coming back in one piece."

I gave a deep huff, rolling my eyes. "You act like I can't succeed without you. Well, I don't have any deals with any more demons. So, I don't need you to cover my butt."

"Yeah, we all saw how good you were against those dark ones back on Charon! If I hadn't been there—"

"Fine!" I interrupted. I knew that if Luke hadn't been there, I'd be in even worse shape than I was. Limos had been kicking my butt pretty bad, and I had no guarantee that my angel form would've proven me victorious. However, that was my convenient excuse. So with all the reluctance one could feel, I agreed to Luke tagging along just as the sky released the first sprinkles of the approaching storm and lightning streaked through the clouds.

Just great, I thought. If Cole found out, I'd never gain his forgiveness, not that I really thought I'd ever get it in the first place.

16

RHEA WASN'T LIKE ANYTHING I'd imagined. I walked along the beach, gazing ahead at the splendid view of a raging ocean sweeping against the base of a rocky cliff. Clouds scattered across the sky like cottage cheese, painted with swirls of pink and purple as the sun descended, peeking over the horizon's edge so its flaming mass seemed to sink within the ocean's depths. There was warmth on my skin that made me feel wrapped in a blanket taken straight out of the dryer, but with such low humidity it was actually tolerable—comfortable even. Earth had come to mind numerous times—the similarities of these two very different worlds were amazingly close. The brisk air carried the scent of the sea, musky and salty, and it filled my lungs as I took a deep breath. Upon my release, Luke's hand brushed against my arm, and I felt his body tense.

Directly ahead of us were two soldier demons. Their bodies were somewhere around six feet tall and they stood on two long and cylindrical legs, the faint light creating darkish green shadows across their scaly skin. Two massive horns protruded from triangular heads, reminding me of a longhorn bull. Fortunately, they didn't seem to notice us yet.

"Do we have to fight them?" he asked with faint astonishment.

"We won't have a choice once they see us. Let's hope they're not immune to my light."

Since we were out in the open with no place to take cover, it didn't take long before they spotted us. Instantly, light exploded from my body, causing both demons to shrink to the ground, arms hovering over their eyes. While they were down, Luke flashed straight to them, and moments later, both soldier demons were lying on their sides, decapitated. Then their bodies vanished inside a cloud of green smoke. Cutting off a demon's head is the only way to kill them, but it was only possible to do that when they were in solid form. Their transparent state was not penetrable. Lucky for us, these two were as solid as they could be.

Luke brushed his hands together. "I guess I'm already coming in handy."

I shook my head. "Come on. We need to at least be somewhere we can take cover, in case there are more of them close by."

"Why?" He shrugged his shoulders. "Can't we just rinse and repeat?"

"Honestly, I'd prefer no killing at all. Hopefully, we'll find the scrolls sooner rather than later."

"This place is huge, though"—his voice full of doubt. "Where do we even start?"

Thankfully, I'd learned the answer to his question as soon as my amnesia had worn off. The essence of demons and dark ones was stronger than I'd ever felt before. I could feel their energy crackling around me like static electricity. This place was crawling with them just as I'd feared. But there was something else I sensed that didn't belong here, and there was a tinge of an angelic presence in it. Nothing I could think of would explain why a weakened angel would be here. Certainly Beck hadn't known or surely he would've told me. At least it gave us a place to start, since otherwise I'd have no idea what direction to go.

Luke and I moved with a renewed purpose along the sand. There was a semi-big mountain ahead, jagged rocks and crooked boulders lining the side that sloped into the ocean—and somewhere on that mountain was where this angelic presence was coming from.

Skirting the mountain, we followed a path formed of rocks and sand, overgrown with thick trees and vine-like bushes, which eventually opened to a field-like area with sparsely placed trees and boulders to finally arrive at the mouth of a cave. The soft light faded to blackness just a couple feet inside it. We'd need to rely on my senses—and Luke's vampire night vision—from this point forward. After a brief hesitation, we plunged on in, moving closer to the mysterious angelic presence.

The inside of the cave was exactly how I'd expected it to be: Damp. Dark. Musky. And this particular cave was narrow and cramped, making it feel extra claustrophobic. We walked in a single file with Luke behind me, maneuvering swiftly around stalagmites and stalactites. Water steadily dripped into shallow, murky puddles, causing creepy reverberations all around us. The air got denser and colder, but since Luke was immune to my light, I allowed my body to glow, brightening and warming the walls and floors around us as we moved deeper inside.

We approached some sort of opening that led to what looked like a room. Luke and I hid off to the side, our necks craning around the rocky doorway to get a good view of the expansive area. At the furthest point away was a makeshift fireplace with a mantle made of logs. Embers glowed bright orange and red, smoke trailing off behind them as if a vent was sucking the air that way. Along the entire right side were old, rustic-looking shelves containing thousands of dusty and withered books. In the center were a couple of antique wooden chairs, an older man with long white hair and matching overgrown beard sitting in one of them. Definitely where the angel presence was coming from. "I know you're there," he called out with a hoarse voice, not looking up from his book.

Shock penetrated through my body, leaving pressure in my chest, cold fear along my back. Luke came to stand beside me, nudging me in the side with his elbow. "How does he know we're here?" he whispered. "I thought you masked us?"

"I did," I said through tight lips.

The old man shut the book, setting it on his lap. He looked straight at us, his dark brown eyes piercing through petite, round glasses. "Don't be rude. Come on over here and let me see you." He motioned to the empty chair next to him. "It has been quite some time since I had a visitor."

When Luke and I didn't move, the old man cleared his throat, then spoke a little louder. "C'mon now. Hurry it up."

We both moved closer, with short, hesitant steps, and I realized his eyes were a soft hazel instead of brown as we came to a stop about six feet away. "How did you know we were back there?" I asked.

His attempted laughter turned into a stream of hacking coughs. Once settled, he replied, "There are protective seals all over this chamber"— he raised his hands, a navy-colored robe hanging down from them as he gestured around the room—"preventing the use of any angelic or demonic magic."

"What?" I asked, flabbergasted. "Why would such seals be in place *here?*"

Luke straightened beside me, his eyes wide with curiosity.

The old man stood and took a step toward us, the oversized robe trailing behind him. "Because the only way I can protect the scrolls," his tone casual, his eyes flitting between me and Luke, "is by having a magical advantage over those who try to steal them."

My breath caught in my throat, remembering how Beck had overheard demons saying the scrolls were heavily guarded, but since lies mostly came out of their mouths, I never gave it a second thought—which had obviously been pretty stupid on my part. But I was a little relieved since I wasn't sensing anything dark or negative coming from the old man, though the magical seals might have had something to do with that.

"Who are you?" Luke asked, his eyes narrowing.

The old man smiled, pushing his glasses up his pudgy nose. "I'm the keeper of the scrolls, dear boy. Name's Ezariah."

"Why are you here, uh, keeping the scrolls?" I asked once I found my voice.

Ezariah let out a deep, long sigh. "Come sit with me. As I said before, I rarely get any visitors." He backed up, then sat down, motioning toward the empty seat.

Luke nudged my arm and once I looked at him, he arched a brow. I answered him with a slight shrug and nervous smile, then we cautiously made our way to the unoccupied chair. Luke directed me to sit. "Here, you take it. I'll just stand."

"Nonsense!" Ezariah exclaimed. "Both of you can sit." He snapped his fingers and a third wooden chair materialized out of nowhere.

Luke gasped, then warily sat down as instructed while I made a mental note of the old man's use of magic. Apparently he was immune to the protective wards.

"Now then." Ezariah looked at me, his arched brow a thin curve of white. "Why are you here with this vampire?"

Luke leaned forward and spoke through clenched teeth. "I'd never let her come here alone!"

I put my arm on Luke's, gently rubbing until his body relaxed some. Then, I focused on Ezariah. "I know this is forbidden, but Luke is my friend. He offered to help me and I thought it was for the best. We both know that me being here is against all rules anyway."

Ezariah gave a knowing smile. "Dear girl, it is okay to break the rules as long as you do so with integrity."

Luke snarled, low and menacing. "What are you talking about, old man?"

Ezariah pushed his glasses up his nose. "Once, I was a guardian just as you are now." He nodded toward me, appearing to relive the memory as he spoke. "After twenty successful years of keeping my charge alive and well, a dark one appeared to me, offering a deal I simply could not refuse. You see, I was smitten with another guardian and the thought of spending some time with her, without our angelic responsibilities, had become too strong a temptation." He shifted in the chair, still seemingly lost in his past. "The dark one promised a few hours of time with my beloved, Aurora, in exchange for a few hours of unguarded time with my charge."

I felt my eyes widen with disbelief. My chest tightened, making it harder to breathe. Now I had both Ezariah and Luke's full attentions, and realizing this washed heat across my cheeks. After I stole another uncomfortable moment to clear my throat, I said with astonishment, "I'm sorry for interrupting you. It's just that our stories seem so similar."

Ezariah tilted his head slightly and studied me for a bit; then at last he said, "I wasn't the first angel who was tempted, and I won't be the last." He leaned back in his chair, adding, "We wouldn't want to stop adding to the demon population, now would we?"

Luke and I just sat there gaping at Ezariah as he chuckled at his own dry humor.

"So what happened to Audra?" Luke asked. "Did you end up meeting her?"

"Aurora," I mumbled under my breath.

"I mean, Aurora."

Ezariah stroked his smooth, white beard. "Long story short, I took the deal, and spent the best two hours of my existence with my beautiful Aurora. Everything had been perfect, even better than perfect. I couldn't have dreamt those moments any better than they were." His smile faltered and his expression became empty as sorrow washed over his features. "When I returned, I discovered my charge had been in an accident. He'd been hunting elk with his friend and was attacked by a bear. The friend had been demon-possessed the moment before coming upon the bear, and he left my charge to fend for himself."

Ezariah's eyes glistened and he seemed uncomfortable with his words. He shifted uneasily a few times, then cleared his throat. "Sorry, this never gets any easier to talk about."

Giving Ezariah of few moments to pull himself together, I glanced over at Luke, who was attentively watching the old man with slanted eyes and arched brows. His dark hair feathered back along the side, revealing the curve of his ear. A pit formed in my stomach and I hurriedly looked away, returning my attention to the former guardian. "Your charge, he died?" I inquired.

Releasing a deep breath, Ezariah replied, "Eventually they all die, dear girl. But he didn't die from the bear attack if that's what you're asking." He leaned forward, peering at me through those thin, round spectacles. "You see, I'd heard about the ancient scrolls of Rhea, and I came here to retrieve them and save my charge. The very reason you both are here, correct?"

A small gasp escaped my lips and my hands rushed up to cover them. Slowly lowering them, I said in astonishment, "It's you! You're the angel I've heard of. You're the one that gave your breath to save your charge!"

Ezariah nodded with a smile. "All the guardians speak of me? I thought I'd be forgotten once I was cast here to be the keeper of the scrolls."

"What do you mean, 'cast here'?" I asked.

"Whenever you're doing something you shouldn't do, you always end up getting caught. That's exactly what happened to me. I came here for the scrolls against my archangel's wishes. There was no keeper at that time. Luckily, I found the scrolls quickly and made it back to my charge undetected. I'd masked my aura just as you attempted to do here. But my archangel was able to penetrate it and he found me standing over my charge, almost finished with the ritual of breath." Ezariah began stroking his beard again. "As I gave my charge my breath, I was ripped away from him and cast here to become the keeper of the scrolls so that no other guardian could attempt it again."

Luke tossed a frustrated hand through his hair. "You're kidding me? We've come all this way and you won't even let Angel take a peek at what they say?"

"I'm afraid I can't, dear boy. Not that I don't want to help you," came Ezariah's weary reply.

A wave of hopelessness settled inside me, along with a penetrating fear for Caitlyn. My eyes welled up with tears and I sniffled, fighting to contain them. Luke reached for my hand, twined our fingers together, then gave a reassuring squeeze. He glared at Ezariah, revealing a glimpse of his fangs. "Either you give us those scrolls, or I will take them from you. Your choice."

"Luke, no! No violence! No more!" Tears flooded my cheeks, racing toward the edge of my chin. I stood up in a rush, tugging my hand free of Luke's grasp, then wiped my fingers across the moist trails. "My charge is dying, Ezariah, and these scrolls are my only way to save her. There is no Plan B."

"Keep your stupid scrolls!" Luke declared. "Please just tell her what to do!"

"Nothing would work without the scrolls," Ezariah replied. "You must hold them in your hand as you speak the words, then exhale your breath into the mouth of the one you're saving."

"Did it work?" I asked. "Did your charge live?"

Reluctantly Ezariah answered, "Yes."

"Angel," Luke said through gritted teeth, "just let me get them for you!"

Ezariah half laughed, which transformed into a slew of coughs. "Dear boy, the only way to obtain the scrolls is if I give them to you. But I am forbidden to do such a thing. Therefore, I cannot help you."

Luke growled and jumped up, dashing toward Ezariah in human speed. When he reached the old man he froze, gaping at his outstretched hands. "What's happening to me? My strength is gone!" he exclaimed with a jolt.

"As I said, you are powerless here," Ezariah stated matter-of-factly. "I am also protected inside this room. You cannot touch me."

Luke lowered his hands until they were about a foot away from Ezariah's head. At that moment it appeared as if he'd hit an invisible wall, unable to move another inch.

"Protective shield," I breathed. Which was odd since angels defended themselves by using the light inside them, meaning there should be no reason to cast such a spell, but then again, protecting the scrolls from other angels would be more difficult since light didn't hurt them the same way it did dark ones. So maybe that meant the former guardian was given extra abilities specifically engineered for his new task of guarding the scrolls.

Ezariah ignored Luke and flashed me a small smile. "Smart girl. Now call your vampire friend back before he hurts himself."

I gave the old man a slight nod. "Luke, please leave him alone. You couldn't get through that magical barrier even if you had your strength." Though a small part of me wondered if I could, the desperate hope of saving Caitlyn pressing on my mind. But violence was never the answer; I'd witnessed too many humans through many millennia make the same mistake. Unless he would willingly give me the scrolls, I'd be leaving here without them—and without any hope of saving my charge.

Luke spat a few protests under his breath, then backed away. Without taking his eyes off Ezariah, he said, "Angel, come on, let's get out of here." He grabbed my hand and jerked me after him.

I pulled free of his grasp. "No wait. We can't leave yet." I peered around Luke's body, meeting the former guardian's eyes. "Please help me. I must save my charge. It's my fault she's dying. Please, Ezariah! You're my only hope."

His face crumbled as if he pitied me. "Girl, if I could help you, I would. There have been dozens to come here before you, with the exact same request." He paused a moment to release a breath. "I would be cast to the demons for assisting you. I'm afraid I just can't take that risk."

"But you don't know that for sure! Do you?" I pushed Luke to the side, then attempted to walk around him, but he grabbed me and held me back. Since he didn't have his vampire strength, it appeared we were on equal ground. I pushed forward again, and Luke twisted around with me so both of us were facing Ezariah. My fists clenched, and a burning chill crept up my spine. "There is only one who can cause us to completely fall. *Him!* Obviously that wasn't *His* will for you, or you'd be fallen and not here!" I thought of the numerous times I'd been granted grace from falling, though I knew without a doubt I deserved no better, yet I'd been spared and offered a new charge, a fresh angelic existence with the return of those powers that had been stripped away. If only Ezariah would take a leap of faith and help me, surely he'd be spared from falling, just like he had been when he was brought here.

His features hardened and his voice grew deeper. "Know your place, girl! Do not make false claims in this room!"

"Angel, what are you talking about?" Luke asked.

"His archangel had to have placed the protection seal in this room and a shield upon him." Because no other being would be powerful enough—except for a high-level demon. I swung my head in Ezariah's direction, concentrating all my energy on him, but not sensing anything that would indicate the former guardian was fallen...but I did pick up something else and I remembered how he'd used magic. "You can remove the seal, lower the shield," I told him, my voice full of certainty.

"What?" Luke asked, dumbfounded as he stared at the old man.

I glared at the former guardian, taking another small step closer. "But you're not going to, are you?" It was less painful thinking the old man couldn't help me even if he wanted to, but to know he'd had the power to help me all along and was simply choosing not to created a dark ember in my gut.

Ezariah snorted. "I am the keeper of the scrolls!"

Unable to contain my fury, my body suddenly went from a faint glow to radiant flashes of light.

"Calm your temper, girl," the former guardian warned.

"Angel," Luke breathed, gripping my arm.

My breaths were deep and short, and my chest felt like I was trapped under a hundred pounds of water—tense pressure boring over me. Then my face dropped into my hands as my light faded. "She's as good as dead, Luke"—my voice muffled against my skin. "There is no other way for me to save her."

"Thanks a lot—for nothing!" Luke spat. He took my hand and started leading me away.

Reluctantly, I followed.

As we approached the doorway we'd entered from, Ezariah called out, "Wait!"

I froze, slowly turning to face the old man.

"What now?" Luke groaned.

Ezariah rubbed his hands together and said, "Maybe there's a way we can help each other."

"Yeah, sure," Luke smarted. "And how's that?"

"Every moment that passes, I grow lonelier, and surely I thought Aurora would find me before now. If she only knew where I was, then I'm certain she'd come. If you'd be willing to get a message to her, let her know where I am, then I could perhaps lower the shield long enough for you to obtain the scrolls. But promise me this!" His voice grew louder. "You will return them here to me as soon as your charge is saved."

Considering his offer, I asked, "But what if my archangel catches me?" Not that I wanted to dissuade the old man's seeming change of heart, though relief wouldn't come unless I was holding those scrolls.

"Then our fates are no longer in my hands," came his warning reply.

"Won't they know how your charge survives anyway?" Luke asked, eyes gliding from Ezariah to me.

"No, dear boy. That's the beauty of miracles. If Selene here can pull the ritual off undetected, then no one will be the wiser."

"But, I expected there'd be no way to pull this off without getting caught. Raphael told me that my future was decided and I'd be receiving a new charge and re-inheriting some of my powers," I noted. "Assuming all of that, I was still willing to risk everything to save my charge."

"Your compassion becomes you, dear girl. Those before you were merely working through guilt and shame; very few really, really cared for their charge beyond their angelic requirement, which is why I've reconsidered my position on this."

"My human form allowed me to experience love in ways most angels don't." A pang struck in my heart, reminding me just how much love I'd been able to feel—both the good and bad of it.

The old man's face softened. "Do not confuse your tenderness for weakness, dear girl. You are far stronger than you give yourself credit for."

"But what about Raphael, my archangel? He'd told me that—"

"Nonsense!" scoffed Ezariah. "He told you what he was shown. Your actions can always change the outcome." He stood up and took a small step closer. "Your archangel is shown new visions all the time. He could never claim your charge had lived by anything other than a miracle. Unless you were caught in the act, of course."

Luke took my hand, giving it a gentle squeeze. "Angel, how can you say no to this?"

Staring at Ezariah's face, I replied, "I can't."

17

THE BLINDS WERE CRACKED OPEN, allowing faint rows of light in the hospital room. Machines buzzed and pumped, providing the only sound. Dusk was fast approaching, the weight of my thoughts pressing heavy on my mind. Yet Caitlyn's face looked peaceful, almost as if she knew what I was about to do for her. I stroked her cheek as a tear slicked down mine. Everything was moving smoothly so far, but that only made me anticipate some type of looming drama. Trouble always had its way of finding you—especially when you were doing something you'd been told not to do. But I was at peace with my decision. It just wasn't Caitlyn's time to go, nor was it the way I'd accept her dying.

After leaving Rhea—sea scrolls in tow—Luke and I had come straight to the hospital in Denver. No time to waste by dropping him off in Virginia Beach—considering he could just run there in a few hours time. But he'd insisted on coming here anyway, offering his help should anything go wrong. Reluctantly, I'd accepted his offer. The invisible ties binding us together were becoming too great to ignore. So was this confusing mixture of emotions I seemed to have for him—all the while beating myself up for how badly things had gone with Cole.

Cole. When would he seek me out? Or would he reach out at all? And even if he could forgive me, how would he react to Luke still lingering around? Sure, I'm a big motivator for forgiveness; it's my job and all that. But really, how could I expect a being of darkness to jump on board? His ability to love me had already been so much greater than I could have ever imagined.

Luke was just outside the room, guarding it like it was the entrance to Fort Knox. In exchange for my generosity in letting him stick around, he'd allowed me privacy while performing the ritual. If anyone were to show up to see Caitlyn, he'd use his vampire magic to make them leave while believing they'd actually visited her. Pretty handy trick leaving no one disappointed.

I gave a long sigh, my fingers tracing my dress's scooped neckline. Just beneath the fabric was where I'd stuffed the sea scrolls. Once Ezariah had handed them to me, I'd initially been surprised at their small size. He'd explained that there were many more pages, but this particular one was all I needed. I retrieved it from my bosom, fingering the texture, an aged papyrus with burnt edges and, along its surface, what felt like hundreds of soft, tiny hairs as it unfolded to its full six-by-nine size. It reminded me of an antique postcard with chunky black script written inside:

For this life,
Precious child of Christ,
My life for your death,
I bestow upon you my breath.

After silently reading it for the twentieth time, I felt confident that I at least wouldn't screw up the words. Releasing a deep, nervous breath, I took Caitlyn's limp hand and gently squeezed. And just when I was about to recite the ritual, all chaos broke loose.

I sensed him seconds before the door flew open, making a loud *whack* when it hit the wall, then he came stomping into the room with Luke pulling him back by the arm. "You can't come in here!" Luke roared.

"The hell I can't," Cole said dryly, jerking his arm free of Luke's grasp.

I released Caitlyn's hand, stepping back until I hit the wall.

Cole kept moving, running his hand through perfectly styled dark hair. He wore a basic black tee with darker black jeans—somehow he made them look incredibly sexy. "What are you still hanging around for?" Cole demanded, throwing a searing look toward Luke. Then his gaze shifted to Caitlyn and his features softened.

Luke came in a few human steps, arms folded in front of his chest. He eyed me confusedly, then glared at Cole. "Leave that human alone!"

Ignoring the order, Cole inched to the side of Caitlyn's bed, standing no more than a foot away from me. He reached down and held her hand, then shifted his attention back on Luke. "This human is my friend! Now tell me, where is Selene?"

My breath caught as I remembered I was still in angel form. With Luke being able to see me, I'd forgotten the fact that no one else could. With a few shakes of my head, I let Luke know to keep quiet about my presence here—and the fact that he could even see me. Then I hurriedly folded the scrolls and shoved them back into my bosom.

Answering Cole's question, Luke shrugged his shoulders and said, "I don't know where she is." He paused a moment, then added, "I'm real sorry about your friend."

"I know why you're still hanging around," Cole said with vehemence. "You gave her your blood, you bastard!"

Luke snarled, a glimpse of fang protruding through his lips. "I was trying to help her! You went and got yourself kidnapped and she was trying to save your worthless life!"

"She's an angel! She doesn't need any saving!" Cole fired back sarcastically.

Luke waved a hand. "It didn't look that way to me!"

Cole turned back toward Caitlyn. "It doesn't matter how it looked to you," he growled.

"Oh yeah?" Luke went on, his voice more steady. "Well I guess I do owe you a 'thank you,' seeing how it's *your* fault she needed my blood!"

Cole released Caitlyn's hand. In a blur of motion, he was standing face-to-face with Luke. He shoved Luke's shoulders, rocking him backward, but my vampire ally straightened with ease. "Go on back to wherever the hell you came from," Cole threatened, "before I kill you!"

"No!" Luke exclaimed, shoving Cole back. "Angel and I, we have a bond. That's something you and her won't ever have!"

"Don't bet your life on that!" Cole snarled.

They lunged forward at once, fists flying. I knew my light wouldn't stop them both—since Luke was immune. So I did the only thing I could, which was to shift into my human form. "Stop it!" I screamed just as they'd thrown another round of punches.

"Selene!" Cole pulled back straight away, and I saw blood pooling in the corner of his mouth. Then he rushed over, placing his arm around my back. "Please tell him to get the hell out of here."

I stared at him a moment, a longing for him searing hot beneath my skin, but now wasn't the time for that. With the threat of running out of time, I needed to stay focused on my charge. So instead of throwing my arms around his neck and pulling him close, I ducked under his grasp, fixing him with a look of regret. "This can't happen right now. Tonight is about Caitlyn! Not either of you!" I glanced at Luke, the gash above his eye Cole had given him was partially healed, hardening my mood. "Look at you two"—my eyes flitted between them—"Both of you must leave. Now!"

"But Angel," Luke whined.

"No 'buts,' Luke. Please let me do this alone." Then my gaze landed back on Cole, a mixture of emotions still churning inside me. "I'm glad you came for me, but I can't do this right now. Caitlyn needs me. We can talk *after* I help her. Please."

Cole blinked in confusion, then his gaze quickly sharpened. "But I have a way to save Caitlyn!"—his tone laced with excitement.

"You're late!" Luke said in a mocking voice. "We've already found a way to save the girl."

"Be quiet, Luke!" My voice rising. "There isn't much time. Please listen to me. I'm not asking you two to be friends, or even get along at all, for that matter! But I am asking you both to leave, and I'm expecting some respect here from both of you!"

"I can turn Caitlyn into a vampire," Cole said in a rush. "And I'll teach her morals and values, and how to survive without killing—"

Luke burst out laughing. "Dude, didn't you hear me? Angel already—"

I held up my hand, ceasing Luke's words (because for once he was listening to me). "Cole," I said calmly. "I already have a way to help her and I need you to leave right now so I can."

"What are you talking about?" Cole asked with suspicion. "You no longer have your healing abilities."

I met Cole's gaze squarely. "I'm not referring to that. I've found another way."

Cole snorted. "What? What is it?"

"I don't have time to get into it right now," I replied curtly, knowing Raphael could orb in at any moment and my whole plan would be a bust.

His brows arched, eyes pressing deeper into mine. I knew he was tempted to take a peek inside my head, so I grabbed his hand and gave it a gentle squeeze. "Please. Trust me."

Luke attempted to say something, but I shot him a single, lasered glance that thankfully silenced his words. Then I returned my attention to Cole. "I love you"—my voice soft and sincere. "Please let me help Caitlyn and then we can talk about everything. And hopefully"—I shrugged my shoulders and took a deep breath—"hopefully, we can work this out."

His hard features softened, brows smoothing back to an even line. "Fine," he said in defeat. "But we have a lot to talk about, so you better come get me when you're finished here. I love you, Selene. We're going to find a way to work this out."

I nodded, swallowing hard, feeling a tightness in my chest that wouldn't budge.

Cole stroked my cheek with his thumb. "I'm sorry about my behavior before. I'm grateful for everything you did for me, even the parts I can't stand to know about." Then his lips covered mine, his tongue sliding between them, seductive and teasing. A fire ignited inside my chest and I threw my arms around his neck, pulling him closer. The kiss deepened, my heart racing, tingles spreading all over my skin like static waves. From across the room, Luke coughed loudly, and even though I tried to ignore his jealous attempt to stop us, Cole and I slowly broke apart. His lips moved to my ear, a chilling breath tickling my lobe. "Even though I can still taste his blood through your skin," he whispered, so faintly I could barely hear him, "I still need you. Always." With that he was gone, and I couldn't help feeling choked up with guilt.

I looked at Luke, still feeling a little stunned from that kiss. He watched me with a hard, penetrating gaze. "What the hell was that?" he spat, venom dripping from each word.

"Don't start!" I warned. "Now is not the time!"

"But I'm helping you!" he shot back. "It's because of *me* that you're even able to help your charge in the first place."

Anger erupted through every pore on my body. "Then I don't need any more of *your* help! Get out of here!"

He gaped at me for a moment, eyes full of jealousy, confusion, and pain. Then at last he said, "Okay. I'll go. But not without this." In a whoosh he was holding me, slightly tilting me back, devouring my mouth with a kiss before I could say anything. It was needy, urgent, and left me breathless when he finally stopped, releasing me with a gentle flick of his arm. I pressed my hand against my mouth, my eyes widening. Then without another word, Luke flashed away.

It took me several minutes to collect my thoughts and pull myself together. My emotions were raw, my human hands shaky. Even shifting back to my angel form didn't seem to help. But I shook it off the best I could and returned to Caitlyn's side. This moment was about her—not me and all my relationship drama.

Scooping up her hand, I retrieved the scrolls, then read aloud, my voice shaking but confident, "For this life, precious child of Christ." My face lowered closer to hers. "My life for your death, I bestow upon you my…*breath.*" As I said the final word, since her mouth was filled with tubes I exhaled deep into her nose, not stopping until every last inch of air was out of my body. Quickly, I rushed to inhale, but instead of finding air, it felt like my lungs were collapsing. In a panic, I grabbed my chest, pressing down as if that would help me breathe. It didn't.

Suddenly, my light flashed on, radiating throughout the room. Then, as quick as it turned on it faded, leaving me depressed and lost. There was a tight twist inside my stomach, making me fall to my knees. My body lit again, then faded, then lit up again. This pattern kept repeating while I was still gasping for air. My lungs were burning; my throat constricting. As I crawled toward the window, I realized that I was now in my human form, not remembering when I'd shifted.

The machines attached to Caitlyn started beeping faster and louder. Lights began flickering like the room was plagued with poltergeists. I got to the window, pulling myself up by the edge of the sill. Somehow I was coherent enough to sense the dozen plus people rushing toward this room. I couldn't risk being seen—especially in the condition I was in. Using the last bit of strength I could muster, I slid the pane open and crawled through the window. Hospital staff rushed into the room just as I jumped off the ledge, swallowed by the night as I fell toward the street below.

18

INSATIABLE HEAT PRESSED AGAINST my skin as if I were wearing a slick, rubber suit. Sweat weaved down my forehead, curving over my brows as I opened my eyes. I cast a sideways glance at hills and dunes coated in red-colored sand—stretching out for miles, an orange hazy mountain range lining the horizon. I'd been lying on my stomach, my face twisted to the side with one of my cheeks pressed against the grainy surface, the other feeling sunburnt from its exposure to the blazing heat. Sitting up, I made a futile attempt to brush away the sand that stuck to me everywhere. Sweating? A strange feeling slithered up my spine, cold and sharp, as I gaped down at my body. How was it that I was sweating while in my angel form? Then I swung a cautious look at my surroundings, wondering the other pertinent question: Where in all the worlds was I?

This desolate place reminded me of Mars—or at least what I'd seen of Mars while watching many documentaries with Caitlyn since I'd never personally visited the planet. I stood up and started walking, my bare feet sinking a few inches with each step. Oh my goodness…the ritual! Was Caitlyn okay? Did she awaken? And what about the scrolls? My stomach turned as I frantically dug into my bosom, then relief flushed through me when I felt the scrolls tucked safely inside. Being in this place was making me crazy. It was time to go. I let out a deep sigh and closed my eyes, concentrating on my charge.

But all I saw when I opened my eyes was this Mars-like place. *Why couldn't I orb?* Feeling a renewed determination, I tried again…and again… and again. But each time was a letdown once I discovered I'd never gone anywhere. Fear was building inside me to the point where I really did think I'd lose my mind. "Raphael!" I screamed, frantically looking around as if he'd appear any moment. But he didn't. I fell to my knees, struck by trembling waves of nausea. I called for my archangel several more times, my voice growing weaker with each attempt. Moments later, I was struck with panic, my breathing shallow, my heart threatening to burst from my chest.

Since time didn't seem to exist here, I had no idea how much had passed or how long I'd even been here. After walking for what felt like miles, I'd arrived at a small fissure in the side of a rocky hill. At least I'd been lucid enough to duck in there and take cover from the blistering heat. Sitting with my knees hugged up against my chest, I stared out at the hazy redness. The winds had picked up, creating a howling sandstorm, grains of sand smacking the stone as if they were tiny shards of ice, and though I couldn't see beyond the mouth of the cave, at least I was deep enough inside that the swirling sand couldn't reach me. It seemed to be getting darker, which meant nightfall would be approaching soon. Since I couldn't get any of my angelic powers to work (and trust me, I'd tried everything—countless times!), I guessed I'd be spending the night in this lovely place after all.

Perhaps I should at least be thankful for having those strange *vibes* I'd inherited after drinking Luke's blood. Everything smelled, well, stale. And the scent was incredibly strong. There was also an alertness to my mind that almost gave me a wired-high type of feeling—including the tingles on my skin and the tiny hairs raised on the back of my neck. *A whole lot of good those senses are going to give me*, I thought while immersing myself in my doom-and-gloom mood.

All of a sudden, I picked up a scent of something between mildew and mud. I wrinkled my nose, covering it with my hand. The smell grew stronger, morphing into something more like roadkill—mildewed roadkill. Yuck! Then there was a deafening screech and the ground started shaking. As much as I'd prefer this to be an earthquake, I knew it wasn't. Something was coming. I could sense it and the harm it meant to cause me. But I didn't have another second to think about it, since something big, hairy, and solid sucked me right out of my makeshift shelter.

I was airborne, flying aimlessly through the sandstorm, then crashing hands-first on a blanket of fresh sand. Another harrowing screech sounded and I swung around to face my attacker. Sharp sand needled against my face, arms, and everywhere else my skin was exposed, keeping my ability to see at a minimum. A blast struck my shoulder, knocking me forward, but I caught my balance and jumped around, fist swinging. My hand collided against something soft, but rock-hard just beneath it like cushioned stone. A menacing groan pierced my ears as the dark silhouette of a giant worm materialized inside the flying sea of sand. I panicked, jumping back, but still took the brunt of the sucker punch this thing just landed in my gut.

"What do you want?" I screamed, fighting the urge to hunch over and cradle my stomach. Then I closed my eyes, felt its approach, and swung my clenched fist with everything I had. Contact. My hand reverberated against the creature's body as it wailed and recoiled back. And I didn't wait to see what would happen next. I turned around and hauled ass.

My speed was fast, even with the sand sucking my feet like suction cups. I seemed to be moving nearly as quick as a vampire, and it wasn't long before I found another place to take cover. This opening on the side of a taller hill—a mini-mountain—was deeper and more cave-like than the one I'd been in before. Once I was far enough inside, I fell to the ground, my body weak and exhausted. The last thing I remembered was gasping for air, before the darkness took me.

The night covered my surroundings like a velvety black blanket. Trees were everywhere, providing an excellent cover for the one I was chasing. A few animals scurried away, fearful of my presence. My feet scrambled to keep up so I used a little angel magic to float over the ground, enabling me to speed up. "Cole?" I sensed he wasn't far, but I still couldn't physically see him.

"This way," a deep voice called from up ahead.

I shimmered a little closer, but then he sped up, stretching the distance between us. "Quit doing that!" I snapped as I made another attempt to reach him.

Laughter rumbled through the silence. "Am I that much better than you?"

His taunting was starting to piss me off. I closed my eyes and orbed, trying to land on top of him. Only I didn't end up where I'd planned.

Salty fumes assaulted my nose before crashing waves hit my ears. Even though it was just past twilight—the orange hue of the sun stained the bottom of the purplish sky—I could still see a man standing about twenty yards away. I rushed for him, but he seemed to be moving away. "Cole, wait!" I called out, picking up my pace.

"I thought you liked playing chase," came his taunting reply, his voice close enough to feel the caress of it against my skin.

Then I was sideswiped and tackled to the ground. We rolled a few times in the sand before his lips pressed against mine. My arms wrapped around his neck, pulling us closer. His tongue stroked around the edges of my lips leaving a musky lavender aftertaste and a few speckles of salty sand. Water rushed underneath us, and I realized I was the one on the bottom. My hair drifted in the current before the sea reclaimed the wave. My dress stuck to my skin like plastic wrap.

I tried to twist on top but was thrust back down, my hands held over my head while his lips slicked across my cheek, descending down my neck and coming to stop right on top of my vein. A low growl vibrated against my chest, rumbled in my ear as his body pressed harder on top of me. Then twin sharp points pricked my sensitive skin. Chills raced down my arms, up my spine, and my head felt like it was flying in the clouds. I arched my back, raising my chin, and he reciprocated, bringing his open mouth tighter against my neck. "Do it," I breathed, unable to say anything else.

"I've wanted this since the day I met you"—his words breathless. Then he bit down hard and I screamed out in ecstasy.

My body grew weightless, and the feeling of euphoria coated every cell inside me. "Yes, yes," I mumbled, when I used words at all.

The slurping stopped just enough for him to mutter indistinctly, "Angel."

That word jolted me back to reality. "What?" I demanded, pushing up against his shoulders.

His body moved with my direction, bringing his face inches away from mine. "Angel, what's wrong?"

"Luke! What are you doing?" I shuffled out from under him just as another wave rushed by. "What happened to Cole?"

"Cole?" he spat, cocking his head to the side. "Cole was never here!"

"You're lying!" I rose and marched off, away from the beach.

"Where do you think you're going?" Luke grabbed my arm, swinging me around to face him. "We need to talk!"

"Where I'm going, is to find COLE!" Anger seared out of me as I pulled free of Luke's hold. But then he just grabbed me again.

"Stop acting like this!"—his voice somewhere between pleading and demanding. Then his lips were on mine, filled with longing and need. I pushed back but his hold on me tightened. Everything warped around me and my surroundings looked strangely fluid, and my bewildered mind raced, yet it remained blank...numb even, as his kisses grew harder, the pressure of him molding into my lips. The warping in my head sped up, everything swirling and shaking. Then, the ground opened up under me and swallowed me whole.

I woke up in the cave gulping for air. What had felt like a memory had really only been a dream—or a nightmare. The temperature had dropped about sixty degrees, and I lay on the bare, rocky floor rubbing my arms for warmth since I'd never been able to find any wood (or anything else that would burn) to build a fire with. Even though it was completely dark out, I could tell the sandstorm had stopped. An eerie calmness settled in my bones, bringing forth a raw, penetrating fear.

The silence was pierced by a wailing screech—similar to the one I'd heard before. In an effort *not* to get sucked out by the relentless, hairy creature, I crawled deeper inside the cave. Again the shrieking sounded, a little more distant this time. I twisted over, sitting on my butt, my back against the stony wall for support. My dress—which I could most likely credit my new vampireish senses for being able to see it in the first place—was no longer white, but stained a hideous orange from all the red sand, draped over my legs and I tucked the muddied edges over my toes. My angel form had never had such human qualities as it did here, in this God-forsaken place. At least I hadn't needed any food or water...yet. With my luck, that would probably be the next issue—if the creature didn't finish me first.

It seemed like three days had passed—blistering hot while the sun was up, freezing once it descended and night claimed the sky. I'd been calling for Raphael nonstop for hours on end; my throat was now raw and my voice had grown hoarse. Sadly, it didn't seem to be healing at all. Still, occasionally I'd try saying his name aloud, hoping for different results. So far, it was a big fat nothing. And my overactive mind was really bringing me down. From wondering if Caitlyn survived the ritual and what had happened to me in that hospital room, to mentally registering if the reason I'd been cast here was because I'd finally fallen, to reflecting on my relationship with Cole, to pondering why I'd been dreaming about Luke. Sure, I'd assumed some answers, but there was just no way to know for certain if anything was true. But what scared me the most was the thought of being trapped here forever, of never seeing anyone I loved again.

At last I shook away those tormenting thoughts and laid my head on the cold, hard ground. It wasn't long before I was far away from this horrible place, smiling and laughing once more.

Caitlyn and I were riding in her brand new, cherry red Eclipse Spider convertible. It was a graduation gift that Caitlyn got six months early, because her grades had been straight A's all through high school. Her parents had even delivered it to her with a big, matching red bow strapped onto the hood. And now we were driving it to the biggest, baddest party of the year, the graduation ceremony being one week away.

We were giggling uncontrollably as we bantered about our day at school, my cheeks becoming tender and sore. "Do you think Ronnie will be there?" I said, my words broken between various chuckles.

Her laughter became a gasp. "I don't like him!" she stated matter-of-factly.

"Are you sure about that?" I asked, my tone arched.

She looked at me momentarily, eyes wide with embarrassment, then returned her attention to the road. "Selene, you can't tell anyone," she warned.

Now no longer laughing, I rubbed my cheeks. "Who would I tell?"

"I don't know, but you just can't say anything to anyone!"

We rounded a sharp corner just when a mother deer and her fawn were crossing the road. Caitlyn shrieked, twisting the wheel in a frantic attempt not to hit them. The car instantly started spinning, tires screeching against the road. But as it steadied, I knew if she didn't turn that steering wheel a bit more, we'd be colliding into the massive tree now looming straight in front of us. I took advantage of her attention on the road and shifted invisible, placing my hands on top of hers, guiding her to move with the same motions I was. Her nerves were racing, but she was able to bend her will to meet my instruction. And when the car finally came to its final stop, we were several feet off the road, just inches away from the tree.

In a flash I jumped in the passenger seat, shifted back into my human form, and quickly leaned over, rubbing Caitlyn's back. "Are you okay?"

Both of her hands held the wheel in a death grip. "I don't...I don't know" was her shaky response.

"Maybe we should just head back home," I suggested, not really wanting to go to the party anyway.

"No! We can't!" She sounded in a panic. "The car. Did I wreck the car?"

After we both got out and assessed the damage—or lack thereof since there wasn't even a scratch on the car—we headed off to the party. A long gravel driveway lined with thick trees spilled into an expansive open field crowded with cars and people. A two-story colonial-style house was sitting just beyond, its lights aglow in the early evening hour. Caitlyn waved at a few friends as we drove closer, coming to a stop between a blue Toyota pickup and a black Jeep.

"Don't tell anyone about our accident...I mean the almost accident," she mumbled just loud enough for me to hear.

I cast a quick glance her way and assured her there was nothing to worry about. We got out of the car, and Caitlyn made a beeline for a small group of friends we'd seen when we pulled in. I started to follow, but there was a man about thirty yards away, standing next to a tree and waving a hand at me. Cole. But how could that be? We hadn't met yet. Still, my insides instantly warmed up as I told Caitlyn I'd catch up with her later. Then I darted off in the direction where I'd seen Cole. It was strange how he ducked behind the trunk for cover as I got closer. I chalked it up to him probably just being playful and kept moving. As I rounded the tree, something firm and hard grabbed my arm, and in the blink of an eye I was somewhere in the middle of the woods, my back pressed against a branch, and Cole's lips crushing mine.

The kiss deepened, and I pressed my body closer against his. Tingles spread along my skin and I grew lightheaded. His arms wrapped around me, cushioning my back from the tree branch as his lips trailed away from my face and down to the tempting spot on my neck. My body burned with need, and moments later it felt like wildfires were scattering all over me, and then I realized he'd bitten me. "I've waited so long for this," he said, his breath both warm and cold on my skin.

I gasped and pushed him back, his words echoing in my head like some kind of crazy déjà vu. And when our eyes locked together, I knew I wasn't with Cole. "How are you here?" I demanded, feeling like all my past memories were being stalked.

Luke shook his head, something smug filling his eyes. "That's what I was trying to tell you before."

"What do you mean 'before'?"

He flung a hand in the air. "I'm in your dream!" He lowered his hand and swung an inquiring gaze at our surroundings. "Where are we anyway?"

"How can you be in my dream?" I wondered aloud, then shrugged. "How is that even possible?" I reached over and grabbed Luke's hand, squeezing. "You feel real," I mumbled with amazement.

"I tried to stop you last time," he explained. "But you took off in a huff and that woke you up, which cut our connection."

I bit my lip, processing everything he'd just said. "But I'm dreaming of Cole...only when I get a better view, it's not Cole at all. It's you"—that last part said with a little vehemence.

"If you don't mind, quit dreaming about that jerk," he said, his voice exasperated. "I can take on the identity of anyone in your dream, maybe next time you'll be thinking of me."

"But how can you do that? You know, become someone else I'm thinking of?"

"It's my blood flowing in you. I just...I just never thought it would work." He eyed me suspiciously, then added, "With you not being human, and all."

I folded my arms in front of my chest. "What are you talking about?"

"It's rare. I've only heard of a few cases like this," he stammered. "Drinking my blood has allowed us to sleepwalk."

"Sleepwalk?" I repeated, unsure exactly what that meant.

His eyes gleamed with excitement. "Angel, it means I can come to you in your dreams. I didn't think it would work with you being an angel, not sleeping and all. But then I remembered your orbing issue and thought it was worth a shot to reach you. So here I am."

I gaped at him. "Why would you try to contact me like this?"

"Because I haven't heard or felt you in almost two weeks. It made me worried and I thought I should at least make sure you're okay."

Two weeks? A fresh wave of panic rolled through my stomach, but I tried to keep positive about this new discovery. I had a way to communicate with Luke, not that I knew what good it would do me.

19

FEAR CLUTCHED MY SPINE. It didn't seem to matter how quick I ran, that monster was gaining ground—and fast. Stupidly, I'd wandered out of the cave to see if there might be any clues as to where I was. Luke needed something to go on if there were any possible way for him to get me out of here. But my exploration had led to a big fat nothing. Now I was running for my life, and there wasn't a thing in sight for miles that I could hide in.

A thunderous shrieking sounded again, followed by the ground rumbling dangerously under my feet. My balance was in question now as I held my arms out, rotating them from front to sides, desperately hoping not to fall. The creature's familiar scent of rotten roadkill tortured my nose. It was close, so close, but my legs kept pushing across the quicksandish terrain. *Keep going, keep pushing*, I encouraged, but my hope was running thin. A girl can only take so much, whether an angel or not.

Not too far ahead, something shimmered along the sand like diamonds. If that's what it was, I might be able to use them as a weapon against the creature. With renewed hope, I pushed harder, picking up a little more speed. Grumbles and screeches threatened immediately behind me, but if I could just buy a little more time…just a little more. But as I got closer, the field of glistening diamonds morphed into a pond. My inspiration immediately deflated like a popped balloon. Now I had no weapon, and no way to defend myself against the monster. Back to square one, only running wouldn't help me much longer.

Pain exploded along the side of my abdomen, and I felt something inside me crack against the impact as it sent me flying through the air. One hand cradled my ribs, as my other one braced for landing. It seemed like the ground opened up as I crashed. The sand ripped through my exposed flesh as if it were razor blades, tearing into my arm and face as I skidded to a stop just before the pond. Ignoring the throbbing in my chest, I swung around to face my attacker, and as I did it was already there, something massive and hard crunching into my left cheek. Instantly, a molten coppery liquid filled my mouth and I spit what I could out as I jumped back, ducking down. One of the creature's arms just missed my face, its great *swoosh* tousling my hair and its stench leaving me nauseous.

The monster howled, screeching in my head like nails on a chalkboard. Then it lunged up out of the sand, revealing that its massive, tubular, segmented body was at least ten feet long. It reminded me of a giant caterpillar, with ten stretched-out black legs extending in a row down its chunky, hairy body. I couldn't see any eyes on its gruesome face, but the mouth on that thing was enough to intimidate me. Razor-sharp teeth the size of my arm glistened with spittle as it gave another shriek, then made its next move. A few legs from both sides compressed together, with me standing helplessly in the middle. I dropped down and lunged forward, both fists landing uppercuts somewhere below its midsection, sending waves of intense pain down my side with the broken bones. The creature howled in agony as it backed up. Instead of standing there, I used its obviously distracted state to pounce forward, both feet out like missiles, colliding into the beast and making it stagger backwards even more. The impact sent me flying in reverse, and I landed with a numbing smack against my back when I hit the water before being swallowed into its depths.

Once my feet reached the murky bottom, I pushed up and fought my way to the surface. As I emerged, my head dipped back, flinging my drenched hair behind my face as I gulped the air. My arms swished at my sides, legs kicking rhythmically, as I watched the creature pace the shore. Shrieks and howls bellowed from its open mouth, and it seemed to nervously ponder how to get me. Each attempt to enter the water left the beast reeling back with more screeching howls. It repeated this pattern a few more times, then stood on the edge of the pond, facing me. Ragged breathing replaced its howls, spittle dripping from its massively sharp teeth. That's when I knew I'd be dog-paddling for a while, even though the sharp bite of pain in my side was making me nauseous. There was no way I'd be leaving this pond until that monster was long gone.

The sun had been gone from the sky for quite some time before I finally built up enough courage to leave the water. The creature had given up what felt like hours ago, but I just couldn't risk it in my weakened state. My arms and legs burned with clenched pressure inside the muscles. I wasn't sure how many ribs had broken, but the excruciating pain in my chest made me think it was more than just one or two, and the left side of my face felt like I'd been hit by a Mack truck. It was going to be real fun not being able to heal these injuries. Sure, yeah, right.

Still, I somehow made the long, horrendous journey back to my little hidey-hole of a cave. Thankfully, no encounters with massive caterpillar monsters were made on the way. I gingerly sat down, my back against the rocky wall. Pain shot through every nerve in my body, intense enough to bring tears to my eyes. Once it got as comfortable as it was going to get, I leaned my head back and closed my eyes, concentrating on anywhere but this wretched place. I opened them a few times, hoping my orbing powers might be working again, only to see that I was still in the cave—and my body a broken mess. Every bone inside me screamed that I was fallen, and this was the hell I'd been sent to. But logic rattled my brain with the fact that there were no demons here attempting to enslave me. Every fallen angel always ended up some demon's bitch. Actually, a lot of the demons *were* fallen angels. The rules couldn't possibly have changed just for little ol' me.

So if I wasn't fallen, then where in all the worlds was I? And did Raphael send me here to punish me? Or was it something else altogether? The changes inside me originated with Cole's bite, but had only intensified once I had Luke's blood flowing in my veins. Could performing the ritual of breath over Caitlyn—pumped full of vampire blood—be the reason I'd experienced those crazy symptoms? And ultimately been sent here as some kind of crazy backfire? Perhaps I should've mentioned those little tidbits of information to Ezariah. Or maybe that didn't have anything to do with it at all.

My fingers traced the edge of the papyrus wedged in my bosom. Somehow the scrolls never got wet, even though they'd been fully submerged in the pond. What a relief, even though I had no idea how to return them to their owner. What if all my efforts had been for nothing? Depressing thoughts deflated me further, bringing forth an exhaustion I couldn't fight off. My mind finally petered out while wondering if Caitlyn had been healed, allowing the dream world to claim me once more.

Techno music thumped in my ears, vibrating in my pulse. There were people—humans—but not too many, so it wasn't overly crowded. I watched them dance from my comfy seat at the bar, sipping on something that definitely wasn't water. My mouth puckered at the bitter, tangy flavor as I turned around, setting my drink on the black granite countertop. Steel framing, fixtures, and appliances adorned the back of the bar in a slickly decorative way. Red bubble-shaped lights hung in various places, further accenting the décor with their red shade. A presence appeared behind me with two cool hands on my shoulders.

"Luke," I breathed, crossing my right leg over my left, the smooth, tight black pants crackling with the friction.

"Hello, Angel"—delight beaming in his azure eyes. He sat down in the empty seat beside me, and I couldn't help but notice how nice he looked in black jeans and a matching black leather jacket. "Thanks for not calling me Cole this time."

The thought of that name stole my breath, and I released a deep sigh of frustration. "You know I love him. That will never change."

A roll of his eyes let me know that he did understand. "I'd rather discuss your feelings for me, not him."

"What feelings?" I asked, indignation in my tone. "Anyway, there is something that I need you—"

"Nah ah ah!" he cautioned with a few flicks of a finger near my face. "You're not changing this up on me! We're talking about this—now!"

I tilted my head, feeling my patience melting. "Luke, this isn't the time. I need to know if that ritual worked. Please. Go to Caitlyn, see if she's awake."

"Maybe I will," he taunted. "But I won't go anywhere until we talk about us."

"There is no 'us,'" I hissed with vehemence. "I'm in love with Cole!"

"I said I don't want to talk about him!" His voice growing louder. "I care about *you*, damn it! I need to know you feel the same!"

If that wasn't putting me on the spot, I didn't know what would be. His pushiness made me want to tell him that I didn't feel a thing. "What does it matter?" was what I settled with instead.

His eyes locked onto mine, emotions best left unspoken revealed inside their depths. "It matters to me," he said at last. "I know you care, but I need to hear it."

My heart lurched in my stomach. Now just wasn't the time to discuss this. Actually, there would never be a good time, but I'd get nowhere suggesting that. "Who knows if I'll ever get out of this hellhole I'm stuck in. But if I do, then I'm going to Cole and working things out with him. I care about you, Luke." I stole a moment to determine the best words to say next. "But my heart belongs to Cole."

Pink moisture welled up in his eyes, and he looked away. My chest tightened, and my eyes stung with my own welling tears, but I fought them back. Not only did it hurt to see Luke upset, but he was also the only one who could help me. Plus, I'd be beyond lonely not having him visit me in my dreams. So when he turned back and looked at me, the sadness in his eyes mimicking my own feelings, my heart froze in a panic.

"Luke," I tried with a soothing voice as a pink tear slicked down his cheek.

"No, I needed to hear that." He closed his eyes, then added, "I really did." He stood up in a blur of motion, then he was gone.

"Luke! Wait!" My shouts brought me back to the hellish cave. My body was still mangled and in agonizing pain. Unable to move, I rested my head further against the rocky wall and closed my eyes, begging my dreams to steal me away. Thankfully, at least I had that going for me.

I was in the same club from before, but all the humans were gone. The dance floor looked like a deserted ghost town. No more pulsing music penetrating my ears, but the silence was eerie and disturbing. Footsteps approached from behind and I swung around, finding Luke on the far side of the bar. "Have a drink with me," he suggested with a smile.

"Don't leave me like that again," I demanded as I walked toward him, then with a softer tone I added, "Please."

He handed over a martini glass filled with a red liquid. I took it without thinking, bringing it to my lips and taking a sip. Instantly, I spit it out. "Yuck!"

"You need to drink it, Angel. I meant to give you some earlier." He rounded his shoulders. "Better late than never."

I frowned, setting down the martini glass. "I'm not drinking that."

"It'll heal you," was his encouraging reply. "Be sure to drink every drop in that glass. Since you're not taking it directly from me, you'll need more of it."

I felt my eyes widen in surprise. "If I drink your blood in this dream, it'll heal me in real life?" I tilted my head and shrugged. "How'd you know I was hurt?"

"We're connected, Angel. I can sense your pain. Even though you broke my heart before, I can't bear to leave you suffering. So go on now and drink that up. Before it goes bad."

Tentatively, I picked up the glass. Then chugged its contents while holding my breath. Wiping my mouth, I set it back down. My body tingled from head to toe, and I knew its healing power had already begun working.

Luke leaned over, folding his arms across the countertop. "Did you figure out where you are?"

I shook my head. "Not a clue. But there are the meanest creatures you wouldn't believe. And all of them want to eat me."

"I'm so sorry you're there." He straightened and slammed a fist against the granite, the countertop rattling with the force of his blow. "I just wish I knew where you were!"

"Even if we knew, how would you help me? I'm stuck here. My powers don't work. And as you know, I can't even heal myself."

"Don't worry about that," he said, his voice reassuringly confident. "If we can figure out where you are, I can come get you out of there."

"How? It's impossible for you to leave Earth!"

A sly smile curved his lips. "Did I tell you that Huron is the epitome of black magic? Once we figure out where you are, he can summon your return. We opened a portal to the underworld last night, offering a reward to anyone that might know anything about what happened to you and where you are."

I stared at him, knowing the truth behind each word he spoke. If Huron really was a voodoo priest, then I knew what Luke promised could really be done. But now I feared getting found would be my biggest problem. At last I asked, "You must be in pretty deep with Huron. Didn't you already cash out your debt?"

"Huron is my friend. His willingness to help me is much deeper than any debt."

I sat down in the padded barstool next to Luke. "Well, then, I owe you both…my life."

"If that's the case, then walk away from Cole," he smarted, but I knew he meant it.

I shook my head, tension building in my chest. "I knew there was a price for your helping me!"

"You know that isn't true," he replied curtly. Then in a monotone of resignation, "When we meet again, I'll let you know what I find with your charge."

That statement got me beaming again. I clapped my hands together. "Thank you!"

In a whoosh of air his lips brushed my cheek, and then he was gone.

20

LIGHT GLINTED TOWARD THE FRONT of the cave, and a musky heat simmered on my skin. I rubbed the sweat from my brow, noticing the small movement didn't hurt. Luke's blood in my dream had really healed my broken body of the real world. The thought brought an instant pang in my heart, though. Once Luke got me out of here, would Cole still want to rekindle our relationship? Would all this extra blood I'd ingested make any kind of difference in Cole's decision to overlook it and be together? Surely, I hoped not. But only time would answer such concerns.

And hopefully time would carry away those confusing feelings I got every time I was with Luke. This whole sleepwalk thing might put some-what of a damper on that, though. I was anxious to hear back from Luke, and not just because I needed to know if Caitlyn was okay and the ritual had worked, but also because I was lonely and he was the only one who could reach me. Okay, maybe I did care for him a little more than that. As boring as this desolate place could be—when I wasn't fighting for my life—I had plenty of time to think about Luke, and my inexplicable con-nection to him. So far, I'd only reasoned it down to this: Sure, I cared for him, maybe even *loved* him on some crazy level, and I knew I couldn't blame it on all the blood he'd loaded me up with. But regardless of that, I was *in love* with Cole.

Distant howls of the worm-like beast kept me from leaving the safety of the cave. I'd nodded off a few times, but with no visits from Luke. My anxiety became desperation—waiting, waiting, waiting. I still called for Raphael, and my prayers sounded more like begging instead of praising. *Please let that ritual have worked. Please let Caitlyn be awake and well. And please help me figure out a way to get the heck out of here.*

By nightfall, the freezing temps had returned. I huddled up against the rocky wall, letting my hair fall over my arms for a little warmth, and trying my best to handle the state of boredom I'd fallen to. In an effort to stay sane, I tried thinking happy thoughts about Cole, focusing on the time we had a picnic near the Rocky Mountain National Park. That had been when the whole idea of him drinking my blood was introduced to our abstinent relationship.

Cool, crisp air brushed along my skin and I cuddled up closer against Cole's body. He was warmer than usual, and I knew that meant he'd just recently fed. Our view from this private little oasis he'd found was spectacular. The snow-tipped mountains on the horizon gave the appearance they'd been dipped in white chocolate. The blueness of the sky was swirled with white fluffy clouds resembling cotton candy. The red- and blue-checkered blanket we sat on was spread out inside a small clearing between the pine trees. My back was nestled against Cole's chest and his arms wrapped around my body from behind.

"How'd you become a vampire?" I asked curiously, hoping the answer wouldn't frighten me.

"You really want to know?" His lips were so close to my ear. The thrum of his soft, sensual voice sent gooseflesh across my arms, and my reply got caught in my throat.

I bobbed my head slightly by way of my answer.

"I'd been discharged from my service in the army for about six months and had been staying with my mom. I could've found some place on my own, but money was hard to come by back then, and my mom had begged me to stay and help her out. My dad had passed on years before that, while I'd been off on one of my missions. So I guess you can say I felt sorry and stuck around for her benefit." His arms squeezed a little firmer around me, then he laced his fingers through mine. "One night I came home from running errands and there was a brand new TV sitting in the corner of the room. Back then, we only got black and white, but it was still the greatest invention we'd ever seen. The Olympics were playing, and she was so excited for us to be able to sit and watch them from our own couch. We'd been doing that for about an hour when there was a pretty loud banging on the door. I got up, but Mom insisted for me to stay and not miss anything on the TV, and then she went for the door."

Cole got choked up. He stole a moment to clear his voice, and continued. "Her screams were the worst sounds I'd ever heard. I ran to the door as fast as I could. There was blood smeared everywhere—along the doorframe, the back of the door, and a big puddle of it on the wooden floors. There was even some red splattered on the yellow curtains at the window several feet away. But my mom wasn't there." His voice was tense and strained. "I ran outside, screaming for her, but I couldn't see her anywhere. It was dark, no moon or stars that night, and our nearest neighbor was two miles away. I searched around the front of the house and out by our shed. Then I thought I heard something over by the house and I sprinted straight over. He was waiting for me on the front porch. I'll never forget watching his creamy white hands brushing along the white railing, leaving a smeared trail of red everywhere he touched. I wanted to run, but I couldn't. It was like my feet were frozen in place. I couldn't take my eyes off him. Selene, he was the most beautiful person I'd ever seen."

When Cole didn't say anything else, I wriggled around and placed my hands on his cheeks. "It's okay," I said soothingly, staring straight into his eyes glistening with pink.

He didn't flinch or try to look away. "I never saw my mom again after that night. It was June 10, 1936. I'll never forget that date for as long as I live—or whatever you call it since I'm technically dead. I've been living seventy-six years as a vampire. I was twenty-seven in human years that night when I was turned."

I wiped a few tears from his cheek, then threw my arms around his shoulders and held him. He returned my embrace without another word. But my curiosity led to a question I hoped wouldn't upset him further. "What was his name? The vampire who turned you." I pulled back enough to look at Cole's face. His eyes had dried up, but he still looked so sad.

"Phoenix"—that name spoken with vehemence. "And once I'd adjusted to my new life, so to speak, I tried to kill him. But he got away and I've never seen him since. Though I've heard plenty of rumors about him and the innocent people he's killed."

I knew this wasn't the best time to ask, but I had to know. "How many people have *you* killed?"

"Selene—"

"I want to know," I pushed. "It won't change how I feel. Trust me."

"Yes it will." His voice full of defeat.

"Cole, I love all of you, even the parts where you made mistakes."

"But you're so freakin' perfect!" he exclaimed, a hand waving at his side.

"No, I'm not," I countered, then sealed my lips. The last thing I needed was him feeling more guilty because of me. And the truth was, I'd never really done anything *wrong* before I fell in love with him. "Wrong" being a questionable word to describe it, since I didn't feel like my love for Cole was anything but perfect.

"Look at us." He shrugged his shoulders, then brushed his fingers through my hair. "You've broken so many rules to be with me...." His words trailed off as our eyes locked together.

"And I'd break them again, and again, and again!" I shot back. "I'm never giving up on you, or us! I love you, Cole." My lips found his in a surge of emotion, full of longing and need. He pulled me closer, deepening our kiss and sending waves of euphoria through my veins. I leaned back, momentarily breaking apart to admire his beautiful features. My fingertips traced along his perfect creamy-white skin, feeling the smoothness of his cheekbones, then exploring his chin, down to his neck, and finally tracing along his collar bone, gently tugging on the neckline of his tee shirt. "You're the most gorgeous person I've ever seen," I panted, lowering my lips to his ear.

"Thirty-two," he said as he unsnapped the top button of my shirt.

"What?" I asked as I nibbled on his earlobe, feeling his body shudder with pleasure.

He pushed me back so we were facing each other. "That's how many people I've killed. Thirty-two. Most of them were accidents. I couldn't help myself when I was a young vampire. But I swear to you, once I was strong enough to control it, I never killed another person."

My whole body went numb. When I didn't respond, he shook me. "Selene, I need you to say something."

I swallowed hard. Thirty-two innocent people. My stomach turned with grief for the humans I never knew. But my eyes were on Cole, looking deep inside at who I knew him to be, and my feelings for him would never dissolve over things he'd done in the past, before we'd ever met. With that realization, I gave a small smile and said, "Thanks for being honest with me."

He cupped my cheeks. "Does this change things between us?"

My head moved slowly right, then left. He could've told me one hundred thirty-two and it wouldn't have made a difference with my feelings for him. A sudden wave of emotion compressed in my chest, making it tighten as my heart sped up. Cole arched a brow—obviously he'd picked up on my increased pulse too. In a blur he was on top of me, arms pressing against my sides, eyes gazing dreamily into mine. There were a few oddly placed pinecones beneath the blanket grinding into my back, but I forgot all about them once his lips meshed with mine. Heat spread across my face, descending down my neck. My body swelled with need and I arched my back trying to get closer. Moans of pleasure rumbled out of my throat, then were swallowed back as the kiss intensified. I locked my legs around him while trying to force his body even closer to mine. His hands trailed up to my head, gently tugging my hair, then grabbing large handfuls and yanking with enough force to make me cry out. But it didn't hurt long. Carnal vibrations rippled down my spine, moving deeper, awakening something inside me that I'd never experienced before.

The fear of becoming fallen forced me to push him away. "We can't," my voice ragged.

"But I want you," he growled, his face barely an inch away. With a hand he held my wrists above my head—I didn't remember him moving them—and with the other traced invisible lines on my face, soft, sensual caresses with his fingertips.

I released a deep breath, my body trembling with need—and caution. "The consequences..."

His lips crushed mine, reigniting the flames that had barely been put out from before. I tried to move my hands but his grip tightened, leaving me unable to budge them. Using his other hand, he rubbed my bare arm, tickling the sensitive skin with his touch. Once he reached the tip of my shirtsleeve, his fingers brushed along the top of my chest, finding the next button and flicking it open. Our kiss grew deeper as he moved to the next button, then the next. It wasn't long before my light pink corset blouse fell to the sides, exposing the pink lace bra beneath.

Low, vibrating groans erupted from his mouth as his lips drifted along my chin and down to that sensitive area on my neck. With my hands still secured above me, I rocked my body against his, my need swelling beyond what I could handle. When his tongue flicked out along my skin, just above my thundering pulse, my whole body erupted with pleasure. I cried out—or maybe that was him as our voices seemed as one—but the sound was drowned out once his lips returned to mine. Realizing my hands were no longer bound, I grabbed the bottom of his tee shirt, yanking it around his shoulders, over his head, and blindly tossing it to the side. My fingernails gently traced the curve of muscle in his lower back, then moved leisurely all the way up to his shoulder blades. Our kisses grew sloppy, his tongue rolling around mine, and I dug my nails into his flesh, making him growl with delight.

Somehow I managed to roll him over. Now I was on top, my legs still straddling his waist. I held him down by his shoulders as I gazed at his beautiful, flawless chest. His skin was soft, yet the muscle underneath was solid as stone. The creamy whiteness reminded me of vanilla ice cream, and the thought made me want to lick him all over. I scooted down his body to where my legs wrapped around his thighs, and when he tried to sit up, I just pushed him back down, my fingers digging into his pectorals with the force. "My turn!"—my voice rough with demand as I leaned over and my lips reached just above the line of his jeans, below his naval. His body shuddered as my tongue touched his skin, but I held him steady with my hands still pressing into his pecks, sliding all the way up to the top of his chiseled, hairless chest. Then I moved to the side and went back down his body, mindful to lick places I'd missed before.

And for whatever reason, that's when fear seized me. In a rush, I jumped to the side, frantically buttoning my shirt. "We can't go any further"—my words breathless and raspy. "I won't be able to stop if we do."

Cole sat up, his brows arching. "I promise I will stop us. I won't let you be punished even more for our love." His facial expression softened as he opened his arms. "Come here. Let me hold you."

I crawled into his awaiting arms with tears streaming down my face. "I'm so sorry. How can you want to be with me? We'll never be able to go any further than what we just did."

"Why?" was the question he asked, and at the moment it was my question too.

Cue my generic answer. "Because I'm a guardian angel. I wasn't made for anything else."

"But there is so much more to who you are, Selene," he said, his voice firm and authoritative. "I'm sorry they don't get who you really are."

A dry chuckle escaped my lips. "And what's that?"

His arms tightened around me, pulling me closer into him. His lips were against my ear when he answered, "The most beautiful, amazing woman I've ever known. I'll be with you no matter what rules we have to follow, and I'll love you with everything I am for as long as I'm on this earth."

A fresh wave of tears flushed my cheeks and I needed a moment before I could speak. "I love you, too," I finally said. "I just wish I could give you all of me, but I promise I've given you everything I can."

"Well, maybe not everything."

I turned to face him. "What? What do you mean?" I sounded as confused as I felt.

"Your blood isn't off limits, is it?"

The creature's shrieking was closer, jolting me out of that memory and straight back to my reality of hell. The ground rumbled and loose pieces of rock rained down from the ceiling. I threw my arms over my head and ducked, hoping to protect myself as best I could. A screeching howl sounded once again—this time at the entrance of the cave. Luckily, the beast's large size would prevent it from coming any closer. Another quake thundered around me, causing bigger rocks to break loose and fall with a crash barely a few feet away. I pressed my back closer against the stone wall behind me, crouching into the smallest ball I could form. But it wasn't enough. Another shake of the earth and I heard something creak and snap above me. Still holding my arms over my head, I peered through them just in time to see the massive boulder falling.

21

MY LASHES FLUTTERED OPEN and I was surrounded by a sea of familiar gray. But it wasn't the cave; it was the basement where Luke lived, and I quickly made a mental note that my vampire ally must be controlling what I dreamed. I sat up in a rush and saw Luke sitting on the sofa where my head had been. "Why was I lying on your lap?" I asked, appalled that he'd done such a thing, especially after our last conversation.

"You needed blood again, but this time you required a lot more of it." He shrugged his shoulders, then added, "Is it a crime that I got comfortable while you drank it?"

More blood? I became fuming mad, glaring straight into his eyes. "No more blood, Luke! I mean it! I don't care what condition I'm in!"

"But Angel, you were really, really messed up. I couldn't just leave you like that."

"I don't care!" I snapped back.

"But I do!" he nearly screamed.

Feeling the need to diffuse, I got up and headed to the table in the back of the room. I took a deep breath, exhaling as I sat down. Luke was watching me, still seated on the sofa. "You can't," I started, but then rethought my choice of words. "I appreciate your concern. I really, really do. But you can't keep giving me your blood. What if…"

He gave me a moment to finish, but when I didn't he asked, "What if what? Spit it out, Angel."

Hesitantly, "Something's happening to me."

"Obviously," he chided, folding his hands in his lap. "Look at you every time I seek you in your dreams. You've been a mess."

"Exactly my point. My body should be healing all on its own, without any help from you. But it's not."

"Which is why I've been giving you my blood," he noted matter-of-factly.

"Right"—my voice doubtful. "But what if your blood in my system is the reason I'm *different*? I mean, I'm quicker now…and more alert. If it weren't for that, I'd be completely human, even though I'm in my angel form. What if"—I stole a second, collecting my thoughts—"What if that's why I'm in this hellhole of a world?"

His gaze hardened. "All the more reason for me to get you the hell out of there then."

"But how?" I wailed, a wave of depression washing over me. "I still have no idea where I am!"

Luke stood up, and slowly approached me. "There's a way you can help me find you." He scooped up my hand and gave it a tight squeeze. "But you're not going to like it."

I craned my neck upward, finding his eyes. "How? You know I'll do anything to get out of here."

The way his eyes seemed to deepen confirmed I probably didn't want to know what he was going to say. So I braced myself the best I could as chills raced up and down my spine.

"Huron would have a better shot at tracking you…if I had some of your blood in me. He could use it—"

"No way!" I yanked my hand out of his grasp and folded my arms over my chest. "No freakin' way! You're not drinking from me!"

"But it could—"

"I don't care! The answer is no!" Then I remembered how he'd already bitten me twice when I thought he was Cole and hotly reminded him of it.

"I couldn't get your blood then since you believed I was someone else. You must willingly give it to *me*." He ran a hand through his hair, seeming extremely frustrated. A few moments passed and when I didn't say anything or soften my glare, he snapped, "Fine, have it your way!" a hint of disgust in his voice.

"Has there been any progress with the Underworld?" I asked, sounding slightly hopeful.

Luke sat down in the chair beside me, then shook his head. "Not really. Some have come forward, but their information didn't add up."

Not wanting to lose hope, but running out of options, I stared at the floor feeling sadness compress my heart.

Luke rubbed my back lightly. "Angel, we're going to find you no matter what. I was just trying to speed things up. I'm sorry. I knew you wouldn't like that idea, but I had to ask."

Then an idea floated to the surface of my mind. And it was definitely worth mentioning. "What about Cole?" I looked at him, feeling a renewed sense of optimism. "He has my blood in him. Can't Huron use that?"

Luke leaned back, fingers rubbing his chin. "Let me get this straight. You want me to find that jerk-off and convince him to come with me to Huron's?"

"Yes! Cole needs to know what's happened to me anyway, and I have no other way of communicating with him...except through you."

I watched Luke as he considered my request—somewhat painfully I might add. When he didn't say anything, I added, "Please," in the most desperate voice I could muster.

"Oh-all-right! I'll do it. But if I can't find him, like I couldn't find your charge, then there's nothing else I can do." He smiled, then added, "Unless you give me your blood directly."

My heart sunk, my mind reeling over the part he'd just said about Caitlyn. "What do you mean you couldn't find her? You're a vampire for goodness' sake! Can't you track her?"

Anger sharpened the angles of his face and he let out an appalled snort. "I *did* track her. But her scent stops immediately outside the hospital!"

"Did you check our dorm? Or Bridgeton Institute?" Would they really have discharged her that quickly?

He shook his head. "I didn't know those locations. Give me the addresses and I'll check them out."

I gave him the info. "Are you going to remember all of that, or should I write it down?"

He cocked his head. "Angel, don't insult me. I've got it all right here." With two fingertips he tapped the side of his head. "It may be a little while before I return. Try not getting hurt, or killed. Will ya?"

I nodded with a small smile. "Promise me, no matter what. No more giving me blood."

Uncertainly. "Fine. Whatever you say."

It felt like a few more days had passed. Thankfully, I'd managed not to get injured so far. My cave was a bit messier—with rocks and boulders strewn all over and a nice layer of dust settled on top of them—thanks to the incident several days back. It actually felt a little more cramped, but I was perfectly fine in this environment. It beat going out and running head to head with one of those worm-things.

My mind was on overload. Worrying about where Caitlyn was, and if she'd recovered. Wondering if Luke had found Cole yet, and what his reaction was to me being missing. Wishing Raphael would respond to my cries for help. Of course, there was also plenty of time to fret over my new vampire-like senses. And why my angelic powers were nonexistent. At least I could find a little comfort in believing I wasn't fallen. Unless that worm thingy was my demon overlord, but I doubted it. That oversized caterpillar seemed more like a guardian of this hellish world than anything else. A hungry one, I might add.

Once the sting of the cold night air hit my skin, I knew it was time to force myself to sleep, hoping this time Luke would be there with good news. I leaned against the rocky wall and closed my eyes. Several minutes passed of my pleading prayers, and then I sat impatiently waiting to fall asleep.

After what felt like an hour, I started dozing off. I was in a cave—but not my cave. Somewhere else. All the walls were black, slick stone, definitely manmade. Antique, rustic-looking fixtures hung from the rock ceiling, casting faint yellow light throughout the enclosed space. There was a solid slab of grey granite in the center of the room, appearing like some type of ancient altar. As I moved closer, I saw red splattered stains on the top. Curious, I ran my fingers across it, feeling a crusty residue. Dried blood. But whose? I cast a wary look around and noticed someone standing against the wall, mostly hidden within a shadow. "Luke?" I said, my voice echoing eerily.

"Hello, Angel," he said, then in a swish of motion was next to me.

I startled. "I hate when you do that." I looked around, then asked, "Where are we?"

"We're in Huron's basement."

"This place is below Huron's bar?"

He nodded, taking my hand. "We're so close, Angel. Huron is working on Cole as we speak."

I let out a deep sigh, feeling a wave of relief wash over me. "You found him. Thank goodness."

Luke half laughed. "No easy feat."

I gave his hand a gentle squeeze. "I owe you, Luke. Thank you."

"We're not out of the woods just yet. A lot has happened since I last saw you."

"What do you mean?" I tugged my hand free and stepped back, finding his eyes.

"I had a little confrontation with a couple of shadow sliders."

"Shadow sliders?" I asked, shocked. Shadow sliders were one of the few types of lower leveled demons that could easily shift from world to world—kind of like the way angels could orb. They're demons, stuck forever in shadow form, but they come in pretty handy when dishing out threats. "Who sent them?"

"Your friend back there on Rhea. I can't believe the nerve of him!"

"Ezariah?" I asked stupidly. I knew it was him. "But why would he send them to you?" *And how would he have any control over demons?* I wondered.

"No, no. Not for me, Angel. For you. But since no one can find you, I was their next target." He shrugged his shoulders. "In a nutshell, they want the scrolls returned."

Of course they did. Obviously I'd had no way to get them back to Rhea since performing the ritual. But excuses never went over that well with shadow sliders. "Well, as soon as you get me out of here, I can take them back."

"They brought a messenger spirit along with them, and it was pretty pissed to be leaving without the scrolls."

Unlike shadow sliders, messenger spirits could take physical form. "I'll never hand the scrolls over to a demon!" was my huffy reply. "This could be a trick. How would Ezariah have the power to control demons? It just doesn't make any sense."

Luke ran a hand through his hair. "I got a feeling there's a lot more going on here than what that old man told you." He shrugged his shoulders. "How would those demons even know you had the scrolls?"

"Maybe they were spying on us in the cave," I offered.

"His magically protected cave?" He snorted in disbelief. "Yeah sure."

I slumped back and felt the cold, hard stone slab against my tailbone. Startled, I jumped forward, rubbing my lower back. "I don't have a good explanation right now, but I'm not giving the scrolls to a messenger spirit, no matter what their threats."

Luke grabbed my shoulders, peering down into my eyes. "Angel, somehow, I'm not sure exactly how, but they claim to have your charge."

"What?" I shrieked, pulling out of Luke's hold. "That isn't...that isn't possible!"

"They had this." He dug into his jeans pocket, then held out his hand, revealing a small vinyl hospital band. I took it from him and read the patient information typed on it: *Caitlyn Harris.*

I shook my head, coldness slithering up my limbs. "No, no, no." My whole body trembled with fear and remorse. I was falling before I realized I'd lost my footing—or was it that I'd just become too weak to stand? The moment before my knees crashed into the chunky rock floor Luke was there, helping me stand back up.

"It's going to be okay," he reassured, but I couldn't find a way to believe him. All of this was my fault. If I'd never left Caitlyn unguarded, she'd never have been hurt so badly. I could've protected her. No, I should've protected her. But instead I was trying to save Cole. And that was all my fault too. I slumped against Luke's chest, allowing him to hold most of my weight. The amount of guilt pressing deep in my heart was making it harder to breathe, impossible to think, and made me feel more broken than ever before.

I gave a long, desperate sigh, but couldn't find the words to say.

It wasn't long before Luke broke the silence. "There's nothing you can do until we get you home. Are you ready to give that a try?"

I nodded, rubbing the moisture under my eyes.

Abruptly, I was sitting on the altar.

"Why did you put me on this thing?" I exclaimed as I tried to get off.

Luke blocked me, saying, "You need to lie down. It's the only way for Huron's magic to work."

Reluctantly, I nodded and scooted back. A casual glance downward gave me too good a view of the dagger in Luke's hand. "What are you doing with that?"

"Blood is the only way for black magic to work. Don't worry, I'm not going to be tasting any of it. I promise."

I felt uneasy, but I knew this was my only option. "Okay, what do I do?"

"Lie back. Keep your arms at your sides, palms facing up."

After I did what Luke instructed, he went to the base of the altar and moved my feet. "They need to be a little more than shoulder-width apart," he explained. I didn't fight him, and my dress fell neatly between my legs.

I stared up at a massive iron fixture until Luke told me to close my eyes.

"Now take deep, slow breaths," he advised. "This may sting a little."

"What—"

"Angel, be quiet!" he interrupted. "You need to do what I say. Please."

My desperation forced me into submission, even though I had a bad feeling about this. Here I was, an angel of light, preparing for dark, black magic. But I had no other options. There was no other way. We had to try this, now more than ever.

That's when a sharp stabbing pain erupted from the heel of my hand as the tip of the knife sliced through my flesh. Since I was in my angel form, that should have been impossible. But I'd already determined something was happening to me, something was different, and now I had more proof—if I even needed any.

Once Luke finished carving my right palm, he swiftly moved over to my left and repeated the same movement. When he was done, his voice filled my ears, echoing throughout the cave. "With blood, we call upon Huron to enter this plane." Luke's fingers rubbed my palms, then smeared the blood across my forehead. "Blood of the angel, all powerful, all spiritual. Here lies the one who calls forth Huron. Her blood welcomes him to this plane. And with my blood, I complete the calling." I heard him moving, but dared not open my eyes. Moments later, I felt power all over me, searing my skin as if I were burning, pressing into my chest, tightening and constricting. My deep, slow breaths increased to sharp, intense pants. My palms were stinging; my forehead felt like it was stuck in a furnace. Panic seized me and I tried to sit up, but my whole body was paralyzed and I couldn't move at all. Then, everything started trembling. I screamed out, hearing my voice reverberate off the cave walls. Suddenly, my voice was halted and my whole body went numb. I couldn't speak; I couldn't feel anything. My eyes shot open but everything was black, then suddenly, I could feel my body pulsing as if my human form was being yanked to the surface.

Something stroked my forehead. With each movement light was filtering in. But I still couldn't see anything—not even a silhouette of the person touching me. I opened my mouth to speak, but quickly realized I still couldn't talk. A second later, I also found out I still couldn't move.

"I call upon the darkness…"Whose voice was that? I didn't recognize it. Definitely masculine with its deep, low tone, but not Luke's.

"…summon the power to return…bring down the walls that imprison…"

The words spoken by whomever this mysterious voice belonged to were interspersed with the sounds of my pounding heartbeat and ragged breathing. Then, all of a sudden, it felt like I was sucked into a vacuum, surrounding me with an eerie silence and complete darkness.

Huron was the first person I saw, his long black hair was pulled back, a hat made of bones and feathers adorning his head. A proud-looking smile spread over his face. "Selene, it's nice to have you back," he said, giving that mysterious voice from before its identity.

I slowly sat up, not surprised to find I was in my human form as I cast a wary gaze around and saw I was still in the voodoo Indian's basement. "Did it work? Am I really awake, or am I still in that dream?"

"Angel, it worked!" Luke came forward and stood next to Huron.

"Selene?" I swung around at the sound of that voice and found Cole standing on my other side.

I felt completely overwhelmed, and skeptical. Glancing back at Huron I asked, "Is this real?"

He nodded. "You are back on Earth now. How were you in Nempha? That is where I found you."

"Nimb-fa?" I asked, unsure of the name since I'd never heard of the place.

"Yes. It is below the Underworld. Hell's hell."

A chill prickled through me. "I don't…I'm not sure." *But that was an excellent question*, I added in my head.

And then, out of nowhere, I was sucked into the vacuum again.

22

WHITE FLUFFY CLOUDS WERE EVERYWHERE. Including the one I was nestled against like a big feather pillow. I glanced down my body, appreciating the fact that my dress matched the cloud I was on—minus the torn, muddy bottom. But at least all that red sand was gone, and for that, I was truly thankful. Even though I could sense that some of my angelic abilities were back, I also felt something was terribly wrong. A quick glance upward gave me an excellent view of the boiling mad archangel standing above me. Wishing I could crawl in a hole, I ducked my head and lowered my body as far as the cloud would let me—which, unfortunately, wasn't very far at all.

"Where in all the worlds have you been?!" Raphael's voice washed over me with an amazing thrust of power, knocking me back several feet.

Once I stood up—a little shaky, I might add—I bravely looked up at his face. "Nem…" I swallowed hard. "…pha."

"Nempha?" he snorted in disbelief. Then his voice hardened. "You better come clean right now and tell me where you've really been." His eyes became flaming blue sapphires, deepening with every threat I could fathom.

Remembering the last time he'd used that fire on me, I fell to my knees before him. "I swear, Raphael. I swear that's where I was. I have no idea how I got there."

"*Selene!*" His voice was louder and madder, if that were possible. "Get up from there. Do not cower from me if you have nothing to hide!"

Oh but I did have something to hide—plenty of somethings actually. Slowly I stood up, careful not to look away from my archangel.

Raphael rubbed his chin as he raked me with a hard, penetrating gaze. "If you really were in Nempha, then that explains why I couldn't sense you anywhere. But I am in no way conceding to your preposterous story."

"I called for you more times than I could count," I noted, feeling despair resurface with the memory. "I thought you'd abandoned me."

"Assuming that's where you were, your powers would not have worked," was his even response.

I felt my eyes widen. "They didn't work. And I couldn't orb either. It was horrible."

Bitter acceptance flashed across his face. "How did you end up there of all places? You must have done something that enabled darkness to take you!" He released a long sigh, shaking his head wearily. "Do I even want to know what you've been up to? I thought you needed time to accept the changes upon you, and respectfully I gave you space to come to those terms. Now, because of your delay, we have lost all contact with your charge. She has not passed on to the light as she should have."

A wave of guilt and fear washed over me. If I told Raphael who had Caitlyn, then I'd have to come clean about everything else. But I couldn't risk my charge's life any longer. My secrets were what caused everything to go wrong. If I became fallen for it, then I deserved no less. I stole a deep breath and swallowed hard. It was time to come clean once and for all— with the exception of having the scrolls in my bosom, and confessing to sharing my blood with a vampire, or having vampire blood in my system, of course.

Well, he didn't strike me, or torture me with blue flames from his eyes. That was a plus. But his expression was punishment enough. His brows furrowed as he shook his head in disgust. In a dramatic motion, he turned around, flinging his white cloak to the side. After taking a few short steps away, he spoke dryly with his back facing me. "So let me get this straight. You went to Rhea behind my back and obtained sea scrolls from some former guardian who is now the keeper of these ancient sea scrolls?"

I nodded. But then realized he couldn't see me so I lamely said, "Yes."

"And then," he continued in a sharp voice, "you performed a ritual over your charge to heal her using those scrolls?"

"Yes"—my voice growing smaller.

He swung around, fury flushing his face. "After I told you your charge's fate had already been decided?" His eyes morphed back into flaming sapphires as his words thundered on. "After I told you to come to terms and make peace with the decision that you were given a second chance?"

I nodded as I dug my nails into my palms, fighting back the tears that threatened to choke me.

"And not only did you save that wretched vampire enabling darkness to torment your charge, you've now also acquired a new friendship with yet another dark one? With whom you participated in black magic to escape Nempha?" With those last words his eyes flared bigger and I closed my eyes, bracing myself for what would come next.

But nothing happened.

Slowly, I peeked at Raphael through my lashes. The flames were gone, and he was shaking his head.

"Raphael, I'm sorry." I meant what I said though I knew we were beyond words.

"Those scrolls were made of darkness"—dread lacing his voice. "And their keeper is the demon lord of that realm."

"Ezariah?" I asked with astonishment. "But he's a former guardian!"

Raphael nodded. "Yes he was. But when he chose to murder his human charge to be with his guardian lover, he was cast down to Rhea to become a slave to the infamous scrolls."

"Murder his charge? But he told me a demon tried to kill the human and the scrolls were his only hope of saving him."

Raphael released a deep sigh. "The scrolls belonged to darkness the moment...Ezariah? Is that what he's calling himself now?...the moment *Ezariah* used them as a fallen angel."

"But that can't be," I argued. "What about the stories told of those sacred scrolls from here? From Europa! Told by other angels of light!"

"Selene, those stories are just that. Stories. They have been fabricated over the centuries. Most never learned of the darkness taking them over. You should have come to me with this! I could have informed you of the truth." He waved his hand. "If you'd only listened to me from the beginning!"

"But it was an archangel that the information came from!" I shot back. "Why would he leave out the most important part?"

Raphael's gaze narrowed. "Who?"

I swallowed hard. I didn't want to get Beck in trouble, but this was too deep, too important. Pertinent information had been left out, and it was my fault for not investigating it further. Shame on me for taking Beck's advice at face value. "Sicily's archangel," I said at last.

He snorted. "Not possible. Elijah does not speak in part truths. Sicily must be your mis-informant."

My chest tightened. It wasn't her at all. "Beck told me," came my reply, waves of anger and dread flushing my bones.

"Why would Beck say such nonsense?" he asked, clearly baffled.

I was wondering the same thing myself. "I don't know. Where is he?"

Raphael's expression hardened. "Stay here. Soon we will be asking the guardian ourselves." Then Raphael was gone, and for the first time ever I was all too eager to listen to him.

Waiting for the return of my archangel, and my obviously confused friend Beck, was no easy feat. What if Beck hadn't been confused? What if he'd told me those details about the scrolls on purpose? But why would he do that knowing I could've ended up fallen? Unless that was his intention all along. But why? What motive would he have to do such a thing? He was my friend. He was a good guy. He wasn't capable of such corrupt behavior. I shook off the thought as shivers raced up and down my arms. Hopefully, soon, I'd have some answers.

Suddenly, blue flames shot up from the fluffy surface, spreading up and whirling until the cloud was completely walled in by fire. Moments later, Raphael, Elijah, Beck, and Beck's archangel Micah appeared. "Selene." Raphael motioned for me to come stand next to him.

Once I was in place, Elijah moved to my archangel's other side. He was a little taller than Raphael, with short, sandy blond hair. His face was youthful, almost boyish, giving him a teenager look. Micah and Beck stood across from us, both of their arms folded in front of their chests. They were about the same height, but the archangel was thicker and broader with rich brown hair falling just below his shoulders. His white cloak covered most of his body, leaving just a trace of his bare chest in view.

"What is the meaning of this?" Micah asked with impatience, as small ripples moved down his cloak.

"The wall of fire is for our privacy," Elijah explained.

"Yes, I already know that," Micah replied. "I want to know what this meeting is about."

Raphael cleared his throat. "I believe we have a problem with your guardian." His eyes fell on Beck.

"Oh, and your angel is such a little saint," Micah shot back, waving a hand in the air.

"No guardian angel is a saint." Raphael's voice was even and firm. "The issues with Selene do not involve any other guardian." His hard gaze shifted to Micah. "However, the problem we have with your angel does."

"Whatever are you referring to?" Micah furrowed his thick, brown eyebrows.

Elijah took a small step forward, his eyes becoming swirling blue embers. "It seems your angel has concocted quite a story, involving words that supposedly came directly from my mouth. Sicily could not be pulled from her charge to be here, but my confrontation with her has already produced the information I need."

Micah turned his gaze to Beck. "Explain yourself. What are they speaking of?"

Beck took a deep breath, then nervously ran a hand through his blond hair, leaving a few pieces behind his ear. "A while back, I told Selene about the ancient scrolls of Rhea. I never in a million years thought she'd actually go there."

"Liar!" I shouted as I moved closer to him.

"No, Selene." Raphael's arm extended around me, pulling me against his chest.

"Your guardian went to Rhea?" Micah asked with widened eyes.

"You're missing the point, old friend," Raphael noted sincerely. "Elijah, please continue."

Elijah nodded, then directed his fiery gaze back on Beck. "Where did you learn of the scrolls?"

Beck anxiously glanced around, then settled his eyes on the cloud floor. "I don't remember," he muttered.

"Yes you do!" I yelled, feeling Raphael's hold tighten around me. "You said Sicily told you, and that her archangel had confirmed it!"

Keeping his eyes on the cloud, Beck replied, "May...be." His words stammered out. "I'm sorry, I just can't remember exactly."

"Why are you lying?"—my voice starting to break, just like my heart was.

When Beck didn't answer me, Elijah spoke up. "Sicily had never heard of the sea scrolls before I spoke with her today. She did, however, see you, Beck, talking with a dark one several weeks back."

A few gasps sounded. Beck shook his head, but never looked up from the cloud. Raphael's hold on me loosened as Elijah pressed on. "You were most concerned with Selene, and you wanted her fallen at all costs. Then you sensed Sicily's presence and you followed her back to Europa, threatening her to keep silent on everything she had heard. Now, will you be forthcoming with the truth we seek, or will I need to burn it from your life force?"

His frown cutting downward, Micah grabbed Beck's shoulders and shook. "Speak now, boy! For I am your archangel, and I demand to know everything. Now!" Micah's eyes widened with the same blue flames in Elijah's. A quick glance at Raphael showed his eyes were also ablaze.

Beck slowly looked up, his attention directed at no one in particular. Tears formed in his eyes as he tried to explain himself. "It's not fair!" he whined, pointing a finger in my direction. "She does everything wrong and is dealt no punishment for her actions! Her boyfriend is a vampire! You heard me, a bloody vampire! How is that acceptable? What horseshoe resides upon her to grant her such grace? She does not belong with us! She is below the world of angels. The darkness wants her, and I will happily deliver her to them!"

"You may not judge another!" Micah declared, a hand over his heart. "How could you? Your behavior is more shameful than Selene's." Micah straightened, grabbing Beck's arm. "You may not play the role of God. You will be dealt with accordingly!"

Beck's eyes widened in disbelief. "But she is the one that—"

"Silence!" Raphael's voice thundered. "Selene is my responsibility. Her mistakes have been addressed. Her guilt does not give you innocence."

Beck started to say, "It's not…," but then Micah shot fire from his eyes into Beck's mouth, silencing him.

"What deal did you make?" I asked, my eyes boring into Beck.

Micah spit more flames into Beck's mouth, then shook him roughly. "Answer her!"

Beck glared at me, then answered, "C-convince you to go t-to Rhea and get the scrolls."

"Which dark one did you strike this deal with?" Raphael asked.

"The d-deal…was with Moros," Beck stammered. "B-but others of higher power w-were involved. I d-don't know who."

Raphael's mouth quirked. "Are you leaving anything out?"

Beck swallowed hard as he raised his hand and pointed in my direction. "She doesn't belong here! I was doing all of us a favor! She's on their side—"

Micah blasted more blue flames at Beck, silencing him for good this time. Then he gave a final nod in our direction. "My guardian will be stripped of his powers, effective immediately. I will seek the remainder of his retribution from *him*. Thank you for bringing this to light, regardless of the pain it also brought forth." At that moment, Micah and Beck vanished.

Completely shaken, I let out a breath without even realizing I'd been holding it in. My face was soaked with tears, my throat constricted and dry. I slumped back against Raphael, feeling complete anguish. "Beck was my friend. How could he have done something so cruel?" I wondered aloud.

"Perhaps he was envious…or jealous," Elijah offered.

I looked his way, seeing just plain blue eyes with no trace of the burning intensity of before. I shrugged, then pulled away from my archangel. "What will happen to him?"

"I must go now," Elijah announced.

Raphael flashed him a smile, then gave a small nod.

"Thank you," I said just as Elijah disappeared, taking with him the flaming blue walls that concealed us. Then I met Raphael's gaze squarely.

"I cannot predict exactly what will happen to Beck," he explained. "Micah will make that decision with *his* guidance just as I must do with you."

"But before you do anything, please let me get Caitlyn back. Please."

"Once she passes, the light will have her, regardless of who has hold over her now," was his answer, but it just wasn't good enough for my taste.

"Raphael, you must let me save her," I pleaded. "Grant me permission to go to my dark friends one last time. They can help me. I swear it on my existence. And then you can do with me as you see fit."

"Selene, I just can't do that." He closed his eyes and shook his head. "What if your so-called dark *friends* are involved with taking your charge?"

"It wasn't my friends!" I shot back, feeling confident in my words. "They would never do anything to hurt me."

"We'll see about that," he replied doubtfully. Then his head twitched as he instantly became alert. "Mihr is close by. I must go now and inform him of the situation with Aurora."

"But what about Caitlyn? Raphael, we can't just leave her—"

"I cannot help you with your charge. Your actions have decided her fate—more than once now. Please let things be. I will summon you once I've decided your consequences." With that he vanished so he could inform Aurora's archangel that Ezariah was looking for her. Maybe Aurora would be all too willing to run right back into the arms of her former lover. I understood all too well how easy it was to love those of darkness—even with the threat of becoming fallen.

My chest tightened. I felt more overwhelmed than I could handle. I'd betrayed my charge, then my friend had betrayed me. Caitlyn. I couldn't just leave her with those wretched shadow sliders, but I had a feeling the only way to get her back was through Ezariah himself. My only chance of fighting that powerful demon (yes, demon; that's what happens to angels when they fall) would be with the help of my forbidden friends. Somehow Ezariah got his hands on some extremely potent magic, but as I'd learned earlier, I knew someone with access to that same level of power. But how far did Luke's favors go with him, and would he be willing to help me? Only one way to find out. Raphael definitely wasn't going to like this.

23

NIGHT HAD FALLEN OVER A COLD, CRISP Denver like a velvety black sheet with stars that resembled sparkling crystals. Surrounding me were trees swallowed by shadows, leaving their true size to a human's imagination. But I could sense their depths, and feel their shapes, and I wondered how much of that ability was still angelic. Everything I could do seemed to have a different vibe. My angel powers still pulsed inside me, but there was a deeper thrum I didn't fully understand. Still, I couldn't focus on that now—I was here to find someone. And I didn't have much time. I'd already lost precious minutes to those annoying orbing side-effects before shimmering into my human form. Thankfully, the one I sought was somewhere in the shadows just ahead.

Suddenly there was a cool rush of wind, and then I was squeezed inside two hard, strong arms. "Selene! I've been so worried. Please tell me this is really you."

"It's really..."—my voice was muffled against his chest—"me." I stretched my arms around him, trying to pull him closer still. Another swish of movement and his soft lips were caressing mine, causing heat to spill across my face, seeping down the back of my neck. Then reality set in, and my ticking time clock started back up. I pushed away from Cole, my breathing heavy and short. "We can't. There's no time. I needed to see you before..." I let my words trail off with the weight of their meaning pressing heavy on my heart. My chest tightened and I sniffled back a few tears.

"Before what?" he asked with concern in his tone. "What happened to you? Where did you go?"

How to put it quickly? "My archangel summoned me to Europa. He's not happy with me, but thankfully there are other issues he must address before handing down my sentence." I shook my head with a sigh. "I'm not sure how much time I have, but I must try to free Caitlyn from those demons with whatever moments I have left."

His lips compressed, but he said nothing. The look in his eyes was all I needed to see anyway.

"Cole, I don't have a choice," I stammered, then filled him in on the rest of my plan.

"You have no guarantee they'll help you, or that it would make a difference even if they did," he said at last, clearly very upset.

"But it's worth a shot. Caitlyn deserves that much at least."

"Why? Because it's all *your* fault?" he shot back. "If you'd never done this, or never done that, then she'd never be in trouble at all?" He rolled his eyes. "Selene, you can't live by hindsight! 'Coulda, shoulda, woulda' doesn't change the reality of the situation. Quit dwelling on that!"

My teeth ground together. "I'm going to dwell on it until I save her! I'm not giving up on my charge!"

Cole waved his hand. "But what about your consequences? If you keep this up, you may lose…" He sighed. "Every thing."

"I may have already lost everything"—my tone sounding subdued. "This might be the last time you ever see me, and this is how you want it to go down?"

"What do you mean by that? Your archangel would never destroy you."

"No, you're probably right about that, but it isn't fully up to him—"

"If that happens, I'll find you!" he shot back with a sharp tone. "If you become fallen, I'm still going to love you." He scooped me up in his arms and his lips crushed mine.

I savored the kiss for a moment longer than I felt comfortable. After all, the heat from that kiss would fuel me for the treacherous journey ahead. My hand cupped his cheek, feeling his jawbone beneath the soft flesh. "I love you, Cole. Always."

"I love you too."

I stepped away, closed my eyes, and had begun focusing on Luke's aura when Cole snatched my hand. "I'm coming with you!"

My eyes shot open. "If anything were to happen to you, it would destroy me. Besides"—I shrugged my shoulders—"you and Luke can barely stand to be in the same room, let alone fight side-by-side in some kind of black-magic-demon war."

"Selene, if the situation was reversed, you'd never stay behind. Please don't ask that of me now." His gaze narrowed. "I'd rather you not be near that vampire without me there with you."

Cole was right. If he were in trouble, I'd be there no matter what he said. So why should I expect it to be any different when I'm the one in hot water? Plus, knowing how jealous vampires were, Cole was actually handling the Luke thing considerably well. I had to give him credit there too. But what if bringing Cole would make Luke not want to help me? Perhaps I could go straight to Huron, but going through Luke would certainly increase my chances of gaining the voodoo Indian's help. I considered my options a few moments longer, then finally decided to let Cole tag along. "But if it poses any kind of problem helping Caitlyn, then you will leave," I added seriously. "No questions asked."

He nodded. "Done."

"Okay." My fingers tightened around his, then once again, I focused on the one who hopefully would help us.

About an hour later, I'd regained my memory, and I was sitting in Cole's lap staring across the table at a very upset Luke. His arms were folded in front of him as he glared at me. "The nerve you have to bring him here," Luke stated irritably, raking Cole over with his eyes.

Cole's hands were on the table, and his fingers started tapping against the wood. I nervously looked over at him, holding my breath, waiting for the verbal assault that was building, I could sense, on Cole's tongue, and it made me wonder what all had been said while I'd been recovering from my orbing side effects. But after a beat, Cole's lips quirked but he didn't speak.

I sighed with relief, then turned my attention back to Luke. "I need your help."

"That's becoming a pattern here," he smarted as his eyes locked on mine.

"Ezariah isn't who he claims," I explained. "He really *is* fallen, and has become the demon ruler of Rhea. Which explains why shadow sliders and messenger demons have gotten involved."

Astonishment flashed across Luke's face. "You know this for sure? How?"

Cole leaned forward, his chest pressing into my back. "Her archangel told her, right before he promised a severe punishment if she tried to do anything about it."

I elbowed Cole's solid stomach. "I'm in big trouble whether I help Caitlyn now or not."

"What am I supposed to do?" Luke asked. "Go back to Rhea and fight every demon that attacks us while you return the scrolls and grab your human?"

I shook my head slowly. "I don't think it will be that easy. There's something else going on here, I just don't know exactly what it is." Then I filled him in on what had happened with Beck in Europa.

"So the whole thing was a setup?" Luke asked, his eyes wide with shock.

A chill gripped my spine as I considered his question. If Beck had been talking with dark ones, then he'd known of the deal I'd made with Moros. Once he confirmed what had happened to my charge, he waited until he saw Raphael and I arguing in Europa, then approached me as if he'd overheard our fight. When, in fact, he'd already known everything and his side of the deal was to get me to Rhea, where Ezariah would be waiting. But what I couldn't wrap my head around was if Ezariah wanted me, then why did he let me leave with the scrolls in the first place? I nodded grimly. "Yeah, I guess the whole thing was a setup."

"Are you going to help us or not?" Cole asked flatly.

Luke's gaze hardened. "If I do choose to help, it will be for her...not you."

Anger and jealousy thick enough to suffocate drizzled out of Cole's aura. I felt the vibrations of a growl building on my back, but surprisingly, Cole stifled it back. I kept my wary eyes on Luke, hopeful he'd agree to help. "Please," I said sincerely. "If we don't have access to the dark ones that helped us on Charon, then we need Cole to come with us. And we definitely need Huron."

Luke studied me a moment. "My favors with Huron have expired, Angel. The only reason he helped me get you from Nempha was because he didn't want to disrupt the natural balance of good and evil. And you being in hell was definitely messing with that balance."

"Isn't it more messed up that they've taken an innocent human?" I asked, fighting tears.

"Selene, forget him!" Cole spat. "Let's just go, return the scrolls and get Caitlyn. If there's trouble, *I'll* back you up."

Luke stood up in a rush, slamming his fists on the table. "I never said I wouldn't help!" He squared his shoulders, fixing his eyes on mine. "You're not going without me."

Cole let out a threatening growl. I nervously rubbed the top of his thigh, hoping to remind him of the promise he'd made. When he didn't do anything else, I let out a sigh of relief and refocused my attention on Luke. "Let's hope we find Huron in a cooperative mood." I reached across the table to grab Luke's hand, twining my fingers around Cole's with my other one.

"No," Luke said, staring at my awaiting hand. "No orbing yet. We'll go to him…my way."

Cole's arm wrapped around my waist, his grasp on my hand unbreakable. "I'm taking her," he warned in a steely tone.

Luke's brows furrowed. "Fine. But if you don't remember where you're going, then you better keep up!" In a swish of movement, he was gone.

"Hold on, Selene," Cole informed. Then we flashed off after Luke.

Huron's bar was packed with preternatural beings, so we were instructed to go to the back room and wait for him. Cole and I sat next to each other at the empty poker table, while Luke paced anxiously along the side of the room. If you'd asked me the other day of I'd ever be in the same room with these two vamps, I would've answered, "never." Yet here we sat, waiting to discover who else would be joining us in the battle to save my charge. And just when I thought things couldn't get any weirder…they did.

The door opened and a petite girl waltzed in the room, her silken red hair flowing behind her. A smile spread across Annabel's smooth, porcelain-looking face as she pulled out a chair across from me and sat down, her eyes an enigma of obsidian that I could feel at the edge of my mind, and I quickly looked away knowing exactly what she intended to do.

Luke came to stand behind her, placing his hand on her shoulder, fingers digging into the skin. "What the hell are you doing here?"

"Relax," she said in a calm, taunting voice. "I only came by to see Miss Angel here." She nodded toward me. "You left so soon before, I totally missed you."

"If I'd known you were still here, I would have *totally* stuck around," was my icy reply.

Annabel frowned, folding her hands in front of her chest. "After everything I did to help you," she scoffed.

Cole scooted closer and scooped my hand inside his, keeping his eyes on the dangerous vampire across from us. "Selene is grateful for your help. And so am I."

Luke's grip tightened on her shoulder. "Leave"—his tone filled with challenge.

Annabel's eyes glistened the color of midnight with a bluish hue, and then transitioned to pitch-black with a pitiless glace of the darkest shade of purple. "I'll leave when I'm ready." Her voice liquid steel.

There was a whoosh of air, then I was standing next to the back wall, Cole's body protectively in front of me. I craned my neck to the side, peering around him. Annabel was pinned against the side wall, Luke holding her by the neck with a single hand. She was snarling, fangs extended and dripping. "We're not playing this again, Annabel," he warned.

"You idiot!" she hissed. "Let me go!"

"You can let her down, Luke."

Huron stood in the doorway, his gaze sliding from one side of the room to the other. He walked in, closing the door behind him. "I assure you she won't touch Selene on my premises."

"But I can smell the desire all over her," Luke countered, still holding tightly to Annabel's neck.

Annabel kicked her feet as she attempted to free herself. Luke released her in the same moment and she tumbled to the ground, her butt breaking the fall. "Imbecile," she mumbled as she slowly stood up, rubbing her neck.

Huron took a seat at the poker table. "Selene, please." He motioned to one of the empty chairs.

I moved around Cole and sat down across from the Indian host. The vampires followed suit and took their seats too—Cole on my right, Luke on my left. Annabel tossed her hair back as she pulled out the chair next to Huron. In one swift motion she was sitting, her hands folded together on the table. I glanced at the vampires on either side of me, and both were casting threatening glares toward the childlike vampire across the way. Huron impatiently cleared his throat, his eyes focused on me. "I know why you're here and I'm afraid I can't help this time."

An argument built up on my tongue, but I swallowed it back. "Even if I'm willing to fall for this?" I asked once I'd regained my voice.

"Selene, no!" Cole exclaimed at the same time Luke said, "Angel!"

I ignored the male vampires and kept my eyes on Huron.

"Just because you're willing to fall," the voodoo Indian explained, "doesn't mean I should risk everything to go up against those demons."

"But they took my charge," I countered, tears clouding my eyes.

Huron rubbed his fingers across his chin. "They only have her because of the ritual you performed with black magic."

"Why? Why would they take her?"—my voice breaking as tears slid down my cheeks. "I had no intention of not returning the scrolls."

Huron considered me for a moment, then answered, "They want you."

A chill gripped my spine, even though I knew the dark ones wanted me. "I know. They could've fought me when I got the scrolls, and then again when I returned them. There would be no reason to take my charge."

"Unless that was the plan all along," Huron suggested. "Maybe they can use your human to their advantage somehow?"

"The whole thing reeks of a trap!" Luke stated.

Cole took my hand and gently squeezed. "There's no chance you'll just destroy the scrolls and leave Caitlyn where she is?"

I met Cole's eyes. "No matter what it takes, I'm not leaving her. Please don't ask me to do that."

Acceptance flashed on his face as he nodded.

"Don't worry, Angel," Luke said. "We're not going to leave your girl."

Annabel's lips quirked, her eyes softening a bluish violet before saying in a shrill voice, "I'll help you."

That statement got everyone's gaze on Annabel. "You'll help, huh?" Luke asked. "At what price though?"

"We're not paying anything," Cole's voice seething, his eyes pure steel. "You're not drinking from Selene!"

"Fine," she pouted, thumping her hands against the table. "Yes, I'd love to taste the angel, but if that isn't an option, I'll still help."

Luke narrowed his gaze at her. "Why?"

"Because I asked her to" was what Huron answered, his lips pulling into a grin. "Luckily for you, she's gone and gotten herself in debt again."

Now all eyes were on me. I nervously bit my bottom lip as I considered the voodoo Indian's offer. "Well if we can't have your help," I told Huron at last, "then this is the next best thing." We'd just gained another ally. Three vampires could do a lot of damage to a horde of low-level demons, and that would free me up to take on Ezariah. A new wave of confidence washed over me. Things really were going to work out.

"There's one more thing I can do for you," Huron went on. "I can cloak you so that whatever black magic that demon uses won't have any effect on you."

His explanation reminded me of the way I could mask auras. And that would definitely come in handy. I bobbed my head and told him thank you, then slid my gaze expectantly around the room. "All right, let's get moving."

"What's the plan?" Cole asked.

"I'll drop us in near the mouth of the cave. There's plenty of thick vegetation and rocks to take cover." My eyes settled on Annabel as I went on. "I need you three to distract the lower-level demons so I can get to Ezariah. He won't be expecting my immunity to his black magic, so whatever his plan is, he'll quickly find out it won't work."

"Angel," Luke said with concern, "what about when we first arrive? I can help you get into position."

Immediately my thoughts were on my orbing issues. Luke was the only one that could get through to me when I was in that amnesiac state. Cole had noticed it earlier at Luke's place, but we hadn't had time to discuss it yet. I'd recognized Luke, and pretty much wanted to go to him, but Cole had refused to give me up and kept me in a death grip on his lap. Still, Rhea would be different. We couldn't take any chances. Cole was not going to like this, but I was hoping he'd keep his promise from before. I swallowed hard and shot Cole a lasered gaze. I needed to choose my words wisely since we couldn't openly discuss this in front of Annabel. The last thing I needed was for her to discover the best time to try to snack on my neck.

Before I had a chance to speak, Cole pulled his hand free and folded his arms in front of his chest. "I know what you're going to say and I absolutely hate it." His eyes became darker, appearing bottomless as he went on, and my chest tightened at the fear of him voicing something I'd hoped would remain a secret. "But I love you" was all he said as he opened his arms, and gently stroked my cheek with his fingertips. "...and I'll do what you need me to do."

Luke started to say, "Give me a bre——," but I swung around and cast him a challenging glare.

When I was certain his lips were sealed for good, I returned my attention to Cole. "Thank you. I love you." I leaned a little in his direction and then he was there. The sensual, gentle suction had me parting my lips so his tongue could tease the tip of mine. My hands pressed against his cheeks, fingers digging into the soft flesh, massaging around the hardness of his cheekbone as I hungrily sucked on his bottom lip. Huron cleared his throat, reminding me we had an audience. Regretfully pulling away from Cole, I swept my lips across his one last time.

In unison, we all stood and followed Huron to the cave below.

24

A LOUD BOOM ERUPTED, followed by a chorus of high-pitched shrieking, wailing, and growling. The ground shook with the force of a medium-level earthquake, but it was enough to make my breath catch in my throat. I remembered the wormish beast that shook the cave in Nempha. And then all my other memories flooded back at once.

My back was pressed against a massive boulder and Luke was crouched over me, shielding me from flying debris that shot sideways at us and rained down from overhead. Trees wrapped with lush green vines and chunky bushes were sparsely scattered around us, a few large stones interspersed amongst the greenery, and the mouth of the cave was no more than twenty yards ahead. I tapped Luke's chest and moved to the side just enough for me to see Cole and Annabel in a raging battle with about a dozen soldier demons. Moments earlier, I'd been cowering under Luke, not remembering where I was or why I was there. But now I remembered what I needed to do, and there wasn't any more time for fear.

"Are you ready?" Luke asked in a loud whisper.

I met his eyes, then nodded, ignoring the growing tightness in my chest.

Luke rose, gesturing toward the battle zone. "I'm gonna go help them. Good luck, Angel. I lo..." He let his words trail off as he lowered his lips to my cheek, his soft touch leaving behind a warmth that sparked an instant wave of guilt. *It's just his blood making me feel that way*, I reminded myself, then gave him a final nod and dashed out from behind the boulder.

As light burst from my body, all the demons suddenly cowered, a few of them wailing in agony. Cole, Annabel, and Luke were immune, however, since I'd added some protection to the mask I'd placed on their auras. Cole and Annabel sprung on the demons closest to them, twisting their necks with a crunch, then yanking their heads off with one swift jerk. Luke dismembered the head off his demon, then sprung to the next one. But as the number of our attackers dwindled, another surge of soldier demons fanned out around us using the trees and boulders for cover, yet I couldn't keep standing here illuminating the area for my allies any longer. I needed to get moving before even more demons showed up to the fight. With a final blast of power, I pushed my light a little further over the expansive space, then hurried inside the cave.

I shifted into my angel form as I ran along the narrow, musky trail that led to Ezariah's room. My bare feet splashed in shallow puddles, then adapted to a coarse surface as I passed a bed of rocks mixed with moist sand. There was a pungent odor that definitely hadn't been there before. Acrid, stale, sulfuric. With my hand I covered my nose and mouth and kept moving. Just as I was about to reach the doorway to the scroll keeper's room, an invisible blast of power hit me with the force of a wrecking ball. My hands went up, shielding the next thrust of dark energy. Yet in the next instant panic seized me when I realized what might be waiting for me in that room. It wouldn't have anything to do with black magic, since thanks to Huron, I was immune. That only left one thing that was powerful enough to hit me with dark energy, and that meant the protective seals in Ezariah's room would have been disabled.

I swallowed my fear and plunged into the room, keeping my arms out as a shield. My body glowed like embers and invisible waves of energy shuddered from my shoulders to my hands. Ezariah stood beside the rustic bookshelves on the right side of the room. But that wasn't what held my attention. Over by the fireplace was a massive demon. He towered about eight or nine feet tall with a horse-like lower body complete with hoofed feet. His top half was more like a man, with slick red skin stretched tightly over large, chiseled muscles. His triangular face featured deep, high cheekbones and sunken black eyes that matched the black claws on his hands as an alternative to fingernails. Instead of hair, two huge spiral horns protruded from the top of his head, their sleek, glossy blackness shining against the pulsing flames of the fireplace. A faint cloud of sulfuric smoke floated around the room. This master demon must have just arrived from hell, bringing some of that wretched odor with him along with that unnerving thrust of power.

His dark, bottomless eyes locked onto me as his thin lips curled into a grin. "Perfect timing, sweet angel of light," his voice rumbled, deep and sadistic.

I lowered my arms and slowly closed my mouth, which had been hanging open in shock. "Typhon"—my words barely audible, but his grin widened so I knew he had heard.

His laughter erupted from the depths of his body and rumbled throughout the room. Everything in me wanted to turn around and run, but I could sense that Caitlyn was close. I cast a quick glance around but didn't see her. Ezariah stroked his beard, his eyes widening with excitement. "Where is she?" I screamed as waves of energy throbbed on my fingertips. Suddenly, my hands burst with swirls of brilliant white light, and the glow over my body increased too.

Typhon swung his gaze toward Ezariah. "Now!" the master demon ordered.

That's when two things happened at once. Ezariah started chanting something in a language I couldn't understand. And the scrolls tucked in my bosom burst into flames. In a panic I grabbed them, burning my hand as I threw them across the room. A sharp sting lingered on my fingers, and that's when I noticed my light had gone out. Ezariah was still babbling that incantation, but his voice became distant background noise when I glanced down at my body. My dress wasn't white anymore. It was an ashy gray color now with the torn, muddy edge draped over my bare feet. I felt my eyes widen as a paralyzing fear spread through me. My chest was sore from where the scrolls had been ablaze, and I delicately rubbed it with my fingertips, gasping when I felt an indentation on my skin. I looked closer and my breath caught again. There was some kind of symbol I'd never seen before etched into my flesh like a tattoo, and that's when I felt my angel form flicker to my human body—still wearing the gray-colored dress.

"The process is almost complete," a cool voice said.

I glanced up to see Typhon with a huge grin on his face, exposing yellowish teeth and fangs. "What have you done?" I asked, disgust in my tone.

"Soon, you will be mine. And the light will no longer reside in you," Typhon replied as he took a few lumbering steps my way.

I looked down at myself, then over at Ezariah, who was still chanting. His eyes were rolled in the back of his head, exposing just the white parts, and his hands were held open in front of him with the palms facing up. "You can't force me out of the light!" I exclaimed, feeling overwhelmed with desperation. "It is not your choice!"

"That's where you're wrong, sweet little angel." Typhon roared with laughter, and once he'd settled down he went on. "By using the sea scrolls to rescue your human, you unleashed the darkness inside you, which began the deterioration of your precious light. Of course, I needed your human unguarded to set the plan in motion. My minions were ready to strike once the deal was made with Moros. And your confidant only made things easier with his willingness to tell you about the ancient sea scrolls. He knew you'd be all too eager to retrieve them and use their power to save your human. And, of course, he would be more believable than any of my demons informing you of the same."

"Beck," I mumbled as anger flushed me with the thought of how involved he'd really been. Then I returned my attention to the master demon, realizing he was still babbling.

"…my advantage, you vanished with the scrolls, giving my servant more time to complete the process. And only to add to my convenience, Luke sent word to the Underworld that he was searching for you, and I knew it was just a matter of time before he'd find you because of his alliance with Huron. So instead of using other resources to help locate you, I sent shadow sliders to relay the message of having your human and then I sat back and waited for you to come straight to me." He lumbered closer, now just a few feet away from me. "You see, you may not be fallen yet…" He rubbed his chin, an eerie grin stretching across his face. "But you will be fallen before you leave this lair."

"No," I replied grimly, shaking my head, the impact of everything the master demon just said throbbing inside my mind. He'd played me from the beginning, using Luke and Huron as pawns in his little game.

Suddenly Typhon roared with laughter again, while Ezariah stopped chanting and thrust both hands up. I sensed invisible waves of power surging right for me, could feel them getting closer as pressure built inside my head and my chest compressed until I thought I'd explode. At the instant I thought the dark energy would overtake me, it suddenly weakened and faded. Yet I could still sense it all around me—like a noxious gas hovering around an unseen force field sheathing my body. The dark magic couldn't touch me. *Thank you, Huron*, I thought with relief. I released a deep breath, regaining some confidence. "You cannot touch me!" I screamed, releasing all the light inside me. But nothing happened. No light, no glow, and my dress was still gray. So I did the next best thing I could think of—act like nothing was wrong.

"Finish it now!" Typhon roared to Ezariah. "Or I will finish you!"

Ezariah attempted to blast me with that black magic again, and even though I felt its weight all over my body, it still couldn't penetrate Huron's protection spell. "It's not…it's not…working," Ezariah mumbled in disbelief.

"But you said if she performed the ritual with the blood of a vampire in her system, she'd be mine!" was Typhon's thunderous response.

Ezariah took a few steps back, cowering from the demon. "It should work!" he wailed in a panic. "Look at her"—his finger pointing at me—"her gown is changing. The ritual worked, but something is stopping it."

"Fix it now!" Typhon ordered with impatience. Then he charged me and grabbed my neck with his massive hand. "Maybe you need more vampire blood in you," he wondered as he raised me off the ground.

My hands flung over his, trying to pry him off my neck. But he was too strong and I couldn't budge him. "Please," my voice wheezing.

"Bring me a vampire!" Typhon demanded as he flung me down like a rag doll. I skidded across the ground, then rolled over and stood up as fast as I could.

As if perfectly timed, about a dozen soldier demons marched into the room with three beaten, restrained vampires. My heart sunk as I watched a demon bash Cole in the side, while another smashed his fist in the back of Luke's head. Annabel was shoved forward, rattling the chains that held her arms against her body.

"It was that one," Ezariah said, gesturing a finger toward Luke.

Meaning the master demon didn't know which vampire had given me blood, but somehow the former guardian did. Typhon trotted over and grabbed Luke by the shoulder. "How much did she take from you?" he asked, digging his claws into Luke's flesh.

Luke turned away, spitting out blood. When he didn't say anything, Typhon squeezed him harder. Crimson trails slicked out, then smoke rose from the wound. Luke screamed out in agony but Typhon didn't loosen his hold on him.

"Stop it!" I screamed, my heart crumbling. "Please! He gave me blood four times. Maybe about two or three pints worth."

"Then that's not the problem," Typhon stated with a grimace. Then, he plunged his clawed hand inside Luke's chest, and with a jerk of his wrist, shredded my vampire ally's heart. Luke cried out, his voice fading from garbled grunts to silence as Typhon removed his crimson-soaked hand and tossed Luke to the floor, my friend's torso resembling bloody, raw meat.

"No!" I screamed, rushing to my vampire ally and kneeling down beside his lifeless body. "Why...would you kill him?" I demanded, casting my glare on the red monstrous demon.

Typhon half laughed, raking me with an expectant gaze. "Do you want to save him?"—his voice taunting.

I nodded, saying "Yes" while cradling Luke in my arms.

"Selene! No! Don't!" Cole shouted, his chains clinking with his movement.

I glanced at Cole and then at Typhon, who was still eagerly watching me. "What do I have to do?" I asked, my eyes settling on the demon.

"He needs the blood of an angel, and then he will be saved," Typhon coaxed by way of explanation.

"No, Selene! Don't do it!" Cole begged. "He's gone. Let him go. That's what he would've wanted."

I gazed at my lover, wanting nothing more than to listen to him, to prove that my heart only belonged to him, and that I could walk away from Luke forever. Cole's brows furrowed as his eyes continued to beg me not to give Luke my blood. Tears welled in my eyes, and I choked them back as I silently mouthed "I'm sorry" to Cole. Then I looked back down at Luke, ready to do whatever I could to save his life.

Cole started to scream and plead, bringing my attention to him once more. A few more soldier demons rushed over to hold him back. His voice became muffled when a demon placed his hand on top of Cole's mouth. I watched helplessly. There was nothing I could do at the moment to help him anyway.

"You'll need this." I glanced up to find Ezariah kneeling beside me with a dagger in his hand. Without a second thought, I took the dagger and sliced it through my wrist.

Suddenly, a deafening explosion blasted through the room, shaking the ground with enough force to rock me backward. I tried to crawl to Luke, but the energy held me down and I couldn't budge. My skin crawled with the invisible force like tiny ants scattering along my flesh. The pressure increased, my insides expanding beyond what I could handle. My heart thundered so hard, I could feel it all the way in my head. The tears I'd fought to contain slicked down my face with a freedom I wished I had. Then everything started warping around me until finally the pressure and energy faded.

Realizing I could move, I crawled to Luke's side, then glanced around the room. The blast had taken everyone down, and a subtle luminescent blue glow hovered over the room like fog, keeping all the dark ones cowered to the floor with their arms shielding their faces. In the center of the room, there were swirls of twinkling white light, and then Raphael appeared. His snow-white cloak was flung back, fully exposing his sculpted upper body shimmering with a golden tan. He moved closer, his white pants flowing with each step.

"You are not welcome here!" Typhon called up while keeping his arm over his face.

"You have no rule over me, demon," Raphael spat. Then he looked at me, his expression grim. "Selene, get away from that dark one!"

I sniffled as tears streamed down my face. "I can't let him die."

"Whether one lives or dies is not up to you. If you give that creature of darkness your blood," Raphael warned, "then you will forever be lost to the light."

"But I've shared my blood before," I admitted, my chest tightening as a pit formed in my stomach.

Raphael's brows furrowed with bitter acceptance of what I'd just said. He shook his head slowly, releasing a disappointed sigh. "Regardless of what you've done, for which there are consequences, you are now marked by darkness. Now, anything you do against what I've told you will strike you from the light without a single shred of mercy."

Swallowing to moisten a throat gone dry, I slowly stared down at Luke's face. A few tears dripped off my chin and splashed on his cheek, and I rubbed my fingers through the wetness, smearing dirt with his blood. "What about Caitlyn?" I asked, glancing at my severed wrist. The bleeding had slowed, and thick dark clots were forming on the edges of the cut.

"She does not belong here," Raphael answered at once.

"Did the ritual work?" My gaze drifted upward, meeting Raphael's eyes.

His frown told me the answer, but then he shook his head, saying, "You never completed the ritual. Your breath for your charge's." He closed his eyes, and as he opened them, Caitlyn materialized in his arms. Even though I could sense my charge was still alive, she hung lifeless in my archangel's arms. A wave of helplessness and sorrow flooded me all at once. My charge would soon be moving on to the light, and I would never see her again. And my friend, and vampire ally, whom I'd grown to feel so strongly for, would be lost forever too. All of this was all because of me. Caitlyn shouldn't be moving on yet; it just wasn't her time. Nor should Luke be fully dead by Typhon crushing his heart. Everything I'd done up to this moment was all for nothing.

Still, Raphael was here to give me another chance. Maybe I could get it right this time around? Even though I was marked by darkness, there was still a way out. Hope for a new tomorrow. And Cole would be there with me—once I'd fulfilled whatever my punishment was. Unless my new lease on life, so to speak, came with the terms of leaving Cole forever. But at least he wouldn't be dead, and I could move on knowing that he was somewhere out there. Unlike Caitlyn or Luke.

"Selene," Raphael called out. "Come now. We must go."

I looked at my archangel with love and admiration. He'd dealt with so much from me, and he was still willing to fight for me. Unconditional love. Something humans weren't able to give. Nor were dark ones supposed to even know what love was, and yet, that had been proven wrong by two vampires. At that moment, my decision became crystal clear. I silently mouthed "I'm sorry" to Raphael, then grabbed the dagger lying about a foot away from me and slid its blade over my existing cut. My archangel screamed my name as I brought my bloody wrist over Luke's mouth. Then I recited the ritual of breath and plunged the blade through my heart. The last thing I heard was Raphael weeping for me, and Typhon shouting something I couldn't understand as a diaphanous wave of energy thrust through my body and a sea of blackness engulfed me.

25

MY SURROUNDINGS WERE PITCH-BLACK. I closed my eyes and focused on my light, but after numerous attempts, nothing happened. Panic clawed up my spine, and my breathing grew short and ragged. My bare feet squished into the muddy floor as I took a careful step forward. Reaching out to my right, my hands brushed something hard and flat. I patted around, finding more of that same solid surface. A wall, I presumed. After another moment speculating, I realized there was another wall on my left. A faint light glinted off in the distance ahead. I swung around, only to find more darkness behind me. I screamed aloud, my voice reverberating both ways down the corridor. That meant there were two ways I could go—head toward the light, or go blindly into the shadows.

After making my decision quickly, I set off toward the light. Uneasiness spread through me with each step, my failed attempts to use my power reminding me of being in Nempha, and it terrified me. *Why wasn't I dead?* I wondered as I moved with cautious steps. I'd sacrificed myself to save Caitlyn and Luke. Why couldn't I sense them? Where were they? Or better yet…where was I? Frantically, I ran my fingers across my chest where the scrolls had left an imprint, then lower where I'd plunged the dagger in my heart, but miraculously there was no hole and my skin was smooth as if nothing had ever happened.

"Raphael," I called out, only to hear my own voice echoing back to me. I gave a long sigh, and kept moving.

Only the light never got any closer. Regardless of how far I'd walked, I never seemed to make any progress. The light still glinted far off in the distance, mocking me with its shimmer. I turned around and the same vast darkness still awaited me. Was I supposed to head that way, since I was now fallen? Was this what had happened to all the angels who fell before me? They kept trying to move to the light, but only the darkness would accept them?

I swallowed hard, feeling gooseflesh scatter across my arms. *Not yet*, I scolded myself, then turned around and took off toward the light once more.

Except the tunnel seemed endless, and I never gained any ground in reaching the light. I felt like a hamster running on its wheel, never really going anywhere. So it was time to embrace the reality of my situation, and as I whirled around to head the other way, a shockwave rattled through the corridor with enough force to topple me over. My knees and hands slammed against the mucky floor, but at least it was soft enough to cushion my fall. As the ground stopped shaking, a thrust of invisible energy blasted through the tunnel, popping my ears with its pressure. It forced me backward against the wall, holding me there. I wriggled back and forth, trying to break free, but I couldn't budge an inch.

Then, a glowing diaphanous being materialized in the darkness in front of me. There was a subtle human resemblance to its transparent features. A hooded gray cloak covered its body, shielding most of its head from view. The squared jaw gave it a more masculine look, though the rest of its face was hidden in shadow. Without seeing it move, it grabbed my shoulders with what appeared to be its hands, and pressed me hard against the stone wall with an unbreakable grasp. Then, suddenly, the being stepped back and I fell to my feet with a *squoosh*. "Who are you?" I asked in surprise.

Something red glowed under its hood, and as the being tilted its head back, I could see it was his eyes. "I am your guide. Your fate has hung in the balance, but now I have come here for you." Its voice was low and gravelly—but definitely masculine.

"What…um…where are we?" My tone throaty.

"Between the realms of physical and spiritual," came his instant reply.

A lump barreled its way up my throat, but I swallowed it back to free my voice. "Am I fallen?" I asked, even though I felt like I already knew the answer.

He gave a slight nod and answered, "Yesss," with a hiss.

I stood nervously for a moment, waiting for something to happen. But when nothing did, I asked, "Aren't you taking me to my demon master?" I mean, wasn't that how this worked? Fallen angels were dominated by the demon ruler of whatever world they were sent to.

"You will not be mastered," was his response. "Never before has an angel of light sacrificed their life for that of a dark one. Let alone, the human you attempted to spare."

I stepped forward in a rush. "Are they alive?" Please God, let them be alive.

"I cannot answer that for you. But your attempts to save them will not go unseen."

"You can't answer because you don't know...or can't tell me?"

His head tilted slightly as if he were studying every feature on my face. His red eyes brightened, and I could see their disturbing glow within his hood. Several long minutes passed and twice I was tempted to ask again— or even beg him. Then finally he said, "Both," only confusing me more.

I shook my head, a desperate plea building up on my tongue. I swallowed it back though, knowing in my heart this thing wasn't going to be of any help.

Suddenly the being moved closer, just inches from me. "Angel of light"—his voice echoing through the tunnel—"guardian of the supreme high, you are now fallen from grace." He raised both translucent hands, the cloak draping from his arms. "You will not be sanctioned to one place, for your ability to orb shall remain. Though some will try, none may reign over you. You will have all the power necessary to keep order to the balance between good and evil. Although I am not your ruler, I am your guide, and thus empowered to remove this privilege should you not heed to your duties. For this is the first and only time a fallen angel will be spared. And you will have but one chance to remain this way. For you, Selene, are fallen, but I have shown you the greatest of mercies for your selfless acts."

Swiftly the being moved into me and I was immersed inside his cloak. Everything was foggy, like entering a dark gray storm cloud, and I couldn't see beyond the sheer thickness. Intense pressure threatened to crush my lungs and my ears were popping uncontrollably. My heart thundered inside my chest, and pressure built up in my head to where I feared it would burst. In my stomach there was a violent rolling and twisting, and I wanted to hunch over and cradle it. Only I couldn't move. I was frozen with intense waves of energy pulsing over my flesh like static electricity, adding chaos to the maddening slew of afflictions I could only pray would cease.

Then, all of a sudden, I was thrown down, the cloak receding from my body like a sheer cover being yanked off. A vast open field lay around me, sheets of greenery coating the ground. It was daylight, the sky a deep shade of blue decorated with large fluffy, white clouds that looked a lot like shredded cotton. Hills lined the horizon, as far as the eye could see, with a faint layer of haziness that blended them into the atmosphere. As I rose I glanced over myself, gasping when I saw the black-styled combat boots covering my feet. My gaze trailed upward, following the stretchy black pants that covered my legs all the way up to the matching tank-styled tee. I ran a hand through my hair, which thankfully was the same wavy caramel hair that I'd always had.

There was a whoosh of air behind me, and I swung around to find the diaphanous man from the tunnel. But as he materialized, his translucent appearance morphed into a more solid form. He raised his hands, pulling the hood back from his head, and it draped behind him with the rest of his cloak. I noticed his glowing red eyes first, but then took in the rest of his appearance. Black pants, matching tee-styled shirt and boots, and a face that put him around fifty in human years. His hair was kept short, and was a mixture of salt and pepper shades with a matching shadow of hair for a beard. Everything about his physical appearance—except the smoldering red eyes—screamed human, while his aura gave off a much different vibe, confirming this was no mere person in front of me.

He placed a hand against his chest. "I'm Darius."

I half smiled, feeling my nerves tumbling inside me. "I'm…um… Selene."

His gaze narrowed. "Yes, I know."

My nervousness left me momentarily speechless. "Where are we?" was what I finally asked when I found my voice.

"Earth." His short, ever so informative response. "Do you not have more relevant questions that require my knowledge?"

I nodded slowly, the lead balloon in my stomach rising to my throat. I anxiously swallowed it back, hoping to keep it together and not let my fear overtake me. "So I get that I'm fallen, but not really. That's not confusing at all." I gave a low, edgy chuckle, then continued. "And now I'm supposed to somehow keep the balance between good and evil, and I'm not limited to any particular place to do it in."

"That is correct"—his tone implied impatience.

Okay great. He'd been real helpful so far. "Well…" I put my hands on my hips, acquiring a new sense of courage. "How am I supposed to know when to intervene in the war between good and evil, and when to leave the situation alone?"

Darius reached forward scooping my wrist in his hand. He chanted something I couldn't understand, then his hand lit up with reddish-orange light. I gasped as an intense burn singed deep into my flesh. Tingles shot up my arm, and then moments later a cooling sensation spread on my skin where he'd touched. Darius released me and stepped back, pointing to my wrist. "The ankh will show you the way."

I stared at a black, cross-shaped tattoo with an oval attached to its crest. It was perfectly centered just below the base of my palm and extended about two inches in diameter around my wrist. A quick glance at Darius' arm, and I noticed he had the same tattoo in the exact same place.

"And how is this"—I shook my wrist at him—"supposed to *show* me?"

His mouth quirked. "The ankh will flare up when it is time to act. It will give you the knowledge of where you must go and what must be done." He grinned, though it didn't appear happy. "I will be here to guide you as you learn your way."

I stole a moment to think about what he'd said, then met his gaze squarely. "Will I be fighting demons?"

He gave a slight bob. "You will have all the power you need to defeat your rivals, though, remember, you no longer have the light within you."

I waved a hand, exasperated. "But the power of light is all I know. How will I defeat anything without its energy?"

Darius' grin widened. "That I will show you." He raised his hands, then thrust them out toward me like he was throwing an object at me. Barely a second later, I was laid out on the ground.

"How'd you do that?" I asked as I got up, wiping grass and debris from my clothes.

"Remember how you called forth the power of light?" He stepped closer, taking my hand and turning it palm up. "Focus on the energy inside you. Feel it expand with your desire for it."

I stared at my palm, concentrating harder than I ever had before. Mainly because when I was an angel, I never really needed to think about using my powers. Faint tingles spread down my arm, like tiny ants crawling under the skin. But as quick as it started, it stopped, and my arm went back to feeling normal. "It's not working," I stated with a grimace.

"Try again."

I shook my arm, loosening it up, then got into position and tried again. With all the strength and concentration I could muster, I commanded the energy to my awaiting palm. The skin prickled up and down my arm, and a warm sensation flushed my hand. *This is it*, I thought with a smile, then squeezed my eyes shut and zeroed in all my thoughts on directing my power. My body shuddered and my arm tingled with intense tremors. Then, all of a sudden, everything just stopped again—like water had been doused over a flame. I glanced at my palm, a defeated whine building up on my tongue.

Before I could say anything, my guide ordered, "Again!"

By my seventh attempt, I could get the energy to my hand, but still couldn't blast it out like Darius had done to me. And trust me, I really, really wanted to take him down. After all, I owed him one…or maybe a few.

"Let's move on," Darius announced, then directed me to stand by his side. "Mimic my movements as best you can." Without warning, he dropped down into a squat, and I hurriedly moved to the same position. He twisted slightly to the left while kicking his right leg out, then immediately sliding it back to his body in one swift motion. "Sometimes your rivals won't expect this and you can bring them down with a swing of your leg."

When I hadn't copied that second part of the move yet, his red eyes narrowed and he urged impatiently, "Do it."

It took me a couple of tries to get it right—well, mostly right since my form wasn't as proper as Darius liked. Then we moved on to other combat moves with punches, upper cuts, elbow hooks, knee tucks, side kicks, front kicks, and jump kicks to name a few. Once Darius realized how horrible my physical fighting skills were, he informed me we'd be here as long as it took.

Four weeks later I was sparring with Darius as if I'd done it all my life. He punched and I threw up my arms, successfully blocking it. Without a moment's hesitation, I thrust sideways, swinging my left leg out in a lower-level kick aimed for his kneecap. Right away he jumped back, but then I twisted around with a jump kick that landed my booted heel in his cheekbone. However, this time instead of worrying if I'd hurt him, I came in for the finish, thrusting my energy-loaded fist for his heart. He dropped and rolled just in the nick of time, then shoved his leg out and tripped me backward. Instead of falling, though, I'd expected the move and sprung up propelling my foot straight for his chest. He grabbed my ankle midair, twisting my whole body around, finally taking me to the ground. And just as he was coming in for the finale, I thrust my hands out, sending a blast of power at him. He flew backwards, his butt crash-landing on the grass.

He proudly smiled at me and simply said, "You're ready."

It was just past midnight and I was crouched behind a large weathered tombstone in the middle of a cemetery somewhere in New Orleans. The name and dates weren't legible, so I had no idea who lay here. But that wasn't the reason I was in some God-forsaken graveyard in the middle of the night. About a yard up the hill from me were two vamps, and some-where in front of them was an innocent human girl about to be drained of all her blood—and then brought back as their vampire slave. According to the blazing red ankh on my wrist, and the churning waves of nausea in my stomach, it was my job not to let this happen.

Darius had been right about the ankh showing me where to go and what to do. When my wrist first ignited with a mild burning sensation, my guide told me to close my eyes and clear my mind, and then the ankh would show me where to go. Once I had the old cemetery plotted in my head, I concentrated on being there—and moments later, I was.

And since there wasn't much time, I needed to get moving. I shook off my overactive nerves, squaring my shoulders as I rose. At the same time, I unmasked my aura, much like I had when I was a guardian angel. It took only seconds for the vamps to turn around. One was an older male with a tall, thin frame, long dark hair flowing over his shoulders. The other was slightly younger with lighter hair, neatly cut around his ears, and a shorter, stockier build. They took a few steps toward me with their fangs already out, their eyes morphing into the deepest shade of blue. The fact that I could see so clearly was because I still had the ability to see at night. Just another perk of my new job.

"Hey boys," I drawled as I moved closer, my boots eerily crunching over sticks and other debris.

"Who the hell are you?" the older one called out through a snarl.

The younger one's gaze narrowed, and then they were both closer and I'd never even seen them move.

My ankh heated up, and I glanced down to see it the brightest fiery red it had ever been. And of course when I did that, the two vampires lunged at me. In a rush I jumped back, just missing a swinging fist from the younger one, but then the older one struck from the other side. I threw up my right arm, blocking him, the impact reverberating like prickling needles, and I knew he'd almost shattered my bone. I ignored it and threw out my left hand, sending an energy ball straight into the younger vampire; at the same time I jumped up and kicked the older one square in his groin. When in doubt, a girl's got to play dirty. Right?

Since I knew the younger vamp would be down for a bit, I focused on the older one hunched over before me, grabbing himself and moaning profanities. As I approached I forced some power into my right hand, bending down to ram my fist straight into his chest. When I yanked out my hand, his gooey-coated heart was cradled in my palm. I squeezed my fingers around it, crushing it to a pulp, and he let out a final shriek and fell back. The remains of his heart were already turning to ashes when I threw it down and wiped my hand, then set off toward the younger vamp that had crawled several feet up the hill.

A painful, feminine moan erupted, and my gaze lifted from the vampire to the girl, draped over a tombstone with crimson trails covering both arms. I fought the urge to go to her, and returned my attention to the younger vampire that was now even further away.

"You can run, but you can't hide," I taunted, taking slow, steady steps.

"What...what...do you want?" he panted as he kept crawling away.

Even though I was taking my time, I was gaining on him pretty quickly. "Oh," I said, bringing my hands to my hips, "I wanted your friend, and now"—I took the final step separating us—"I just want you." I reached down, scooping a massive handful of his hair in my left hand and pulling him up to stand beside me. But since he was still having balance problems thanks to my little energy ball, I needed to keep holding him up.

The girl moaned again. She'd be awake soon and I needed to finish this creep off before that happened. "Sorry I don't have more time to chat," I said musingly.

"No, please," he begged. "I'll leave the girl alone. I promise never to mess with her again."

"I'm sorry," I said at once, not feeling the least bit of remorse. "It's not up to me." I glanced down at the blazing ankh on my skin, then sent all my power to it and thrust my fist inside his chest. Moments later, his heart was ashes, blowing from my hand in the soft breeze.

Then I rushed to the girl and gently slid her off the tombstone, rolling her over and catching her in my arms. Some of her soft brown hair stuck to her face, held there by dried tears or blood. I brushed it back as I lowered her to the ground, feeling an instant pit form in my stomach. She looked young—really young, barely sixteen, I guessed. Her clothes were bloody and torn, and chunks of dirt were caked underneath her fingernails. She sighed, low and deep, then her body shuddered and wriggled. *No time left*, my cautious mind warned. I needed to tap into her aura to see where her home was. I nervously glanced around, hoping to see Darius lurking somewhere nearby. But when another minute of searching turned up nothing, I returned my attention to the girl.

There was movement behind her eyelids. They fluttered and twitched and she seemed to be gaining a sense of awareness. I gazed at the crimson streams on her arm, still moist, and smelled the wafting scent of metallic spice—yet somehow it was inviting me closer, tempting me with its fresh aroma. I'd raised her arm to my watering mouth without even realizing I had moved. My breath caught and I tried to draw back, but I didn't want to. It was like a part of me I didn't recognize was in charge, reminding me of the changes my body underwent when I'd still been a guardian. And now, it'd grown strong enough that my doubts—or even common sense for that matter—couldn't stop it. My tongue lashed out and slid down her arm, her blood coating my tongue and slicking down my throat. I growled with delight, then slightly turned her, exposing more of the warm, red fluid on her neck. Another sigh escaped her lips, followed by a few more moans. Panic slithered up my spine, momentarily bringing me to my senses and forcing me to focus on her essence. Even though I'd become aware of what I was doing—really, really aware—it still didn't stop me from lapping her blood. Then, suddenly, an image of a room rose up in my mind. After casting my view a full three hundred sixty degrees and confirming no one else was around, I pushed with my entire mind to go there.

At once, we were in the room, definitely her bedroom with a white and pink canopy bed in the center and a small white desk and matching dressers on either side. Since I couldn't shape-shift her into something clean, I gently laid her on the bed and rushed to the nearest bathroom—which thankfully was attached to her bedroom. Moving as quickly and stealthily as possible, I grabbed a few washcloths, wetting them in the sink and lathering one of them with a little hand soap.

Five minutes later, she was as cleaned up as I could get her without a full-on shower, and I was rummaging through her dresser for some nightclothes. Her dress came off in one swift tug over her head, and just as I was putting on the tank that matched the pajama shorts, she gave one last sigh and opened her eyes. My breath caught, but thankfully I remembered to turn translucent. She stared in my direction, straining to see, and I knew she'd think there was a ghost standing over her if I didn't leave. So I pushed all my thoughts to the field where Darius trained me and silently mouthed "good-bye" to the girl as I vanished.

"Well done," I heard my guide's voice moments before my eyes landed on him. He stood in the open field, sun shimmering on his light-colored skin, and his red eyes seeming even more vibrant than the last time I'd looked at them.

"Thanks," was my sincere reply.

His lips quirked, then curled into a frown. "Though I fear we may have a problem."

I felt my eyes widen. Without a doubt, me drinking that girl's blood was definitely what he was talking about.

"It appears that vampire blood still thrives inside you," he said, confirming my fear with a grimace. "Even in your renewed body."

"I…I told…I told Raphael—"

"You told your former archangel that you had given blood," he interrupted with fury, "not that you'd ingested theirs!"

"My friend…um…the vampire, he thought I was dying," I stammered as my nerves twisted inside me. "He was only trying…to help."

Darius folded an arm in front of him, rubbing his chin with his other hand. "Perhaps that is why you were chosen for this, although it seems some details have been kept secret, even from me."

"I'll tell you everything!" I exclaimed, waving a hand in the air. "I'm not trying to keep any secrets from you!"

He lowered his hand from his chin and held it up, palm toward me as if gesturing me to stop talking. "There is nothing else for you to tell me.

When you were a guardian angel you could sense the aura of any being, anywhere. But now, you must taste their blood to acquire information from them." He lowered his hands to his sides, giving me a sincere look. "It seems we are still learning what gifts you possess, and what you can no longer do. The more power you have within you, the better you will perform your job and keep the balance between good and evil."

"So I shouldn't be worried about the fact I just drank that girl's blood as if it were nothing? Like I'd been doing it all my life?"

He shook his head, his jaw tightening. "I do not believe so. Nothing happens by accident."

I mulled over his statement for a moment, then my mind shifted to Cole, Caitlyn, and Luke for at least the thousandth time. I'd brought them up a few times while Darius was training me, only to get nowhere with his riddle-themed answers. But now felt like good a time as any to try asking again. Hopefully this time, I'd actually get somewhere with him.

"Darius," I called out, feeling a wave of boldness come over me as I stepped forward. "I need to know that I didn't sacrifice myself in vain. I need to see them. Please."

He considered me for a bit. "And if they no longer live, what difference would it make to see that?" was what he ended up asking. Good, at least I didn't get shot down.

A lump barreled its way up my throat, but I swallowed it back and found my voice, saying, "Please. I just need to know. I promise it won't affect my job." I glanced down at my wrist and the ankh was its normal black color—when it wasn't alerting me to battle good and evil, of course.

Several tense moments passed, and just when I thought he'd respond with all the reasons I couldn't find Caitlyn and Luke, or even Cole for that matter, he surprisingly came back with something else instead. "You are free to find them," he looked at me hard, his gaze unfathomable, "but you must remain hidden from them should they be alive. Because you can no longer sense their auras without first drinking their blood, it will be most difficult to locate them. That is, of course, if they live." He paused and I waited for him to change his mind. "I will summon you if I need you before the ankh's next call" was all he added, then he vanished without another word. Anxiety thickened inside me as I blankly gazed across the expansive, plush field, wondering how I could possibly remain unseen if in fact Caitlyn and Luke were alive. Or better yet, would I really be able to stay hidden from Cole?

The last time we'd been together, he watched me kill myself for someone else. He'd probably be so disgusted with me that it really would be best not to ever show my face around him again. But I love him, and love has a funny way of pulling you close to those you feel that way for. So even though Cole wouldn't be the first person, or vampire, that I'd be visiting, I still knew without a doubt that I'd be seeing him soon enough.

26

I COULD ONLY SENSE ONE BEATING HEART in my old dorm room, even though the commotion I'd just heard sounded like there were several people in there. I bit my bottom lip as I hovered in my ghostly form at the door, hesitant to float inside and see what was causing the noise. It was nighttime, and since no light shone at the base of the door, I knew whomever the heartbeat belonged to was sleeping and oblivious to the spiritual ruckus. Darius had warned not to show myself to my friends, but he hadn't said anything about other demons and beings. But just to take precaution anyway, I masked my aura as I glided into the room.

I felt my eyes widen at the sight of two demons and one guardian angel in the middle of a heated argument. I recognized Morton, but didn't know the angel or the other demon. The angel stopped talking mid-sentence, his gaze hardening as he searched around the room. "Who's there?" he called out in an annoyed tone, waiting a few short moments before setting his eyes back on Morton and the other demon.

The trio became background noise once I realized the angel could only sense my presence but couldn't see me or determine where I was in the room, and the demons didn't seem to have a clue I was there at all. All my mind could focus on was that Morton, one of Caitlyn's demons, was here. In a whoosh of air, I was at her bed, my gaze trailing up the mass of blankets and landing on her face. Only it wasn't Caitlyn's face I was looking at. It was a young lady, about her same size and age, with flaming red hair and an abundance of freckles coating her cheeks and forehead. "Damn it," I muttered as my heart twisted with sharp, stinging pain. Then I shook my head, feeling waves of unbearable sadness wash through me.

Since I didn't know who this girl was—I'd never seen her before on campus—she must have just enrolled. And I guess that meant Caitlyn had un-enrolled. Most likely, not by choice either. My chest tightened and my breathing grew short and ragged. My translucent hand pressed against the cotton material of my shirt just over my heart, but the pain didn't ease up—actually it worsened a little. Tears formed, then gushed over the ledge of my eyelids. Even with my diaphanous body, my face still felt wet and sticky, and after a beat my eyes started to burn. Crying wasn't going to bring my charge back, though, nor would it answer any of my questions. I needed to pull it together and move on. Especially not knowing when my ankh would be calling again with another mission.

"...can threaten us all you want, but we're not going anywhere."

I glanced behind me, choking back the last of my sobs, and saw a challenging grin formed in Morton's blobby shape. I closed my eyes, fighting the urge to blast him with an energy ball. Sharp pains reignited, now prickling everywhere inside me, combining with a fresh eruption of anger, and I wanted desperately to materialize and demand that Morton tell me if Caitlyn was dead. But since he hadn't been her primary demon—that position belonged to Grote—then it was quite possible that Morton didn't know anything. So I made a quick decision to keep the mask over my aura. No point in getting in trouble just yet.

The other demon caught my attention as he shuffled over to the bed, casting a malicious gaze down at the girl. He was in human form and appeared to be a sixteen-year-old boy with dark brown hair and a slender figure—too young and innocent looking to be an evil, soulless demon. But the way he looked at this innocent human girl was sinister, diabolically evil in its most raw form. They'd hurt her for no reason other than their inner desire to hurt and destroy people, and at that moment I really, really wanted so desperately to intervene and kick both these demons' butts. If I didn't hurry up and get out of here, I'd end up getting involved in something my gut told me I shouldn't.

Suddenly, there was an explosion of light radiating throughout the room. I dropped to the floor, throwing my arms over my eyes, feeling the searing light burn deep in my flesh. The air around me compressed like the pressure of a storm, and my ears needed to pop. Even though I wasn't visible to the angel, obviously he could still bring me down with his power. That made me wonder how I'd fight—or rather win—against a guardian if it ever came down to it. I peered around my makeshift shield and saw both demons cowering to the floor, crying out for the angel to stop. I wanted to cry out too: that angel's light energy hurt like hell, and it made me miss having that old ability. A twinge of remorse, then my chest tightened with grief—both for Caitlyn and myself—and then I closed my eyes and focused on my next destination.

Moments later it felt as if my ears had finally popped, my skin no longer smoldered, and I was standing in an alley just outside Luke's basement apartment. It was dark on this side of the continent too, just as it had been on the outskirts of the Midwest. Since I could no longer feel Luke's aura, I couldn't sense if he was home. There was no heartbeat behind the door, beneath the stairs, or anywhere else within the confines of Luke's personal space—which only meant no humans were in there. I did, however, pick up a slightly familiar scent that I knew belonged to the one I sought. But I had no way to know if it was old or new; it could be his residual essence from hours ago, days ago, or even months ago. Although I was hoping beyond hope that if I didn't see him in person once I entered his apartment, I'd at least find some form of evidence proving he'd recently been here—and confirming he was still alive.

I squared my shoulders and floated through the door, down the stairs, and into his studio-styled living quarters. My breath caught in stunned surprise as I took in the disheveled view of the room. Luke had always been a neat and orderly kind of vampire, but what I saw here was the exact opposite. Sofa cushions were stacked on their sides, one of them completely tipped over. Clothes were strewn all over, hanging over the back of a few chairs and lying in heaps on the floor. I drifted through the room, noticing broken glass littering the floor around the coffee table, glistening in the soft lamp light like jewels in the sun. The back table was covered by at least a dozen hardcover books. An observing glance told me most of them were about raising the dead. Even though I was certain that no one was here, I decided not to materialize and rummage through the books. Instead I lowered my face closer to a stack of two of them, and inhaled deeply, filling my nose with an unfamiliar scent—and just beneath it was Luke's.

I gasped with excitement, but quickly shook that feeling away. It didn't prove Luke had been here recently. It only proved that *someone* had been here, trying to raise the dead. Either Luke was alive, and he thought I was dead—thus trying to find a way to bring me back. Or Luke was dead and someone was trying to get *him* back. But I didn't sense Huron on those books, and he was the only one I knew powerful enough to even attempt such a thing. I stuck around and searched the place more thoroughly, not finding anything else that would give me any clues. I guessed my next stop would be the voodoo Indian's bar. But just as I started concentrating on going there, the ankh flared up, pulling me somewhere else altogether.

Water was everywhere. No land in sight as far as my eyes could see. Masses of downy white and pale silvery clouds drifted in the sky above as if in a hurry to get somewhere. I hovered about a half foot above the sea, in my diaphanous form, feeling thankful for the first time for being what I was now—whatever that was. Darius was so mysterious about a lot of things, especially what we were. He'd summed it up with him being my guide. But my questions remained: What was I? What was he? Had he been keeping the balance between good and evil all along? And better yet: Why the heck was I in Anthemusa?

I stared at the blazing ankh waiting for it to tell me the answers I sought. But when I opened my mind, allowing it to show me what to do, it gave me an image of a siren—in big trouble. And it wanted me to help her. A vaporous demon had been wandering throughout Anthemusa sucking the energy from every water demon it came across, and killing them off along with their precious sea snakes. Somewhere farther out at sea, the weakened, petrified siren was trapped inside an orb of inky fumes—AKA, the vapor demon—and it wouldn't be long before it finished her off. But what the ankh showed me next only brought more irony to my situation. The siren in danger was the same one who'd threatened me twice before when I'd accidentally orbed here as an angel.

"*Just great*," I mumbled through a sigh. I really didn't want to help her. She'd driven me crazy with her stupid whiny challenges, and now I'd have to suck all of that up and save her? My wrist burned hotter, the ankh flaring brighter and redder, and I knew it was letting me know that time was running out. I took a deep, unsatisfying breath and focused on the siren.

Though once I got there a few seconds later, I didn't know what to do. I couldn't fight the vapor demon with combat force, not only because my fist would go straight through it with no effect, but also because I was in my ghostly form so I could stay afloat above the water. I could blast it from a distance with my energy, but how do I keep my electrifying power from frying the siren? The vapor demon held most of her helpless body above the water, but there was still a small part of her dangling beneath the surface. The scorching symbol on my wrist forced me to figure it out quick, so I unmasked my aura and approached the demon. "Release her," I called out, sounding authoritative. Goody for me.

The vaporous demon's hazy, inky blue shape rippled the way perfectly still water does when you poke it with your fingertips, and it hissed a warning low and deep. But with it lacking a mouth—or a face for that matter—it was hard to tell where exactly it'd come from. I could vaguely see the siren inside the vapor cloud. It looked like her aqueous body was somehow melting like the way hot wax drips over the edge of a votive candle. Thick, wet streams slid down her body, the small drops splashing into the sea just below her. The indentations where her eyes were, on her water-formed face—which had been so much more lovely the last two times I saw her—were now deeper and sagging at the lids. It seemed like the thin line of her mouth was frowning as I moved a little closer.

"I said let her go"—again spoken with confidence, even though I was praying on the inside this thing would just listen to me so I wouldn't have to fight it.

Another threatening hiss—the same sound you'd hear if you got too close to a rattlesnake a second before the warning shake of its tail. But even as fear thickened inside me, I still kept heading toward it.

All at once, a handless, pellucid arm extended out from the vapor demon's body and struck me across the chest with the force of a battering ram. I hunched over, grabbing my stomach, but keeping my eyes locked on my attacker as I steadied myself for its next move. Only instead of coming at me again, its arm folded back into the rest of its body. Just great, that thing can touch me in my ghost form—not good at all. I quickly cast my hardened gaze around, hoping to see Darius but doubting I would; therefore I wasn't surprised when I didn't find my guide. Regardless, I needed to do something bolder, since my verbal requests weren't getting me anywhere. I pushed all my focus on the power inside me, being careful not to use the full force of it, then thrust it outward in an invisible burst. It knocked the inky cloud back several feet, freeing the siren of its hold so that she dropped into the sea with a faint splash. Her body automatically blended with the water, but her human-like form still held enough shape so I could see her floating on top.

I swung my attention back to the vapor demon just as it flew into me, enveloping my body inside its smoky form. The air was heavier, thicker, building up pressure in my head and against my chest, making me feel like I weighed a ton. Panic rushed up my spine as I fought to get out, but I was barely able to move and couldn't break free of its hold. I was trapped, and scared beyond what my mind could handle, but I fought to hold myself together since freaking out never really helps anyways. Okay, so maybe I was freaking out a little.

The minutes seemed to creep along and I hadn't made any progress. I was still trapped within the demon's cloudy, bubble-shaped body, the sea an indistinct view beyond it. When my countless attempts to blast this thing with more of my power failed, I frantically tried to think of some other way to free myself. Then it occurred to me that maybe this demon couldn't hold me up if I was in my physical form. I shimmered—just as I'd always done since being with Darius—but nothing happened. I was still diaphanous, and the demon still had its unbreakable hold on me. A rush of mixed emotions washed over me, sending shudders of panic through my body. My wrist grew hotter, pulling my gaze to it. The ankh was still fiery red but was now warping in and out, gaining about an inch in size, then shrinking to its normal shape. It kept repeating that process over and over, burning hotter and hotter. I closed my eyes, squeezing them shut, and willed all my thoughts away from the pain, away from the fear, away from the doubt and hopelessness. Once I felt the clearing in my mind, I pushed all my energy into the ankh, fighting to embrace it and touch its energy. More excruciating pain shot through me and I knew without a doubt that the demon was trying to suck my life force, just as it had been doing with the siren's. I could sense some of my power being pulled out of my body, slowly—like pulling a bucket filled with water from a well.

Terror seeped back up, but I shook it off and kept my mind open to the ankh. I could feel its power rippling along my skin like tiny electric currents. After that, there was an image in my mind—crystal clear—and I knew what I needed to do. With all the strength I could muster, I pushed my foot against the vapor floor, straining and forcing it through the cloud's thick barrier. Slowly, I moved half inch by half inch until the toe of my boot was free—and just barely under the water's surface. And that's when I thrust all my energy outward.

Electrifying shockwaves jolted through the vapor demon, rapidly intensifying with the connection to the water. The vapor demon's whole body trembled, it howled and hissed…and then it pulled away. Once my body was free, I shimmered into my human form and fell to the water with a splash, everything submerged but my head. The ankh was still burning, so I clenched that fist as tightly as I could as I swam the few feet to where the demon hovered. In a rush, I kicked up and thrust the top half of my body above the water, then jabbed my hand into the vaporous cloud, releasing the full amount of my power into it. An explosion rocked me backward, and plunged me deep beneath the surface. Water surrounded me as I desperately treaded upward. Only I never made it. Darkness came, and I was swallowed into the sea's abyss.

My lashes fluttered open and I saw a middle-aged man with graying brown hair, chiseled, squared facial features, and beaming red eyes. "Darius!" I gasped, sitting up in a rush. I sat on a black sheet that had been laid on the ground, and beyond the guide standing before me was the training field.

"You did good" was his response, even though I'd expected him to explain what had happened instead.

When he didn't elaborate, I stood up, asking, "What happened to me?!"—sounding more like a demand than a curious question.

He gave me a look that made me feel like he was the proud parent—and I was the child. The thin line of his lips curved into a slight smile. "You've mastered the use of your inner power." He paused a moment as if considering his next choice of words carefully. "And you are much stronger than I thought you would be."

"But I…but…," I stammered, getting frustrated that my mind was moving faster than my mouth. "After I threw my energy into that horrible demon…" My words trailed off, flashbacks racing through my head like fast-forwarding a video.

Darius nodded, a suggestive look expressed on his face, and anger sparked alive inside me.

"You were there the whole time." My voice low and accusatory. "Watching me." I shook my head with frustration, vaguely registering we were both in our solid, more human-like forms. "Well," I scoffed, "did I put on a good enough show?"

His brows furrowed, and his lips arched into a frown. "I was observing you, yes," was all he said.

"I called for you"—my voice seething with anger. Then I said in barely a whisper, "I called for you and you never came."

His features softened. "I came when you truly needed me. Not a moment before that." He stepped closer, placing his hands on my shoulders. "Selene…"

My chest tightened at the sound of my name. He'd never called me that before. I swallowed hard, slowly raising my face to meet his eyes, and as I did, a tear slid down my cheek.

"Your power is great, but you still have much to learn of this new life. When you destroyed the vaporous demon, you were plunged several hundred feet into the sea, and your bearings were lost. Instead of swimming for the surface, you treaded parallel with it. You panicked. Your nerves got the best of you and then you lost consciousness." He released me, stepping back. "You can't drown. You can't suffocate. Selene, you simply cannot die. Next time, do not let your fear control you. Let your confidence reenergize and strengthen you."

"Are you saying I blacked out because my mind couldn't handle the situation?"

He nodded by way of an answer. Then he added, "If ever you lose a battle, it will not be because you lack strength and power."

Good to know, I thought, feeling less upset and a little more secure in myself.

Darius knelt down on the sheet, folding his legs together in front of him and resting his hands—palms face up—on his knees.

"What are you doing?" I asked, staring curiously at him.

With his head, he gestured for me to sit next to him. "We're learning better control of our minds through prayer."

I snorted in disbelief. "You pray?"

"Of course I pray." Sounding more like "Duh!"

Hesitantly, I sat down, mimicking Darius' position.

"After all," he went on. "Who is it, do you think, that requires our existence in keeping the balance between good and evil?"

"I guess that means I'm not a demon, even though all other fallen angels are?"

Darius flashed a knowing smile. "As I told you, you are not like any other fallen one before you…or after you."

"Well, what am I then?"

"We are many things." Another vague, uninformative answer.

"Fine," I replied curtly, sitting up straight and squaring my shoulders. "Let's pray."

27

EVEN THOUGH IT WAS NIGHTTIME the light from the half moon glimmered between tree branches, creating mysterious shadows with their dying leaves. I floated over a few darkened snow patches, the dim light illuminating them into silvery smears on the ground. The thickness of the trees fanned out into a more open terrain with shorter, stick-like bushes scattered here and there. Even though I was in my diaphanous form, I could feel the chill of the wind out here as it rustled more urgently without the protection of the forest. It blew through my body, yet my shape remained solid and untouched like a vent with air blowing through it. Other than the breeze, the night was eerily quiet, and I wondered if all the wildlife had already migrated or had taken refuge for the fast approaching winter.

A *snap, pop, crunch* came from directly in front of me. My body froze and something tight constricted in my gut. It was probably him but I needed to be sure, so I got moving in that direction. It wasn't long before I could make out a silhouette of a man just on the other side of the bend. My heart started racing. I really hoped he'd be receptive to me. And I prayed with every ounce of my being that when I asked him the important question, his answer wouldn't be the one I feared.

Once I confirmed his identity, I stealthily came up behind him and paused. A few doubts swirled in my mind, mostly about what Darius would do to me if he found out what I was about to do. But I shook them off and materialized. Then I reached out my hand, gently gripping his shoulder from behind.

"What the hell?" The vampire swung around, fangs extended.

I smiled nervously. "Hi, Croix."

"Who's asking?" he replied icily, narrowing his gaze.

"It's me... Selene."

He cocked his head to the side, and his auburn hair spilled in luscious waves over the shoulder of his black button-up shirt. The moonlight seemed to create yellowy highlights, though I didn't remember him having those before. His eyes deepened as they slid up and down my body, most likely taking in my new combat attire. "Selene? What the hell are you wearing?" he asked with a raised right eyebrow.

"Um, I can get into all of that later," I explained in a rush. "I need to know if you've seen Cole at all in the past month."

He considered me a moment, then shook his head. "No, I ain't seen him. But I just figured he'd gone off somewhere with you."

A chill spread through my body and my knees felt weak. I threw out my arms to steady myself as I wobbled to one side, but it wasn't balance that was taking me down. My emotions roiled, charged with the heaviest anguish just as my legs gave out. Everything swam in slow motion as I dropped, and I barely registered that Croix was holding me up by my arm.

"Selene, what is it?" he asked, concern spilling over his features.

I barely tilted my head to stare at his smooth, perfect face, since he wasn't that much taller than me. His lips were pressed in a thin line and his brows arched just enough to make one small wrinkle crease on his otherwise flawless forehead. As I met his eyes, they seemed to swirl with a bottomless depth. "Don't," I managed to say once I realized that if I didn't start talking, he'd try to roll me with his eyes. And my deepest thoughts were none of his damn business.

He shook his head, a faint smile tugging the corners of those thin, pale lips. "Sorry. I didn't mean it. You just... you just got me all worried." He shrugged his decent-sized shoulders—not too broad, but not too narrow either—still keeping a firm grip on my arm, and I realized he was still holding me up.

"I'm sorry... I'm sorry too," I stammered as I kept staring at his face, only I wasn't really looking at him. Everything was blank, my body numb.

Croix let me go and I managed to stay on my feet. He stepped back, running a hand through his long, voluminous hair. I remembered how I'd thought, the first time I met him, that any human girl I knew would've killed to have his hair. Croix frequented one of Cole's favorite lounges to pass time at. I'd been introduced as Cole's girlfriend, and as I'd spent more time with Croix, eventually I had told him my secret of being an angel. I'd mostly told him because he could smell something different about me and he pestered me until I finally caved and confirmed it. He'd left me alone about it ever since. Goody for him. When I hadn't seen Croix at the lounge earlier, luckily I'd overheard another vamp mentioning Croix's whereabouts, which led me out here in the middle of nowhere.

My head lowered as the current situation expanded in my chest, leaving it difficult to breathe. "You haven't seen Cole and no one else has mentioned seeing him?" My voice came out strained and I stared harder at the ground.

"You ain't been with him." It didn't sound like a question, more an acceptance of the fact Cole was missing.

I didn't look up because now my eyes were welling up with tears. This entire day had been somewhat productive, but very painfully so. Since the ankh hadn't flared since my rendezvous with the siren and vapor demon, I'd gone to Huron's bar. It had taken me three long, drawn-out hours to finally learn that Luke, and Annabel for that matter, hadn't been seen since Rhea. I'd hovered against the wall on the far right side, mostly hidden in shadows while waiting to overhear the information I sought. No one had paid me any attention whatsoever. Cloaking my aura seemed to be a sure thing around every species I'd encountered so far except guardians, and fortunately for me they could only sense there was a presence, nothing more. The jackpot hit once an old vamp friend of the voodoo Indian's had come in and thankfully asked just the right questions. Even though Huron's answers had been vague, I'd still been able to make out what I needed. And now Croix had pretty much confirmed my biggest fear: Cole hadn't been seen either. Whether or not Luke was alive still couldn't be answered, but my heart told me going to Rhea would be the only way to find out—and get Cole back to Earth. Annabel's fate would be decided when I saw her. If she pissed me off, she was definitely staying behind.

Croix firmly grabbed my shoulder and gave me a small shake, bringing me out of my thoughts, and I finally raised my eyes to meet his. A lone tear streamed out of the corner of my eye and he gently wiped it away with his finger, mostly smearing it into my skin. "Do you know where he is?" Croix asked, his tone sincere.

I took a deep, confident breath as I nodded. "I've got to get going."

"Well don't hurt him too bad when you find him," was Croix's nervous response.

"What do you m…?" I started to ask but then realization sparked in my mind. I bet Croix thought Cole was with another woman, and that made me curious and I just had to know. "Has he ever mentioned someone else?"

"No," he answered right away. And the way he looked at me with unflinching eyes made it believable.

I swallowed the lump that had moved up my throat, then told him, "Thank you," as I turned on my heel and started walking. After a few minutes, when I was certain Croix hadn't followed, I closed my eyes and focused on my next destination.

Moments later, I was sitting on the black sheet laid across the grass in the middle of the vast meadow where Darius had helped me after my accident in Anthemusa. I really needed to talk to him before I did anything stupid, and I was hoping to keep a more honest relationship with him than I'd had with Raphael—well, sort of. I definitely wasn't telling him that I'd revealed myself to an old vampire acquaintance. But there were several questions looping in my head, and Darius was the only one who could answer them.

I laid back, my hair spilling out as I settled against the soft cottony fabric. It was dusk here—wherever that was—and the sky swirled with vibrant shades of blue and purple, splashed with tinges of yellow and gold. There were only a few remnant clouds, and they seemed to gather around the setting sun as if it were pulling them below the horizon with it. I stretched my arms over my head, twining my fingers together, then extending them as far as they would go while I inhaled deeply. As I exhaled, I felt the sheet move beside me. I rolled to the side, finding Darius.

"Hey," I said sweetly. "I was wondering when you'd get here."

My guide's legs were stretched out in front of him, and he crossed his right leg over his left as he replied, "Did you find your friends?"

"No…but I, uh, I think I know where they are."

His red eyes locked onto mine, and I wanted nothing more than to look away. But I held my ground and returned his gaze. "I believe they're still on

Rhea." I swallowed hard, then forced myself to ask the looming question in my head. "Can I orb someone with me while I'm...uh...*ghost-like?*"

He compressed his mouth and said nothing.

That made my whole body shudder with a fresh blast of nerves. But I ignored the tightness in my stomach and pressed him again. "What I'm asking is if I can bring them back to Earth *undetected*." A little emphasis on that last word so he'd know I was trying to follow his rules.

"Yes," was all he said, and it was all I'd wanted to hear.

My anxiousness eased up, and without thinking I leaned over and threw out my arms to hug my guide. But I stopped with my arms in the air and slowly brought them back to my sides. "Sorry, I was just really happy with your answer," I told him. Aside from combat training, we'd never touched before, let alone hugged, and I felt awkward about almost doing it.

He seemed to notice my inner struggle, but he didn't do anything to reassure me. But after a beat, he finally asked, "When are you going?"

I shrugged. "I figured I'd go now, since this thing"—I shook my wrist, exposing the tattoo—"hasn't flared up yet."

"Remember to stay..."

"Unseen," we finished together.

"I have one more question," I stated uncertainly.

Darius' gaze was hard again, penetrating, and unreadable. It took me a minute to find the words I wanted to use. "There's a demon that I have some issues with, and I'd really like to kill him."

"No" was his instant reply.

"Darius..."

"You must always listen to the ankh. If it tells you to kill the demon, then you may. But you cannot kill him of your own regard."

Fine. Not exactly what I was hoping to hear, but at least I did get some good news. Finally, I nodded in submission. "Okay."

Darius jumped up in one rapid move and held out a hand to me. "Come." That one word spoken with authority and conviction and I took his hand right away. He pulled me up, saying, "I think we should go over what we practiced before you go to Rhea."

"Why do I need to practice more fighting? I can't use that unless I'm like this." I gestured up and down my body with my hands.

"I'm not referring to physical combat." He turned on his heel and headed off through the expansive meadow.

I chased behind him, my boots whisking in the short, plush grass. "What do you mean then?"

"Your mind still has much control to learn." He stopped walking and spun around to face me, eyes penetrating. "What if your friends are in danger? What will your emotions provoke from you? I fear your control. Or should I say lack of control?"

"I knew it! You've known all along they were trapped on Rhea and you never told me!"

His gaze narrowed. "Should your friends not be there, I would not be worried. I am only preparing you in the event that they are."

The word *liar* built up on my tongue, but I swallowed it back and took a few deep, lasting breaths, then rotated my neck until it popped. "Fine. Let's get this over with so I can go."

My guide turned around and headed off without saying another word. The vast open field seemed to go on for miles and it felt like hours that I followed him, but since I didn't have a watch I had no idea how long it really was. Finally the terrain became rocky and uneven. A few times I tripped and needed to use my hands to push up off the rocks. It was almost full night, the sun barely clinging to a lower corner of the sky, and all those vibrant lights had dulled as the darkness moved in to swallow them. I was just about to ask, "Are we there yet?" when Darius finally stopped. He didn't turn to face me, just held his hand out to the side, gesturing for me to come stand beside him. Once I did, my breath caught in my throat.

We stood on the edge of an incredibly high cliff, overlooking the most beautiful scenery I'd ever seen. The faint light the sun gave out cast hazy shadows on the landscape below us. The view reminded me of the Grand Canyon—only this ravine wasn't a desert-like place. It was robust with tree-covered hills and a few small lakes separating them. Soft light glistened on the massive, shiny, granite-like stones that jutted up in various places like beacons lighting the way. There was a waterfall somewhere off in the distance. I could hear the raging water splashing into the depths below, could sense the moisture building in the air, but I couldn't see it with my eyes. A serene peacefulness washed over me, and I let it embrace me. It was the most beautiful feeling I'd experienced in a long while, and I wanted it to take over and thrive inside me.

All of a sudden, I was giggling and I didn't remember having started. But it continued, the joy of the moment spreading through me with a pleasant burn along my flesh. And I savored it. I reveled in it. Rapturous laughter now spilled off my tongue, making it hard to breathe, and I grabbed my chest as if that would help me. Darius' hand was on my back, steadying me, supporting me, and, oddly, comforting me. It was the first time my guide had ever touched me in a compassionate way. He was always so hard, so tough to read, and impossible to really feel close to. But in this moment, I felt close. For the first time he felt like a friend.

And then the moment ended as swiftly as it had come. My guide sat down on the edge of the cliff, staring out at the breathtaking world below us. His legs were crossed in front of him and his palms rested on his knees facing the sky. This time, I didn't need his invitation. I sat down next to him, copying his stance. Our eyes were closed, our breathing deep and slow. Moments later, I could feel his mind inside me and mine inside him. We were one, opening our hearts in silent prayer. Asking for strength, guidance, and control just as we had done before.

Then surprisingly, Darius requested loyalty to one another. I could feel his desire to trust me swirling inside my own head, and before I could stop it, guilt pushed to the surface and interspersed with our already shared emotions. I startled, jolting out of our incorporeal connection, tears forming in a rush of regret. I stared ahead because I couldn't handle looking at my guide—even though I could feel his eyes burning the side of my face. "I'm sorry," I offered with a strained voice.

"What did you do?" He didn't sound mad, but worse than that—disappointed.

"I needed to confirm my suspicions of Rhea. I was able to do most of it without being detected." I hesitated, nervously shrugging my shoulders, fighting the tears that threatened to choke me. Then I told him about my confrontation with Croix.

"You mustn't show yourself to anyone," he scolded.

"I know." I peered over at him. "I'm sorry."

"Sorry won't keep our identities protected," he went on, raking me with his hardened gaze. "If others find out about you, about us, we risk them learning of what we do. Darkness and light alike do not favor anyone who can tamper with their works. If they learn our identity, they will seek us out."

"We can't die. You said so yourself."

"But what they will do to us will make us pray for death."

"I can see a demon trying to torture us, but a guardian angel?"

He looked away, exhaling slowly. "Most of all…guardians. If we inter-fere with their ability to protect their human charge, they will attack us with the full force of their inner light."

The memory of my encounter with the guardian in Caitlyn's old dorm room flashed in my head. And he hadn't even attacked me. It had been the run-off of his power he'd thrown to the demons that had brought me to my knees—and kept me there until he turned off his light. My body shuddered and I rubbed my arms with my hands. My throat constricted, making it impossible to speak—not that I really wanted to anyway.

"Take me to him," my guide requested, all his anger seeming to have faded.

"Take you to who?"

"This Croix. The one who knows what he cannot know."

I felt my eyes widen. "What are you going to do?"—my voice laced with panic.

"I'm going to protect us."

"No!" I exclaimed, scooting over and grabbing Darius by the arm, shaking him. "You can't kill him! You told me we could only kill when the ankh allows us!"

Darius brought his wrist over toward me, exposing the same black tat-too that was on mine. "I will protect this power at all costs. Once I go to this vampire, the energy will be there for me to harness."

So the magical symbol wouldn't lead him to Croix since technically Croix hadn't done anything to disrupt the balance—yet. "Please," I begged. "Let me talk to him. I can explain our situation. He won't say anything to anyone."

Darius' eyes glowed brighter, the eerie redness seeping over the lines of his lids. "Can you guarantee his silence? Are you able to bet your life, and mine, that he can be trusted?"

My mouth opened to say yes. I desperately wanted to say yes. But I couldn't get the word off my tongue, like it was frozen in the depths of my throat. Could I trust Croix? Even though he was Cole's friend, I just wasn't sure that I could trust him with a secret such as this. All it would take was one little slip of the tongue, him telling someone that he'd seen me and then blabbing on about the outfit he'd seen me wearing. Would those details be enough to endanger me? Maybe. And at that moment grim reality hit me. I knew with a one hundred percent certainty that Croix would tell Cole. And if Croix would tell one person, he'd be capable of telling more. It was just the simple way gossip worked. My insides rolled with regret, wishing I'd never shown myself to Croix. If only I'd been more patient, perhaps I still could've gotten the information I needed. But I was in a hurry, and now it would cost someone I knew their life.

"It is a hard lesson to learn, and I am sorry for what must be done," Darius said with a gentle tone.

"Please. There has to be another way." Because Croix's death on my shoulders was too heavy for me to bear.

He assessed me, his expression tight. When he didn't say anything I knew his threat was final.

I nodded by way of my answer, glancing down at my lap. At last, tears spilled down my cheeks and I lowered my head to hide them. My hair fell forward and Darius brushed it back with the softest of strokes, then pulled me into his arms and held me as I cried.

28

THE CAVE THAT LED TO EZARIAH'S LAIR was swarming with demons. But since none of them could see me, I was feeling pretty lucky. I hugged the rocky wall as I floated along, keeping my diaphanous body concealed within the shadows. Being in my ghostly form kept me from stepping in those murky puddles with the slimy bottoms, and the rest of the slick, rocky path. The demons—all lower-leveled and mostly soldiers—carelessly marched back and forth, several holding torches with flames dancing and pulsing as they moved. Suddenly, a few fights broke out all at once. One soldier demon was blindsided, a Frankenstein-like demon punching him in the side of the head. The soldier demon growled a warning and carelessly flung the lit torch toward the other. When that happened, the torch struck another soldier's face, and that commotion caused several others to get involved. You simply couldn't have this many demons in one room without some head bumping, so to speak. Unless, of course Typhon was still here to whip them into shape. But their foolhardy behavior had me doubting I'd see the master demon, and for that I was relieved. Mostly because Darius had told me that without the ankh's power, I couldn't kill him. I rolled my eyes at the thought, and started moving a little faster.

Moments later, I rounded the doorway and spilled into the expansive room, conveniently finding more shadows near the shelves by the wall to keep me fully concealed. A few torches lined the walls in various places, and my eyes followed them until I saw about a half dozen soldier demons standing in a half circle, as if huddling around something—or someone. I glanced the other way, finding Ezariah sitting in one of his wooden chairs over by the fireplace, thumbing through one of his worn hardcover books. With each careful flip, he seemed to be looking for something within the old, torn pages.

The rattling of chains pulled my attention to the far left side of the room, across from where the soldier demons stood. Annabel sat on the ground, her back against the bare stone wall and silver chains wrapped around her body with cuffs at her wrists and ankles. She was barefoot and filthy, her jeans were torn, and she was down to just a black cotton bra. Her red hair was matted with knots, and dirt was smeared across her porcelain cheeks and forehead. The look on her face told me she'd been kept this way the entire past month. And I was willing to bet she hadn't been fed either.

Thank God, I mouthed silently. If Annabel was here, then I hoped Cole would be here too. And if Luke was alive.... I let my thoughts trail off. I could only handle one thing at a time. I drifted through the massive bookshelf and over by the group of soldier demons, and as I came around them, ever so careful to stay in the shadows, my heart caught in my throat.

Cole. He was chained just like Annabel, and seemed to be in her same condition: barefoot, dirty, his shirt missing. Only he didn't have a wall to sit against. His legs were pulled against his body and his face was pressed against the tops of his knees. Relief gushed through me, a few tears of joy slicking down my cheek. I wanted to go to him, throw my arms around him and feel the cool firmness of his perfect body against mine. And that's exactly what I'd be doing to get him back to Earth. Only he'd never see me or feel me, and I wouldn't feel the physical connection I craved, only the essence of his body touching the essence of mine. It saddened me and made me smile all at the same time. At least he'd be home where he belonged, and not in this hellhole of a prison serving a punishment for something *I* did.

But before I could take Cole home, I needed to find...Luke. As I thought his name, a body came into view lying in a heap of bloodied chains and clothes several feet away from Cole in the corner of the room. I hovered a little closer and confirmed it was a man, curled in a fetal position with his back facing me. His brown hair was caked with blood—thick, chunky tufts matted to his head—and I knew at that instant it was Luke. Yet since technically I wasn't supposed to have that old angel ability, there was no way for me to understand why I was so certain, but the feeling in my gut was undeniable. This beat-up vamp was definitely Luke, and unlike the other two vampires, his shirt was still on and stained with various shades of red.

Another sharp glance around the room proved Caitlyn wasn't in here. Even though my heart sunk at the thought, at least she wasn't being held against her will and tormented like the others. A simple human just couldn't handle things a vampire could—even if my sacrifice had healed her. I remembered Raphael holding her limp body in his arms. She hadn't been dead, but she'd been so very close, and after everything I'd just seen, I needed to believe Raphael had taken her with him. I needed to have faith that my old archangel wouldn't have left her here. Whether or not that meant she moved on to the light, I didn't know. But I breathed a sigh of relief just simply knowing she wasn't here.

I returned my concentration to the vampires I'd come to save. I wished with everything inside me that I could save them all at once—Annabel included. Even though I didn't like her, she still didn't deserve such inhumane torture. After all, she'd helped me...twice. And I owed it to her to get her out of here. I took a few minutes to assess the situation. Once I was finished, I reluctantly came to terms with the fact that since she didn't have any guards near her, Annabel would be the easiest to save. As much as I wanted to get Cole and Luke before her, I just simply couldn't risk it. If I took either of the boys, someone would notice right away, and then the demons would be on high alert when I returned. Nope, it had to be Annabel first or no Annabel at all.

With my final decision made, I slid back to the doorway, hugging the shadows lining the walls. Then I curved around and started moving toward Annabel. There were fewer torches on this side of the room, making it easier for me to stay hidden. Once I got within a few feet of her, I paused to confirm that no one was paying attention to this side of the room, and quickly discovered they weren't. Ezariah still leafed through his book, and the demons in the back of the room still huddled around Cole, nearby Luke. *Now or never*, I urged myself, then flashed forward, swallowing Annabel inside my ghostly body. The childlike vampire never moved; she never noticed a thing. A new rush of boldness washed over me as I swirled around her body—tighter and tighter, my energy whirling between her skin and the cold hardness of her chains. I concentrated on my power, willing it to silence the chains. Then I closed my eyes, visualizing the only place I knew to go.

A few seconds later I opened my eyes, and I was no longer in the cave. Soft light glowed from a few hanging fixtures in the back room of Huron's bar. The poker table was directly in front of me, and thankfully it was empty. A quick search around showed there was no one else in the room, and I breathed a sigh of relief. I could feel Annabel's essence cradled inside my body as if she were part of my skin. Then she let out a panicked yelp. In a rush of air, I was hiding in the far corner of the ceiling, carefully watching the young-looking vampire. Wet trails glistened on her dirt-covered cheeks as she swung her head around the room with wide, disbelieving eyes. I could feel her emotions rushing to the surface, tingling along my arms like thousands of ants marching. A small part of her essence was still connected to me, and I could taste her fear, pure and raw. But there was also a soothing wave of relief as she began to accept she was no longer on Rhea—even though her mind couldn't begin to grasp how she'd left. And that's when the tears fell in violent sobs and she hugged her knees against her body, shaking and trembling as she let loose her harbored emotions. The harder she cried, the less I could see inside her, and I knew my connection to her was breaking. As her voice carried throughout the room, creating pained, eerie echoes, I knew it was just a matter of time before Huron heard her and came back here to help. And I still had two more friends to save. It was time to get back to Rhea. I closed my eyes, focusing on Cole and Luke, and praying for guidance on whom to save next.

When I opened my eyes I was in the demon's lair, floating in the shadows against the wall in the back of the room. Nothing had changed. All the demons still held their same stances—including the one I hated most who sat by the fireplace. I glanced over to where Annabel had been held prisoner and saw the empty, dangling chains. Relief flushed my body like small waves of heat spreading across my sheer skin. No one seemed to notice Annabel was gone. I breathed a quick sigh, then started contemplating my next step. There weren't any guards directly around Luke, but they were still close enough to make me think that grabbing him next might not be the smartest move. Still the demons surrounding Cole brought their own level of intimidation—even though soldier demons had proven not to be the sharpest tool in the shed when it came to thinking. Brute force was their main strength. Maybe I could be so lucky as to steal Cole right out from under their noses. Since they wouldn't be expecting that, they wouldn't know what to watch out for. Plus, deep in my heart, I felt that if anything went wrong, I needed to know Cole was safe.

My chest tightened with the realization that Luke would be left behind just a little bit longer, but I was confident in my decision and needed to act fast. I slowly looked at each of the soldier demons, and saw that none of their eyes were on Cole. They blankly stared toward the wall, seemingly in some kind of trance. In a rush of wind, my body engulfed Cole's and I was swirling in tight circles around him just like I'd done with Annabel. I could feel his face pressing hard enough against his knees to nearly crush bone if he were human. My energy coursed along his body, conforming to his skin, and gently holding the chains to prevent any clinking. My upward view of the demons showed they hadn't changed position, or even bothered to glance our way. I moved quicker, churning around Cole like a mini-cyclone. Then I opened my mind to one of the places we'd gone to in Colorado, willing all my power to take us there.

A short moment later, I was on the edge of a small pond with water spilling into it from an overhead rocky ledge. Sunlight poked through layers of clouds like sheer yellow ribbons, glistening across the wave pool—sparkling and ethereal. A faded green clearing opened up behind me filled with fuzzy white flowers that were swaying in the chilly afternoon breeze, interspersed with minuscule patches of ground frost. I breathlessly gazed down and relaxed upon seeing Cole. *We made it*, I thought with a satisfied smile. He was sitting in the same position as in the demon's lair: hunched over and cradling his legs, and his face was still buried into his knees. With my ghostly form wrapped around him like a blanket, I could feel his body stiffen and then his face begin to rise slowly.

Panic seized me. I couldn't risk Cole seeing me even though he'd most likely just assume he'd seen a ghost. After what had happened to Croix... No! I couldn't take any chances. Not with the man I loved. There were groves of trees, and thick, overgrown brush just on the other side of the small clearing. Their dark shadows would be the perfect place to hide. I focused on keeping some of my energy around Cole's body. The sunlight wouldn't kill him, but it was still uncomfortable for a vampire to be in, especially in his condition. Then, in a brush of motion, I was hovering inside the safety of the forest, watching my vampire lover—or former lover—from a safe distance, willing my power to shield his body. The faint light shimmered on his fair skin, revealing muddy smears on his arms and back, and what appeared to be lacerations as if he'd been beaten with leather whips. His brown hair looked darker, matted and stained with blood. My heart caught in my throat and I swallowed back the tears that threatened to invade my eyes, wishing with every part of me that I could go to him and hold him inside my arms. But for now, I'd have to feel him through the essence of my power. His skin that was once smooth like silk now felt crusted from the dirt and dried blood. I could feel his body tighten with fear, could taste his panic on my tongue like a bad aftertaste. I watched his eyes widen, and I could sense their disbelief at what they saw. He slowly cast his gaze around, looking completely bewildered, unsure. I knew he couldn't believe what he was seeing. I could sense his mind telling him this was just an illusion. Doubt, fear, and sadness so thick with despair filled him, and because I was open to him, because I was feeling all of him, my own thoughts began to mimic his. As he released the tight grip he held around his legs, I could feel the tenderness in his muscles—aching, burning from lack of use. His arms dropped to his sides, and slowly his gaze rose up, up, eyes squinting against the veiled light. He gasped aloud, throwing a hand over his eyes, then hesitantly lowered it, his brows furrowing with confusion. I could feel his amazement that the sun wasn't hurting him, yet an urgency built up inside him, pushing him to take cover in the shadows of the trees. He painfully rolled over, getting on his hands and knees, then began crawling toward me. I'd stay with him until he made it to the edge of the forest, then I'd draw back my power and go, though I was not ready to leave him.

But I knew time was running out for Luke, and I needed to get back to Rhea—hopefully before anyone noticed the missing prisoners. Fat chance, I knew. Surely at least one of those demon imbeciles noticed Cole wasn't beneath their noses any longer. And if they caught that, they'd most likely have seen the empty chains on Annabel's side of the cave too. What measures would they take to keep Luke imprisoned? Or worse—what condition would he be in when I returned? As Cole moved closer, I could feel his essence on my skin getting warmer. Just as he reached the line of trees, I closed my eyes and pulled back the reins of my power, then vanished once more from Earth.

29

THE PULSING TORCHLIGHT CAST EERIE shadows on the bare stone walls. The soldier demons were gone. Ezariah was still by the fireplace, except now he was standing and there was no book in his hands. He angrily glanced around the room as if trying to see something—so much for hoping that the vampire disappearances would go unnoticed. Luke's body had been moved closer to fireplace, and still lay in a bloody heap, silver chains dangled around him, the side of his face pressed against the rocky floor. Ezariah's foot stuck out from underneath his thick robe, revealing a worn brown, gladiator-styled sandal. He ground it into Luke's back like he was trying to rub something off his shoe. "He's barely in this world," the scroll keeper called out in a warning tone. "If you attempt to get him, I'll finish him off!" His eyes moved around the room, as if he were talking to the empty air. But I knew those words were meant for me, and they sent chills along my ghostly flesh. I moved closer to the bookshelf, morphing my body into the wooden shelves and books for extra coverage.

At that moment, I prayed harder than I ever had before for permission to kill the demon scroll keeper. I stared at my ankh tattoo, willing it to flare up with crimson. *Please*, I silently begged, *please*. A few minutes dragged along, and nothing happened. No throbbing warmth at my wrist to confirm what I knew I needed to do—or really wanted to do. My teeth ground together as I contemplated my next move. The fireplace emitted too much light by Ezariah, and that would make it impossible to remain unseen. Plus, the demon's foot still ground into Luke's back. So not only would he see me, but he'd feel me when I encircled Luke. And there was no other way for me to orb him out of here.

"Damn it," I said under my breath as I impatiently hovered between wood and shadows. Ezariah seemed to be focusing on something at the other side of the room—which meant he didn't have the slightest clue where I was, or what to look for. But there was nothing I could do...yet. I'd bide my time. And once Ezariah stepped away from his position by the fireplace, that would be my moment to act.

The minutes dragged on, and a sense of urgency was building in my bones, rolling along my skin like electric waves. Ezariah hesitantly re- moved his foot from Luke's back, while lowering his arms to his side and slowly casting uneasy glances all around. "Guards!" he called out.

A moment later two soldier demons scurried into the room. They swiftly approached Ezariah and knelt down on one knee in front of the old man.

"What did you find?" Ezariah asked, anticipation in his voice.

"Nothing. No trace of whoever has taken the prisoners."

The demon scroll keeper's eyes narrowed. "That's impossible!"

"It's true," the other soldier demon squealed. "There's no one in the cave. No signs. No clues."

"Search the perimeter!" Ezariah exclaimed. He took a few deep breaths, then rubbed his beard as if contemplating any further instruction for the lower-leveled demons. "Those vampires could not have been taken right out from under our noses! Find them! Typhon will be outraged if he learns of this!"

Both soldier demons nodded, then abruptly stood and left the room.

So Typhon had taken my friends as prisoners—just one more reason to go ahead and kill the master demon. His absence right now was not only keeping him alive but also preventing me from disobeying the strict rules I was given of not killing him. Goody for both of us. Ezariah turned around, mumbling something under his breath. It was obvious he had no clue I was here or even believed that someone or something was in his lair. He took a few careful steps toward the fireplace, then turned around, his back facing me, and placed his hands (palms out) close to the vibrant, throbbing flames. I didn't need to see what he did next since I could hear his voice vibrating throughout the room as he chanted strange words in a language I couldn't understand. My body stiffened with anxiety. This was bad—really, really bad. Whatever spell he was trying to cast, I knew it was too dangerous to be here. I needed to get Luke and leave as soon as possible—before the demon scroll keeper finished his incantation.

The seconds ticked by. My heart thundered so hard I could feel it pulsing in my skull. Ezariah's head tilted back, his face toward the ceiling of the cave. I couldn't tell if his eyes were open or closed, but I remembered how his eyes had rolled in the back of his head the last time I'd witnessed him doing this. All of a sudden, I could feel a power building like clouds accumulating just before a storm. My body shivered at the strength of the dark energy that was beginning to surround me. I had to go. There was no more time. I gazed at Luke with a longing need rising in my chest. *You can't die*, Darius had told me. And it was time to put that to the test.

After finishing a quick prayer, I sprung out of the shadows in a whoosh of air, and my body wrapped around Luke's like a diaphanous blanket. Suddenly, an unrecognizable power blasted into me, intense enough I thought I'd been struck by lightning. I shook it off the best I could and kept swirling around Luke—tighter and tighter, faster and faster. Sharp tingles jolted through me again, but I fought them, willing my power to take control. Ezariah's chanting stopped and then he broke out in laughter, deep and sinister. He'd finished his spell and I wasn't out of the room yet. *Crap, crap, crap!* My heart was racing, but I kept moving…until everything in the room became nothing but a blur. With all my strength, I pushed away from this place, far, far away, with Luke locked inside my core.

The smell of sulfur filled my nose. Heat pressed against my skin, ever-present and suffocating. I opened my eyes and my breath caught at what I saw. Fire everywhere. Rivers of lava flowing through ravines and spilling over their ledges like thick, flaming waterfalls. The bare stone ground was splattered with the molten, fiery soup, some of it drying in dark, grayish-black clumps. Smoke hovered like a stale fog, hazy and unmoving since there was no wind. This place reminded me of what Hawaii must have looked like before it was transformed into the beautiful tropical paradise it is today. However, this definitely was not Hawaii.

I pulled Luke's body closer into me, casting a protective gaze at my unwelcoming surroundings. I could sense his aura was already starting to gain strength now that those silver chains were no longer binding him. And no sooner did I think I needed to get us out of here than the ground began rumbling and quaking violently. Rocks fell off some of the higher ledges, splashing into the ponds of lava below them. Large cracks ripped open on the surface, oozing more of that smoldering orange liquid. Once Luke's body began to teeter uncontrollably, I raised him up on a wave of my power like he was riding on an invisible magic carpet. I'd seen enough of this wretched place. Now it was really time to go.

But as I closed my eyes, I felt *his* presence like static electricity inside my ghostly flesh. The distraction was just enough for him to blast me with a fireball, and knock my hold loose of Luke. The vampire fell several feet and landed on the rocky surface with a *thud*. I willed my power to retrieve him, and at the same time thrust some of my energy out toward our attacker. But since there were three sets of fireballs coming my way, my power collided into them with an eruption that shook me from the inside out. Then another round of fireballs shot into me, burning, scorching, and I lost my hold of Luke once more.

And that really pissed me off.

Anger washed over me as I propelled another blast of energy ten times stronger than the last one. It burst through the oncoming fireballs as if they were made of feathers instead of solid, pulsing flames. Barely a second later, it struck the assailant with the force of a giant boulder, and he was blown backward before he crashed into a massive mound of dried lava. He peered at me, snarling, black eyes wide with disbelief. Then, using the wall of rock for help, he slowly pulled himself up to stand on his hooves. His gaze narrowed, spittle dripping from his sharp, stained teeth. "Reveal yourself or this vampire is dead"—his tone seething with vehemence.

My voice caught in my throat as I glimpsed Luke several yards away, at the foot of the master demon. Now what the heck was I going to do? I couldn't kill the red, horned enemy, and I could only continue fighting him in self-defense. There was no way to keep Luke safe without obeying the demon's demands. But I couldn't materialize without a whole other set of consequences. *Show yourself to no one* was what Darius had warned. My body tensed with anxiety, knowing I should orb away right now. But I couldn't leave Luke. We'd made it this far, and there was no way I could turn my back on him now. Not when we were this close to his freedom.

"Release him and I'll let you live," I said harshly, hoping to scare the demon into giving me Luke.

Typhon's head swiveled back as he burst into deep, thunderous laughter. The seconds ticked by as I pondered any other options. So far, I was coming up blank.

"I'll ask once more, but let me warn you, my patience has almost run out." He raised his clawed fist in the air. "If you do not show yourself right now, I will crush his heart—again. And there is no angel blood here to save him this time."

The clenching in my stomach returned, restless and tight. My eyes met Typhon's levelly, though I wondered if he could see them since I was still in my hazy form. Even now, I knew he'd be seeing me soon enough and I wondered if he'd recognize me in my black combat attire. *Only one way to find out*, I thought with the mildest twist of regret. I'd come clean with Darius the minute I saw him next, though I wished he'd appear right this instant and help me get out of this mess.

And that's when Typhon's patience ran out. His fist pivoted downward, rushing toward Luke's limp body. "Wait!" I called out as my body materialized. The master demon's fist stopped, hovering just above the center of the vampire's back as he raked me over with speculative eyes.

"What have we here?" he asked in a hushed voice, as if talking to himself. "I know you," he stated accusingly as he straightened.

"I know you too, pal" was my dry response. I took a few cautious steps toward him, feeling my gaze harden. "Give me the vampire"—sounding more a demand than a request. I was rather proud of myself for at least not acting scared.

"But you're fallen!" Typhon stammered, but holding his ground. "You were cast into another world for all eternity."

"I guess you could say that, though my eternity will be much different than you're thinking."

A soft snort escaped him. "It appears you're finally where you belong," he said, his voice almost purring with delight.

His statement reminded me that I was somewhere hot and horrible that I hadn't deliberately orbed to. "Where am I exactly?"

He half smiled, yet it looked more evil than anything else. "You're in my home now."

Cold slithered up my limbs, clinging to my insides like twisting, razor-edged vines. I was in the Underworld. Not Nempha (AKA faux hell) where I'd been trapped, but the real place of torturous fire and the home of a master demon, his many thousands of minions, and possibly the ultimate head devil of them all. A massive lump barreled its way up my throat and I clenched my fists, fingernails digging into my palms. Never had I so wanted to orb away. I had no business being here, but as I glanced down at Luke, my body remained frozen in place. And as I let my eyes roam my surroundings once more, making sure no other demons were around, I remembered something Darius had said that made me smile. "Give me the vampire," I said in a calm, steely voice. Then I added, "This is the last time I'll ask," for my own taunting amusement.

"No!" came his icy reply as he crouched down over Luke in a guarded stance. Then he hurled another series of fireballs toward me.

I dodged them easily with confident laughter rolling off my lips. The last of the flaming balls whizzed my way, and I ducked under it with grace and surety.

"*What* are you?" Typhon roared and thrust several more pulsing fireballs right for me.

I bent to the side avoiding two of them, then whirled around and jumped up, missing three more. And as I dropped to the ground, allowing a few more to hurtle by, I felt the much-anticipated heat flare up on my wrist. I stood up, straightening my body in one rapid motion. I flashed Typhon the widest of grins as I brushed my hands along my pants.

"What the hell are you smiling at?" was the last thing he ever said.

30

I RUSHED TO THE DARKEST CORNER of the back room at Huron's bar as Luke stirred to life on the sofa. Once the voodoo Indian had found Luke on the poker table moments after I'd left him there, he'd sent Annabel—who seemed to be doing much better—to bring in the same sofa they'd used with Cole. Two plasma bags hung from the metal holder, one jumbo-sized tube lodged down Luke's throat. Huron and Annabel had been taking shifts watching him, and the last time Annabel had been in here she'd cleaned him up with a damp cloth. He was still wearing the torn, bloody clothes, but at least his beautiful creamy skin was perfectly healed and sparkling clean. After being alone in the room for a bit, Luke finally came to. He sat up in a rush, eyes wide as he yanked the tube from his throat. His nostrils flared as his gaze roamed heavily around the room, confusion wavering across his hardened expression. I was certain he'd never pick up my scent, though, since it's impossible to get a whiff of a ghost—if that's even what you'd call me—so I remained confidently hidden in the shadows. I watched him get up slowly, his face softening as he must have recognized where he was. I'd brought him to Huron's since I still didn't know who had been at his apartment. I couldn't risk putting Luke in more danger while he was recovering.

He took a few steady steps in my direction and I knew it was time to go. Though I didn't doubt he'd be taken care of here, I couldn't bear to leave him without seeing for myself that he was okay. And he was going to be just fine. The only thing left for me to worry about was finding out what happened at his apartment, and I planned on going straight there and doing just that. Hopefully whoever had been there had returned, and I could deal with them and let Luke be none the wiser. I closed my eyes, a smile tugging the corners of my lips as I willed all my energy to take me away.

"Angel…"

I froze, eyes opening, my awareness centering back to this room. Luke moved to the side of the poker table, his gaze probing up and down the walls, his empty hands clenched at his sides. I waited, the seconds ticking by, but after a beat, his shoulders slumped and his face softened.

And just when I began to think I'd heard him wrong, he called out the pet name he'd given me once more.

My chest tightened and a cold chill raced up my spine. It wasn't possible for him to know I was here. I shook my head, floating deeper into shadows, burying most of my body inside the cracked, off-white wall. Luke moved closer. Panic surged up. I was already on the other side of the table, pressed deep enough into the ceiling and wall that only my eyes still hovered in the blackness. There's no way he could see me. No freaking way. And it was also impossible for him to pick up my scent. Absolutely impossible. I'd learned that from Darius in one of our many training lessons. So why in all the worlds was he saying my old nickname?

In a whir of motion, he was on the poker table. I never even saw him move. He was just there, crouching, the tops of his fingers resting on the green padding like a cat about to pounce. He closed his eyes and sniffed the air, inhaling deeply. Suddenly he was standing, his face just a couple feet away from mine. And as he opened his eyes, there was a knowingness in them, a satisfaction that he'd found what he was looking for.

The world stilled around me.

"Angel, I know you're there," he said with confidence, and all I could do was continue to stare.

Then the door opened and Annabel walked in. "What are you doing up there?" she asked, her tone filled with surprise. She shut the door and walked to the edge of the table, smiling as she peered up at Luke.

His brows furrowed, then, hesitantly, he gazed down. His lips compressed but he said nothing, and then he jumped off the table to embrace her. "You're okay," he finally said. "How did you, how did I…how did we get out of there?"

My tension eased a little. At least he wasn't going to tell Annabel he thought I was here.

"I don't know," she replied, pulling away. "I just opened my eyes and here I was. Huron's place. Thought it wasn't real at first. Huron had to stab me with a knife to get me to come around." She chuckled at the memory. "And then *you* show up out of nowhere."

Luke shrugged. "I don't know how I got here either." He ran a hand through his messy brown hair, a small frown dipping the corners of his mouth. "Maybe I need you to grab that knife."

Annabel giggled, squeaky and childlike. With a finger she tapped him on the chest a few times, then said, "It's not every day a vampire gets a miracle. But I promise you, we're home, we're safe, and *that* is our reality."

"Did that other vampire…Cole…is he back too?"

She shook her head. "I haven't seen him yet. But, who knows." She shrugged. "Maybe we should keep an eye out for him."

A slight nod was his only response.

Annabel raised a hand to his face, grazing his cheek with her fingertips. "You look good"—her voice low and giddy.

Luke stepped back, putting a small space between them. I could sense his uneasiness, could see it in his eyes as he glanced back my way. "Do you mind giving me a little time in here?" was what he finally asked.

"Sure, of course. I needed some alone time too, once Huron convinced me where I was. I'll be out in the bar, and I'll be sure to tell Huron to give you a little time before coming back here."

Luke met her gaze levelly. "Thanks."

"No problem." She turned on her heel, then stopped in the doorway. "You might need some *real* food soon, but I'll wait 'til you're ready." With that she closed the door, and Luke's eyes were already boring into my little, dark corner.

And I didn't plan on sticking around to figure out how he knew I was there. Not even Annabel considered the possibility I'd brought them home; she certainly would've said something if she had. But after my suicide attempt—which she'd witnessed firsthand—why would she? With my mind heavy in thought and my heart shuddering beneath my chest, I floated above the ceiling, then closed my eyes and orbed away.

After a beat, I was in Luke's apartment, nestled in blackness within the curve of walls and ceiling. I sensed its presence before I opened my eyes. My old enemy wasn't in his komodo-dragon-looking form. Nope, he was in somewhat of a human form—yet the sex was questionable even though I'd always referred to it as a "him." There was a gas can in his lizard-like hands with claws that looked like half moons with sharp points at the tips. A pair of jeans cut off at the knees and a tee was all he wore. Dark green scaly skin covered the rest of his body, and his feet were bare and looked similar to his hands. His face was also reptilian with the sunken nose, angular jaw, and definitely more male than female. With a last probing gaze around the room, he focused on the table, tipping the gas can and splashing its contents all over the books.

And as Moros moved on to the sofa, I was faced with a tough question: Do I stop him from blowing up Luke's place? Added to the fact that I'd also love to know why he was even here with books about raising the dead in the first place. I watched the demon soak the entire apartment, feeling worry, concern, and the strongest emotion of them all—curiosity. I wanted—no, needed—to know what the heck had been going on in here. Even though I knew Darius would be angry, a part of me built my confidence up with the fact that my guide was probably already beyond furious with me. I'd killed Typhon. Yes, the ankh had lit up, but only because Typhon had begun plotting in his mind everyone he would tell my little secret to, and since Darius hadn't shown up, it had been my pleasure to take care of it. If I materialized now, I was certain my wrist would eventually flare again, leaving me no choice but to get rid of Moros too. Which, the more I thought about it, sounded like a really good idea.

With the force of a crashing train, I thrust some of my power at the demon as I materialized. Moros flew over the table, colliding into the wall beyond it with a *bang*. He slowly stood up, head shaking rapidly, obviously dazed. And when his beady black eyes landed on me, his gaze hardened with a snarl. "It can't be," he hissed, the words sounding thick with a Russian accent.

"How ya been, Moros?" I asked with a more chipper-sounding tone. "It's been a while…" I let my last statement trail off as I blasted him with another energy ball—this one not quite as intense as the last.

After he recovered, he stared squarely at me, his reptilian eyes wide with surprise. "But we tried everything. Nothing worked. You were gone." Those last words he mumbled under his breath.

"What do you mean, 'we tried everything'?"

He cowered with no more room to move, his body pressing against the wall. "Pleas-s-s-s-e. Don't hurt me again."

I folded my arms in front of my chest. "That's entirely up to you, demon. Tell me what you were doing with books about raising the dead. And while you're at it, I'd also love to know who you were working with." I moved a little closer, my voice deepening. "Don't make me ask again."

"We were trying to raise *you*," he stammered through hisses. "Typhon knew you'd been—"

"Typhon is who you were working with?"

"Yes-s-s-s." The word slithered through my ears.

"But Typhon thought I was cast to another desolated world for all eternity?" I made it a question even though that's what the master demon had told me.

Moros bobbed his head. "My master wanted to raise you back in this world." He straightened but held his position against the wall. "But we weren't able to locate you." He slid an observing gaze beyond me, then added, "Even with your essence, which was difficult to find."

So that's why they'd torn up the place—looking for a small piece of my old existence with hopes of bringing me back and having me serve him. Just what Typhon had always wanted. I guess the blood I'd given Luke simply wasn't enough, and obviously they were clueless to the parts of me I'd shared with Cole. A small chirp of laughter escaped my lips as I thought of the irony, such a shame the master demon wouldn't be here to enjoy the fact that I was back. I dropped my arms to my sides, hands clenched tightly with power throbbing just beneath the skin. "Why are you burning the place down? Why not just take the books and abandon it?"

"It was my master's orders-s-s. Destroy the evidence permanently."

I was just going to love breaking the news to him. "Typhon is dead. No reason to burn anything now."

He eyed me suspiciously. "I don't believe you."

Then the heat scorched the flesh on my wrist, tugging my mouth into a smile. "Well, it *is* true, but you're not going to be able to confirm it," I smarted, raising my right hand straight out in front of me, pointing my closed fist at him. I could feel the power surging with the gusto of a veiled raging inferno, and just as I was about to release its horror, Darius shimmered to life beside me.

"What are you doing?" Simple question but spoken from the depths of his anger, and it rattled my insides with fear.

"Who are you?" Moros called out, but I barely registered that he was speaking and didn't hear anything else.

In a gut reaction I held out my flaring wrist. "I'm doing my job"—spoken confidently. Goody for me.

"You're creating jobs. And this must stop."

"I can explain...," I started, words rushing off my tongue as I dove into what had happened when Ezariah sent me to the Underworld. As I summed things up, I noticed that Darius' ankh was glowing just like mine.

He considered me a short moment, then turned his attention to Moros.

"You can let me go. I won't say anything. Pleas-s-s-e," the demon begged.

But I wasn't surprised when Darius sprung toward him and thrust his fist through Moros' neck, instantly decapitating him. The demon's remains became an oozing black smoke, which moments later evaporated into nothing.

My guide was next to me in the next heartbeat. "I'm assuming he was blowing the place up."

I nodded.

Darius' eyes roamed the room, then he sighed deeply. "Let's get this cleaned up. The only thing we're taking is those." He gestured toward the books.

After we finished scrubbing the place down in complete silence, we grabbed all the books—both of us carrying more than we could handle—and orbed back to our training field. There, we combined our powers to destroy the demonic grimoires. They vaporized, leaving trails of smoke in their wake. All the while, I'd been wondering why Darius never came to help me when I was in Hell. That and wanting an explanation as to why Luke could sense me in the back room at Huron's. Since our ankhs were dark with ink instead of blazing crimson, no better time than now to address my concerns.

"Why didn't you come help me when I was in the Underworld?"—my voice more accusing than inquiring.

He stared at me, knowledge sizzling beneath the depths of his flaming red eyes. "I would have come had the threat not been destroyed before I could get to you."

Well, that removed my suspicions that Darius had been following me around, and brought me to my next question, which I was afraid to ask. It must've shown in my eyes, because my guide raised a brow. "You're scared of something."

I grimaced. "Yes I am. But I respect you and I know I must talk to you about this." I stepped forward, grabbing his arm. "Promise me you won't do anything—yet." I shook his arm. "Promise me!"

Instead of the argument I'd expected, my guide just nodded.

But since I wasn't convinced, I added, "Is that a promise? Your word?"

"Yes."

At first, the words were difficult to find as I tried explaining what had happened with Luke at Huron's bar. Once I got going though, the story flew out of my mouth. Moments later, when I finished, I gazed at Darius expectantly.

"This is the vampire whom you shared blood with?"

I bobbed my head slowly. "Uh huh."

"And he could feel your aura when you were still a guardian too?"

"Yep. Once he gave me his blood."

Darius ran a hand through his hair. "But if he were to tell anyone—"

"He won't. I know we can trust him. Plus, I didn't purposely show myself, so he can't be punished for simply *thinking* he felt me."

"You said that about your other vampire friend, but by the time I arrived, his essence was swarming with the prospect of gossip, and the ankh was ready with fire."

I clenched my fists at my sides, hard enough my nails pierced the tender flesh on my palms. "I didn't know Croix as well. He was more Cole's friend than mine. And I never swore his secrecy." My teeth ground together. "But I'm swearing on my existence that Luke can be trusted."

Darius stared at his wrist as if he was seeking it for advice. And after a few beats, his fiery gaze found me. "Selene…"

My heart thundered beneath my chest, waiting for him to spit it out.

"If the ankh should alert us," he went on, "I have no choice but to obey."

The clenching in my stomach returned. "But it hasn't"—my tone argumentative. "And I know for a fact Luke saw me. In my spirit form."

My guide rubbed his chin and paced for a minute. When he stopped, he scooped up my right hand and closed his eyes. He slowly brought my hand to his nose and inhaled the back of my palm deeply. Then he turned it over, sniffing the tattoo. His eyelids fluttered and then they slowly opened. I stared at him expectantly. "I believe the reason he scented you was because of his blood within you," he explained, his brows creasing. "And perhaps that same connection will keep your friend safe from true death."

I tugged my hand free, a wave of relief washing through me. "Does that mean I can reveal myself to him?"

Darius shook his head. "I don't know for sure. It would be risky."

Would it even be fair to do that with Luke, when I knew I definitely couldn't show myself to Cole? If only I'd taken some of Cole's blood instead of him just drinking mine. A heavy feeling sunk inside my chest, then began to rise with my next thought. Since Cole didn't seem to notice me before, I'd just assumed he couldn't—like most others. But now that I knew Luke could sense me, it made me wonder if Cole's drinking my blood would give us a stronger connection. Even though it might never be as strong as Luke's, I needed to know if something else was there. I strongly hoped there would be.

But then my chest tightened with despair. What did it matter if Cole could sense me if I couldn't show myself to him? What kind of relationship could be built on that? Me lingering in the shadows and him calling my name, but nothing more. Suddenly my throat constricted and instant tears fled from my eyes. My guide patted my back a few times, but chose not to say anything. There really was nothing he could say anyways. More tears rained down and I buried my face in my hands. Time seemed to stand still, and no matter how much of it passed, I was still broken.

31

I WRAPPED MY BODY IN SHADOWS, then fell in step behind the vampire in the alley. His boots thudded against the asphalt with each heavy, swift step. His body was covered by a full-length black trench coat, its hood shielding his head. His hands were buried inside the pockets, and there was a hunch to his back suggesting that he was cold. But I knew better. Vampires didn't get cold like humans did. And this vampire was acting like a human—to blend in better, and, more than likely, to score his next meal. But I wasn't here to stop him from doing that. I was only following him to see if he could sense me. Yes, I'm a glutton for punishment, I know.

Cole rounded the corner and I picked up my pace, staying hot on his tail. I got as close as I dared, afraid to fully leave the safety of the shadows. Sadly, my old boyfriend never seemed to notice my presence. But I just wasn't ready to give up on him yet.

There was movement not too far ahead of us; a quick glance showed it was a couple of people, and as we neared them, their foul, musky scents told me they were either homeless, drug addicts, or both. Cole's steps quickened, and then in a blur he was standing right behind them. Both were turned away, their backs facing my former boyfriend. "Hello, gentlemen." Cole's voice floated in the air like a song, and it made my heart skip a beat.

Slowly, the man in a torn gray blazer turned around. The way the light from the full moon shone on his face revealed a lot of wrinkles, and his half smile exposed missing teeth. His graying dark hair was a mess, some of it sticking to his forehead. "Hey buddy, where the heck did you just come from?" he asked with a surprised tone.

The other person didn't turn around, but did turn his head enough to show it was a man. He was a lot younger, with a smoother face and lighter, short hair. He wore a burgundy sweatshirt with some kind of collared shirt underneath that didn't really match. He considered Cole for a moment, then turned away, seemingly disinterested.

"I need a favor from you," Cole explained to the older man still gazing at him.

"Look around, buddy. There ain't much I can do for ya."

"Please," Cole begged. "I will pay you for your trouble."

The older man's eyes widened, and that got the attention of the other guy too. "Well, what's the favor?"—asked with anticipation. And it made me reconsider this guy being on drugs. His responses were too alert and his voice wasn't dragging.

"I need you to put this through my heart." From the pocket of his trench coat, Cole pulled out a dagger the size of his wrist to his elbow.

My breath caught in stunned surprise, and my heart started hammering. Why would Cole want a dagger jammed in his heart? Just the thought alone brought tears to my eyes, but I choked them back.

The older man let out a gasping whistle. "I don't know, man, I ain't never killed anyone before."

The younger guy grabbed his buddy's arm. "Wait just a second…how much money?"

"One thousand dollars. Cash." Cole brought his hand out from the other pocket, holding a wad of money. Presumably the thousand dollars.

The two men considered it for a moment, a hushed bickering passing between them. All the while, I was sinking deeper in a sea of dread, desperately praying the guys would politely decline and walk away. If only I could appear to Cole and talk to him. Surely, then, everything would be okay. But if I did that, I'd be risking his life in a whole other way, and he'd eventually find the same fate. I brushed the few tears that had managed to escape my eyelids, feeling a sharp tightness in my stomach—twisting, turning, and stabbing. Yet regardless of my silent pleas, no solutions presented themselves. Then, at last, the older man stepped forward. "Sorry, buddy. As much as we need the cash, we're just not willing to murder you for it."

A deep sigh rushed off my lips. Thank God Cole picked *these* guys. Most other people roaming the alleys would've done his favor without thinking twice. But my relief was short-lived when I realized that both men were locked in a vampire's trance. Cole had rolled their minds in a matter of seconds, and he was most likely instructing them to move forward with his demands. *Crap, crap, crap! What should I do? What can I do?* Tears rained down the sides of my face as the older man took the dagger from Cole. *I can stop this. I can stop this right now. This is madness. I can't watch Cole die the true death.* Vampires are extremely hard to kill. You can't do it by stabbing them through the heart alone. You have to twist the blade while it's inside the heart, rupturing it, and then the process of death will begin. That's why when I killed them, I pulled their hearts straight out of their chests. No waiting that way. But what my old lover was asking these humans to do would surely be a slow, painful death. One he definitely did not deserve.

Cole opened his arms wide, exposing his bare, sculpted chest. His perfect creamy skin glimmered in the brilliant light of the moon. With a dazed look on his face and glossed-over eyes, the younger guy moved back a few steps. That's when the older guy struck Cole with the dagger, shoving it deep inside his heart. But before he could twist the blade, I thrust a wave of my power straight at him. It blasted into the homeless men, throwing them through the air several feet before they crashed into a concrete wall. My lasered gaze was back on Cole, just in time to see him stagger to the side, his hands gripped firmly around the base of the blade. His body swayed a few times, then fell. In a rush of wind, I was there, holding him up with the energy of my diaphanous body. I opened all my senses to him, pushing my power through him like invisible electrical waves. I couldn't heal him, but I was doing my best to comfort him. A gargled noise came out of his mouth, deep from in his throat. Just hearing his pain cued more tears out of my eyes. I closed them, squeezing them shut, willing all my power to gently remove the blade from his heart so his body would begin regenerating. Once the dagger was free of his chest, I cast it to the side. It skidded across the asphalt, its clinking making eerie echoes inside the alley. I waited impatiently, the tension pressing against me like a boulder crashing on top of me. The seconds dragged by, and there weren't any signs that Cole was recovering. Hesitantly, I opened myself further to him, advancing dangerously close to the limit I was forbidden to show him. Yet, as I did that, something horrible was revealed to me. Cole wasn't healing…he was dying.

Suddenly I materialized and summoned the dagger, bringing it on invisible waves of energy to my awaiting hand. I moved swiftly, without thinking, my mind just focused on one thing: saving Cole. Nothing else mattered. I couldn't bear to watch him die. I sliced my wrist, vaguely noticing that I'd cut right through the ankh. There were instant rivers of crimson streaming from the wound as I urgently placed it over Cole's mouth. I wriggled his lips apart, pressing more firmly against his teeth. Tears choked out; I could barely catch my breath as I begged Cole to drink from me. But his body was limp, his lips unmoving. No suction, no licking—nothing. Anguish gnawed inside me. What if it was too late? What if vampires really did die quickly, unlike what I'd thought before?

"Drink, damn it! Drink my blood!" I screamed, my voice breaking with each word. "Cole, please! Drink!"

When nothing happened, I screamed again, this time wordless wailing that echoed throughout the night air. I bellowed louder, crying out to God. When He didn't respond, I called for Darius, willing my power to summon him. But Darius didn't come, nor did God ever answer me. I was alone with my dying former boyfriend, and there was nothing I could do.

It wasn't long before I could feel my wound stitching itself back together. I cried out again, raising my wrist and slicing the blade through the existing cut. Fresh blood instantly bubbled at the surface, and I pressed my wrist back against Cole's mouth in a panicked, shaky movement. My teeth ground together as I grabbed his chin with my other hand, forcing his mouth to open as I pressed my fingers deep into his skin and tendons. Then, I clenched the fist of my wounded arm, tightening my grip, then releasing it, creating a pulsating movement. In a steady stream blood dripped inside Cole's lips, like a trickling waterfall, splashing on his fangs and teeth, then seeping into the depths of his mouth. I let it flow for several thundering heartbeats, then I turned my wrist over and the blood pooled at the edge of the cut before I was able to move it over his heart, then twist it back over so my blood would flow on his stab wound too. Another several heartbeats passed, maybe more since I wasn't paying any attention to that, or anything else except helping Cole. My cut was starting to heal again, even as I pulsed my tightened fist. In blind desperation I raised it up to slice it again, but Cole coughed, and I froze, blade suspended midair.

Another single cough, and then he started hacking as if he were chok-ing on the blood. My breath caught with excitement and I lowered my hand to the ground, releasing the dagger. Then I gently grazed my fingers across his forehead. "It's okay. You're okay," I reassured both him and my-self. "Everything is going to be just fine."

The seconds ticked by and his coughing finally eased up. His eyes flut-tered, and then he slowly opened them. A tender warmth vibrated through my insides, relaxing the tension, as our eyes locked together for the first time since he watched me attempt suicide. A mixture of emotions danced within his twin sapphire orbs, swirling with doubt and disbelief. He pulled away, his head bumping against the asphalt, then he swung an anxious gaze at his surroundings. "No, it can't be..." His words broken in a whisper as he scooted away on his elbows and heels.

I sniffled, my eyes filling with tears. "I'm sorry." I shook my head, the reality of the situation sinking in. "You were dying! I couldn't just sit back and watch. I love you too much for that. But now..." My shoulders slumped and I stared at the ground. "Now you may end up with the same fate regardless. Cole"—I raised my face and met his gaze levelly—"I have no words except I'm sorry." I paused a moment, then added, "And I love you."

He furrowed his brows. "Selene?"—spoken with doubt. "But you were cast to a demon. I watched you plunge the knife through your chest."

It was pointless to hold anything back now since I knew I'd already gone too far by revealing myself. "I am not fallen, Cole. I've been spared because of my sacrifice. This is what I am now...something I'm not even sure what to call it. I'm a defender of balance between good and evil." I held out the wrist with the tattoo, and noticed it was completely healed as if I'd never sliced it. "This is what I am."

His eyes widened in disbelief.

"And by revealing all of this to you," I went on in a rush, "I have brought death upon you." My gaze narrowed. "Though it seems you were already working on that." Those last words seething with anger.

Pink moisture glistened in Cole's eyes. Then he was on me, the weight of his body knocking me over and crushing my back against the ground. His arms were stretched around my neck like thick, muscular snakes, and when his lips locked onto mine, my whole world began to spin. My body shuddered with delight as warm waves flushed my face. Our kisses grew urgent, needy, hungry, and I panted for air between each one. He moved inside my mouth, sucking on the tip of my tongue then pushing deeper, slurping and sliding, taking all of me inside him. His arms released just enough for his hands to find my hair, pulling and tugging. My hands were on his cheeks, my fingers digging into the soft, silky flesh, directing his movements as we kissed. "I missed you so much," he growled, then his mouth was crushing mine all over again. His body pressed harder against me as his right hand trailed down my side, coming to a stop at my waist. Then he gently moved under the hemline of my tank, his touch softly grazing along my skin until he reached the button of my pants. With a flick of his wrist, the button released; the zipper was down a split-second after that. My body tensed with anticipation. I'd never been more ready to give myself fully to the man I loved. And now that I was no longer an angel, I didn't feel those restrictions. So instead of stopping him—like I had all the times before—I tore off his coat, seeing that though his chest was smeared with blood the knife wound had completely healed, and got busy unfastening his jeans. As if I wasn't moving fast enough, Cole intervened and ripped them off, tearing the rest of my clothes away too. And for the first time, we lay together with the heat of my flesh burning into the coolness of his. Our kisses were slow and sensual, filled with more tenderness than I'd ever felt. He slowly traced the lines of my body with the tips of his fingers, leaving gooseflesh in the wake of his touch. I released a deep breath, and locked my eyes on his. They swirled with mysterious hunger, burning with the intensity of his need. I nodded with silent agreement and closed my eyes, tilting my head to the side. A moan tore from my throat as his fangs sunk into my neck, sending waves of pleasure throughout my body. Then I lost all sense of reality as we made love there in the alley, under the light of the full moon.

I awoke to searing flesh on my wrist. The night was now a suffocating darkness with no moon or stars casting down any light. I was cuddled against Cole, his arms snuggly holding me. His trench coat was wrapped around us, and as I sat up in a rush, I realized we were still naked. "What's wrong?" he asked as I fumbled for my clothes.

"Nothing," I lied, my mind racing with panic.

"I've always been fond of the truth," a familiar voice echoed throughout the alley.

I startled, and then in a flash Cole was standing, snarling, fists clenched in front of him.

My chest tightened as I looked up at my vampire lover. This was the moment I'd dreaded, and all along I knew it was coming. At least I was able to experience what it was like to be with him, and the memories of our special moments would stay with me forever. I swallowed hard and held up a hand toward Cole, gesturing for him not to move. Then I turned, letting my gaze roam the alley until I found *him* lurking in the shadows.

Darius—in his human form—moved closer, his boots crunching the ground with each step. I braced myself for the fight, because I surely wouldn't let Cole go without one. "Get dressed" was all my guide said as he folded his arms in front of his chest.

"Who are you?" Cole demanded through a growl.

Darius half laughed, his eyes glowing like red beacons in the darkness. "Who am I, Selene?"

I swallowed hard, rushing to pull up my pants. "This is…um…my boss," I informed him as I pulled my tank over my head. Then I retrieved Cole's jeans and handed them to him. "Put these on."

"No!" Cole spat. "I won't weaken my position for him to attack."

"Just do it"—my voice laced with warning. "Now!"

Once Cole got his jeans on, Darius took a few steps closer. That's when I noticed the flaring ankh on his wrist.

"I called for you," I stammered, my gaze locked on my guide. "Cole was dying. I couldn't…" I shook my head, panic swirling inside me.

Darius held his arm up, exposing his flashing tattoo to us. "I will never sacrifice this power!" he cried, his voice roaring throughout the alley. "I will fight for its honor always." His eyes locked on me as he continued, "I warned you not to show yourself to anyone. I even showed you what happens to those who see you." He gave a long sigh, his shoulders slumping as he lowered his arm.

"Selene explained everything to me," Cole exclaimed. "I would never betray her. You must know that!"

Though I was pretty sure it wouldn't matter, I still confirmed his words with my guide. "He wouldn't!" I called out as I stepped forward. "And I will not let you take him without a fight."

"I will crush you!" Darius warned.

"You won't touch her!" Cole yelled, moving beside me.

I pressed my hand against my lover's chest, cautioning him not to move. "You are no match for him. Please, Cole, stay out of this," I begged.

"I will not," Cole shot back, his gaze narrowing. "I love you and I can't lose you again. I'd rather truly die than be without you. That's why I had those men stab me."

"Your wish is mine to grant," Darius said as he moved toward my lover with death in his eyes.

"No!" I screamed, throwing myself in front of Darius, falling to my knees before him. "Please, spare him. Kill me instead. Please."

"I'm sorry, but you are too valuable to lose." Darius thrust me to the side with an enormous blast of power, sending me hurtling into the concrete wall. After a few seconds of stars dancing in my head, I jumped up and swung around. My guide struck at Cole, but missed when Cole dropped to the ground and kicked out his leg. Darius effortlessly jumped up as Cole's leg swooped under him, then my guide leapt back and shoved his hands outward, firing an energy ball and landing it on Cole's chest. My vampire lover flew back several feet and landed on the ground with a *thud*. He was out cold, and Darius was moving in to finish him.

I closed my eyes, harnessing all of the power inside me. My body tingled with electric vibrations and all the hairs on my arms rose up. I willed the energy to my awaiting fingers, then pushed all of it into Darius. Upon impact, my guide was knocked back several feet, and he crashed to the ground, his arm breaking his fall. "What are you doing?" he demanded as he got back up. His body was shaky and his balance seemed off. Good, I'd meant that to happen.

Keeping my eyes on Darius, I went to Cole. He was still out, but I could sense that he was okay. No major damage had been done—yet. "I will not sit back and watch you kill the man I…" As I said "love," I blasted another wave of power toward my guide, but he was ready and blocked it with an invisible shield of his own. Then he thrust a diaphanous orb of energy at me, knocking my head back hard enough I'd have whiplash if I were human. Something moist and tangy dripped over my lips. I licked it, tasting my blood, and smiled. "Is that all you got?"—my voice laced with ice. With the speed of a vampire I rushed Darius, while my power vibrated off my skin like sound waves. His gaze hardened, then he shot toward me at the same speed. Energy pulsed out from his body, and as we collided, there was a spectacular explosion of white flames. He swung high, I ducked, but he was ready with an uppercut that landed in my gut. Air flew from my lungs, and though I was gasping, I jumped up and kicked out my heel, crushing my guide's cheekbone. I fell back into a warrior's stance: my right leg a foot in front of my left, knees slightly bent, and my fists raised in front of my chest. Astonishment flashed on Darius' face—obviously he didn't think I'd have the momentum after he'd given me that punch, and I was happy to surprise him. He rolled his head to the right, then the left, releasing a few pops from his neck. Then he rushed forward, throwing out a right hook, but I dropped and slid out my leg to take him down. He sprung upward, sending another blast of energy when he thrust out his palms. I threw my arm over my face to block it, feeling tingles racing just beneath my skin with the force of my power. Then, sensing where my guide stood, I used my free hand to send a series of energy waves at him. As soon as I couldn't feel his power against my shield, I pushed up, did two forward flips, then kicked him in the chest as hard as I could. That's when I smelled his blood. In a raging whir, I was on him like a savage animal, fighting to hold down his arms so I could get to his neck. Blood dripped from the corners of his lips as he screamed for me to stop. My power was building and building, seeping out of my pores—and penetrating through all of my guide's invisible defenses. Sensing his moment of weakness, I pressed my mouth into the soft flesh of his neck and bit down with the force of a vampire. Even though I didn't have fangs, blood gushed into my mouth, coating my tongue and warming my throat.

Darius roared with anger, screaming for me to stop. His power was pulsing at the edges of mine, but he wasn't strong enough to break through. And that meant he couldn't stop me, so I kept drinking, the warmth of his existence filling me completely. And when I finished, I moved my lips to his ear and said in a mocking voice, "I have tasted your power and you are no match for me. I will crush you if you do not grant my desire."

"What…what do you want?" he stammered, his voice weak and out of breath.

I licked my lips and swung my gaze to where Cole was just beginning to stir. "I want him to live."

Darius followed the direction of my eyes. His lips compressed, but he didn't say anything. I pressed his arms harder into the ground as I shook him. "Your answer!" I demanded through a growl.

"Selene, what are you doing?" Cole called out. I heard movement behind me and I knew he was approaching.

"Stay out of this, Cole!" I warned icily without taking my lasered gaze off my guide. "What is your decision?"

He swallowed, then nodded. "Your vampire will not die by my hand."

"Swear it!" I roared. "I want your word with blood!" Then I glanced at Cole, who was standing directly behind me with wide eyes. "Bring me the dagger," I instructed him.

He did as I requested without a word. I released Darius to take the blade, and sat up, slicing my tattoo once more. Even though it was blazing hot, my skin still split open with ease and blood instantly pooled to the surface. Power and heat throbbed while blood flowed in streams of dark red. When I grabbed my guide's arm, he resisted at first, but a hardened glare from me seemed to help him loosen up, and as I raised his wrist, I brought the blade through its fiery center. Crimson spilled out, trailing down his arm as I brought our glowing ankhs together. Sparks of power shot out from us as the tender flesh of our wounds rubbed together, bonding his promise to me in blood. "Cole's afterlife will be spared, on your honor," I said, staring into Darius' flaming eyes.

"On my honor," he repeated with defeat in his tone.

Pulsing waves of heat shot out from our wrists, visible the way heat simmers off asphalt roads in the dead of summer. The throbbing in my cut increased, sending sharp pain up my arm. Darius jerked away, gingerly rubbing his wound. Though it was coated in blood, I could still see the dullness of the tattoo's ink and I quickly glanced down at mine. A long sigh pushed from my lips when I saw the fire was out on my ankh too.

Cole helped me stand, then pulled me inside his arms. Relief flushed over me and I released a deep, warm breath against his bare, cool chest. We held each other a brief moment, then I pulled back enough to turn around. Darius was standing, his eyes focused intently on us, frowning. "I had such a love once," he said by way of an explanation. "They all eventually die. No one, nothing, can outlive us. We are the true immortals. Remember that."

I stepped forward, feeling a tightness spread out in my chest. "What are we?"

"We are defenders of balance."

I shook my head, my gaze falling to the ground with disappointment. He'd already told me that version of what we were at least a hundred times now.

"We are *Immortals*, Selene," my guide went on. "We can take physical and spiritual form at will. And with the power of the ankh, we are unstoppable."

"But I tasted your death," I wondered aloud.

"Yes, but it was only the death of my physical form," Darius replied.

"You can die one way, only to live in another?" Cole asked, stepping beside me and taking my hand.

Darius nodded. "Something like that."

"But if you're both undefeatable," Cole pressed on, "how did Selene overpower you?"

My guide and I stared at each other, both of us knowing the answer, but neither willing to be the one to say it.

I felt Cole's eyes burning the side of my face, so I slowly turned to him. "There was vampire blood inside me when I was cast down into this existence." I swallowed hard, seeing the pain in Cole's eyes. "Because of that, I'm not *exactly* like Darius."

My lover grimaced. "Luke." His brows furrowed. "Did you bring him back from Rhea?"

My head bobbed slowly up and down, unable to speak over the lump in my throat. I glanced away, the pressure of his gaze too intense to look at. That's when I noticed my guide was gone. He'd orbed away undetected with my mind fully on the vampire in front of me. But that was the least of my worries at the moment. Though it was forced, Darius and I had an understanding, and until he understood my extra powers, he definitely wouldn't be challenging me.

Cole gripped my shoulders, shaking me roughly, regaining my full attention. "Has he seen you..."—he shrugged—"like this?" His gaze slid up and down my body, suggesting my new look.

"No," I shot back defensively. "I have not shown myself to him." I struggled to find my next words and knew no matter what I said, it just wouldn't sound good. "But I think Luke was able to sense my presence."

"Sense your presence?" Cole released me and ran a hand through his hair. "How could he...?" Realization dawned on his face and he raised a brow. "It's the bond of his blood inside you."

My stomach clenched as I nodded. "But if I reveal myself to him..."

"Then you'll have to kill him," Cole finished for me. "Or the other Immortal will do it for you."

I nodded. "But there is a small chance that Luke wouldn't be affected since he can already sense me. It would be risky to try it, though."

Cole frowned and cupped his hands on my face. "I don't want you to see him again. Though, honestly, if it meant his death I wouldn't be upset." The chill of his fingers pressed deeper into my skin, his blue eyes burning into mine. "Please. Baby, I love you. We can get on with our new lives now...without him."

My teeth grazed my bottom lip as I considered his request. Could I really abandon Luke and never see him again? Our blood bond was strong and I hated how Cole and I didn't have that same connection. Was that really the only reason I was holding on to Luke? Would I care for him the same if he hadn't given me his blood? Yet, I'd never be able to answer those questions since there was no way to rewind the clock. But there was a way to deepen my bond with Cole. "I want to drink your blood," I said with conviction.

"Selene," he growled, his eyes swirling like bottomless pools of mystery. "Are you sure?" he asked as he brought his wrist to his mouth.

"I want to be one with you," I said, watching his fangs rip through his skin, blood trickling over his hand.

At once, he grabbed my face. I could feel the tips of his fingers smearing *his* blood on my cheeks. I felt my eyes widen with anticipation as his glistening red lips lowered toward me. The first drop of crimson moved from his tongue to mine, and my whole head zinged with delight. My body felt light as feathers as our kiss deepened, bringing a raging hunger to the surface. When he pulled back, I gasped with need, but then he brought his wrist to my mouth and I greedily bit into it. As I ravaged him, slurping and sucking his blood, I could feel our bond growing, the final door opening between us. A groan slipped through my lips, muffled against his skin. I'd never felt more in love with him, and the intensity of those feelings pressed into my heart, constricting it with unbreakable passion.

And just when I thought my body would burst of euphoria, Cole took his wrist away and gently brushed his lips across mine. "I love you." His breath caressing me with a chill, and my body trembling with need.

"I love you, too." I rubbed a hand across my mouth, and it came back smeared with red. "If I'd known how delicious you were"—a sly smile tugging the corners of my lips—"I'd never have waited this long to taste you." Then I licked my hand, the metallic taste sending waves of pleasure through my mouth.

He chuckled, then took me inside his arms. "I've never been happier, Selene. We are going to have a great after-afterlife together."

I stopped licking my hand and giggled. Then I pulled him tighter against me. "I completely agree."

We held onto each other as though our lives depended on it, then his lips crushed mine once more. As the kiss deepened, a strong sense of happiness poured over me, and I knew without a doubt that Cole was that one being in all the worlds that was my soul mate. And I would fight to the death to be with him always and preserve our perfect love.

****

Want to read more by Ashley? Here is the first (unedited) chapter of her upcoming urban fantasy/paranormal thriller, *Crimson Flames*—Book Two in *The Crimson Series*. Content within this chapter is subject to change prior to final publication.

Crimson Flames
By Ashley Robertson

1

The Deal

MY STOMACH CLENCHED as I sensed the vampire's approach. He was close. So close I could feel the thrum of his power vibrating along my skin. The hairs on the back of my neck rose, and I knew if I was going to use my power for defense, then I needed to bring it forth now. I closed my eyes, forcing myself to breathe as deeply as I could—which thankfully had gotten easier with practice. I focused on the energy inside me, willing it to the surface, and as I felt it swelling, building like an approaching storm, I threw out my hand, gripping Stone's shirtsleeve and urging him to the floor. "Get down! He's here!"

Stone raked me with a look that told me he was not too pleased, but then fear swept over his face when he realized just how little time we had.

That's when the wooden door to the pub burst open—bits of wood and dust raining down from the force. Even though Stone should've cowered behind me—since his gift of reading blood wasn't something he could fight with—somehow he'd found some bravery and boldly stood to my side. Though I appreciated it, I didn't like it, and desperately wished he had listened to me. But I couldn't think about that *and* call forth the fire within me at the same time. So I pushed Stone to the back of my mind with the silent promise of dealing with him later. Then I returned my attention to the power building inside me. One last deep breath and my heart shuddered to life inside my chest, making a rhythmic pattern with my faux breathing. A tingling warmth spread from head to toe, then settled on my awaiting hands. Seconds later, there was a glowing orb of fire (about the size of a basketball) cupped inside my palms. And just as the vampire appeared through the settling fog, I called out, "Not another step, Tristan, or it will be your last!"

"I think you should reconsider your threat," Tristan shot back with caution. "We are on the same side."

That, I sincerely doubted, but I knew killing a member of the Head Council would definitely put me on the Most Wanted listed. Which I might already be on, since I'd helped the human this vampire was here to claim escape.

"She's not bluffing!" Stone said through a snarl. I wanted to glare him into silence, but I refused to take my eyes off of the vampire standing in the broken doorway, wearing a black Armani-looking suit—now lightly covered with dust. It was a custom for all the members of the Head Council to wear black suits, but each of them would wear shoes and an undershirt of their own choosing. I guess it was a way to express their individual personalities. Yet this one seemed to express himself through his spiked, platinum blond hair, not the basic black undershirt and matching boots— which seemed so boring compared to what I'd seen a few of the other Council members wearing. But this vampire was far from boring. He was a tracker for the Council—one of the best hunters on earth. And he was after my human boyfriend.

"You know why I'm here, Abigail," Tristan said in a scolding tone. "The human was here."

I felt my gaze narrow as I carefully took a step forward, the ball of flames growing hotter on my hands. "Yes, he was. It's my fault he wasn't captured."

"That's not exactly true," Stone said as he moved up beside me.

I stole a few deep breaths, fighting the urge to throw my fireball at him instead of the blond vampire in the suit.

"Please explain!" Tristan ordered with impatience. But as Stone attempted a reply, he was cut off. "Not you! I want to hear this directly from Abigail!"

"Abby," I corrected, feeling sweat forming above my brows.

The vampire smirked, folding his arms in front of his chest.

"I did not restrain him because I do not believe he will be kept safe once in your hands," I went on. "And until I can prove his innocence in all of this, I feel it's best that he stay far away from *you*."

A tinge of red formed a ring around Tristan's irises as he scowled. "That is not your decision. He must pay for his involvement with those rogue vampires, including Bronx. He cannot get away with helping them try to destroy our stronghold."

"I made an agreement with the other Council members," I reminded him. "Doesn't that count for something? Your word is nothing if your actions do not back up what you say!" My voice was getting louder, my patience thinning. And the angrier I got, the more difficult it became to control the fire in my hands.

"Yes. We have a deal," Tristan assured. "We will not kill him or harm him—Just as we told you—But that does not mean he won't be punished some other way."

"I don't believe you," I shot back through gritted teeth.

Stone put his hand on my shoulder. "Abby, what are you—"

In a flash of movement, the vampire closed the distance between us and held Stone in a headlock from behind with his fangs hovering over my friend's neck. And since it wasn't to drink Stone's blood—since Stone was also a vampire—then that meant it was a threat to rip out my friend's jugular. From there it would be too easy to finish Stone by ripping off his head. And that's when my patience snapped. There were only two ways to kill a vampire—burning to death or decapitation—and he was about to find out first hand just how very dangerous I was. Sure, he could threaten to kill my friend, but he'd be burned alive before Stone's head hit the ground. I placed all my focus on the orb of heat in my hand, willing it to retract to half its size while intensifying with heat, then I thrust it at Tristan's face. In a blur of motion, he ducked, throwing Stone to the floor, as the fireball grazed over his head, singeing the soft tips of his hair. A snarl swept from his throat as his fiery gaze locked onto mine. There was a brief hesitation, burnt hair and musk filling my scents, then something similar to curiosity flashed over his eyes and he was airborne, charging straight for me. My body shuddered as heat blasted out of every pore, radiating from me like invisible steam. The vampire immediately jumped back, throwing his arms over his face, and retreated back by the door from which he'd entered. Satisfied I'd made my point, I pulled all the heat back inside me, then I rushed over to Stone and helped him up. "You okay?" I asked.

He nodded by way of an answer, then ran his hand through his brown hair—which was completely messed up now.

I felt my gaze narrow as I glanced across the bar, by the door. "Do that again and I'll kill you," I warned with vehemence as I helped Stone get up.

Tristan brushed some of the dust off his pants. "Abigail, I'd rather not have to repeat that again. Hopefully I've made my point by now," his mouth curling into an amusing grin. "I would not have harmed your friend, as I'm sure Mr. Rayver here is already aware." He glanced at my disheveled friend, a smirk still pulling at his lips, then his gaze slid back to me. "Your powers make you far greater than just any other Enforcer. You are an equal with us. We should work side by side, you making the sixth, and final member of the Council. But you must not argue with our protocol. If rules are broken, there are, and will always be, consequences. There are no exceptions to this. Ever. The rules of our kind are ageless. It's been that way for centuries and shall remain that way indefinitely."

Well that was news to me. I knew the Head Council wanted my services but I'd thought they just wanted me to be one of their many Enforcers. Enforcers were gifted vampires like me. Well, kind of. A few months ago I'd been kidnapped by Bronx and turned into a vampire, which awakened the sorceress' bloodline inside me, unbeknownst to me. But Bronx knew all about it, and he'd planned to use my powers to defeat the Head Council. Only I'd killed him before he got the chance. Later on, I'd learned about my real mother being an all-powerful sorceress and she'd used her magic to impregnate her vampire lover—my father. So I never really was just another vampire. Or even an Enforcer. I was always more than that. A whole new species altogether, a hybrid, and a hot commodity among the vampire world—since there was no other like me. Yet if the Head Council really wanted my partnership, then I just gained a whole lot of leverage. My chest tightened with anxiety. "If you want me to work with you, and of course the others, then I will need you to be more flexible. Rules are always in place for guidance, but we both know they are not in stone. Especially when I believe innocence is a key component."

"When there is proof of ones innocence, then we have a trial," Tristan explained. "But there is no proof of that with this human."

I thought about that for a moment. Sure, I didn't have "proof" per say, but I had Tyler's word. And though he'd lied to me about his alliance with Bronx, and the fact he'd known about my father's death all along, for some crazy reason I believed him now. "Allow me the time to find the proof you require and I will consider partnering with you."

Tristan shot me a lasered glare. His face softened but I had absolutely no idea what his thoughts were. Mind reading wasn't one of my gifts—yet. Since no one could predict what other gifts I'd inherit.

"How can you possibly believe this human didn't help those rogue vampires?" he asked at last.

I shook my head, keeping my eyes on Tristan's. "He was involved. I'm not saying I can prove that differently. He's innocent of not knowing what Bronx's intentions were, what those rogue vampires' intentions were." I paused a moment to suppress some of the heat inside me, though I didn't completely extinguish it, just in case things got hostile again. "He thought he was helping them," I went on with my explanation. "He thought they were in trouble. He didn't realize he was working for the bad guys until... until it was too late."

Stone snorted in disbelief, but kept his mouth shut. Smart vampire.

Tristan's eyes widened. "How can you possibly believe that? He must have you brain washed!"

"That isn't possible," I told him.

"What are you speaking of?" confusion in Tristan's voice. "Bronx would have claimed you with his mind control had you not killed him first."

"No, it's not possible to brainwash me," I explained. "And that is how I *was* able to kill Bronx." Saying that struck a pang inside my chest, I didn't want to be a murderer any more than I wanted to be a vampire, err hybrid. "I have the ability of blocking powers."

A wave of surprise flashed over the Tristan's face. "There is so much to learn about you, Abigail," he said.

"So do we have a deal?" I asked, taking a couple steps toward him.

Tristan raised a brow. "How much time are you asking for?"

"As long as it takes," I shot back instantly. "I have a feeling you and the others will delay me, since we are all curious to learn more about me and my powers."

Tristan closed his eyes momentarily, presumably using his telepathic powers to confer with the other members of the Council. I stole a moment to look at Stone. He was shaking his head slowly, azure eyes with hints of red wide with shock. I shrugged my shoulders warily, knowing fully that to keep Tyler safe, I'd break this deal and the neck of anyone who attacked him. Obviously Stone knew that too.

"We have a deal," Tristan finally announced.

I smiled. Relief flushed through me as the remnant heat within finally extinguished. Moments later, my breathing slowed and my heartbeat completely stopped. Oh the joys of being a vampire hybrid. "I have one more favor to ask," I said, a whole new confidence exuding in my voice.

Stone called out, "Abby, what are you—"

"Silence, Mr. Rayver," Tristan stated. "I am very interested in what Abigail will ask for now."

"I want to speak to Madelaine. Will Elliott do that for me?" My real sorceress mother, Madelaine, had died long ago, and I'd never even had the chance to meet her. My father and one of his female blood donors, all the while believing she was my mother, had raised me. And though I'd love for Elliott to connect me to my father, I simply couldn't risk giving away the fact he was dead too. Who knew how that little piece of info would affect the deal I'd just made, or the innocence I wanted to prove for Tyler. Bronx killed my father. But it was because of Tyler's gift of premonitions that Bronx was able to find my dad in the first place. So I guess you could say Tyler did carry some of the blame. But he'd sworn that he never thought Bronx would've killed him. And I believed him, hopefully not foolishly. So far I was taking the news of my fathers death okay. Maybe my estranged relationship with him was helping me through the mourning process. After all, he'd left me when I was ten. Eleven years later, I'd finally gotten a phone call from him, warning me I was in danger. I never had a chance to thank him for trying to help me…or see him again.

"Abigail," Tristan said, bringing me out of those thoughts. "You're going to make a great addition to our team. You're already very good at negotiations." He chuckled lightly. "It will be our pleasure to call upon Madelaine for you and an honor to introduce you to your real mother." He moved closer, holding out his hand. "So we have a deal?"

I nodded, taking his hand inside mine. "We have a deal." Then I asked, "When do we leave?"

His answer was one simple word. "Dusk."

I felt my chest tighten as he said it, then I went to Stone and threw my arms around his neck, burying my face against the softness of his tee-shirt, yet I could feel the solid muscle just beneath. "I will miss you," my voice muffled.

He gently grabbed my shoulders and pushed me back, just enough for him to look at my face. "Abby, what in the hell are you talking about? Do you actually think you can get rid of me that easy?"

"What do you mean?" I asked feeling confused.

"I'm coming with you."

"No, you're not!" Tristan shouted from behind me.

I shrugged as a plan formed in my mind. "Wait a second. I think it's a great idea for Stone to come."

"No," Tristan repeated.

"Actually, sir," Stone said, "I can be of help to both Abby and the Council. I can help look for the information Abby seeks to clear her human while she is tied up with business affairs with you. It would make her that much more available."

I felt my eyes widen. That was actually better than my plan. "But you hate Tyler." And he did—with a passion.

"Oh I still hate him, but I think the world of you." Stone gently gripped my chin, caressing it with his fingertips.

I smiled, a lone tear I hadn't felt before dripping from my eye. Stone wiped it, as I glanced over at Tristan. "Please allow Stone to come with us. He would be a true asset. And he is my friend. Please."

Tristan was quiet for a short moment, face hard, eyes studying us intently. "Very well."

"Where are we going exactly?" I asked.

"Boston," Tristan replied. "We have a few stronghold locations, but we are operating out of Boston right now. It's good to move around. Staying in the same place for centuries can get quite boring. And it's not as safe."

I nodded. I'd never been to Boston before, but I'd heard it was an interesting place. A huge part of me was looking forward to seeing it, checking out all the historic monuments and buildings, and meeting the statue of Sam Adams, if there would be any time for sightseeing. With Stone coming, we would certainly accomplish twice as much, twice as fast. I trusted that he would work diligently on finding a way to prove Tyler's innocence. Though Stone despised Tyler, I was certain that he cared enough about me to do as he said he would. Yet Stone wouldn't be upset in the slightest if he was unable to find the proof we needed to clear Tyler's name.

There was also the uncertainty over what kind of situation I'd be getting myself into with the Head Council. Learning vampire politics and more about the new species I'd become once Bronx turned me, well, that could take more time from me than I could ever imagine. Plus meeting my mother for the first time and finding out more about her set my emotions swirling with anxiety.

I closed my eyes and let out a deep, long sigh. *Just take one thing at a time, Abby. One thing at a time. Quit worrying about things that haven't happened yet.* Bronx was dead. Tyler was alive and pardoned for the moment. Lily, my closet human friend and old blood donor, was okay. Stone was here with me now and would stay with me at the Head Council's stronghold. And I'd gotten pretty good control over my amazing, awesome, and insanely strong powers. I'd say my life, afterlife, whatever, was going pretty darn good at the moment. Pretty good indeed. Yet, at the time, I had no idea just how quickly everything was about to change.

www.ingramcontent.com/pod-product-compliance
Lightning Source LLC
Chambersburg PA
CBHW071118170626

46809CB00002B/415